TWO UNIT

LAURENCE TODD

TWO UNIT

The Choir Press

First published in the United Kingdom in 2020 by
The Choir Press

ISBN 978-1-78963-133-3

ONE

Monday, early evening, 19th March 1972

He was shaking with fear. He'd been roughly snatched off the street, he'd been gagged and hooded, and now he was lying face-down in the back of a van, with his hands tied behind his back. He knew he'd been pulled in by soldiers from the Parachute Regiment as he'd seen their red berets before the hood had gone over his eyes.

He was thinking hard but could come up with no reason why he'd been abducted and trussed up like this. He wasn't involved with any paramilitary organisation or any of their many clandestine support groups. Everyone in his community had heard the whispered stories of people who'd been kidnapped, interrogated and sometimes tortured, either because they'd strayed onto the wrong side of the tribal divide or, more likely, because they were suspected of touting. In the eyes of the fighting men and women on both sides of the sectarian divide, no sin could possibly be graver than this, no matter what the Bible said.

He could feel a dampness around his groin. The thought of what might be about to happen to him had caused him to lose bladder control.

Not twenty minutes back he'd told his parents he was off out, going to visit his girlfriend, who lived several streets away, but he'd not be late back as he had to be at the factory by seven thirty tomorrow morning. There'd been a rush order for several boxes of machine tools which needed to be completed by the end of the working day, for immediate shipping over to the firm's main production facility in Bromsgrove, on the mainland. If the deadline was met, he'd be in his boss's good books for once.

Brendan Morgan was twenty and known by his family and friends to be something of a dreamer. He was the fourth and youngest child of Reggie and Mary Morgan and, though a Catholic by confirmation and upbringing, did not involve himself with the politics of the country he lived in. He'd managed not to take the side of the IRA against either the Proddies or the hated

British army, and had refused to become part of what was known somewhat bizarrely as *the Troubles* when, to the outside world, it looked like a full-blown civil war. Bloody Sunday had occurred not six weeks back, and the hideous brutality of the Parachute Regiment had led to many young Catholic boys queuing up to fight back by joining the Provos, but Brendan had always refused their entreaties, despite the constant cajoling from his friends and the local brigade commander. His older brother and several of his schoolfriends had joined up, and were now either in jail, in an early grave or on the run, hiding out in the south or over on the mainland.

Brendan's continually recurring dream, shared with his girlfriend, Jackie, was for them to escape from war-torn Belfast and seek a new life together elsewhere. This was what they were saving all their money towards. They wanted to marry but refused to do so until they were away from Northern Ireland, so any children they had could be raised without having a civil war being waged around them by the men and women of violence, and away from the eyes of the British armed forces who constantly patrolled the streets. If he kept his nose clean at the factory, and did good work, his hope was that he and Jackie could get jobs at the firm's main facility in England.

He'd walked along his road and had turned right onto the busy main road, walking towards an army checkpoint two hundred yards away. He'd seen the soldiers searching bags and checking identities, and he was readying himself to be aggressively searched, patted down and probably insulted: *On your way, you Fenian bastard* being one of the more polite insults used by armed squaddies.

He had been turning out his pockets, confirming he was carrying nothing the British soldiers might construe as being a weapon, when he became aware of a shuffling movement behind him. As he had turned two paras had grabbed him, one taking each arm, squeezing his muscles hard and lifting him from the ground slightly to keep him off-balance. "Over here, you Fenian scum," one had said, loudly and menacingly, as they'd dragged him to a parked van on the corner of the road.

The back of the van had immediately been opened by another soldier, and Brendan had been roughly pushed inside. He had been told in no uncertain terms, "Get down, face to the floor, and don't fucking move." He'd complied and was then bound, gagged and hooded. The van had driven away. It'd been all he could do not to cry and soil his trousers.

He was disoriented and didn't know how long he'd been inside the van. He'd had the sense that the van had been driving around a number of narrow bends when it suddenly screeched to a stop. He heard muffled voices and then the doors at the front of the van slamming shut; footsteps moved quickly around the side of the van, and then the back doors opened.

He was dragged roughly out of the van, thrown onto the ground and then hauled upright. He felt dizzy from nausea as he was dragged along, and he had to walk quickly or fall down. After a while the walking stopped. He was pushed back against something hard and the hood over his head was removed.

It was dark, but, as he blinked rapidly and his eyes adjusted to the absence of light, he knew he was near a clump of trees. He immediately realised he must have been driven several miles away because there were no woods or forests around his hometown. The van was on the road, about fifteen yards away, with its headlights still on; there were no other lights beyond it.

He then saw three men in front of him, standing ten feet away. He knew they were paras because of their red berets, and the paras were intensely hated amongst his community because of Bloody Sunday: the Bogside Massacre, as the nationalists called it. Two were the paras who'd snatched him off the streets, both probably around late teens, maybe twenty. They were standing in the alert position, glaring at him and holding their rifles in a manner suggesting they were ready to shoot in an instant.

But the other man was a little older, mid-twenties perhaps, and from the way he carried himself, wearing a cap instead of the red berets worn by the other paras, it was clear he was in command of this little unit.

The man in the cap took a step forward, looked at Brendan and didn't like what he was looking at. He could see the fear in Brendan's eyes and he let the silence continue for several seconds to build on that fear.

"You fucking Irish, you never learn, do you? If there's one thing history's taught us, it's that the Irish never fucking learn." He said this quietly, the words echoing slightly in the silence of the woods. He was well spoken, probably a university man from the sound of him.

Brendan didn't know what to say in reply. *Learn what?* he was thinking to himself, but he was afraid to say it.

The officer walked forward and stood a foot away from Brendan. "Do you?" he shouted into Brendan's face.

Brendan was too scared to respond.

Three seconds later the officer nodded to one of the paras. He stepped forward and backhanded Brendan hard across the face.

"Answer when being addressed by an officer," the para shouted firmly. He stepped back and resumed his position, clutching his rifle and looking menacingly at Brendan.

"What ... what do you want me to say?" Brendan's voice sounded very weak to him.

"Ah, much better; he can speak." The officer gave a sarcastic smile, nodding slowly. "Now, you bog Irish Mick, your name's Morgan, isn't it, and what I wanna know is very simple: where the fuck have all those weapons been hidden? You know the ones I mean: the ones the IRA took possession of last week. We know they have them, and we know they're being stored away somewhere on the sinkhole estate you live on." He spat the words out. "So *I* wanna know where they're being stashed, then we can go and retrieve them before any of you Fenian scum can use them to kill another one of my soldiers. Tell me where they are and you'll be returned home safely."

"I-I-I don't know any ... any ... anything about weapons," Brendan stammered out. He was trembling, as though he were shivering in the cold.

The officer nodded to the other para. He stepped forward and rammed the stock of his rifle into Brendan's stomach. Hard.

Brendan yelled out in pain and fell to the ground, lying in the foetal position, sobbing.

"We can do this easy or hard, son; it's your choice," the officer stated calmly, indifferent to the pain Brendan was feeling. "But don't take too long deciding; we've not got all fucking night to wait on you." The threat in the voice was evident.

"I don't know anything about any weapons, honestly, I don't," Brendan said through his tears. "I don't know what you're talking about."

The officer sighed loudly. "Oh, fuck this." He shook his head. "We don't have time for this."

He nodded again to the first para, who stepped forward and kicked Brendan hard in the base of his spine with his steel toe-capped boots. Brendan screamed with pain and started to cry harder. He was then hauled roughly to his feet and forced to stand upright, both paras holding him up by his arms, with his back against a tree.

The officer produced a pistol from the holster on his belt. He pointed it at Brendan, aiming right between his eyes. There was no chance he could miss from twelve feet away.

"I'm going to count down from five," he said, slowly, "and if you don't tell me what I wanna hear, sonny, it'll be the end of your war. So it's your choice; you decide."

"Oh, please, *please*." Brendan was now crying full-on, tears streaming down his face and begging, pleading for his life, shaking and more terrified than he'd ever thought he could be. He didn't want to die, not like this. He thought of his mother.

"*Five*." The countdown began.

"I don't know anything . . ." His voice was breaking through the tears.

"*Four*."

". . . about any guns, honestly, I swear to God I don't . . ."

"*Three*." The officer's voice remained firm.

"Please, *please,* I'm telling you the truth . . ." Brendan struggled, but he was being held firmly in place and couldn't move.

"*Two*."

"Oh, God, please . . ." He was sobbing and screaming now.

"*One*." The officer's tone hadn't changed whilst counting downwards. He was firm in his delivery and his eyes never left Brendan's face.

"I don't know . . ."

The officer nodded, and the two paras released their grip and quickly stepped away laterally. In the next instant the officer fired three shots, two into his stomach and one into his throat. Brendan was dead before he'd even begun to fall to the ground.

The first para ran to the van and returned with an old bolt-action Armalite rifle, a favourite weapon of the Provisional IRA, which had been wiped clean of all fingerprints. Brendan's wrists were untied and he was dragged alongside the tree and dropped to the ground, his fingers wrapped around the trigger of the rifle, which had been left lying next to him.

"Another IRA man taken out," the officer said formally. "One less to contend with. Lucky we were passing by and spotted this sniper hiding with his rifle." He paused for a few seconds. "Everyone clear on our story?"

"Yes, sir," both paras immediately responded.

They placed Brendan's dead body into the back of the van. All three men got in and they drove off.

"What if this kid was telling the truth, though?" the second para asked quietly. "What if he *really* didn't know where those weapons were? You see the look on his face?"

"Yeah, right," the other laughed, slapping him on the shoulder. "Come on, it's your round."

TWO

Tuesday evening, forty-something years later

Seven twenty-six: I was approaching the door of a house in Flood Street, Chelsea, with a young uniformed officer. The man I was here to take into custody had a flat on the ground floor as his London base during the working week, as well as a small country pile for spending his weekends somewhere in the Hampshire countryside. He'd been surreptitiously followed home, and his presence in the flat had been confirmed, so I knew where he was. As we exited the car, the uniform was looking around. He was smiling and nodding to himself, as though he were on a promise later tonight.

We walked up the short front path and, as I rang the bell, the uniform said, "Did you know, sir, Margaret Thatcher used to live in the house just over there?" He nodded to a house directly across the road. "This is where she was living when she was elected leader of the Conservative party in 1975, and she was still there when she became Prime Minister."

He was obviously a fan.

"They should put up a blue plaque to commemorate her living there," he eulogised. "She was a great woman, sir, don't you think?"

I said no, I didn't think she was a great woman at all, not even in the slightest. He looked horrified, like I'd muttered an apostasy in front of an archbishop.

"Didn't you vote for her, sir?" he enquired.

I tried not to feel too insulted as I explained I was just starting primary school the last time she'd left Downing Street.

"But would you have voted for her if you'd been able to?"

I shook my head. "Definitely not."

"You have a problem with her politics, sir?"

"I have a problem with everyone's politics."

He looked disappointed. I focused on who I was here to see.

Sir Alexander Bressington was sixty-two and a top career civil servant, joining after coming down from Cambridge, where he had achieved a double first in Greats from Trinity. He'd worked his way up to his current exalted position, as the permanent under-secretary at the Ministry of Defence, through the sheer force of his intellect, and his ability to smarm his way into the confidence of the ministers he'd served down the years. The smart money inside the service had him tipped as the favourite to become the next secretary to the Cabinet when the incumbent retired early next year, making him potentially the most powerful unelected figure in the country. As well as controlling the agenda at Cabinet meetings, he would get to see many other top secret papers from Cabinet committees, not to mention having the ear of the Prime Minister at all times.

His elevated position and stature in the Ministry meant he was a leading member of the Whitehall mandarin elite, the top-level policymakers who worked alongside and advised the Government of the day. He was undeniably a fully paid-up member of the establishment elite, a bona fide member of the Great and the Good. Earlier today, before coming here, I'd looked him up in *Who's Who*, and his entry took up more space than my life story to date would.

So it was a matter of utter astonishment that a man of his repute and eminent stature had been caught up in an elaborate pornography scam. It was especially worrying because the pornography in question hadn't even been, for want of a better term, 'ordinary'.

As I understood it, the scam had worked something like this. Advertisements had been placed in certain discreet voyeur, private subscription only magazines, the kind newsagents don't keep on the top shelves, and also posted on selected discreet pornography sites, offering something *out of the ordinary for the discerning voyeur*, with tantalising pictures of very scantily clad, beautiful women of many different nationalities as the hook. Anyone sufficiently interested was required to log on to the website address given, give their name and email address, and complete a short questionnaire. If accepted, they would be given a unique individual password and told to follow a link to a different website.

Having followed the link, the punter was to learn this site was actually a private club. To be considered for membership, and to have access to the materials advertised, as well as to the women in the pictures, the individual then had to complete another questionnaire, which included leaving an address where tangible materials like DVDs and magazines could be dispatched to, plus details of online downloads and streaming facilities.

There was also a request for details of bank accounts for standing orders to be paid out from, plus credit card details for a one-off non-refundable *admin fee* of £250.

Once these preliminaries had been completed, the £250 received, and permission to join the club given, the punter was given an access code to go online and begin streaming the materials they'd paid for, using their unique individual password. What had been discovered when the site opened, however, had been empty cyberspace. It had all been an elaborate scam.

To their horror, what they'd next discovered, when they contacted their banks to close down the standing order, was that the first month's payment had already been taken, alongside the £250 admin fee. Some punters, who'd placed orders for some of the more salacious materials the bogus site had advertised, also found they'd had several hundred pounds charged against their credit cards.

The beauty of this scam, for those responsible, was that most punters who'd been ripped off in this manner had been too embarrassed to report these losses to the police, and put the experience of being taken for hundreds of pounds down to a very expensive learning experience. It was evidently what the scamsters had been counting on.

One punter, though, had been sufficiently aggrieved by the loss of his money, in his case over £600, to report the matter to the police. The investigation had been passed on to the Cybercrimes Unit, who'd been investigating similar online scams, and they'd discovered the address given on the website had originally been put up somewhere in Eastern Europe, with Ukraine the most likely destination as several such scams had been run out of there before. Since then, the site had been taken down and had vanished into cyberspace altogether, with the perpetrators now several thousand pounds richer and the money extorted nestling in an untraceable tax haven somewhere.

Through an Eastern European source, however, believed to be in Croatia, the Cybercrimes Unit had discovered the website had also offered a portal into a secretive paedophile network, where known sex offenders from across Europe filmed themselves having sex with children and made the films available to others through the Dark Web.

Police had trawled through the names on the list of site users given by their Croatian source and, through this, had inadvertently uncovered Alexander Bressington. He'd signed in under an alias, James Murray, and given as his mailing address a newsagent's just off the west end of the King's Road, in Chelsea. Police had visited the newsagent's and asked for details of Mr Murray, and had been told he'd visited the shop two days ago to enquire if any packages had arrived for him. The shop was fitted with CCTV, and police had viewed the tape as it hadn't yet been wiped. The newsagent pointed out the man who'd entered the shop mid-evening, saying, "Him, he's James Murray," and claiming he'd no idea what was in the packages Murray had been receiving as he was just offering a mailing address for a small fee. Had Murray always collected his own packages? Usually, yes; initially someone else had collected them, though no names had been given.

When police had fed Murray's picture into the system, the answer had come back with a red flag attached, meaning there was a security connection, which had been disconcerting. Further inquiries revealed Mr James Murray was in fact one Sir Alexander Bressington, high-flying mandarin and someone with the requisite security clearance to see almost everything crossing his Secretary of State's desk.

The matter had been passed on to Special Branch where, amongst other things, it'd been revealed he'd sat as one of the members of the Finality Committee, investigating paedophile activity in the Republic of Ireland involving senior politicians and several Catholic priests, which had had connections to the political establishment in Westminster and Northern Ireland. I was interested in this as I'd been involved in the investigation into the murders of three prominent individuals with connections to the Finality Committee. I believed all three to have been killed by an Irishman named Martin Riley, who'd since returned to Eire and disappeared.

For the security service, given the very sensitive position Bressington held, with its access to top Government ministers and state secrets, what had been most alarming was the discovery that two of the perpetrators of the scam were Russians with known connections to the Federal Security Bureau, the successor to the KGB, and Bressington would have been a prime candidate for being blackmailed if details of this had ever came to light.

The other main worry for the security service: how many other people knew James Murray was in fact Alexander Bressington, with a significant role in the Government?

*

"I just don't get it." Smitherman had looked mystified when, an hour earlier, I'd been informed I was to go and take a Knight of the Realm into custody. He'd explained what Bressington was suspected of being involved with, evidently repulsed. "Why would a career civil servant in the higher echelons, a man who has the ear of the Defence Minister, someone tipped to get the Cabinet Secretary's job, engage in this type of conduct? What does he hope to gain? His record's so spotless, you'd think he'd been born without the stain of original sin on his soul." He shook his head. "How did he even get through security vetting? How'd he manage to keep this perversion a secret for so long?"

"I was about to ask that," I said.

"The other worrying thing is, how did the FSB even *know* he was inclined towards this kind of activity? MI6 will want to know how much they've got on him."

The question was rhetorical and I attempted no answer.

Smitherman sighed. "Oh well, go and bring Sir Alexander in. You know where to take him."

"If I'm gonna be interrogating him, can I at least see his case notes?"

"Oh, you won't be doing it," he casually informed me. "MI5'll take the case over once you've delivered him to Paddington Green. Any security implications will be theirs to consider. All you're going to be doing is taking him in to be questioned."

I was curious. Were there any particular protocols involved in taking someone who'd been touched on both shoulders by Her Majesty's sword, a Knight of the Realm, into custody, especially on a potentially explosive charge relating to the exploitation of young children? No, I was informed, but be courteous and ensure all the rules are followed to the letter as he'd be likely to cause a stink in high places if established procedures were not followed.

I'd never taken in a Knight of the Realm, and I wondered how he would react when I explained why I was there.

*

I rang the doorbell again and a well-presented woman with perfectly coiffured hair and a warm smile answered a few seconds later. She was about five foot five, wearing glasses and dressed mostly in various shades of light fawn-coloured clothing: cardigan, blouse and trousers. I assumed she was Elizabeth, Lady Bressington. I showed ID.

"DS McGraw, Special Branch, I'd like to speak to Alexander Bressington, please."

Immediately I realised my *faux pas* as I'd not used his title. Fortunately, she didn't pull me up.

"Er, ah, yes." She suddenly appeared nervous. "Is this about William? Has he actually gone ahead and done it this time?"

"William? I don't know who that is. I'm here to speak to your husband."

"Oh." She smiled. "Oh, in that case he's in the study." She sounded almost relieved.

She stood aside to allow me and the young PC to enter into the hallway. She then opened the door on her left.

We entered the room and I saw Bressington sitting in an armchair reading the *Daily Telegraph*. The room was well lit and very spacious, as well as exquisitely and tastefully furnished.

He stood up and put the paper down on the coffee table after I'd shown ID to him. He was my height, pencil-thin and wearing a blue shirt with the tie slightly loosened, plus a pair of smart casual slacks. His hair was grey, short and expensively trimmed. He was tanned and looked as though he'd spent time in the sun. The young police officer stood by the door and remained alert.

"Can I help you, detective?" Bressington smiled. His accent was straight from Oxbridge high table.

"Yes, I believe you can."

I asked him to identify himself, for the record. He looked curious but complied, stating his name, then asked why I'd wanted him to do this.

I informed him I'd like him to accompany me to Paddington Green police station to answer questions concerning his potential involvement in a conspiracy to commit offences contrary to public morality. I heard his wife gasp and whisper, "Good Lord," as I finished speaking. I then cautioned him, informing him of his rights. He looked nonplussed and didn't reply for several seconds.

"Am I being arrested, detective?" He had the condescending look which seemed to suggest he was thinking, *Things like this aren't supposed to happen to people like me.*

"No, but if you don't come voluntarily then, yes, I'll arrest you."

Given what I'd been told he was involved in, I'd have been delighted to grab his scrawny wrists and slip the bracelets on them, tightly, but I kept my feelings in check.

"Are you sure you've got the right person, detective? Do you know who I am and what position I hold in Government?" He narrowed his eyes and looked at me suspiciously as he spoke.

I explained, yes, I knew who he was as he'd just told me his name, and I was here to take a person answering to this name into custody. He smiled benignly.

"Call Gilbert," he said to Lady Bressington, looking remarkably calm as he took a jacket from the back of the chair. "Tell him what's happened. He'll know where I'm being taken; he can meet me there."

I assumed Gilbert was a lawyer.

"I'll be back in a couple of hours, dear." He gave his wife a peck on the cheek as he slid easily into his jacket. I was doubtful about this as the matter was a serious one, and there was no presumption of bail, or even access to a lawyer, when such offences were at issue, especially if security matters were included.

"Shall we?" He nodded graciously to the door.

*

I'd been expected and, as I arrived at Paddington Green and entered the foyer, I was met by two men, neither of whom identified themselves beyond saying they were from MI5. Bressington, who'd been casually looking around as if waiting for the maître d' to show him to his table, was greeted almost warmly and deferentially. The two MI5 men took turns to shake hands with Bressington. One then seemed to gesture in a kind of *this way, please, Sir Alexander, if you're ready* way, and the other thanked me for bringing Bressington in: "We'll take things from here, detective, and thank you."

Bressington was escorted away, all three chatting amiably. I noticed all three men were around the same age. It was a strange sight, as though they were there to accompany him to where a meeting was to be held. I'd no sense he was being taken into custody to answer questions on what sounded to me like very serious offences against public morality.

As they walked away I was about to leave when I heard my name being called. I turned and saw a smiling woman approaching me from along the corridor. It was my friend Christine Simmons. I thanked the uniform for his help and he turned and left.

Simmons formally thanked me for my assistance, and then told me I'd have no involvement with the questioning of her distinguished guest as this was well above my pay grade, given the sensitivity of the subject matter and the person involved. I'd already been told this, so I thanked her and, after a quick chat, was about to leave when she looked quizzically at me and asked if I'd time for a quick coffee. I agreed I did.

We went to the mostly empty cafeteria in the basement. She bought two coffees and we took a table. She thanked me again for bringing Bressington into custody. I nodded but was puzzled. I knew she hadn't asked me for a coffee just to offer thanks for what I'd done, and I was sure she had something on her mind. I soon discovered what it was.

"Well, Sally certainly shook things up last month, didn't she?" She smiled broadly.

Five weeks back the *Evening Standard* magazine had run a lengthy article, written by the love of my life, my wife Sally Taylor, in collaboration with a freelancer, Steve Jacobs, about the decision to sell a block of flats in Covent Garden to a property company run by Yuri Krachnikhov, a Russian businessman of dubious repute, as well as about some of the lamentable financial transgressions of the Mayor of London, James Blatchford. Blatchford had resigned because of the controversy the article had generated; in fact, he'd stepped down on the same day the article had been published. His deputy, Arthur Woodley, had now stepped up to become the new mayor. Blatchford had subsequently been the subject of an investigation by the Serious Fraud Office, as well as the police, and had been arrested and charged with, amongst other things, several offences contravening accounts law and company law, including trading whilst insolvent. MI5 was also taking an interest in the proceedings due to his connection with a shadowy company called Cartillian, based in Gibraltar. Blatchford's immediate future wasn't looking too promising.

I agreed that Taylor had indeed made waves, and added that she was beginning to make a name for herself as a journo, and was now the paper's deputy political editor. I mentioned how very proud I was of her, which brought a smile to Simmons' face.

"We learned a few things about Blatchford and some of his Gibraltar dealings, things we'd no idea about. Quite eye-opening, some of them, as well. What your wife and Jacobs discovered led us to look into other things and we've found lots of dark corners, lots of things hidden." She nodded and looked me straight in the eyes. I knew what was coming.

"Off the record, strictly between you and me." She paused for a moment. "Do you have *any* idea who she spoke to to get what she wrote? Give you my solemn word as a friend it'll go no further. It'll certainly aid our investigations if we knew."

"No, I don't." I immediately shook my head. This was true. I knew who Jacobs had spoken to, but not Taylor. "And she'd not tell me even if I asked."

"Yes, I can imagine." She smiled but sounded disappointed. "I only ask because Stimpson's dying to know where all this information came from."

Colonel Peter Stimpson was her section chief inside MI5, a man I'd had a few run-ins with.

"But no matter." She nodded knowingly. "As she's done us an unsolicited favour, I'm gonna do an unofficial one for her."

"Oh yeah?" I was curious. "Does she *need* a favour?"

"Yes, I think she might." She looked serious.

She leaned forward so our heads were only twelve inches apart.

"You might wanna whisper quietly in Sally's ear she really shouldn't be spending too much time associating with Steve Jacobs," she said quietly, looking me in the eye.

I paused for a moment. "And this's the favour you're doing her? You want me to tell her what you've just said?"

Simmons nodded.

"Why's this?"

"I can't tell you too much, for obvious reasons, but, hmm, let's just say he's a person of interest to my section," she said. "He hasn't committed any major offences we know of; it's just ..." She paused. "It's just, I don't know, he seems to have some extraordinarily good sources, some of whom are telling tales outside the classroom, so to speak. I mean, how on earth did he ever know about Cartillian, for instance?"

I shook my head. "I've no idea." I did know, but I wasn't saying.

"Lots of other little snippets keep appearing in the press under his name, or he feeds them to others to print, so we're just keeping our eye on him."

We sipped our drinks for several seconds. She read my thoughts correctly from the expression on my face.

"Oh, don't worry about Sally, if that's what you're thinking," she assured me, patting my hand. "She's not a person of interest to us and we've nothing about her on file, other than the routine stuff we keep on journalists on all the major newspapers. She's on the side of the angels, so far as we're concerned."

I was pleased to hear this, but then she paused. From her expression I could sense a *but* was coming. I was right.

"But, if she spends too much time with Steve Jacobs, well, it could be guilt by association, if you get my meaning." She raised her eyebrows. "And you know who my section chief is, don't you?"

I did. Colonel Peter Stimpson. I'd been told by Smitherman that Stimpson had not been at all happy about some of the information Taylor and Jacobs' article had contained, because of the consequences which'd followed.

"So, she spends too much time with Jacobs, she'll get marked down with him, and, as Sally's now joined at the hip to you, take a wild guess at what Stimpson'll think."

I didn't need to guess. I'd already been told by Smitherman the repercussions from their article about Blatchford could well come back and haunt me. I realised I was being given a friendly heads-up.

"What's Jacobs done, then?" I was now very curious. "Are you saying Taylor should keep her distance from him just because he has some good sources?"

"Now, you know I can't answer that." She smiled. "Well, not at this moment, anyway."

She was right. I'd not expected an answer.

"So, next time you're whispering sweet nothings into Sally's ear, or having post-coital pillow talk" – she raised her eyebrows and grinned evilly – "you might wanna whisper this as well."

"Okay, thanks. I'll whisper this in her ear, though it probably won't be on a pillow."

After a brief chat about married life – *yes, meeting and marrying Sally is the best thing ever to happen to me* – I thanked her for the information she'd given me about Harry Ferguson several weeks back, which'd been extremely useful. I asked about any progress looking for him, but she just smiled enigmatically.

As I watched her walk away a thought struck me: about a year back, I'd been convinced I was in love with Christine Simmons, but I'd simply become infatuated with her. It hadn't lasted too long and, fortunately, I'd not gone so far as to make a fool of myself.

I smiled at the memory, then left to go home, wondering what Jacobs was doing which meant Taylor should be careful around him.

THREE

Friday

Three days on and the fact of Sir Alexander Bressington being taken into custody had yet to be mentioned anywhere. It was as though it hadn't happened. I knew he'd been taken into custody. I'd taken him. Yet his name was conspicuously absent from the news.

Maybe he was still being interrogated. Given his position, the security service would want to know the likelihood of his being compromised in some way by his indiscretions and, in particular, whether blackmail was a possibility, given the FSB being implicated in the scam he'd fallen for.

The seriousness of these issues, if true, would be more than sufficient to see him damned in the eyes of public opinion, assuming they ever made the press, and they'd carry a degree of societal opprobrium which would follow him like a bad smell for the remainder of his lifetime. A distinguished thirty-five-year career would be snuffed out like a candle in a breeze, and all for what?

I couldn't ask Smitherman about this as, this morning, he was attending a high-level meeting of top security chiefs at the Home Office, so I was familiarising myself with my current assignment when my mobile rang. I answered.

"Hi, Rob. What about poor old Sir Alexander, eh?" The sarcastic delight in the voice was almost tangible.

It was Richard Clements. He was a journalist on the left-wing magazine *New Focus*, and someone I'd known and not particularly liked at King's. However, in the past eighteen months or so, some kind of friendship had evolved between us and we did each other the occasional favour. It'd been to him I'd leaked the information about James Blatchford's usage of insider trading, alongside the suggestion he pass it on to Sally Taylor at the *Evening Standard*. The fact he was also Smitherman's son-in-law, and a perpetual source of irritation to him, was a thing of constant amusement to me.

"I've heard he's been taken into custody by Special Branch," Clements said. "You involved in doing this?"

I was momentarily stunned. The news of this hadn't been released, I reasoned, because security needed to know who or what, if anything, had been compromised by Bressington's indiscretions. So Clements knowing about it was disconcerting.

"How did you hear about this?" I asked.

"Oh, come on, Rob, it's all over the Lobby. There's not a political journo in London who doesn't know about it." He sounded amused. "I'll bet Sally and her editor know about it as well. I heard about it yesterday at the Thursday gathering of Lobby correspondents. So, as I asked, were you involved in taking him into custody? Also, *why* would someone like him be taken into custody? He's one of the pillars of the establishment, straight out of the Sir Humphrey Appleby mould."

I'd taken Sir Alexander into custody, but I didn't want Clements knowing this. I told him I couldn't comment.

"Oh, don't worry, Rob, no one's gonna be publishing anything about it in the papers. There's not even been an acknowledgement of the situation from the security people. Nobody even knows why he was taken in. The speculation is, of course, espionage of some form or another, leaking secrets or something, but nobody knows anything definitive yet."

The *yet* sounded ominous. I wondered whether Taylor had in fact picked up on this at the *Evening Standard*.

"I can't help you," I said. "I don't know anything other than the fact he was taken into custody." This was true. I didn't know what had happened since Tuesday evening.

"I'll await developments, then. I'll get back to you soon, mate. There's something I wanna talk to you about, though the situation might have changed by then."

I intimated that this would be okay. We rang off.

Clements calling me *mate* eighteen months ago would have left me thinking about hitting him, but we were now friends of a kind, and we both went to considerable lengths to ensure Smitherman never discovered this.

*

Taylor and I were in a restaurant we both particularly liked, the little Italian place close by South Kensington tube station, Grazie

Dei Bei Fiori, which I think I remember being told by one of the waiters meant something like *thank you for beautiful flowers*. Despite its location, prices were very reasonable. The overhead lights were kept low, the food was always excellent, especially the antipasto, it stocked my favourite Italian beer on draught, the music was unobtrusive, the tables were small and conducive to intimate discussion, and every table was lit by scented candlelight. Just looking at Taylor through the soft glow of a scented candle was like experiencing the first warm day of spring after a long winter.

This was one of our go-to places when we felt like eating out or, like tonight, when we had something to celebrate. Taylor had been told a few months back that she was in line to become the *Standard*'s deputy political editor when the incumbent retired, and he'd finally left the paper, after deferring his retirement one month for family reasons, so we were belatedly celebrating her promotion.

We'd both come straight from work, so we spent a little time talking about our respective days before she told me her news.

"Oh yeah, I got a call from Steve Jacobs this afternoon. Remember him?"

I nodded my agreement whilst quaffing a Birra Moretti.

"I'm meeting him tomorrow lunchtime. He's got another idea about an in-depth story for the magazine, and he's already talked to Hugh about working with me again." Hugh was the *Standard*'s editor. "He thinks it could be a major story. Hugh's okay with the general principle behind it, so he's told Jacobs to firm up his idea and get back to him. I'm gonna meet up with him tomorrow and he's gonna clue me in." She smiled.

"Any idea what it might be?"

"None at all. I'll find out tomorrow." She nodded. "If I like the sound of the story he's looking at covering, I may well help him out. I enjoyed working on the big feature we ran about Blatchford. It was really exciting getting my teeth into something so substantive."

I then remembered what Christine Simmons had told me, three nights back, about how Taylor shouldn't get too closely involved with Steve Jacobs. I'd not mentioned it at the time as Taylor hadn't even mentioned Jacobs since the article about Blatchford, which had been published five weeks ago, so I hadn't thought too much about it. But hearing Taylor say she was meeting him again made me wonder whether to tell her what Simmons had said.

For the moment, though, I stayed quiet. I'd wait till she told me what Jacobs had to offer before deciding.

I must have looked miles away, as Taylor leaned forward and put her left hand on top of my right, squeezing it lightly.

"What you thinking about?" She smiled softly. "For about ten seconds you were away with the fairies."

"Oh, nothing really," I airily replied.

We locked eyes for a few seconds, smiling all the while.

We settled the bill and took a taxi back to Battersea. In the cab she sat up close, linked arms and rested her head on my shoulder. I loved it when she did this. It was the warmest feeling. Whatever shampoo she'd used to wash her hair was still giving off an aromatic scent and it smelt enticing.

Just inside the entrance to our maisonette block, heady from a few drinks and the excitement we felt just being with each other, we spent several seconds frantically kissing each other, her back pressed up against the wall. After a while we both started laughing because it'd dawned on us we'd been acting like lovesick teenagers on a first date. Just as well the lobby had been empty.

"Your place or mine?" I asked as I tickled her and squeezed her gorgeous bum playfully.

"Mine. Lead on, Macduff," she laughed, returning the squeeze. It felt good.

FOUR

Saturday

Before I did anything else today I decided I wanted to know more about Steve Jacobs. He was a well-connected freelance writer who specialised in rubbing the political establishment the wrong way, and he had worked with Taylor on a major story for her newspaper's weekly magazine. Beyond that and the half-hour I'd spent with him in a Westminster pub, when he'd given me some very pertinent information about Charles Garlinge, I knew nothing about him. But Christine Simmons had advised me Taylor ought to be cautious about too close an association with him. Was he involved in something which might have repercussions for Taylor? I entered his name into Special Branch's file on journalists of interest and brought up his details.

Steven David Jacobs was thirty-eight and a Cambridge PPE graduate. He appeared to have surprised everyone by not following in the family tradition of joining the military, as his older brother, younger sister, grandfather, father, uncle and other relatives had done. Instead he'd taken a job as a trainee journalist on a local newspaper, near the family home in Hendon, North London, and, after five years learning his trade, had secured a plum job as a staff reporter at the *Guardian*. But he'd quit after less than three years because the then-editor had spiked a story he'd believed deserving of publication.

Somehow, Jacobs'd managed to acquire details of how the British government was acting in collusion with the Americans concerning what was known as *extraordinary rendition*: government-sponsored abduction of suspects believed to have been involved in terrorist actions but hiding in other countries and protected by the laws of those countries. This practice bypassed the process of law theoretically required before someone could be sent to another country to answer charges relating to terrorism. The UK was on record as being opposed to extradition to countries where torture was known to be practiced, but even with the UK government's certain knowledge that suspects were to be taken to Guantanamo Bay and tortured, they'd still colluded with the US. The UN regarded this as *torture by proxy* and declared it to be a crime against humanity.

Jacobs had somehow managed to obtain details of how the Prime Minister himself, on a personal request from the US president, had overridden all opposition and agreed to US planes using UK airbases to refuel on their way back to the USA, knowing the planes carried suspects who'd been kidnapped and were on their way to be tortured. But Government law officers had instructed his paper's managing editor not to publish the full details, or even to allude to this information, on grounds of protecting the national interest, and the editor had agreed to withhold publication.

Unknown to Jacobs, the information he'd obtained had triggered a major alert inside the Government, as well as an intense security service trawl amongst top officials at GCHQ and the Cabinet Office. Someone in the know had to have leaked all these details to Jacobs, and the Government desperately wanted to know who, but no one had ever been identified as the source of the leak, and no arrests made.

Disgusted by what he'd referred to in his letter of resignation as the editor's shameful kowtowing to the entreaties of the security service where the public interest had been involved, Jacobs had walked out and had the story placed with newspapers abroad, where its impact in the UK had been minimal as few outlets had chosen to report it. The story was eventually published in the UK press, when the issue had become less controversial.

Special Branch detectives had questioned him about his story, concerned particularly with whom he'd spoken to to obtain this information, but he'd refused to name his sources. And, going by the details on his file, this wasn't the only time he'd fallen foul of the security services.

Over the past decade he'd made his name as a freelance journo, and he'd been partly or wholly involved with several stories which had made national headline news. He'd had syndicated articles published in several European and American magazines, such as *Le Monde* and the *Nation*. The *Observer* and, surprisingly, since he'd walked out on them, the *Guardian* had also carried his stories, plus *New Focus* and other left-leaning magazines. His work usually related to intelligence and defence matters, but not exclusively.

Taylor had been involved in his most recent story concerning the fall from grace of James Blatchford, of course, and what Jacobs had uncovered about the late Charles Garlinge had been the basis for a follow-up story in the *Evening Standard*. I'd been in on this case, and I knew who'd killed Garlinge, but I had no evidence a court of law would accept. The fact the person I'd identified as the suspect had admitted *mea culpa* to me in private didn't count as evidence.

Jacobs was listed as being politically non-aligned and wasn't a member of any party, though it was noted he was believed to be an anarchist, as was his partner, Trish, who worked for the London branch of Lantanis, an American think tank. On two occasions they'd been seen together at demonstrations, either with a known anarchist section or with Jacobs carrying a black anarchist flag. Trish was suspected of being the source of some of the information Jacobs received, though it was noted he'd contacts in many media outlets as well as in Government departments, some of whom had leaked very confidential information to him. He was also known to have contacts inside a few London embassies, notably the US embassy.

His partner, Trish, interested me, so I also checked her out. Her full name was Patricia Campbell-Berron. She was the daughter of a baronet from a family line which owned a large estate in north-west Somerset, given to the family by King James I, and her grandfather was currently something like two hundred and sixty-second in line to the throne. She too was a Cambridge graduate. After leaving university and backpacking around south-east Asia for eighteen months, she had worked for a while as a journalist, where she'd met Jacobs, before obtaining her current post working for Lantanis. Other than her connection to Jacobs, little else was listed about her.

There was a lengthy list of articles written by Jacobs, and most were what one would expect from him, mainly covering current events and terrorist-related matters. He had also co-written *The Last Imperial Spasm*, a book dealing with the events leading up to Bloody Sunday in 1972. The book's central point was that the killing of thirteen innocent Irish demonstrators, which the authors described as a *slaughter*, was just the latest in a long line of similar atrocities, stretching all the way back through Amritsar in India, 1919, to the Boer war, where it'd been noted the British had given the world its first concentration camp. He'd devoted a lengthy chapter to what he referred to as the Suez Debacle 1956, which he'd gleefully stated was the death knell of Britain's imperial delusions of being a world power.

Despite its leftist slant, the book had been well regarded by historians, and had drawn some very favourable reviews in many serious newspapers and magazines, including several which wouldn't normally share the authors' left-wing perspective. Its damning conclusions had been controversial and attracted much critical comment, but publications including, somewhat surprisingly, the *Sunday Times* and the *Spectator* had praised the book for its historical and analytical insight, as well as its intellectual rigour, though not necessarily the political conclusions drawn. It had made the lists of bestselling publications, was considered essential reading on Modern History and Politics courses at several universities, and had sold particularly well abroad.

I remembered Jacobs saying his brother had been with Charles Garlinge's unit as a young squaddie when Alecks Krachnikhov had killed another recruit, so I wondered what was known about the brother.

Major Neil Jacobs was forty-one and a career army man. He was regarded as a good soldier and officer and nothing was listed against his name, other than that he was the older brother of a known radical journalist. The rest of the family line consisted of military personnel who'd all served their country with honour and distinction, and no black marks were listed against any of them.

I paused. Whilst what was written about Steve Jacobs was interesting, there was nothing to suggest why Christine Simmons had told me Taylor ought not associate too closely with him. It was noted that Jacobs had been spoken to by Special Branch on a couple of occasions, but he'd no criminal record, no major money issues and a positive credit rating.

There were several pictures which'd been taken at various demonstrations he'd attended. I already knew he had been seen carrying a small anarchist black flag on the Stop the City march. I looked at a few more pictures, and, in one, I noticed he was walking alongside Richard Clements, and they appeared to be conversing. This shouldn't have surprised me, and it didn't. Both fervent supporters of left-wing causes, and both of them journos. I'd have been more than amazed had they *not* known each other.

I entered Clements' name into the database and cross-checked it against Jacobs. They'd collaborated on a couple of articles for *New Focus* and had been pictured together at a few demonstrations, but they weren't listed as being close associates. Neither appeared on any current watchlist, though Clements being the son-in-law of Commander Jack Smitherman, head of Special Branch, was noted.

I was still curious but, for the moment, logged off and returned to work.

*

Nine o'clock. After an afternoon at an interminable meeting devoted to the firming up of an investigation that was currently going nowhere, and a lengthy though fruitful early evening meeting with a source, I was on my way to a pub near World's End, at the far west end of the King's Road, Chelsea. Someone once told me this was one of the central London pubs where footballing legend Georgie Best had drunk himself to death.

One of the perks of Taylor's position as a journo on the *Evening Standard* was the continuous flow of invitations to various high-profile and, occasionally, very exclusive events across the capital. Tickets to film premieres, opening or preview nights of new plays, new exhibitions at major art galleries, gigs at major London venues by top rock acts or a table on the opening night of a trendy new restaurant were usually easy to come by. I'd even been to Twickenham recently to watch England play Australia and had had a great seat in the Upper West Stand, with complimentary alcohol as part of the package, courtesy of a freebie from the paper's sports editor.

This evening, Taylor and a few work colleagues had been to see the preview night of a new play at Sloane Square's Royal Court theatre, in which *Othello* had been rewritten as a contemporary political drama. She'd been invited to the after-show party in the pub by the paper's political editor, although it'd also been a working invitation. The political editor's fiancée had just obtained the nomination to be the Conservative party's prospective parliamentary candidate for a marginal seat in Norfolk, currently held by the Lib Dems but deemed by top party strategists to be eminently winnable, and the editor had particularly wanted Taylor to meet her because he thought a story about her might help her cause, particularly if the interview was conducted by another young woman. I'd not been able to make the play but had said I'd be at the pub later.

I entered the pub and found it packed with journos and drama types, fondly referred to by *Private Eye* as *luvvies*, all talking loudly and in varying stages of insobriety. I felt about as out of place as a mouse in a cattery.

I inched my way through the crowd, looked around till I spotted Taylor standing by a table in the far corner. She was talking to a woman who had her back to me. I had no clear line of sight on the woman, but, even from this angle, something about her struck a chord with me. I sensed there was a familiarity about her as I inched my way through the crowd.

Taylor spotted me and smiled. I finally made it and we gave each other a warm hug. I turned to face the woman she'd been conversing with and received what felt like a mild electric shock down my spine. The woman Taylor had been talking to saw me and immediately her eyes also opened wide in surprise.

"I was just talking to this lady about a possible interview as she's hoping to become an MP," Taylor said, excitedly. "She's just got engaged to my political editor and also got the nod to be a PPC, a prospective parliamentary candidate."

I turned to face the woman. She was smartly dressed, wearing a midnight blue jacket that matched her trousers, and a white silk blouse with a matching scarf. Her dark hair was slightly shorter than when I'd last seen her, and styled very professionally. Her eyes were a little glazed over, and she was slightly rosy-cheeked from one too many glasses of red wine, but she was still oozing all the class and confidence which comes from an expensive private education, followed by Oxbridge, and she still looked as smug as ever.

"Well, congratulations, Debbie; you've finally found a seat to contest."

"Thank you, DS McGraw." She sort of smiled at me. Her voice was slightly slurred.

The woman was Debbie Frost, someone I'd encountered on a few previous occasions, not all of them pleasurable. She held a senior position in the Conservative party's research department and, featuring on the party's list of approved candidates, had been attempting to win the nomination to be a Tory candidate and stand for Parliament for a few years. It would appear she'd finally succeeded.

Frost was thirty-four and still undeniably a very attractive woman, though of course nowhere near Taylor's class, but I didn't like her at all. She was arrogant, vain and very self-centred, not to mention amoral and venal where money and success were concerned. She'd only been prevented from being prosecuted in a case involving her late fiancé, Darren Ritchie, and his role in money laundering on behalf of a terrorist organisation, by the unwelcome intervention of an ex-lover of hers, a very senior Tory MP with connections in the security service.

For two seconds, Taylor stood with her mouth and eyes open wide.

"You two *know* each other?" She sounded amazed.

"Yes, we're old friends, aren't we?" Frost said, casually touching my arm before I could speak.

"Indeed we are," I replied, playing along. "How you doing?"

"Pretty darn good, actually. I've just got engaged to Sally's political editor and I've got a good chance of becoming an MP if I can get the support and goodwill of the constituency activists, so life's currently on an upswing."

"Nice," I said neutrally, "and congratulations on your engagement."

I looked at the crowd, three deep in places, forming around the bar. I really wanted a beer but realised my chances of getting one were negligible, so I didn't bother. Probably explained why Georgie Best always sat at the bar the whole time he was here.

"Thank you." Frost smiled, almost warmly. She took a sip from her glass of wine, and, as she did so, her eyes flitted, curious and quizzical, between Taylor and me, as if she couldn't quite believe what she was seeing. "So, how do *you* two know each other?"

"Oh, Rob's my husband," Taylor replied, smiling and linking arms with me. "We got married a couple of months ago."

"Ah-ha," she said slowly, looking at me. "So *you're* the police officer who married Paul's new deputy. He just said she was marrying a detective named Robert so I knew who to address the card to. I didn't twig it might be you."

Paul was Paul Grayley, the *Standard*'s political editor.

"But you were with a doctor not too long ago, weren't you?" she asked innocently, though I suspected there was a motive behind the question.

I was immediately curious. How would Debbie Frost have known this? I'd never shared any personal details with her. For the moment, though, I decided not to ask how she knew. "At one time, yeah, though some while back now."

"So, where do you two know each other from?" Taylor was curious.

"From an investigation." I leapt in before Frost could reply. "Debbie's car was stolen and, because of the political sensitivity of her role inside the Conservative party, the Branch was called in as it was suspected there might've been some important Government papers in there. Turned out not to be the case, so there was nothing for the Branch to investigate; it was a straight robbery." I shrugged. "So CID took the case, rather than us."

"Yeah, that sounds about right," Frost agreed, "*and* I got my car back as well, undamaged." She finished the drink she was holding. "Well, I'm gonna have to love and leave you. I'd better go and schmooze, keep Paul happy. He wants me to talk to his editor."

She turned to Taylor. "Good to finally meet you, Sally. I've heard a lot about you. Contact my office sometime early next week; we can firm up a date for our interview. The end of next week's looking good for me."

Taylor agreed she would do this.

Frost then turned to me. "Nice meeting you again, DS McGraw."

She didn't mean this at all. She'd probably sooner have smallpox than be friendly to me, but I smiled at her, said something anodyne in response and watched her disappear into the crowd.

We stayed at the pub another half-hour. I made some small talk with an excitable female drama critic about whatever it was, most of which I forgot as we were still talking, while counting down the seconds until I could finally leave.

*

Back in the flat I was still wired, so I made myself a cappuccino, and a latte for Taylor, as eleven twenty-five was too late for the first beer of the evening.

The pub hadn't been too far away, about a twenty-five-minute walk, so we'd strolled along Cheyne Walk, wondering which house was Mick Jagger's, crossed over Battersea Bridge, stopping for a few moments to look at a bright waxing gibbous moon reflected on the still waters of the Thames, and then continued along Battersea Bridge Road to our third-floor maisonette.

All the way back I'd been thinking about Debbie Frost and the fact she'd now taken the first tentative steps towards achieving her long-held ambition of a seat in Parliament. For her, though, this would only be step one. I knew she'd never be satisfied with just being a backbench MP, as I was aware, from previous conversations with her, that she nurtured ambitions to rise so much higher in the political firmament.

Reaching Cheyne Walk, I'd briefly looked right and remembered how Frost's then-fiancé, Darren Ritchie, had been murdered in nearby Cremorne Gardens, only a couple of hours after I'd interviewed him and her together. In the interview she'd all but admitted she'd known he was involved in the process of money laundering and, even when she'd eventually realised his actions had been helping the terrorist group Red Heaven, she'd still gone along with this because Darren had pocketed a sizeable sum from his financial transgressions. I'd surreptitiously recorded the interview and still had a copy of it.

I wondered exactly what it was that party members in the constituency she'd soon be contesting actually knew about her. It was a safe assumption they didn't know everything I did.

Taylor and I were reclining against the back of the couch, shoes off and feet up on the coffee table, her head on my shoulder and my arm around her. After a hectic work day and a night being buffeted in a crowded pub, relaxing at home and just being alone with Taylor was the doorway to paradise.

After sitting silently for a few minutes, she turned towards me and showed some remarkable insight into what had occurred earlier. "You and this Debbie Frost woman, you're not really friends at all, are you?" She was smiling cryptically as she spoke.

"Now, why would you think that?" I looked at her and grinned playfully.

"Why? Oh, come on, McGraw." Her smile turned slightly evil. "The way you both looked at each other; you each had that *oh, God, not you again* look, despite the stuck-on smiles. That's why. I'm a journalist; I see expressions like this all the time. But it's obvious you know each other, so how *do* you know her?"

I told Taylor *everything* she was about to hear was extremely confidential, and she wasn't to let on she knew *anything* about Debbie Frost when she met her again to interview her. She agreed to this proviso.

I began explaining how the Branch had uncovered a money laundering scam at the investment bank Karris and Millers, which Michael Mendoccini had been instrumental in helping to organise. I'd found evidence Frost's then-fiancé, Darren Ritchie, was implicated in this laundering, mainly through doctoring books and the manipulation of accounts to disguise the movement of funds. I'd interviewed Ritchie and Frost about this in her Chelsea flat, and I'd cautioned them both afterwards but, in the moment, hadn't arrested either of them as I didn't want the main player involved being tipped off.

An hour or so later the same evening, Ritchie'd been murdered, killed by a single blow to the back of the neck, almost certainly delivered by Bartlett 'Post' Poe, when Red Heaven's money laundering scheme was being wound up and loose ends were being tidied up. I'd good reason to believe it'd been Michael Mendoccini who'd given the order to kill, but I didn't tell Taylor this as I had suspicion aplenty but nothing constituting hard evidence. Ritchie had been murdered, as had Roger Bradley, an investment manager at the same bank who'd been the main organiser and overseer of the scheme.

Debbie Frost had been aware of what Ritchie had been doing, and I was certain she also knew a freelance journo, who'd been investigating allegations of money laundering, had been murdered just after he'd met with Ritchie at a pub in Canary Wharf. During my interview with her and Ritchie, Frost had tacitly admitted she'd known, or at least reasonably suspected, everything that'd been going on.

I'd secretly taped this conversation and had intended to use it to bring charges against Frost, but we'd been unable to act upon what the Branch knew. She'd been protected by a senior Tory MP, Christian Perkins, who'd used his security connections, including a long-standing friendship with Colonel Peter Stimpson, to claim she was in fact helping MI5 with the allegations by passing on what she'd heard from her fiancé, who was also helping. His story had been a total crock, but Stimpson had believed it and no charges had ever been brought.

I concluded with my opinion she was a wholly venal character obsessed with her ambition to be an MP, and then a Cabinet minister, and she'd let *nothing* stand in the way of this aspiration.

Taylor listened carefully and absorbed what I'd said. She registered surprise at a couple of points I mentioned about the delectable Ms Frost, but I trusted Taylor's discretion absolutely, so I had no concerns talking to her about this.

"And this is all true, McGraw?" She looked and sounded amazed by what she'd heard.

"Very much so. Scout's honour." I smiled and gave her my Scouts salute.

"So, what you said earlier about her car being stolen . . .?"

"Oh, her car *did* get stolen, which is how I first came across her. She'd initially thought she'd lost some classified papers in her bag, which were thought to be the minutes from a Cabinet committee meeting, which is why the Branch was initially involved. They were found elsewhere, so, as I said, the Branch withdrew; CID took the case over. I'm not sure how the investigation concluded; the Branch wasn't involved by then."

I was being somewhat economical with the truth. I didn't tell Taylor I'd discovered Debbie Frost had actually been attempting to blackmail Christian Perkins about the details of their affair, which Perkins had recently ended, and which had also involved a terminated pregnancy, though his actions in protecting her from prosecution seemed to suggest they'd resolved whatever enmity there'd been between them.

I also didn't tell her it'd been me who'd found the letters Frost had been hoping to use for blackmail purposes, or that the person who'd had possession of them had died from severe injuries inflicted by Christian Perkins' son, Richard Rhodes, not too long afterwards.

I also omitted the fact that Debbie Frost had been instrumental in recruiting the man who'd shot and killed Louis and Paulie Phipps, the men who'd stolen her car and had been attempting to sell the contents back to her, including a letter to Christian Perkins stating she was pregnant and naming him as the father. Had this story become public knowledge, as the Phipps brothers were planning if she didn't come up with the payment they were asking for, Perkins' career might well have hit the buffers.

"So she's got some previous, then?" Taylor asked with a fey smile.

"Oh, God, yeah. She's got her hands dirty more than once." I returned her smile. "So, as she now knows about us, it's likely she'll assume you know most of this already. If she *does* ask, don't let on you do. Just act surprised if she tells you *anything* about what I've just told you."

"Okay." Taylor nodded. "I'm gonna be contacting her office either Monday or Tuesday to arrange an interview, and hopefully it'll be in the following week's paper."

"Good luck with interviewing *her*," I said, disdainfully. "You want me to come along and bodyguard you?"

At this point Taylor, who'd been smiling lasciviously and moving closer to me by the second as I'd been speaking, knelt astride me on the couch and, unbuttoning and sliding her hands inside my shirt, kissed me with a tenderness and an intensity which lifted me out of my skin.

"You can guard my body *any time*, Detective Sergeant Robert McGraw," she whispered sexily. She lightly nibbled my ear, stroking my chest with her fingernails. It sent shockwaves of excitement coursing through me.

"Hmm, it's a dangerous world out there," I said softly, returning her kiss while unbuttoning her blouse. "You think it might need guarding now?"

"What do *you* think?" she whispered, her eyes sparkling.

I'm a trained police officer. My answer was in the affirmative.

FIVE

Sunday

Both of us were off duty, so, after last night's exertions, we had a leisurely breakfast and spent the morning reading the Sunday papers. Just after lunchtime we decided to go for a tea over in Battersea Park at the open-air café we occasionally visited, the Pear Tree, which was next to the tennis courts. We took the long way around, passing the football ground and the boating lake. It was a slow casual stroll through the park, holding hands, enjoying the scenery and avoiding the cyclists, the joggers and the Frisbee players, plus the Alsatian dog off the leash which tried unsuccessfully to untie the laces on my trainers.

Taylor went to buy two teas and I took a table with a clear view of the boating lake. It was a cool but pleasantly sunny early afternoon with just a slight breeze, and I was enjoying looking around the park. Despite being so close to the centre of a major city, the park always radiated a peaceful sense of calm and tranquillity, irrespective of the time of year, and it was a delightful place to sit, unwind and watch the world pass by. From here, you could also see the tops of the chimney stacks of the iconic Battersea power station, now sadly disused with the site being converted into luxury flats.

Battersea Park has nothing like the renown of Kensington Gardens or Hyde Park, but it's pleasing to live so close to it, and it's a lovely place to stroll around and, very occasionally, stop for a tea.

I watched Taylor walking back. She was wearing tight black jeans and a white T-shirt under her denim jacket and silk scarf, and her wavy mop of strawberry blonde hair was being shifted around by the breeze. She kept shaking her head slightly as hair fell over her glasses. Just looking at her gave me goosebumps. Staring at Taylor, sometimes I even forget how to breathe.

Taylor passed me a tea and sat opposite. She smiled.

"Don't look now, McGraw, but behind you to your left, about eight o'clock, there're four teenagers sitting at a table, and they're all staring at you and whispering. Do they know you?"

I waited a few minutes and then casually looked round, like I was checking something. When I saw who Taylor had been referring to, I realised I knew who they were.

Several weeks back I'd apprehended these four getting off a bus. The ginger-haired guy, who'd been the ringleader, had been carrying a bag of psychoactive substances: legal highs, as well as some top-grade marijuana. But, rather than arresting them, I'd just confiscated the drugs and given them a verbal warning.

The dark-haired girl looked up and spotted me looking at them. She slightly nudged the ginger guy sitting next to her and delicately nodded in my direction. His eyes opened wide. They all stopped talking, hastily gathered their phones, books and bags and got up to leave. Their way out of the park took them towards our table.

"Hello, detective," the dark-haired girl said demurely. The rest nodded at me.

"Hi." I smiled, looking between all four of them. "You all keeping out of trouble?"

"Of course we are," the blonde said, jokingly indignant. "We have to. We're all hoping to go up to Oxbridge next academic year."

"Good for you."

All four were students at St Anne's in Pimlico, a day school charging jaw-dropping fees but specialising in getting the children of wealthy Londoners into Oxbridge colleges.

"Did you know Eduardo's been arrested and put in prison?" the ginger-haired kid asked.

"No, I wasn't aware of this," I said innocently. They nodded and walked away.

I was lying. I did know. I'd set the ball in motion. Following my encounter with the four youths, when I'd learnt Eduardo de Salvio sold drugs to schoolkids at the school gates, which was an *infamita* as far as I was concerned, I'd whispered his name into the ear of someone I knew in the drugs squad. A few days later, Eduardo had been picked up outside St Anne's, in possession of several hundred pounds' worth of psychoactive substances and marijuana, and, as it was a third offence, jailed for four years. Dealing to consenting adults is one thing, but selling drugs to schoolkids was beyond the pale.

We drank our teas and took in the scenery for a while. I settled back and listened to the birds singing in the trees. I watched Taylor trying to keep her hair under control in the breeze. She saw me looking at her and smiled.

"Oh yeah," Taylor suddenly said, leaning forward. "I was gonna tell you this last night, but we, ah, kind of got distracted, didn't we?"

"Distracted? I was guarding your body, I seem to recall." I grinned.

She laughed. "I met up with Steve Jacobs yesterday lunchtime."

I remembered her telling me on Friday evening she was going to be doing this. I'd forgotten to ask her yesterday how it'd gone.

"I met him in Covent Garden," she said. "He'd just finished interviewing someone there for another piece he's working on, so it seemed convenient to meet there."

"So, what's his new storyline?" As I asked I was remembering Christine Simmons' warning against getting involved with Steve Jacobs.

She told me Jacobs had been put in touch with an ex-soldier who was claiming he'd a quite sensational story he wanted to get published, despite the controversy its publication would probably generate. So he'd met up with the soldier, initially on his own because he wanted to be certain there was at least the basis of a viable investigation in the man's story; there was no point in two people wasting their time if there wasn't. But the man, Jacobs said, had *absolutely rocked him* with the story he'd told. Taylor emphasised the point firmly.

"What was his story?" I was very curious.

Taylor leaned across the table towards me, conspiratorially.

"You probably won't believe this," she said, quietly, "but Jacobs said the guy he was talking to, this ex-soldier, claimed to have served as part of a covert British army unit going after the IRA and following a shoot-to-kill policy in Northern Ireland in the early seventies."

"What, a *British army death squad?*" I asked in disbelief.

"That's what Jacobs says he was told by this guy."

I thought for a moment. Death squads operated in places like South America, places with major heroin and cocaine producing facilities, organised and run by powerful drug cartels, or places like south-east Asia, usually with some degree of covert government involvement, but they didn't operate here in the UK. Did they?

I was already sceptical. "So who was it they shot and killed?"

"Jacobs said this guy's an ex-paratrooper and he and a few others from the paras either went after and shot known IRA gunmen or bombers, or they claimed those killed were snipers they'd managed to get the better of, and they'd returned fire only."

She paused to drink some tea; I did the same.

"He hinted at a couple of other things as well, such as they weren't always a hundred percent sure the people the unit killed *were* IRA. He implied a number of innocent people died as well, and it's this he wants to talk about, as well as the one they tortured to death."

An army death squad. Did the British army ever have such a unit?

Taylor read the doubt on my face.

"Oh, it wasn't official, if that's what you're thinking," she explained, sitting forward. "The unit operated completely under the radar and was never officially sanctioned by anyone. But this guy said it was part of an unofficial military reaction force the army had in operation in the early seventies."

"A military reaction force? How many were in this unit?"

"In his little unit, usually about three or four, depending on who they were after. An officer, a sergeant and one or two ordinary squaddies. Guy talking to Jacobs had been one of the squaddies."

"How long did this unit operate for?" I asked.

"On and off, he says a year or so, maybe a bit longer, until the officer was deployed elsewhere, then it all came to a halt."

I then remembered there being a BBC *Panorama* programme about this very issue a couple of years back. Had whoever'd been talking to Jacobs been part of this? If so, why did he want to make the points that had been raised in the programme known again?

"Did this guy offer any exact numbers about how many they killed?" I was trying to imagine the headlines a story like this would generate, if it was true.

"No, but he estimated his little unit alone killed or injured at least twenty suspected IRA personnel."

"Twenty?"

"At least, according to this guy, but that's for the whole unit, not just this one guy."

I sat quietly for several seconds, turning over what I'd just heard. This was quite a story and I briefly speculated about the reaction were it ever to be made public. I remembered there being some controversy when the BBC had broadcast its programme about there being a supposed *shoot-to-kill* policy in operation, but the claims made by the programme, or by soldiers saying they'd been part of such a unit, had been categorically and emphatically denied by the army and the MOD. After a few days, the mainstream media had stopped reporting the story, and no further mention of this issue had been made.

I'd little doubt not every death wrought by British soldiers operating in the province had been four-square according to the guidelines issued to soldiers in times of insurrection. Armed conflict doesn't exactly follow the Queensbury rules, I knew this only too well from my own experience, but an undercover, unofficial policy of actually *seeking* targets to kill?

"How were they killed?" I asked.

"Shot, mainly. In a couple of cases, they took the victim to a quiet place, then they'd shoot him from behind and claim he'd been arrested but was escaping from custody."

I chewed over what I'd just heard, and I wasn't certain how much of it I believed. For the moment, though, I kept my reservations to myself. But I *was* curious about one thing.

"So, why's this guy coming forward now? From the timeline you've mentioned, these events took place, what, forty-five years back, so why now? What's he hoping to gain by talking about this now?"

"Jacobs asked him the same question." Taylor leant forward in her seat. "He said he told the guy he could have made this public any time in the last forty or so years. He said he could have even helped out with the *Panorama* programme, so why's he coming forward now? What's he hoping to gain by going public now?"

She sipped her drink, put the cup down, then leant forward again, resting her elbows and the palms of her hands on the table. "He gave two reasons. He's says he'd been carrying the guilt of his involvement for years but, since he converted to Roman Catholicism in 2010 and became a practising communicant, the feelings of guilt and remorse have really been biting into him. Evidently, some of the deaths he was involved in have been playing on his mind for a while."

She paused for a moment to brush hair away from the top of her glasses. "He'd also watched the *Panorama* programme about the shoot-to-kill policy, and claimed everything said had been watered down and sanitised. Those interviewed were making it sound like they only went after top IRA personnel, those the RUC knew to be guilty, but he knew this wasn't true. He said there were several deaths of people known to be innocent of any involvement with the IRA. He knew this was true because he'd been a part of it."

She looked around the park for several seconds. "The other reason is, a few months ago, he was diagnosed with an inoperable brain cancer, and he fervently believes his eternal soul won't get into Heaven until he confesses all his sins in public, which is what he says God's telling him to do. Doctors have said he'll probably be dead before too much longer, so it's now or never."

I was curious about something. I had remembered something from catechism class at school. "So why doesn't he just go to church and confess it all to a Catholic priest? What is it they say about there being greater joy in Heaven over one sinner who repenteth his sins, that kind of thing? He'd be given absolution, told to say some Hail Marys as penance, then it'll all be off his conscience, and his place in Heaven'll be assured," I said, somewhat irreverently for a Sunday.

"Jacobs also pointed this out to him." Taylor was grinning at my irreverence. "But what's tipped the balance is this guy says one of the people his unit killed was a young kid, aged twenty, and this kid had absolutely nothing to do with the IRA."

"What happened here?"

"They pulled him in off the street because his older brother'd had some kind of peripheral involvement with the IRA, and army intelligence believed weapons were being hidden on the estate he lived on. The assumption was this lad had to know something about them, and he didn't, but he says they still killed him," she explained.

"Why's he focusing on this case?" I asked.

"He was watching a Channel 4 programme a while back, something about the Good Friday agreement, and this kid's surviving family were interviewed. He recognised the surname, did some checking of notes he'd made at the time, and realised the timeline fitted; he'd been part of the unit which'd killed their son. He wants to make a full public confession so the kid's family can get some kind of closure, and he also wants to offer a public apology to the family for what he did, because he was a party to the killing of an innocent person."

Taylor sat back in her seat and drank more tea. She was looking at me and, I suspect, wondering whether I was believing her story. She sat forward again.

"The guy Jacobs talked to said, when they reported the death of this kid, they'd claimed he'd been an IRA sniper in hiding, waiting to ambush the army vehicle as it went past, and they'd surprised him by coming up on him and shooting him. They even showed a rifle they'd supposedly taken from this young kid, but it'd caused a ruckus at army HQ. The boy's name wasn't known or listed as being IRA, he'd never come to the attention of the police *or* the military, apart from being searched at army checkpoints, that kind of thing. The IRA officially disowned him, said he was not one of their volunteers and had *nothing* to do with them, and it issued a statement accusing the British army of cold-blooded murder. His family and the RUC said they knew he wasn't a paramilitary. Kid was a churchgoer, an ex-altar boy, and his parish priest said he was innocent. Even the local UVF said they knew this kid was nothing to do with the IRA."

She paused to finish her drink, then sat quietly for several seconds.

"The shooting of this kid was investigated, and he says the army brass weren't wholly convinced by the officer's explanation of why they were even in the area where the shooting occurred. The way this man told it, they were supposed to have been on duty in Belfast that evening. The officer's story couldn't actually be disproved because the two soldiers with him had backed it. But, whatever, soon after, the officer was transferred out of Northern Ireland. And, just after he left, their little unit ceased operations."

I was quiet for a moment, contemplating everything I'd heard. "Are there many more cases like this one?"

"Don't know. Jacobs is gonna ask him when he meets him again."

"Did this guy himself kill anyone?"

"Says he didn't." She shook her head. "Says he fired shots at several people with a handgun or rifle, and he thinks he injured a few, but doesn't think he killed anyone directly. He said they shot one guy IRA execution style, down on his knees and shot in the back of the neck, making it look like he was an informer." She put down her empty cup and looked around for a moment. "It's things like this causing his crisis of conscience."

We were silent for several more seconds.

"So, what's *your* sense of what Jacobs told you?" I asked.

She looked thoughtful. I was noticing how the breeze was still moving her hair around.

"I think, on balance, Jacobs believes this guy, thinks he has a story deserving of being looked into," she finally answered. "So far, he's only heard the broad outline. He's gonna talk to the guy again soon, but this time he wants *me* to come with him, wants me to listen and see what I think. Jacobs told me, next time they talk, the guy's gonna give the names of everyone he was involved in killing, as well as the names of all the soldiers in his unit. We'll research the circumstances of each death, work the story from there."

"You gonna help him if he thinks there's a story there?" I asked.

"If what he says sounds plausible, then oh yeah." She nodded, looking serious. "I mean, even if only part of it's true, it'll still be a major story."

"So where you meeting this guy?"

"Somewhere in Bedfordshire, near where he lives. Jacobs is gonna meet him again this week sometime; he'll let me know when. He's seeing the editor tomorrow and, assuming he gets the go-ahead to develop the story, we'll take it from there."

We set off for home, taking a slow walk around the park, holding hands and just enjoying being with each other. It began to drizzle slightly as the wind picked up, so we sped up.

But I was somewhat distracted. Did what she'd just told me have anything to do with why Simmons had told me to warn her away from Jacobs?

SIX

Wednesday

Jacobs had talked to the *Standard*'s editor, Hugh Blackbourne, Monday afternoon. The soldier's story had been relayed in as much detail as was currently known, and Jacobs had outlined the angle he was looking to develop with the story. He'd suggested there would be considerable public interest if it could be established that British soldiers had pursued an unlawful *shoot-to-kill* policy, despite repeated categoric Government denials such a policy had ever existed. This would be in direct contravention of long-standing official Government policy, as well as international human rights law. When British soldiers were engaged in armed conflict, the Yellow Card policy was to be followed, meaning soldiers were only permitted to discharge their weapons when they reasonably believed their lives to be at extreme risk. Soldiers were not permitted to discharge their weapons simply because they disliked a particular situation.

After careful consideration, Blackbourne had agreed there was the nucleus of a disturbing revelation in the man's confession. He'd stated the story could be pursued, *but only* if what this man was claiming could be established as the truth, *and* any further information he gave could be independently verified. As an ex-Cabinet minister, Blackbourne would be all too aware of the acute political embarrassment Government would suffer if such a story was made public without all due care and attention paid, given all the official denials which had been issued. More importantly, he'd also be aware of the damage to the reputation of the paper if the story was published and then proven to be wholly incorrect.

Blackbourne had laid down the ground rules. Before it would be considered for publication, the article had to be based upon *one hundred percent concrete evidence*, grounded in *proven and established facts*, and everything was to be validated by authoritative and independent experts. Anyone making claims would need to give a sworn statement. The soldier's story, whilst interesting, was *not* to be believed verbatim. No one source was to be wholly relied upon. *Only* if a source's account could be supported by someone else, preferably someone the source didn't know, was credence to be given to any claims made.

Blackbourne also emphasised that the story was *not* to be written from the angle of questioning the UK's role in Northern Ireland. The article's sole focus was to be the ascertaining of any truth about an army shoot-to-kill policy.

After all his provisos had been agreed to by Jacobs, Blackbourne had greenlit the enterprise. At Jacobs' request, he had told Taylor she could work the story with Jacobs, should she wish to do so, which she did. After the impact of their story about Yuri Krachnikhov and James Blatchford, the editor had been looking for another public-interest topic to turn into a major investigation, and Jacobs had now found one which, *prima facie*, fitted the criteria, even though this wasn't exclusively about an issue which affected Londoners.

So, today, Jacobs and Taylor had taken the train to Bedfordshire to talk to this ex-soldier. He lived in a cottage in Houghton Regis, a village just north of Luton, and they'd met with him and his wife, who was now also his live-in carer. The soldier was Barry Pencourt, now aged sixty-four. According to his recent medical prognosis, if he saw sixty-five in five months' time, he'd be a very lucky man, because his cancer was now well advanced and the tumours on his brain were inoperable.

Pencourt had been wearing his regimental tie and a jacket bearing the emblem of the Parachute Regiment when they'd arrived at his house just before midday. His hair was clumped and there were red blotches on his skull, the result of chemotherapy sessions. Taylor and Jacobs had spent the next couple of hours listening to and, as he'd no objections, each taping the man's story.

As per his original promise, Pencourt had supplied the names of twenty-three people he believed his unit had been involved in the killing of over the time it'd been covertly operating. He'd listed the name and rank of every soldier, officer and sergeant he could remember serving in his little unit, which had been given the designation *Two Unit*, stating his belief every person mentioned was as culpable as he was for the killings that had occurred. His wife had made tea for everyone and sat next to her husband, occasionally holding his hand and offering moral support.

They'd begun the session by asking Pencourt how he'd become involved with this unit in the first place. Pencourt had sat very quietly, lost in his memories for a long moment, before he answered the question.

"Always wanted to be a soldier, I did, right from when I was a kiddie. It's the only thing I ever wanted to be. Even at school. They'd ask, *What you gonna do when you leave?* Join the army, I'd say. Proud of being a soldier, I was, proud to be the first one in my family line ever to be in uniform, apart from when my dad did his national service in 1954, just after Korea."

He'd spoken quietly, pushed his chest forward, puffing himself up with pride.

"Always wanted to join the Parachute Regiment as well." He paused for a moment. "You know how bloody hard it is to become a para? You have *any* idea how hard the training is, or how tough, both physically and mentally, you have to be to successfully complete it?"

Question had been rhetorical. Nobody answered.

"Anyway, I was proud to be a para as well, proud to wear the red beret. A bloody great achievement to become one, it was. They're a proud regiment. We were damn good soldiers, the best in the army: well trained, fit, disciplined and very tough. No matter what sins I later committed, nothing'll ever tarnish the memory of the pride I felt the first time I earned the right to put the red beret on. You remember the advert about the army, *Be the best you can be*? Well, we were the best. It's no coincidence the SAS draws most of its recruits from the paras."

For a few seconds he'd drifted off into some uncharted corner of his mind, looking at the people asking questions but seemingly not seeing them. He'd then exhaled and continued.

"Being a para meant taking shit from nobody. I remember, on leave once, I was with a mate in a pub, and these six skinheads nearby keep swearing loudly and being obnoxious, so my friend tells them to shut up. This loudmouth leaps to his feet, comes over and says something like, *Want some, do you, mate?* So we say, *Outside.* You know what? We beat the crap out of four of them. The other two? They ran. *That's* what being a para means." He was smiling at the memory. "Either of you two ever been in uniform?"

"Only if school uniform counts," Jacobs had replied with a grin. Taylor shook her head.

"Didn't think you had." He'd smiled cryptically. "Neither of you look the type."

He was quiet for a few more seconds.

"So, how'd I get involved? Me and a mate, we were called in to see our captain one Sunday morning. This would have been sometime early autumn, 1971, don't remember the exact date. I initially thought we were in the shit for something. I mean, captains don't usually call to speak to privates, do they? If we're due a bollocking, it's usually done by sergeants, so all the way to his office we were wondering what the hell we'd done wrong. When we arrived, we were told to go straight in, and the captain was there with another officer."

"You know who he was?"

"No. He was never introduced by name, and I didn't recognise him, but from his uniform and the pips on his shoulder I guessed he was a higher rank, something like a lieutenant colonel. We were told to sit; we did." He paused for a moment. "The captain then started talking to us about the current military thinking on how to deal with the increasing threat posed by the IRA. Peacekeeping didn't seem to be working and the thinking amongst the senior officers was, if top IRA personnel could be taken out of the picture, this would help disrupt their capability to wage war." He'd nodded knowingly. "He said something like, *You remember those three young Scottish soldiers who'd been murdered not too long back?* I said we did, and he said it was incidents like this making the politicians think it was time to take the war to the IRA, rather than letting them bring it to us. He said it'd been decided to change course because by then we'd been in Ireland two years and we were no nearer to resolving the conflict. Politicians were worrying about the death count."

He'd stopped for a moment to draw a deep breath. "He talked about how the British army had many years' experience of jungle warfare and insurrections in places like Kenya and Malaysia, but no experience of fighting urban guerrilla warfare in its own backyard, especially against an indigenous population where many were actually supporting what these IRA terrorists were doing."

He'd then looked directly at Jacobs and Taylor. "So he told us, straight up, we'd both been selected to join a special undercover unit being put together, which was going to play a leading role in taking the war to the IRA. I asked him what he meant by this, and he said the plan was, rather than just keeping the two sides of the sectarian divide apart while the politicians tried to find a solution, to go under the radar and eliminate known IRA personnel, take out as many of their foot soldiers as we could, disrupt their lines of communication and their ability to wage war. He asked how we felt about this. We both said yes straight away, didn't even need to consider it. I mean, my battalion'd lost a couple of squaddies, and I was no friend of the IRA, so we both said we were pleased we'd been selected. The officer dismissed us and said someone would be in touch soon."

"Had he spelt out exactly what was meant by the term *eliminate*?" Jacobs had asked.

"Not specifically, no, but I think I just initially assumed it meant getting them off the streets, getting them put into Long Kesh or some other prison like Castlereagh, so they couldn't shoot at soldiers or plant bombs any longer. The RUC was struggling to hold the line and, as we were better trained and better equipped for this kind of thing, I just thought we'd be helping the police by getting more directly involved."

"Why'd you think they'd selected *you* to be involved?"

"They said I fitted the profile and I had the qualities required. I was good with firearms, I'd qualified as a marksman, and I was calm under fire, is what I was told."

"At this point, did you have any notion at all of what the unit would be?" Taylor had asked.

"No." He'd shaken his head firmly. "I was under the impression, from what this officer had said, we'd be working alongside the RUC and going into IRA-held areas to make arrests. I thought we were gonna be something like an elite snatch squad, going to republican strongholds and picking up IRA bigwigs and bombers."

"So, just to be clear at this point, you're saying you'd *no* idea at this time what you were getting into," Taylor said.

Staring directly at Taylor and Jacobs, Pencourt had raised his right hand. "I swear before Almighty God, at this time, I'd no idea we were gonna be an assassination squad."

So now there was an unspoken question in the air: how long had it been before he'd found out the reality? He'd anticipated this and answered before the question could be asked.

"The killings began on our second trip out. First time out, we were dispatched to pick up someone suspected of being involved in the shooting of an RUC officer. We found him coming out of a pub, just where the RUC'd said he'd be. We cornered him, he surrendered, no problem, and we brought him in. Piss-easy, it was. I thought it was all gonna be like this." He nodded. "But, on our second time out, we drove out early one morning, about seven or so, to a house where someone suspected by the RUC of being an IRA gunnie lived. They thought he was the one who'd shot and killed an RUC man. So we sat and waited in the car for a while."

"*Suspected?* You didn't know if he was or wasn't?" Jacobs had asked.

Pencourt had shook his head as an answer.

"Didn't this bother you?"

"Not at the time, no. I'd no reason to disbelieve the intelligence we'd been given." He'd nodded to himself for a moment, looking pensive. "After about an hour the person we were waiting for came out and turned left. We knew he was going to work, so we followed for a short distance, then we pulled up by him as he walked past a couple of disused shops. I assumed we'd be getting out to pick him up as there was no one around, but the officer sitting behind me called out the man's name and, as he turned, the officer fired three shots at him. Killed him outright, he did, *and* he'd used a handgun we'd found on an IRA man we'd taken in but never reported he'd had. We sped off before anyone spotted us."

He'd sighed. "The bloke never knew what hit him. The story was quickly put around he'd been done by loyalists, and we did nothing to dispel this suspicion, even though nationalists staged a small-scale riot in the centre of Belfast the same evening." He'd paused. "And that's really when it all kicked off."

"How did you feel about it once it'd started, once you'd found out what this unit was really all about?" Taylor had asked him.

Pencourt had sat silently for a moment, thinking of the right way to answer. "I watched this bloke get gunned down in cold blood and I suppose, if I'm honest . . ." He'd been quiet for several seconds. "It didn't bother me too much to begin with. At this time, I was assuming everyone we went after was IRA in some way or other. The notion of innocent people being killed hadn't yet dawned on me."

He'd looked upwards for a few seconds, then continued. "After this shooting, when the officer asked if anyone had a problem with what he'd just done, I wasn't too upset. I suppose I was thinking something along the lines of the greatest good of the greatest number being served by these people dying and, as I said, we were acting on RUC information about these people being involved in the IRA, so I suppose I didn't lose too much sleep." He'd spoken slowly and solemnly. "I mean, our next hit, the RUC had stone cold proof this bloke had been one of the IRA team who'd recently planted the bomb in Belfast which'd killed several people, including women and children, so I guess I wasn't too upset at the manner of his death either, shot coming out of a bookie's. I still hadn't fully realised this was what the unit was all about."

He'd gone quiet.

"So, how did the situation change for you?" Jacobs had asked.

"Over a period of weeks, I began hearing stories of people being shot and killed almost at random, people who weren't involved with any terror group, and I started to realise some in my regiment didn't seem too concerned whether someone was innocent or not. *That* was when it started to bother me. Because the official records will say we killed a certain number of people but, trust me, we took out a bloody lot more than the records suggest, including several IRA people they never acknowledged as being killed. We did more damage than will ever be admitted by anyone. I was there; I *know* we did. And not all of them were IRA either."

He'd then sat quietly contemplative for almost half a minute. It appeared he was finding it hard to talk about the situation.

"But what *really* got me thinking, what *really* got to me, was . . ." He took a deep breath. "I was there when this one bloke was shot dead because he'd been scoped in the company of someone we knew for a fact to be an IRA quartermaster. We pulled up in the car and confronted them. The one we were after, the IRA man, he sees us and takes off, scarpers down a back alley, across someone's back garden and escapes. But this other bloke? He just stands where he was, doesn't move, and we put several bullets in him."

He stopped talking for a long moment, breathing deeply.

"It came through on the news the same night. He wasn't *anything* to do with the IRA. He was a civilian and'd only gone to see this other man because they both played in the same Gaelic football team. His wife said he'd just been checking to see if this person could be available for a game at the weekend, because they were struggling to get a team together." He'd sat looking at the floor for a number of seconds. "He lost his life for being with the wrong person at the wrong time. The man was only early thirties and had five children, all under nine." He'd shaken his head, mournfully. "I'd been involved in an action which had led to the murder of an innocent man. At this point I knew something was very wrong with what we were doing."

He'd been breathing deeply and sighing heavily by now. At one point, Taylor had thought he was wiping tears from his eyes. This was clearly a painful memory.

"And there was no apology given from the army either," he'd sighed. He'd stopped, wiped a tear from his eyes and then blown his nose. "Sorry about this."

"No problem. Take all the time you need," Taylor had replied.

"Soon after this, we pick up someone off the street. I thought we were taking him in for the RUC to question, but the officer orders us to drive elsewhere. We take this guy to a deserted barn a few miles north of Belfast. I was told to stand outside and keep watch. The officer, the sergeant and another bloke dragged him inside and they did a real number on him. I could hear what was happening, could hear his screams as they were beating him. I looked inside and I saw the officer kick this bloke in the head, right here." He had pointed to his chin. "You know what happened? He drove the bloke's jawbone right up into his brain, killed him instantly."

He'd laughed ironically. "We took him with us and said we'd found him in the road, said he'd probably been hit by a vehicle and killed. They signed off on that as well, even though it must have been obvious his injuries couldn't have been from being hit by a car." He had shaken his head in disbelief.

Silence for several more seconds.

"Did anyone in your squad suspect you were having these doubts?" Taylor had asked. "Did you ever tell anyone at all about how you were feeling?"

"No. No, I didn't tell anybody." He had sat grimly silent again for a moment. "I mean, who could I tell? It was a senior officer, a captain, who'd offered me the chance to be involved with this supposedly elite team, and who'd have believed me even if I'd told them?" He'd shrugged. "Also, telling someone how I felt would've meant I'd be dropping the men I was serving with into the crapper, and they were all good soldiers, doing what they thought was the right thing for their country, so I just kept my doubts to myself. Didn't say anything to anyone. But, since I left the army, down the years, those doubts've grown."

"Couldn't you have just asked not to be involved any longer?"

"Wouldn't have been possible. I ask not to be involved, they'd wanna know why. I'd be admitting to having doubts, and that'd raise questions with the top brass, not to mention the others in the team, so I just kept my head down."

He'd paused at this point and spent some time breathing deeply, according to Taylor.

"And it's been burning up inside me for years, and now I can't live with myself any longer. I have to atone for my sins before I die. If not, I go straight to Hell and burn for all eternity."

Jacobs had then come straight to the central point. "I wanna be clear on what you've told us so far, so there's no misunderstanding. For the record, you're saying there *definitely was* an official shoot-to-kill policy employed by the British army against the IRA, instigated by the British government. You're claiming the British army, operating in Northern Ireland in an official peacekeeping capacity, was targeting and killing IRA personnel, and occasionally innocent civilians, as part of its shoot-to-kill strategy."

"As far as I'm aware, the unit never knowingly targeted anyone not involved with the IRA, and I'm not sure if what we did was ever officially sanctioned," Pencourt had replied, "but we'd been told by our captain, who was also involved, what we were doing had the blessing of those on high, which I assumed meant Government. So, yes, that is what I'm saying."

Silence for several more seconds.

"And you're happy to be quoted on this?" Jacobs had asked.

"Yes," he'd replied firmly, "because at all times, even when I was having my doubts, I thought as soldiers we were simply doing our political masters' bidding."

He'd then told them about the case of Brendan Morgan, which was the last action he'd been involved in. He had recited the circumstances of his apprehension, where they'd taken him to, how he'd been interrogated and then shot by an officer.

"Kid was scared fucking shitless, he was," he'd said quietly and sorrowfully, shaking his head. "Poor little bastard had no idea what was happening to him or why. He wasn't involved with the paramilitaries and'd never held a rifle in his life. His family said he'd been off to his girlfriend's house when we'd picked him up off the streets and then shot the poor sod. We'd roughed him up a bit beforehand as well."

As he'd finished saying this, he'd looked down and started crying. Not full-on; just tears rolling down his cheeks as he spoke. His wife had put her arm round him and given him a hug. He had taken a few seconds to compose himself.

"I remember seeing his mother and sisters, his grandmother and girlfriend, all crying at the kid's funeral; local TV news covered it. I thought to myself, *I'm responsible for all those poor women's tears.* I was absolutely certain at this point something was very wrong."

He'd paused again to wipe the tears from his cheeks with a tissue.

"I've found out the kid's mother and sister are still alive, so, before I die, I want to meet these women and offer my heartfelt apologies for the murder of their son and brother."

"Why this particular kid?" Jacobs had asked. "Why'd *he* been picked up?"

"Army intelligence had informed us who his older brother was; he'd been some kind of IRA volunteer. He wasn't a soldier, just a runner, passing messages and storing things, stuff like that, so the assumption was ..." He'd shrugged and hadn't completed the sentence.

He'd sat in silence for several seconds, tears rolling down his cheeks again.

"You know," he'd said quietly, "I can still hear the kid's screams as the officer was pointing his gun at him. Bloodcurdling, they were. I've had nightmares about this for some time now, months, years in fact. Several nights I've just lain in bed and thought about what I did to this kid, and I can't sleep. I have nightmares about what I've done, about the sins I've committed and the pain and heartache my actions must have caused. I have to make my peace with God the Father before I die," – he'd made the sign of the cross as he spoke – "because I won't get into Heaven if my sins aren't forgiven and, if I die unconfessed, my soul goes straight to Hell, so it's got to be a public confession, which is why I'm telling you two as writers my story. I'm prepared to take my share of the blame for what I did, and if it means my dying in prison, then so be it." He had paused for a few seconds. "I can't go to meet the Good Lord" – he'd crossed himself again – "with the stain of mortal sin on my soul. I must be confessed in order to be ready to meet God."

Taylor and Jacobs had spent a couple of minutes comparing notes whilst Pencourt had excused himself and gone to the toilet. He had returned and sat down again, ready to continue.

Jacobs had then asked him the pivotal question: "This is all very interesting, but how do we know what you've told us is true?"

Pencourt had nodded at his wife, who'd produced a memory stick and passed it to Taylor.

"There was something about the way this kid was protesting his innocence as we were interrogating him," Pencourt had said. "I'd slapped him around the face when he didn't respond to the first question we asked. He'd denied knowing anything. I mean, that's normal procedure, but there was something in his tone of voice. We stood him up against a tree and you could see looking at his eyes he was just a scared kid. All the way back to barracks, it was eating away at me: *We've killed an innocent person.* It kept going round and round in my head. So, when I was alone, I wrote his name and details down, and then spent some time doing the same with all the others I'd been involved in the deaths of, when I got the chance. I've listed everyone I can remember and made some notes about where we apprehended them, what we did to them, where they were killed and who did it." He had taken a deep breath again. "They're all on this," – he'd nodded at the memory stick Taylor was holding – "and you can follow it all up from there. There's your starting point."

As they'd been leaving the house, Pencourt had spoken again.

"You know, some years ago, I went to a reunion evening for my old regiment, the paras, and I met up with someone I'd served with in Two Unit." He'd looked significantly at Taylor and Jacobs.

"We got on to talking about some of the things we did in Northern Ireland, and this one person was absolutely proud of what we'd done. I asked him if he'd ever thought we might've killed any innocent people. You know what his reply was? *What if we did? Fucking animals, the Irish were. They were bombing and killing us on the mainland, so we exacted revenge on them. Nobody died who didn't deserve to.* Straight up, that's what he said."

"Who said this?" Jacobs had asked.

"All the names and details are on the memory stick."

*

"So, where's this memory stick now?"

Taylor and I were in the kitchen, preparing dinner. Or, rather, she was. I'd been leaning back against the counter and listening attentively to the story she'd just finished telling me. It was an astonishing story and I was thinking about the response of the *Standard*'s editor if everything they'd been told could be confirmed as fact. What would the next step be?

"Steve has it. He's gonna examine the contents and get back to me," she said. "He'll also make copies of it."

"You were there; you saw and heard this Pencourt guy speak. Do *you* think he's telling you the truth?" I asked in all seriousness.

She stopped what she was doing and looked seriously contemplative for a moment.

"On balance, yeah, I do," she finally said. "You only had to look at his eyes and hear his voice to know he was telling the truth. Either he's an Academy Award winning actor or there's a lot of truth in what he's saying, but obviously we're not just gonna accept what he said at face value. I'm gonna start researching military codes of conduct and what the law was at the time, as well as what Government did and said about this, and Steve is gonna check out the people named on the memory stick, and then we'll take it from there. If it looks like there's something in what he's told us, we'll start putting together an approach for this story."

I was curious about one thing. "How did Steve Jacobs even get put onto this guy in the first place?"

"Through his older brother. Steve's brother, I mean. He's in the army; I think he's a major. He'd told Steve he'd come across someone at a regimental reunion who'd kept going on and on about this *Panorama* programme on shoot-to-kill, and said what'd been reported didn't tell the whole story, because nothing'd been said about the role Government played. Steve asked to be put in touch with the man who'd said it, so the brother got him in contact with Pencourt."

"Does his brother think there's something there, then?"

"Didn't say, though he did tell Steve he'd be very lucky if he found *any* press outlet willing to believe or print Pencourt's claims."

Was now the time to tell Taylor about Simmons' warning against too close an association with Steve Jacobs? For the moment I said nothing. Something said *not yet.*

"Just be careful with this one, okay?" I slid my arms around her from behind and started nibbling her neck. "Don't want you getting in trouble with the MOD."

I released my grip and she turned to face me.

"That's sweet, McGraw, but don't worry." She smiled and lightly kissed me. "I'll be careful."

SEVEN

Friday

From the memory stick he'd been given, Jacobs had printed off a list of names of those Pencourt claimed had been killed by his squad, Two Unit, and in the past two days, according to Taylor, he'd unearthed details of all of them from news reports. He'd somehow managed to track down the person Pencourt had stated was in command of his little unit, though he didn't say how he'd managed this, and was planning to go and see this officer, who was now living in secluded retirement somewhere in the West Country. Jacobs had also discovered one person killed by the unit had a relative in America who'd once been active in NORAID, the pro-Irish-nationalist American group which raised funds for the IRA, but was now living in Ireland, and Jacobs was attempting to make contact with him.

Jacobs had told the editor, after everything his research had uncovered, he was now more convinced than ever that there was a story waiting to be told here. Blackbourne, after hearing what he had to say and giving it careful thought, had agreed with him and told him to continue working on the story, mindful of the caveats he'd stressed earlier in the week.

Taylor was in on the story, and had been checking the legal position concerning British soldiers charged with keeping the peace during civil insurrection, as well as researching what members of the Government had said at the time about claims of a shoot-to-kill policy being utilised against the IRA. She'd managed to identify an ex-Government junior minister who'd been in the Home Office at the time, but he was currently away on holiday, so she'd left a message asking him to call her. She'd also requested a copy of the BBC's *Panorama* programme which had made the claim. One was due to be sent to her.

The objective was to have the article researched and ready to be written inside the next five to six weeks. Two weeks later, if all went to plan, it would be ready for publication.

*

Just after twelve thirty: I'd now finished writing up my report relating to two LSE 'students' I'd been monitoring the activities of, who, it'd been claimed by a security service source, had been holding radicalisation sessions with new entrants to the university, with the specific intent of converting them to radical Islamist beliefs. They'd been holding sessions both at the university and at the same Islington mosque where the late, unlamented Khaled al-Ebouli had conducted similar sessions. Two such talks had been secretly recorded by MI5's man on the inside and translated into English, but, after careful scrutiny by Special Branch and the security service, it'd been decided, for the moment, no action was to be taken, despite the repeated use of terms like *jihad*, *caliphate* and *sharia law*. Special Branch had been given orders to keep both men under ongoing surveillance, though, around the clock.

One of the two men, a Turk named Mehmet Tabzouni, was a mature student supposedly studying international comparative politics and a known associate of persons connected with the terrorist organisation Muearada in Iraq and France, several of whom had been the main suspects in a car bombing near the Pompidou Centre in Paris some months back, which'd caused considerable damage in the immediate vicinity but, fortunately, no fatalities. Tabzouni had been in Paris at the time, and CCTV had caught him several times in and around the Pompidou Centre, though neither he nor anyone else had been charged after being pulled in by the GIGN, the counter-terrorist branch of the French National Gendarmerie. No reason for the bombing had ever been given either.

I'd spent some part of the morning reviewing Tabzouni's file and wondering just whose immigration fuck-up had allowed this joker to enter the country on a student visa, given what we knew about him. Student? I spent more time every day cleaning my teeth than he spent studying every week. The only way he'd ever be in the main lecture hall would be if he'd lost his way and entered it by mistake.

I'd been owed a few hours in lieu because of the extra time I'd put in following Tabzouni and his acolyte, a British-born Muslim on the same course, Sam Alorami, over the past several days.

Alorami, also a mature student, had attended the radicalising talks given by Tabzouni. His profile by MI5 psychologists maintained he was, despite the improbability of his being an LSE student, easily manipulated and not particularly bright, and therefore he was considered susceptible to the notions of pursuing the jihad against the west that Tabzouni was preaching, which meant MI5 had profiled him as a potential suicide bomber. He would need to be watched very carefully.

I'd spent this past week as part of a team of followers trailing both men, who seemed to spend a lot of time in the refectory talking to others, several of whom were also known to the security service through their attendance at the mosque. The only time they'd spent elsewhere in the LSE was when they'd played backgammon in one of the common rooms, apparently for cash sums equivalent to my and Taylor's annual salaries.

So, having spent most of yesterday either in the refectory at the LSE or in a Bloomsbury café, watching both men talking animatedly to other individuals about, from the later translation, how Israel could and should be destroyed and whether germ warfare should be the method employed, I'd signed out just after midday today. I was now on my way to talk to someone who, frankly, I loathed and detested in every way possible but who, nonetheless, would probably be a goldmine of information concerning the topic I was looking for details about.

It was nothing to do with my current assignment from Smitherman.

After hearing what Taylor had said Wednesday evening, I'd decided yesterday morning on the way to work that *I* was going to do a little surreptitious checking, without her knowing, into Pencourt's claims of an undercover army unit enacting a shoot-to-kill policy in Northern Ireland in the seventies. Frankly I was sceptical such a unit had ever existed. I knew a couple of guys who'd been soldiers in the early seventies, and both had done time in Northern Ireland, so I was curious to learn what they knew about this claim.

There were a couple of reasons why I'd decided to do this. For one thing, I didn't know whether this story was in any way connected to the warning Simmons had given about working too closely with Jacobs, and I was still agonising over whether I ought to tell Taylor what Simmons had said.

But the more important reason, for me, was that, if Taylor was being hooked into a story with no credibility, or potentially damaging repercussions for her, I could attempt to safely extricate her before any serious consequences arose. I was indifferent about what happened to Jacobs. He was a big boy; he could look out for himself.

I was going to see this particular person first as I'd had previous dealings with him. I knew he'd been a soldier around the time the alleged unlawful killings had been committed, and I knew from his Special Branch file he'd done two tours in Northern Ireland in the early seventies.

George Selwood was a self-professed *ageing fascist*, now in his early seventies but no less vitriolic in his hatreds, of which he nursed many. He could hate for his country. Any dictionary definition of the word *hatred* should include his picture alongside it, and time had done nothing to mellow how he felt about the objects of his pet hatreds. If anything, his hatreds had intensified as he'd got older, and they included just about everything and everyone. He was deeply embedded in the intense depths of pessimism about the state of humanity that all extreme right-wing adherents I've ever encountered seem to use as a lodestar for their actions.

He was proud of being the only son of parents who'd both been interned, imprisoned without trial, alongside Oswald Mosley and others in the British Union of Fascists, in May 1940, because of their overt Nazi sympathies. They had publically campaigned for Britain to accept the peace deal Hitler had offered rather than going to war against Germany, as it would still leave Britain in control of its monarchy and its empire. His father had also faced charges under the Incitement to Disaffection Act 1934, after he'd been arrested for circulating leaflets urging soldiers to disobey their lawful orders and not go to war against Germany, just after the British Government had declared war on 3rd September 1939.

George Selwood was someone who'd spent his entire adult life seeing conspiracies organised by Jews behind every closed door. He'd once told me he firmly believed the world financial system was run by a sinister cabal of Zionists operating out of their base on Wall Street, which he always referred to as *Jewrusalem,* and he maintained the financial crash of 2008 had been instigated by Jews to tighten their grip on the world financial system.

And it wasn't only Jews he hated, though these he hated almost viscerally. He was an avowed and unreconstructed racist who'd devoted his life to fighting against what he referred to as the *increasing mongrelisation* of the 'indigenous' white British population, which he was convinced was on the near-horizon. He particularly despised intermarriage between black and white people, which, he'd once written in a Dutch far-right magazine, should be outlawed, as well as his particular *bête noire*, interracial pregnancy, which he'd written should be punishable by death, with any foetuses compulsorily aborted. In the same article, he'd justified this view by claiming, *A cat born in a kennel doesn't make it a dog.*

Before coming I'd read through his file again. Since his early youth, he'd been active in many of the more extreme right-wing groups, such as the League of Empire Loyalists, the White Defence League and, in the 1970s, the National Front. In 1958, while still only thirteen, he'd been part of a group of young thugs who'd taken part in the Notting Hill riots, attacking black immigrants and throwing stones and bottles at the police as they attempted to break up the fighting.

When Rhodesia had declared its independence from the United Kingdom in November 1965, so as to preserve white minority rule, he'd been active in supporting this decision, earning the first of his several arrests at a pro-white colonial rule demonstration in Trafalgar Square. In April 1968 he'd organised a march in London for people who supported Enoch Powell's warnings about *rivers of blood* flowing through the nation. On 11th February 1990, the day Nelson Mandela had been released from Robben Island, he'd staged a solitary protest outside the South African High Commission in Trafalgar Square, with a homemade placard insisting that Mandela, rather than being released, should have been hanged as a communist-backed terrorist. His response to Mandela later becoming president of a South African rainbow nation hadn't been recorded, though it probably wasn't too hard to guess.

He'd been active in every major right-wing cause for more than sixty years, opposing independence for British colonies, mass immigration to the UK, joining the then-European Economic Community, Hong Kong reverting to Chinese control and many others. In fact, such was his notoriety on the extreme right that the anti-fascist magazine *Searchlight* had once included him in a special edition it'd published about leading racists and their beliefs. In conversations with him, his worldview and his extremism were starkly illustrated, and I'd long suspected it was only his intense hatreds which gave him any reason to stay alive.

I'd first encountered Selwood when, after not being in uniform too long, I'd helped to arrest him at a demonstration against British involvement in Iraq. He'd thrown a plastic bottle filled with urine at marchers.

He still lived in a hard-to-let block of flats on Rockingham, Elephant & Castle, just by the tube station, ironically only a few floors away from leading gay activist Peter Tatchell. Entering the building, I saw a group of four black youths, mid-to-late teens, loitering by the stairwell and blocking access to the stairs, laughing loudly and joking around. They wore baggy jeans and hooded sweaters like a uniform, plus the latest design of Nike trainers, and, as I approached the stairs, they all stopped talking and stared hard at me. There was tension for a moment as I stopped a few feet away from them, but then one smiled broadly, revealing very discoloured teeth.

"You're wiv the police, ain't ya, boss?" His accent was hard to place.

I was wearing a black leather jacket, black Levi jeans, a dark shirt and scuffed trainers, so I was surprised he'd made this observation.

"You're quite sure about this?" I asked with a smile, looking between all four of them.

"Yeah, boss, I'm sure. It's in the eyes, you got the look, know what I mean?" another replied. I couldn't place his accent either.

"And what would the look be, huh?" I stared right into his eyes as I spoke. He turned away.

"You don't turn away when we look at ya. You keep looking at us," the first youth said.

I was about to respond when he spoke again.

"You here about that old racist motherfucker upstairs, the old fucking Nazi?" he snarled. "You should do something about 'im, boss. You wanna know what? He walked past here the other day, like, and he eyeballs us and shouts out, *Why don't you all go back to swinging on trees in the jungle?*" He'd raised his voice in indignation. "I'd had a blade with me, I'd have fuckin' done 'im in, like."

"Yeah, we shoulda run the racist bastard through. Do the world and us a favour, like," another youth snarled, somewhat too aggressively. "Maybe next time we will."

"Not advisable, and you should be careful who you say it to." I stared directly at him and, as I spoke, I produced ID, flashing it to all four youths. "Because, if anything happens to him, I now have four suspects, and I've clocked every one of you. You really think it'd be hard for me to find you four around here?"

I kept my ID up for a few more seconds.

"Yes to both questions. I'm police and I'm here to see Mr Selwood, but not for the reason you've suggested, though I'll certainly mention this to him. In the meantime, you four, go find somewhere else to play." I stared at all four of them and nodded towards the door.

They took my meaning, stared hard at me for the obligatory few seconds, then turned and walked away, laughing and high-fiving amongst themselves. I took the stairs up to Selwood's flat, which was on the second floor.

He opened the door almost as soon as I pressed the buzzer. He looked hard at me for a moment, like he was trying to focus.

"I've seen you before, haven't I?" He smiled. It was an unattractive sight.

I was about to produce ID.

"Don't bother. I know you're police." He stood aside and allowed me to enter.

I'd been to his flat once before and I knew where his cramped lounge was. From the small window, I could see the block opposite his.

I knew Selwood was a virulent anti-Semite, so it didn't surprise me to see a shelf full of extreme right-wing texts about the 'Jew Problem'. I saw a hardback copy of *Hitler's War,* a book written by David Irving, an unashamed Holocaust denier, whose central premise was whitewashing Hitler by claiming the extermination of Jews had been carried out without Hitler knowing anything about it, plus several equally unpalatable pro-Nazi tracts, including one entitled *The Myth of the Concentration Camps.* There was a framed black-and-white picture of Adolf Hitler speaking at the 1938 Nuremberg Rally on the wall above the mantelpiece, but at least there wasn't a swastika on display.

The room had a morbid feel, an aura of intense melancholy, and I felt a degree of nausea just being in it. Looking at the books on his shelf, I thought, *Didn't my grandfather fight in a world war to help crush this repulsive ideology only seventy-odd years back?*

I heard the door close behind me. Selwood walked across the small room and sat down in an armchair.

Even though I'd last seen him around a year ago, he looked older, as though carrying so much hatred was sapping his essential life force. He was clean-shaven, though his face looked as though it'd been carved out of stone. He was smartly dressed in a short-sleeved white shirt, tie and suit trousers, and he still had a full head of hair, which was now steel grey and cut militarily short. I could see, on his left forearm, the fading outline of a tattoo: a Union Jack overlaid by three large initials, *KBW*, which I knew stood for *Keep Britain White.* I wondered how often he left the flat, because his skin looked pale and anaemic, like it was hardly ever exposed to sunlight.

He sat facing me, looking stern, like a headteacher about to admonish a recalcitrant student.

"You're a detective. Special Branch, if I remember correctly. You came to see me a while back about those pictures you'd found regarding the abortive coup in the mid-seventies," he stated formally.

"Yeah, that's right, I did. You've a good memory."

"Whatever happened to those pictures?"

"Oh, nothing came of it," I breezily replied. "The investigation was wound up soon after I spoke to you, and the pictures are now locked away in an evidence room somewhere."

The last part was true, but the first part wasn't. I'd been investigating the theft from Debbie Frost's car, and I'd eventually found what had been taken. It'd been a detailed series of notes, pictures and a manifesto relating what was supposed to have been the plans for a military coup in the mid-1970s, staged by disaffected army officers alarmed by the direction the UK was heading in. The man I'd located in possession of them had been found beaten to death soon afterwards, and I was certain I knew who by, but I had no proof.

The supposed coup had never been a serious proposition and, I later discovered, had been connected with an elaborate MI5 sting operation in some way, though I never learnt exactly what, or even whether it had been successful. What I *had* learnt was that Frost had intended to use the pictures to blackmail Christian Perkins, now a Conservative MP but, at the time, one of the leading participants in the sting operation. I'd also found out Selwood had been a minor participant in the plan, but, as I didn't want to be here any longer than was necessary, I didn't bother explaining all this to him. I also said no to his offer of tea or coffee.

"I just passed some of your fan club on the way up here," I began lightly.

"What, you mean the gang of surly niggers who hang around at the foot of the stairs, intimidating old people and conducting their drug business?" he replied formally.

"They intimidate an old soldier like you? Surely not." I smiled sarcastically.

"They're black, aren't they? Probably all got knives or guns in their back pockets. You know how many people have died from knife crime in London this year, most of them blacks or some other off-white colour?"

There was nothing to be gained from responding to this. "Do yourself a favour: moderate your language in public, eh?"

"Bloody niggers," he snapped instantly, scowling, "but I won't debate the point because I don't suppose you're here to discuss *race relations*."

"You're right, I'm not. Just remember what I've said."

He nodded and frowned. "So, what *are* you here for?"

Without being invited to do so, I pulled out a chair and sat by the table, adjacent to him. He sat back, radiating calm and ready to answer questions. He was well spoken and smartly dressed, in a shirt and tie. If you didn't know him, you might have thought he was a retired diplomat or senior banker, though the hatred in his heart negated his potential for any such occupation. I suspected being camp commandant at a death camp like Treblinka would have been his dream career.

I began. "You were in the army for a few years, weren't you?"

He looked surprised for a second or two but quickly regained his composure.

"I was, yes. I was a soldier, put in eleven years. Proud to serve my country, I was." He pushed out his chest with pride. "No higher honour or calling than fighting for your country."

I was just relieved he hadn't said *serving the Fatherland*.

"I'm from a line of soldiers, y'know," he said proudly. "My grandfather even won the Pip, Squeak and Wilfred in the First World War, and he was only a young man when he was honoured for bravery under fire, kept firing even though he'd been wounded. His actions saved several of his squadron's lives that day." He paused for a moment and his face screwed up into a snarl. "But that was back in the days when this was still a country worth fighting for. Not today, it isn't."

He pulled a face like he'd just bitten into rotten fruit. "You know what this once-great nation is today? It's a country full of niggers, like those four downstairs, as well as Muslim terrorists, welfare cheats, black drug dealers and black single mothers, most of them having their first kids before they even leave school, and bringing up their three or four half-caste bastard rugrats born from three or four different fathers." He shook his head, looking and sounding disgusted. "And an enfeebled political class in hock to the EU who cling pathetically to the coattails of the USA for any influence we might still have. I were a young man today, *not a chance* I'd be a soldier," he said scornfully. "Fight for the scum living around here? You think any of *these people* care about their country's proud heritage?"

I was beginning to wish I hadn't come, but I took a deep breath to speak.

He refocused himself before I did. "Anyway, what about the army?"

"You served in Northern Ireland, didn't you?"

"Yes, I did two tours of duty there."

"When was this?"

"In 1971 and again in 1972." He was wondering why I was asking these questions.

"See any action?"

"A little." He almost smiled.

I paused for a moment, then leapt straight in with a caveat. "What I'm gonna ask you is off the record, right? *Anything* you can tell me which helps will *never* be attributed to you. You got my word on this."

He looked around for a moment. "Okay."

I began.

"When you served in Ireland, were you aware of, or did you ever hear anything about, small army units pursuing a shoot-to-kill policy? You know, people intentionally targeted and killed, rather than arrested? Before you ask, I'm also asking other ex-soldiers if they'd heard anything about this. As I said, you won't get into trouble with any answers you care to give me."

He sat back in his chair and folded his arms. He fixed me with a stare I found hard to penetrate for a few seconds, then he smiled. At least, I think it was a smile. Does anyone who carries as much hatred in their heart as him *ever* smile?

"I did, yes," he said casually. "In our barracks one night, we heard about the shooting of some IRA man, shot dead on his way home from work. Initially we assumed he'd been shooting at us and we'd returned fire, but soon afterwards we began to hear the whispers about this being a deliberate shooting, about how there'd never been any intention of bringing this person in. We heard rumours of small undercover units going out looking for IRA men, and one'd found this person and killed him." He looked as though this was something he'd approved of. "Over the next few months there were a few more such killings, IRA personnel being shot and killed where they stood."

"This would have been around . . . when?"

"I don't remember exact dates, but I'd say probably around early 1972, during my first tour of duty."

"How many would you say were killed?"

"Oh, I don't know for sure." He looked thoughtful for a moment. "If I had to guess, I'd say there were probably around fifteen or so I heard of, but there were quite likely others we never got to hear about."

"Were the people carrying out these shootings *absolutely certain* all those who died were IRA personnel? No innocent casualties?" I was thinking about what Barry Pencourt had told Taylor and Jacobs about the young kid, Brendan Morgan, and Pencourt's certainty he was innocent.

"Oh, yes, they were sure." He paused for a moment. "Well, mostly sure."

"What do you mean, *mostly* sure?" I didn't like the sound of this. "Was there ever *any* doubt about *anyone* who was killed?"

He looked directly at me for several seconds. I suspected he didn't like what he saw. Even as police, I probably still made it onto his hate list. He looked as though he was thinking how to phrase his next comment.

"What you simply have to understand, detective," he said firmly, settling back into his chair and unfolding his arms, "is this country was at war. You, you're too young to know what it was like back in the early-to-mid-seventies, with bombs being randomly planted all over the place killing innocent civilians, like in that pub in Birmingham, killing about twenty young kids. It was worse than the Blitz at times. At least back then there were air raid sirens giving warnings of attacks, but there weren't with the IRA." He sounded outraged. "People were living in fear the whole time. Anywhere in the country could have been a target. The bastards even bombed a pub in Aldershot, killing several off-duty soldiers just having a beer." He paused for a moment, then shrugged casually. "Anyway, the SAS were involved in it, and they're the best at what they do. They're professionals; they wouldn't kill the innocent."

"The *SAS*?" This took me by surprise. Taylor hadn't mentioned Pencourt referring to the SAS. Did Pencourt even know? If so, had it been included on the memory stick? It would be a different ball game if they were involved.

"Of course they were." He stated this as though it were common knowledge. "When you're engaging in guerrilla warfare in unfamiliar terrain, detective, you need experts who know how to conduct such operations to fight your battles, and the SAS are experts. They've their own rules of engagement and, when they get deployed, it's because they're acting under political orders. The shoot-to-kill action we heard about was guided by intelligence provided by an SAS major, who we heard was liaising with our CO. He'd provide the details of who was an IRA combatant and where he'd be likely to be at a given time, and if the SAS weren't dispatched, then we'd be used and he'd be taken out soon afterwards."

I thought about the implications of this for several seconds.

"You're quite sure about this?" I wanted to be certain I'd heard correctly. The official position was the SAS weren't even *in*

Northern Ireland in the early seventies, so hearing they may have been part of any shoot-to-kill policy was disconcerting.

"Oh, yes, I'm certain. I knew one or two individuals who were involved in the shootings. They'd come back and tell us what they'd done." He sounded proud of these actions.

The SAS. It occurred to me to wonder whether this was what Christine Simmons had in mind when warning me about Taylor getting too involved with Jacobs. Did Jacobs already know about this? Was he investigating this angle?

I probably knew the answer to my next question before I even asked it.

"You just said *we'd* be used. Were *you* ever, personally, involved in any such shootings?"

He sat quietly, looking at me. I wondered what he was thinking.

"Are you investigating these shootings, detective? Is this why the questions?"

"Oh, no, nothing of the kind. We're just doing a background check for a book some ex-senior military figure's writing." I used the lie I'd planned on using if he asked why I was asking such questions. It was plausible, one he'd be likely to believe. "He's writing his memoirs, and his book's going to be claiming there *was* a shoot-to-kill attitude amongst leading military and political figures of the time. He's admitting his involvement, and also planning to name names concerning top political figures who were involved in formulating this policy, so we're asking any ex-soldiers we know of who'd served in Ireland about what they'd heard."

"Oh, let him publish the damn thing," he snapped sharply. "Why should we be ashamed of what was done? It's true. There *was* a shoot-to-kill operation carried out in Northern Ireland. How official it was I don't know, but I know such a mindset existed amongst some of the officers I knew, and several IRA men who might otherwise have gone on to kill soldiers or civilians with their car bombs and Armalites or their Russian-made Kalashnikovs were no longer able to do so."

He sat quietly for about ten seconds. "You've never had to go up against the IRA, have you, detective? You've never had to police the streets during a civil war, have you?"

I was about to say I'd had an IRA bomber, Cormac McGreely,

pointing a gun at me not too long back and, but for the arrival of the anti-terrorism squad, I might well have ended up as a corpse, but decided not to. "No. The Troubles were before my time."

"*The Troubles*," Selwood sneered. "It was a civil insurrection, is what it was. The IRA had declared war on the Crown, detective, and so our soldiers were entirely justified in shooting to kill enemy personnel, rather than wasting time with arrests and all this *human rights* rubbish. I'm proud of my actions."

"You *were* involved in this, then?" I looked directly at him.

"Not directly, but I shot at this IRA bastard when we cornered him out on patrol one night, and I'd do it again. He ran when he saw us coming, but we caught up with him, by a builder's yard, and I'd love to have shot him, right here." He pointed to his chest.

As detestable as spending any time in George Selwood's company was, I'd at least confirmed the notion of a shoot-to-kill policy with someone who'd served in the province. Selwood had been an ordinary squaddie, but, if he'd heard about army units pursuing a shoot-to-kill policy, the likelihood of one having been in existence was all the greater.

But unlike Barry Pencourt, who was now racked with guilt for his actions, and seeking absolution for what he'd done as his ticket to a better afterlife, George Selwood positively gloried in what had occurred.

I wasn't surprised to have this confirmed, but I'd been *very* surprised to learn the SAS had played a role. The official position was that the SAS, or the Hereford Gun Club to those in the know, hadn't even been in the province back then, though received IRA folklore is full of stories of heroic resistance to SAS activities directed against them.

"If we'd gone in hard, right at the beginning, detective, we could have crushed the IRA decisively and saved ourselves several years of civil war and many British soldiers' lives, as well as innocent civilians. But it's typical of the spineless, craven, cowardly politicians in a country like this to worry about the rights of bombers and care less for the lives of soldiers fighting these traitors."

There were so many things wrong with this statement I didn't even know where to begin, but I wasn't about to debate them with someone like George Selwood. I also didn't want to be in this room any longer.

"Anything else you wanna add?" I asked, standing up.

"Do you think this book'll be published, detective? It's about time the truth was told."

I shrugged. "Not my decision; this'll get decided well above *my* pay grade. I'm just assisting with checking out this officer's story."

I walked along the short corridor to the door of the flat. I stopped and turned to face Selwood. I stood close up and glared at him.

"You wouldn't be lying with what you've just told me, would you, George?" I said, quietly but firmly. "'Cause I find out you've misled me . . ." I didn't finish the sentence.

"I'm not lying, detective." He sounded almost offended. "Why would I lie about something like this, which incidentally I supported very strongly? I took part in such an action myself, and I'm glad I did. I helped capture an IRA traitor." He was smiling as he spoke. Or at least I think it resembled a smile. His eyes told me he was being truthful. I believed him.

I left, feeling relieved to be away from the presence of such an obnoxious and hateful man. Compared to him, being in the same room as Colonel Stimpson was almost a pleasure. If there was one positive thing about Selwood, it was that he'd never sired children and, as he had no living relatives, his family line was likely to die out with him. Thank God for small mercies.

*

At the same time I'd been breathing the nauseating air surrounding George Selwood, Taylor had been interviewing Debbie Frost at Conservative party headquarters, in Westminster's Matthew Parker Street. Taylor had prepared for the interview assiduously, researching her subject, talking to several people who knew Frost, and compiling several pages of detailed notes.

Whereas I'd had to take a deep breath and psych myself up before talking to George Selwood, Taylor had been excited about talking to Debbie Frost. Her boss was convinced his fiancée was certain to win the seat at the next election, and then go on to make her mark in the Tory parliamentary party, so, thinking careerwise, Taylor was hoping she could cultivate a source to approach for future comments. A constructive and positive interview with Debbie Frost would also earn her kudos with her boss. Her interviews with the Home Secretary and with the leader of the opposition, Ian Mulvehill, had been well received, so she was hoping this one would go equally well.

"She asks if you've ever talked about her, or told me anything about her, what should I say?" Taylor had asked earlier as we were getting ready for work.

"Tell her the half-truth." I'd grinned. "No, I haven't."

I was wondering how Taylor's interview had gone as I got on the Bakerloo line after leaving Selwood's flat. I rode it as far as Baker Street, changed to the Metropolitan line and travelled north-west to Watford, the terminus, to talk to an ex-soldier I'd once spoken to about an incident in the mid-1970s which had led to somebody dying. Come to think of it, that had also had an indirect connection with what had been stolen from Debbie Frost's car, though this wasn't why I'd spoken to him. From his files I'd learnt he too had served in Northern Ireland in the early seventies.

Jonathan Rothery was home when I arrived at three fifty. He seemed surprised to see me again, but he invited me in. He was still wheelchair-bound, the result of a collision with a parked van on the M1 while driving a juggernaut lorry which had left him paralysed from the waist downwards.

"You came to see me a while back about all that nonsense in the mid-seventies, if I recall rightly. Did anything ever come of it?"

"Nah, nothing," I assured him. "Matter was wound up just after I spoke to you. No action was ever taken and it's all been forgotten."

The second part was true. Again, I didn't bother explaining the full story.

"So this visit isn't connected to it?"

"No, no." I shook my head. "I just wanna ask you a few points about something else which occurred a little earlier than this. You okay with this?"

"Yeah, I think so."

He made himself comfortable in his wheelchair and I began.

"When you were in the army, you served in Northern Ireland, didn't you?"

"Yes, I did," he said guardedly.

"When you were stationed in Belfast, did you ever hear anything about unofficial army units carrying out a shoot-to-kill policy?"

I gave him my practised lie about a senior military figure

writing his memoirs, and how Special Branch had been asked to do a little fact verification concerning the details. Individual soldiers weren't being investigated, I assured him. He could talk freely about anything he knew, and nothing would ever come back to him.

He sat nodding for several seconds. Whilst he did I glanced around the room. It was spacious and comfortable and laid out for easy wheelchair mobility.

My gaze settled on a large colour photograph on the mantel. While he was considering what I'd said, I walked across the room to get a closer look at it. It was a group of about twenty soldiers, smiling and looking relaxed. Rothery followed, and I spotted Christian Perkins in the middle.

"There's me." Rothery pointed to a young, fresh-faced soldier in the front row. "Taken at the training camp I told you about last time you were here. Couple of them blokes are dead now, and this one's an MP." He pointed at Christian Perkins. "He was in command of the unit." He wheeled himself back to his chosen spot, opposite the television.

During the next fifteen minutes I heard about his experiences in Northern Ireland. Yes, he'd heard the whispers about the deliberate targeting and killing of known or suspected IRA personnel, but, no, he'd not taken part in it and neither was he aware of anyone who had. His commanding officer had dismissed the rumours as repulsive republican propaganda and not to be believed. No, he'd heard nothing about the SAS. So far as he knew, the SAS weren't even in Northern Ireland then.

What did other soldiers think when they heard the shoot-to-kill rumours? Most seemed to think, so long as the *right* people were eliminated, it was all well and good. Few had shed any tears. Would he have become involved if asked? He replied he was never asked but, had he been, he couldn't honestly say what he'd have thought.

"I mean, you've gotta have nerves of steel and no qualms about the sanctity of life to be part of any hit squad, you know what I'm saying? Returning fire to someone shooting at you in a war situation's one thing. That's a survival reaction: you return fire or die, simple as that. But killing in cold blood's something else altogether." He paused, shaking his head. "I still feel bad about the bloke whose death I was involved in. I'm not sure if I'd have had the bottle to have joined."

*

On the tube back into central London, I considered everything I'd been told in the past few hours. Following Barry Pencourt telling Taylor and Jacobs about a military reaction force pursuing a shoot-to-kill policy, I'd now spoken to two ex-soldiers who'd served in Northern Ireland around the same time. One had said the fact of a shoot-to-kill policy was known to him, and the other was at least aware of the rumours relating to it.

It now seemed increasingly likely to me that Taylor and Jacobs had been told the truth by Pencourt. So I'd now have to wait to learn just how much they'd discover about the reality, if any, of this policy, and whether any other ex-soldiers would be prepared to admit to them what they'd done when serving in Northern Ireland.

Of course, my unofficial probings weren't going to be made known to Taylor. Not yet, anyway.

*

Taylor's interview with Debbie Frost had gone well, for the most part, and she was pleased with her work. She'd arrived early for her one o'clock interview and, after getting her tape recorder ready and arranging her notes and questions, had grilled Frost with questions about her background, her political philosophy and what she believed in, why she wanted to be an MP, which politicians had inspired her to want to become one herself, where she stood on several contentious political issues of the day, her work in the Conservative party, all questions she would have expected to be asked. Frost had been dogmatic in espousing what she stood for and her political credo, and such was the rapport between the two women that the interview had extended twenty-five minutes beyond the hour Frost had initially allocated for it. She'd even deferred a meeting she was supposed to be chairing early afternoon to continue her dialogue with Taylor.

Afterwards, however, whilst Taylor had been packing things up and checking the recording levels on her tape recorder, ensuring everything had come out clearly, Frost had sat closer to her and looked at her in what Taylor would later describe as *a curious way*, then had asked if she wanted another coffee. Taylor'd said she'd time for one more, so Debbie had got her secretary to bring in two more coffees, then sat down opposite.

After a few initial comments like *how'd you think it all went, was I forthright enough, did my answers make any sense, did I go on too long, should I have made my answers shorter, when do you think the interview will be published*, all of which was post-interview normality for a journo, Taylor had been surprised by Debbie Frost's next question.

"So, how did you and Robert McGraw get together?" She'd smiled.

After her initial surprise at the question had receded, Taylor had given her the potted version: I'd been investigating a case, she'd been reporting on it, she'd asked me a few questions, we'd then met for a coffee, and it'd all started from there. Which was more or less true.

Frost had sat quietly for several seconds while Taylor drank her coffee.

"Before we did this interview, did he talk to you about me?" Frost had asked. "Did he tell you *anything* at all about me?"

"Like what?" Taylor replied innocently.

"Oh, I don't know, just . . . anything." She'd looked and sounded apprehensive.

Taylor had waited a moment before replying. "No, he didn't say anything. Why? Was he supposed to?"

Debbie Frost hadn't responded.

"The only time we talked about you was walking back home from the pub last Saturday evening. I'd asked a couple more questions about the case where your car was stolen, which McGraw said was when he first met you, but he said nothing came of it, Special Branch wasn't needed and CID took the case over. The only other time your name came up was when I told him Tuesday evening I'd arranged this interview with you, and he said to say hi from him. And I did, remember?"

"*Really*? He didn't say *anything* about me?" According to Taylor, Frost's expression had almost radiated disbelief and then, a few seconds later, disappointment.

"No, he didn't. Why, should he have done?" Taylor had grinned. "Am I missing out on some good gossip then?"

At which point Frost had stood up and thanked Taylor for the interview and hoped it read well when published. The two women had parted on good terms.

*

Taylor was sipping her wine, sitting in the pub we liked near the main entrance to Battersea Park. For a Friday evening, the place was pleasantly rather than uncomfortably full. She'd been recounting how her interview with Debbie Frost had gone.

"Honestly, McGraw, she asked more about you than I asked her about herself. You'd have thought we were BFFs. She knows a lot about you, *and* about us. She knew where we lived, how long we'd lived there, she knew you'd had a relationship with a junior doctor. She even knew about my ex-boyfriend in the City. Why would she want to know all this?"

"No idea." I shrugged. "But, next time I see her, I may well ask her why.

"I know." Taylor grinned, sipping her wine. "She fancies you, McGraw."

"Oh, *please*." I grimaced and drank some beer. I'd rather Smitherman fancied me.

"No, it's true. I saw it in her eyes; they lit up when she mentioned your name and asked about you. I'm a woman, McGraw; women know these things. We pick up on signals a lot quicker than guys do." She smiled at me as she spoke.

This was too absurd. I moved on. "Did you just talk about the election?"

"No, a few social issues as well: women's rights, abortion reform, things like that."

This I was interested in. "Abortion reform?"

"Yeah, she'd like to see the law tightened up a little. Apparently she thinks it's currently too easy to get an abortion without a good reason. She thinks the law's being abused as abortion's being used as a form of birth control."

This interested me as I knew Debbie Frost'd had an abortion after discovering she was pregnant by Christian Perkins. It was to keep the knowledge of this out of the public eye that Frost had engaged the services of Phil Gant to stop the blackmailers in their tracks, and both men were now dead, killed by Gant. I didn't tell Taylor.

Taylor looked at me excitedly. "Anyway, Steve's been going

through the names on the memory stick. Pencourt's given us a lot of detail to work with. He'd listed every soldier he served with in his little unit" – we both knew what this referred to – "and also the names of everyone he thinks his unit was responsible for killing, plus which soldier killed which person, so far as he can remember. Steve's spent the past two days looking up details of all the victims and compiling a document of where and when they were killed. He's logging them all in chronological sequence: when they died, how they died, and so on."

"How many victims?"

"He says Pencourt's listed twenty-one he's certain Two Unit was responsible for killing. There're a few others as well, but his unit wasn't involved, and he's certain there were a lot more."

"Anything not quite kosher about any of these deaths, other than the kid he said was innocent?"

"Steve hasn't mentioned anything so far. He'll tell me if anything turns up."

"What's your role at this stage?"

"I've been trawling through the newspaper coverage from the time, looking at reports of killings in the province and Government's response to the shoot-to-kill rumours, looking at it from several different angles and making notes about it. Someone I was at Queen Mary's with now works for the BBC and she's gonna send me a DVD of the *Panorama* programme from 2013, plus a DVD of stuff that didn't make it in. We can watch it together if you like. You can tell me what you think afterwards."

I decided to take her up on this. After what I'd heard earlier today, it'd be interesting to learn what soldiers who claimed to have been involved had to say. My scepticism was gradually being eroded by what I'd been hearing.

EIGHT

Saturday

I was meeting an informant in Camden Town, someone I occasionally used for low-key errands, usually ones that had minimal risk attached and required little thought. Andy Harris was known to police as a tea leaf and pickpocket who operated in and around the Camden Market area, and his especial delight was in robbing foreign students, whom he regarded as easy pickings. His philosophy was that, if they could afford to be in the UK, they had to be rich, therefore they could afford to lose a few quid. The amount of money foreign students had lost to Harris' thieving down the years probably ran into the thousands.

I used him as he had the enviable knack of being invisible, able to fit in without being noticed. On quite a few occasions he'd passed on titbits of information concerning imminent criminality, or suggested whom police might want to look at more closely for a particular offence, which, in the right police hands, had been extremely useful.

One time, several months back, when police had been searching for the person believed to be responsible for the killing of three members of the Finality Committee, it'd been Harris who'd given police their initial starting point, simply through a conversation he'd overheard in a Stoke Newington pub.

Through Harris, police had also eventually caught a serial rapist who'd been plaguing the Camden and Kentish Town area for several months, because Harris had overheard the owner of a stall at Camden Market telling his friend about a man who'd tried to sell him a woman's expensive, Italian brand name handbag, with no plausible story as to how he'd acquired it. The bag had in fact been stolen during an attempted rape, which happily hadn't succeeded. Harris'd pointed out the stallholder and, through him, police had been able to identify and apprehend the attempted rapist, who was now serving eleven years in prison.

So long as police continued to get good tips from Harris, and so long as his kleptomania remained low-level and, most importantly, non-violent, I turned a blind eye to his thieving.

When I'd first made Harris' acquaintance his flat, on the top floor of a building on a side road off the Chalk Farm road, had been only slightly tidier than a landfill. It'd been cluttered with fast food wrappers and empty pizza boxes, dirty crockery with remnants of meals eaten days before still evident, and stacks of empty beer cans, surrounded by piles of clothes in varying states of cleanliness. There'd been enough dust on all surfaces to write your name very clearly. On the kitchen counter had been half a loaf of uncut bread with more mould than you'd expect to find in a biology lab. The flat had reeked of neglect, stale food, unemptied bins and body odour, and the windows had been so grimy I'd initially thought he had art nouveau stained glass. His approach to housework had been to ignore it and hope it went away.

But, remarkably, he'd recently become attached to a North London woman somewhere around forty, a lady named Stella, who'd taken pity on Harris and, for reasons far beyond my feeble comprehension, had seen partner material in him. She'd succeeded in smartening him up to the point where he was now only scruffy, and she'd cleaned, dusted, polished and hoovered the flat so thoroughly even Harris hadn't recognised it. First time I met her I'd wanted to know who she was and what'd she done with Andy Harris. But at least now I no longer had to be concerned about the slimy-looking film floating on the surface whenever Harris made tea or coffee, because Stella'd washed all his crockery.

Looking around his flat, I noticed he'd gone upmarket. He now had a brand new microwave, a washing machine, a tumble dryer and a dishwasher in his small kitchen area. Each of them was new, in pristine condition and top-of-the-range.

"How'd you afford all these, Andy?" I nodded towards his kitchen area. "Pickings good at the market, are they? You got receipts for all these?"

"Well, you know how things is, Mr Jack," he said with a wicked leering smile. *Mr Jack* was what he referred to me as whenever he phoned. "Things fall out the backs of vans if the doors ain't properly shut, don't they?"

I didn't pursue the conversation. I decided I didn't want to know where he'd acquired these white goods from.

I was here to see Harris because, at a Special Branch briefing this morning, Smitherman had informed those present that MI5 had obtained credible intelligence from one of its undercover operatives concerning a plot to perpetrate a terrorist atrocity somewhere in central London. The exact nature of the plot had yet to be revealed, though the implication was that it would either be a suicide bomber or an IED planted somewhere. This had been heard spoken of in whispers at a midweek prayer meeting in a North London mosque recently, the same mosque Mehmet Tabzouni and Sam Alorami attended, by two known supporters of Muearada who'd been talking about *something which'll bring London to its knees.* What was particularly worrying was that one of them had mentioned *finally having the resources and the person to do this.*

While there's always such talk inside these groups, the credibility of the source and the fact that the speakers were persons of interest meant that security had now been ratcheted up to a state of official high alert. All sources were being mobilised, and police had been told to be even more vigilant. Security around the Westminster area, as well as Government buildings and mainline railway stations, was now being subtly tightened.

From how Smitherman had addressed the Branch meeting this morning, my assumption was that this tip-off had to have come from MI5's man inside Muearada. This source had said Mehmet Tabzouni and Sam Alorami had been seen later on, after the prayer meeting, talking to Asou el-Taccouli, a Syrian immigrant to the UK, suspected by MI5 of being a leading talent spotter inside Muearada. He didn't plant bombs himself; his skill came from identifying those who had the makings of a successful suicide bomber, ones who'd carry out this despicable deed, inflicting maximum damage with no remorse. It appeared volunteers were in no short supply, which was worrying. All three men were known to have been involved in the planning or the perpetrating of terrorist activities in other countries. According to his visa, Tabzouni was a student, as was Alorami, but I was certain this was simply a cover for what Tabzouni was really here for.

But what had made me really perk up at this briefing was hearing that, outside the mosque the same evening, el-Taccouli had been clocked talking excitedly to someone who'd been photographed and, later, identified as Drake Mahoney.

This had made me sit up because I knew Mahoney. I'd questioned him recently concerning a series of car bombs in London, one of which had killed the driver carrying the bomb before he'd had time to park the car and walk away. The driver, once enough of him had been pieced together to allow for identification, had turned out to be a friend of Mahoney's. Mahoney was also known to be on the periphery of the Chackarti family, possibly the most successful and violent London-based crime family you've never heard of, carrying out ground-level jobs like driving, door security, debt collecting and other small-time functions helping make the Chackartis what they are. But why was Mahoney now being seen in the company of people like Asou el-Taccouli? Did he have a role in whatever was being planned?

Mahoney lived in Camden Town, and was known to frequent several of the pubs in the area, so I was hoping to use Harris again. Recently, I'd got Harris to steal Mahoney's wallet in Camden Market, and from this I'd learnt there was a connection between Mahoney and my late colleague, DI Paul Glett.

Mahoney had claimed, when I'd spoken to him, that Glett was *dirty police* and in the pay of the Chackartis. I'd refused to believe this, but Glett had died soon after, suffering a cardiac arrest from an infection which had developed after he'd been stabbed while arresting a murder suspect, so I'd been unable to have my belief in his innocence vindicated.

However, as well as my superior officer, Glett was my friend, and I still wasn't going to believe any stories about his being corrupt until incontrovertible evidence was offered.

But the more worrying aspect of Smitherman's talk earlier was when he'd introduced an unnamed serving officer from MI5, who said this same source had claimed Mahoney had been clocked in a Camden pub talking with someone later identified as Adrian Bowketts, a forty-year-old home-grown terrorist suspect who'd fled the country after Red Heaven's ultimately futile attempt to cause an explosion outside the Albert Hall, an operation I'd had a role in thwarting. He was one of the people suspected of helping the late David Kader put the explosive device together, using a stolen top-secret chemical compound called hydroxilyn.

If *he* was now back in the UK, after security being tipped off about a possible terrorist attack, then *something* had to be in the pipeline, MI5 was thinking. Prior to this, Bowketts was known to have been active on the fringes of terrorist activity and seen in the company of several persons associated with Muearada, and he'd been on MI5's watchlist until he'd dropped out of sight some while back.

Police had learnt Bowketts was in London due to a quite fortuitous break. On a tip-off from French customs officials, a British juggernaut lorry had been pulled aside at Dover, suspected of carrying items other than the industrial machinery described on its manifest. A search of the lorry had found a considerable amount of tobacco, wine and spirits being smuggled into the country to avoid customs duties, probably destined for the Chackartis, though the driver didn't know who they were for. Confronted by customs officials about the consequences of his actions, the driver'd then surprised everyone by asking to speak to a detective because he'd information he'd be willing to offer in return for a lesser charge. A local detective had told him that, if his information led to something, it'd be taken into consideration.

The driver'd said, on his previous return trip from Germany to the UK six days ago, he'd been coerced into smuggling somebody into England from France. He'd been confronted by three men he didn't know at Farthing Corner service station, on the M2, who'd told him they wanted him to do them a favour. To emphasise this hadn't been a request, they'd shown him a picture of his wife and daughter. They'd known where he lived, where his wife worked and his nine-year-old daughter's route to school, and they'd made comments about how, unfortunately, some people have accidents on their way to school. This he'd taken to be a threat, so he'd told them when his next load was being taken to France.

The men had been in touch with him again and had told him, on his next return trip through France, at a layby nine kilometres south-east of Calais, he'd be flashed. He was to pull over, and there'd be a man waiting for him. Who was this man? They'd not said, just told him where to pull over to collect a passenger.

The passenger had been waiting with another man, who'd flagged the lorry down. He'd been put into the back of the lorry, hidden inside a box of machine tools which had been left partly empty for this man.

A few miles outside Dover, along the A2 heading towards London, the driver had been told to pull over at a layby where a car was waiting with two other men. The passenger had then exited the lorry and got into the car with the waiting men. What kind of car? The driver had thought it was a Vauxhall Astra, but, as it had been getting dark, he wasn't completely certain, and he'd not thought to get the registration plate. Were these the same men as before? Yes. One was English and the other an Arab. The third one hadn't been there.

The driver'd then been shown a laptop with a 'rogues' gallery' of pictures and, after twenty-four minutes, he'd picked out Adrian Bowketts. "I'm certain this is the bloke who got into my lorry in France," he'd said.

If Bowketts was in the country, the MI5 guy had said, it was absolutely imperative that we pick him up, and soon, because it *had* to mean something was being planned. Getting him out of circulation was now our absolute A1 priority.

Which was why I was putting Harris to work. If Bowketts had been seen with Drake Mahoney, it was possible that Bowketts was staying somewhere in the same area. He'd lie low until it was time to do whatever it was he was in the country for.

Sitting in Harris' main room, which I was now able to do because all the clothes had been washed, ironed, neatly folded and put away, I noticed several cases of wine, beer and spirits piled high in the corner. A quick count revealed there were twenty such cases. I looked at Harris.

"You having a party, Andy? I do hope Sally and I are getting invites." I grinned.

"Leave it out, Mr Jack," he laughed. "I ain't 'aving a party. I'm just holding them for a friend, ain't I?"

"Oh, really? So, if I run a check with local CID for details of any recent robberies from off-licences or wine warehouses, I won't find anything. Is that what you're saying?"

I knew I wouldn't. The brand names on all the cases suggested these had been obtained in France and Belgium, and they were probably just a small percentage of a much larger load which had probably been smuggled into the country in the back of a juggernaut lorry. Soon, no doubt, they'd be sold on the black market, either to private individuals at boot fairs, to clubs like Las Vargas in Wood Green, a known Chackarti family hangout, or to small shopkeepers happy to obtain alcohol and liquor they could sell without VAT. This was made possible because it was known the Chackartis had several bent customs personnel in their pockets, so obtaining forged receipts wouldn't be an issue for them.

Harris looked away and said nothing. I knew, and he knew I knew, he was storing quantities of contraband for someone working for the Chackartis. One way they always stayed ahead of police investigations was by breaking up large bulks and storing them across several different locations, which made life much harder for the police. Harris wasn't known to be connected to the Chackartis, so he wouldn't be suspected.

"Helps to pay my rent, Mr Jack. I get a few hundred just for storing them for a while, you know what I'm saying? I get cheap booze from them as well."

"And Stella's okay with you doing this?"

"You kidding me?" He nodded at the cases, grinning inanely. "It's her brother what brings 'em here. He works for the Chackartis. We're keeping it all in the family."

I shook my head and sighed. It was time to focus Harris.

"Right, Andy." I moved across and sat down next to him. I produced two pictures. "You see these two?"

He nodded.

"Look at them closely and memorise their faces, because I want you to keep your eyes open for them. This one" – I held up Mahoney's picture – "lives down the road from here and he's known to use a few of the local pubs." I mentioned a few pubs Mahoney was known to frequent. "So, you see him in the street or the pub, keep an eye on him. I wanna know who he talks to, who he's with, what he does, where he goes, you know the drill."

Harris nodded and looked at the picture again for several seconds, squinted, then pulled a worried face. "Hang on, that's the bloke you got me to nick the wallet from in the market, innit? He ever finds out it was me, he'll kick my fuckin' 'ead in."

"Yeah, he probably would, so be *very* careful if you see him. Don't do anything to upset or antagonise him."

"Saw him the other night, didn't I, Wednesday or Thursday? He was in the pub up the road by Chalk Farm tube station."

I knew the one he meant. "He with anyone?"

"Just talking to a coupla blokes, didn't recognise them." He sounded nervous. "I was hoping he didn't remember me from the market that time."

"Would you recognise either of those guys again?"

"Yeah, I think so," he eventually responded.

"Good. That'll make your job easier."

"What about this other geezer?" Harris pointed at the other picture.

"His name's Adrian Bowketts, goes by Ada or Ade. This bastard blows people up, and he's *also* a nasty piece of work, suspected of involvement in several terrorist incidents."

He was indeed. Harris would need to keep his wits about him now.

"What they done, then?"

"For the moment, what they've done isn't important. It's what we think they might be about to do that's important, so listen *very* carefully, Andy. This guy here" – I nodded at Bowketts' picture – "we think could be residing in the Camden or Kentish Town area, so I want you to keep your eyes and ears open. As I said, he's a nasty bastard and we want him off the street as quick as possible. So, you see this guy, *or* this one," – I pointed to Mahoney – "I particularly wanna know *who* they're with and *where* you saw them. Be careful around them, though; don't take any unnecessary chances. If you're think you're in any kind of danger, pull out immediately. Don't get too close." I produced five £20 notes from my wallet and gave them to Harris. "These are *not* nice people, Andy."

NINE

Monday

Taylor had met her friend at the BBC for lunch earlier today, and she'd received a DVD copy of the BBC *Panorama* programme about the alleged shoot-to-kill policy, plus another DVD of outtakes from the programme, featuring comments from interviewees which, for whatever reason, had not been included. According to Taylor's friend, the second DVD contained some quite sensational comments, which hadn't been included in the original broadcast due to their potential incendiary impact. Taylor planned to watch the show this evening and asked if I wanted to watch it with her.

I did. Taylor had no idea I'd been making under-the-radar inquiries concerning whether such a policy had ever existed, but I'd been assured by George Selwood it had, so I was interested in hearing what had been said on this programme.

We had dinner, I made coffee and then we sat on the couch, ready to watch. Our usual position would be sitting slumped back on the couch, her head on my lap or my shoulder, my arm around her and thoughts of intimacy prevalent, but, as she was going to be taking notes and wanted to concentrate fully, she sat in the other chair.

"So, how's your research going?" I asked as she slid the disc into the machine.

"So far, all going well. Steve's making good progress. He's compiled a list of all the victims Pencourt claimed his little unit killed, listed when, where and how they died, and then matched these up against the official record of how they died, and he's working back through them. He's found several discrepancies between the official army version of how victims died and how Pencourt says they actually did, and he's following these up."

"What do you mean, discrepancies?" I was curious.

"The Brendan Morgan killing, for instance."

She explained. According to the official transcript of Morgan's death, which Jacobs had somehow been able to obtain a copy of,

Morgan had been lying in wait in a heavily wooded area outside Belfast, a few miles south of the city: an area where several other assassination attempts on British soldiers had been made. The army's story was that the soldiers had spotted Morgan crouching beside a tree, aiming his rifle at the military vehicle, and had *got their response in first*, firing several shots at the would-be assassin before he could fire his Armalite rifle. Once he'd realised he'd been spotted he had got up to run and been hit in the back by two bullets, and had died from his injuries.

The soldiers had stated they'd been extra vigilant when travelling through this area, as they knew it was favoured by the IRA. There were any number of potential escape routes from the area, meaning several shots could be fired, and the rifleman could escape, before any retaliatory response could be made. This extra vigilance had been how the soldiers had spotted the rifleman kneeling next to a tree and opened fire before he could shoot, and he'd been hit attempting to escape. All three soldiers in the vehicle had stated this was what had occurred, and this version had been accepted and listed as the official record of how Morgan died.

I was dubious about this story, even discounting what I'd already heard. Why had someone planning to shoot at soldiers not hidden themselves more covertly than this? IRA volunteers weren't usually so careless as to allow themselves to be seen when firing. And soldiers in a hostile combat area are trained for extra vigilance at all times, regardless of the situation, because danger can come from anywhere.

Also, most IRA 'hits' were two-man operations. The lone IRA gunman simply didn't exist. And why use firearms when IEDs would have been more appropriate if the area was as remote as the soldiers claimed it was? Whoever planted the device could have been miles away upon detonation.

"But, according to Pencourt, this isn't how it happened at all," Taylor went on. "He says they pulled Morgan off the street in Belfast as he was approaching an army checkpoint, bound and gagged him, drove him out into the woods someplace and, after a few questions, the officer shot him."

"In cold blood?"

"According to Pencourt," Taylor said firmly. "The kid had no weapons when they pulled him. They stood him up against a tree, threw a few questions at him, and then the officer shot him. Pencourt says they also slapped him about a bit."

"What kind of questions they ask?"

"The IRA were supposed to have weapons hidden somewhere on the estate Morgan lived on. The officer wanted to know where they were."

"He give any answers before he was shot?"

"Not according to Pencourt. Kid said he knew nothing about any weapons, but the officer still shot him."

"Why'd they pick this Morgan kid up? I mean, what was so special about him?"

"His older brother had once been an IRA volunteer, so I can only assume they thought Morgan was IRA as well, but he wasn't; he'd nothing to do with the IRA," she said. "Apparently, even the local UVF commander came forward and said he knew who *all* the local IRA men were, and Morgan had nothing to do with the Provos. The commander also worked with Morgan's father at the same factory, one of the few where there was no sectarian divide, and he knew the kid had no connection to the paramilitaries. His parish priest said the same thing. This was when Pencourt says he began making detailed notes on everything he'd been involved with, because he was now certain innocent people were being killed."

Taylor was quiet for a few moments while she lined up the programme.

"Pencourt's adamant there has to have been official connivance with persons higher up in the regiment, because there're several points which don't add up," she said at last.

"Such as?" I was now intrigued.

"Such as . . ." She paused for a moment. "His parents' story contradicts the army's version of events. The officer in charge had reported the shooting of Morgan occurring at seven-oh-four, but his parents' affidavit claimed he was just leaving their house around seven to go to his girlfriend's place. If he really *was* the shooter, he'd have had to have left their house at least a couple of hours beforehand to check out the location and find a good vantage spot, *and* someone would have had to drive him there and bring him back as Brendan didn't drive, hadn't got a driving licence. But there were no reports of any vehicles found in the area, so how was he expected to return?"

She looked at her notes for a couple of seconds. "Also, he didn't finish at the factory until five, and he went straight home. His factory manager told the police he saw Brendan clocking out; he produced Brendan's clock card, which showed five-oh-one. So how could he have been lying in wait outside Belfast when he didn't leave work till five, and his mother said he arrived home at twenty past? There're two major inconsistencies right there. The timelines just don't add up."

I thought about this for a moment.

"And there's something else as well." She was now warming to her theme. "The rifle Morgan was supposedly going to use to shoot at the soldiers was defective."

"*Defective?*" This didn't make sense.

"Yeah, the firing pin was jammed. He couldn't have shot anyone with that rifle, even if he'd wanted to."

"How did you . . ."

"Pencourt included this in the notes he made." Taylor had anticipated my question. "The officer, realising they'd got a dud, had the rifle disposed of. It was never submitted in the official report as evidence."

"And nobody asked to see the weapon he was going to use?"

"Apparently not." Taylor shrugged. She looked thoughtful for several more seconds. "So the position as we see it is either his parents and the factory manager were lying about the times involved, or . . ."

She didn't complete the sentence, but I knew what she meant. These were *major* discrepancies; why hadn't they been picked up on?

"The army went overboard trying to rubbish the parents' story, claiming it was no surprise they were blaming the army because their older son was IRA. Steve found the Belfast newspaper reports for the time and the army's story was given prominence." Taylor glanced at her notes again. "Pencourt says the officer shot Morgan three times, twice in the chest, once in the neck, front on, but Steve obtained a copy of the death certificate, and it records the cause of death as being twice shot in the back." She paused for a moment. "So, if Pencourt's claim is true, McGraw, someone covered up the real cause of death."

"And the officiating medic didn't spot this discrepancy?"

"Even the dumbest doctor knows the front from the back," she said, with a laugh, "so perhaps they were never given the opportunity to. Steve's trying to locate the doctor concerned, see if they're still around, so we can put this discrepancy to them."

This one case suggested the real story was at odds with the official story, just as Pencourt had said. What if there were more examples like this?

I could see why Jacobs had thought there was a story here.

"Shall we watch this?" She smiled at me.

She settled back, yellow legal notepad on her lap, and pressed the play button.

The programme, entitled *Britain's Secret Terror Force*, had originally been broadcast in November 2013. It began with some context, describing why soldiers had originally been sent to Northern Ireland and acknowledging the major difficulties soldiers on the ground had faced, attempting to keep the peace between two seemingly implacably opposed communities and to prevent a full-scale civil war from breaking out.

However, *Panorama* then went on to claim, on several occasions, British soldiers had overstepped the mark and had used lethal force in circumstances where it wasn't officially authorised. As well as suspected IRA personnel, innocent people, people uninvolved in any paramilitary activity, had died as a result: people who'd simply been in the wrong place at the wrong time. The programme stated these killings, of IRA personnel or otherwise, had been carried out by a secret army unit: a *military reaction force*.

The more sensational claim, though, was that this shoot-to-kill policy had been endorsed at the very highest level of Government. One contributor, said to be an officer on the ground at the time and who'd agreed to speak only under conditions of strict anonymity, readily admitted to this being the situation, but had justified this action by claiming that, as the terror threat had been escalating and the IRA widening its sphere of operations, the army had needed to become more proactive in its approach. The thinking had been that, if the IRA was seen to be losing key men and volunteers lower down in the ranks, this would have a demoralising impact and they'd be less inclined to continue with their struggle.

This was the rationale for a military reaction force, an MRF, though it had never been officially sanctioned. There'd never been any written evidence of shoot-to-kill orders issued by the then-Government or the top brass in the army, but the clear nod-and-a-wink implication was that officers on the ground were expected to enforce one. One officer said the guiding principle was clear and simple: *just don't get caught.*

The MRF had consisted of around forty hand-picked soldiers from across the army. It'd operated in Northern Ireland between 1971 and 1973, putting into practice the manoeuvres and tactics outlined in a book written by Brigadier Frank Kitson, the officer in command of the MRF, entitled *Low Intensity Operations.* Kitson had been someone with considerable experience of policing troubled parts of the British empire and who, it was said, wasn't really too fussed about who was killed, or even how, so long as order on the streets was restored.

The mission of the MRF, one soldier stated, was to *draw out the IRA and minimise their activities, and, if they needed shooting, to shoot them.*

Panorama claimed it'd contacted several former soldiers who'd served with the MRF, and they had admitted they'd been charged with *hunting down* the IRA in Belfast, rather than fulfilling their role as a peacekeeping force, with one soldier freely admitting, "We broke the law while doing so."

Another soldier categorically stated, "We weren't there to act as an army unit; we were there to act like a terror group. We were put in a position to go after the IRA and kill them wherever we found them."

If this was true, it was in direct violation of the official military line when any level of armed engagement was being considered. This was the Yellow Card policy, whereby soldiers were permitted to open fire *only when the risk to soldiers' lives was very real.* It was a court-martial offence to violate this policy.

Special Branch operated under similar rules. As someone who routinely carried a lethal weapon, a firearm, I knew I would face serious consequences if I used it unnecessarily. But the soldier said the Yellow Card policy was *just a fuzzy line* and didn't apply to them.

Several former participants in the MRF stated quite candidly they'd killed IRA personnel, and had shot them irrespective of whether they were armed or not. One soldier admitted unarmed targets had been shot as they'd driven past groups of people, even if they couldn't see anyone holding a weapon. But it hadn't been possible to identify exactly how many had been killed, as any official records of the MRF had long been destroyed.

One soldier attempted to justify the policy by claiming the actions of the MRF had saved many lives, though no evidence of this was produced.

The programme finished with the restating of the soldiers' difficulties in Northern Ireland, but expressed concern at the number of innocent people who'd died in the pursuit of what several soldiers had said was a definite shoot-to-kill strategy, with the clear implication the UK had violated its responsibilities under international law.

All through the programme, Taylor sat scribbling notes on her legal notepad in shorthand. When it concluded, she substituted one disc for another.

This was a shorter programme, mainly interviews with serving or ex-military personnel whose comments had been considered too inflammatory for inclusion. Several soldiers who'd appeared in the main programme were also included. One soldier admitted that, not only had he killed three IRA personnel, he wished it could have been more. He made reference to Bloody Sunday, approving wholeheartedly of the paras' actions that day and saying, quite calmly, he'd have liked to be where the paras were shooting from, but armed with a flamethrower instead of a rifle. Most of the other comments were either attempts at justification for the soldiers' actions or a kind of dismissive *so what* attitude towards any suggestion of unofficial deaths.

The programme's presenter, John Ware, had said to one ex-soldier, "We believe our investigations suggest several innocent people lost their lives in the army's pursuing a shoot-to-kill strategy."

The response was a shrug of the shoulders. "People die in war, don't they, even innocent ones. It's sad, but it happens."

The second DVD was only twenty minutes and, when it finished, Taylor ejected the disc and switched the machine off. She finished scribbling something in her legal pad, closed it and sat down next to me. "So, what'd you think, McGraw?"

I said I was still getting my head around the idea of a Government-endorsed shoot-to-kill policy, but it seemed pretty conclusive, from what had been said in the programme, that one had existed. I didn't say it also tallied with what I'd been told by George Selwood.

Taylor sat nodding slowly for a few seconds. "Yeah, fair enough. I mean, when Steve first told me about this ex-soldier, Pencourt, I was initially sceptical as well. I wasn't aware death squads had *ever* existed in the UK, but I agreed to go with him to see this guy and hear what he had to say. But then, when I heard his story, and saw the look in his eyes, I began to think maybe there's something in what he's saying. And now, hearing those soldiers on this programme" – she nodded at the TV – "and what our research has uncovered, I'm inclined to think Pencourt's telling the truth; there really *were* units of British soldiers in Northern Ireland engaged in illegal acts, killing innocent non-combatants as well as IRA. I'm now pretty clear Two Unit existed *and* it did what Pencourt claims they did." She shuffled the notes from her pad. "Anyway, I'm gonna go type these up while it's all still fresh in my mind."

She leaned across, kissed me on the cheek and went into the second bedroom which we'd turned into an office-cum-workroom. I remained seated and spent a while thinking about what I'd just seen. There was a lot to think about. Not the least of which was: what might Taylor be getting herself into?

TEN

Tuesday

I was in the office early because the trial of Cormac McGreely was due to begin today at the Central Criminal Court, the Old Bailey. He'd been arrested a few months back after I'd apprehended him in the flat belonging to rogue MI5 agent Harry Ferguson, who'd somehow evaded arrest and disappeared when anti-terrorism police arrived.

McGreely had been charged under the 2006 Terrorism Act with engaging in acts preparatory to terrorism, as well as the commission of acts of terrorism themselves, both in London and in Belfast. I'd also learnt he was suspected of being one of the IRA men who'd helped smuggle Semtex out of Libya, in an operation which had cost an MI6 man his life, but McGreely's participation had never been demonstrably proven.

I'd spent some part of yesterday brushing up on the statement I'd made soon after the arrest, which had been accepted by the prosecution, and refreshing my memory of the exact sequence of events leading up to McGreely's apprehension. Just before the anti-terrorist unit had arrived, McGreely had been holding me at gunpoint, and the thought had crossed my mind I was about to take my final breath. I didn't doubt, had he had longer holding a gun on me, I'd have been a dead man fairly soon, and possibly not killed with his first shot either. This had been occurring in the presence of Harry Ferguson, a man who, for a few years, had been someone I'd thought of as a friend I could talk to about matters relating to terrorism.

But when McGreely's attention had been distracted by the sound of police sirens and squad cars outside, he and I had grappled for his gun and, in the ensuing struggle, I'd managed to break his nose, which I would have enjoyed doing had I known it at the time. Just afterwards, though, Ferguson had clocked me over the back of the neck with my own gun. He knew the exact spot to strike to obtain maximum impact, and I'd lost consciousness for twelve minutes.

I was sitting at my desk looking over my statement, psyching myself up for my court appearance, when Smitherman asked me to come to his office. I went to sit in my usual seat.

"I've some bad news, I'm afraid. John McGreely's not going to be put on trial." He came straight out with it as I was sitting down. "Well, not just yet, anyway."

"Huh?"

"MI5 have decided, at this time, the evidence we have against him's only circumstantial, so for the moment . . ." He shrugged and spread his hands out in a *what you gonna do* gesture. "I mean, we can't place him directly at the scene of any bombings, and we haven't got his image on any CCTV connected to them. Seamus Drew's dead, so he can't point any fingers, and, yes," – he'd seen I was about to say something – "I know you arrested McGreely at a lock-up where explosives, including Semtex, were found, but *no* fingerprints belonging to him were found there, were they?"

I remembered this. My delight at thinking we'd caught one of the bombers had turned to despair when no fingerprints had been found. McGreely had said he was simply checking out the availability of a lock-up he'd been thinking of renting.

I was about to say we'd a statement made under oath by Chapman Watts about him and Gary White subletting the lock-up to McGreely, which would be a major contributor to McGreely being found guilty, but Smitherman had anticipated my next comment.

"I know, you're about to tell me we've a sworn statement about him renting the lock-up, but White's dead and Watts has disappeared." Smitherman sighed and shook his head. "We'd need him to give evidence at the trial, but no one knows where he is. Supposed to have gone abroad with his girlfriend, though border control says no one answering to his name's left or entered the country recently."

"Disappeared? What, you mean gone into hiding?"

"Who knows?"

"Do we know why?" I could feel a rising sense of frustration. The reason John McGreely had stayed at large as long as he had was partly due to Chappy Watts' initial reluctance to make a statement. By the time he'd finally given one, McGreely had gone into hiding.

"No. When the legal team were assembling the case against John McGreely, they looked at Watts' statement and the authorities tried to inform him he was going to be called as a witness to give evidence, but his father said his son had left a while back."

"His family know where he is?"

"Don't appear to." Smitherman shook his head. "Police've spoken to both parents, and they claim not to know where he's gone."

This was a body blow. Chappy's testimony would have been crucial against John McGreely. His unavailability now raised real problems.

"So," Smitherman said, "with the evidence we currently have, you can just imagine what a QC like Timothy Smythe would do to it, can't you? We'd be laughed out of court."

"What about McGreely entering the USA on a false UK passport?" I suggested. He'd been picked up by Homeland Security in Boston when I'd come across him on my honeymoon, travelling under the name Peter Redlands, a surname his father had also used.

"What about it? He entered the US after flying from Paris, so it isn't our call." He shrugged. "And he's in the UK now, so, as things stand, I don't know what the Americans want done."

I sat forlornly. The idea John McGreely might go free despite two deaths, one being my friend Paul Glett, was depressing.

"The top brass want to nail him for terrorism," Smitherman said. "Just having a false identity document won't put him away for as long as security wants, so, for the moment, they're holding back."

"So what happens to him now?" I was despondent.

"He'll be kept in custody until it's decided what to do with him. His dad's another story, but, as for John, for the moment we're buggered."

I sighed.

Smitherman then attempted to lift my spirits. "But at least there's one piece of good news." He smiled. "You're no longer required to give evidence today."

"What?" I was now confused.

"The other McGreely's lawyer entered a plea of guilty yesterday."

"Cormac McGreely's actually spoken?" I let out a surprised laugh. Since his arrest, he'd been maintaining his right not to incriminate himself by keeping silent, both in pre-trial questioning and at the magistrates' court. He'd been following the tactics of hardline IRA men down the years and refusing to recognise the jurisdiction of the courts trying him.

"Finally spoke to his counsel, the learned Timothy Smythe QC." He sneered at the name. "McGreely knew he was gonna go down because of the weight of evidence against him, both from this country and Northern Ireland, so Smythe was telling him what he intended to say today when, to his and everyone else's amazement, McGreely spoke up. He told Smythe to plead guilty to whatever charges were laid, and he especially wanted him to read out these words."

Smitherman picked up a piece of paper on his desk and read aloud. "*In the fight for an Ireland freed from the colonial yoke of English imperialism, I was and still am a proud and dedicated soldier of the Irish Republican Army, fighting for my country's right to self-determination, and I'm proud to have done my bit fighting in the cause of freeing my country from the tyranny of the Brits. I apologise for nothing I've done, I regret nothing I've done and, if people have died whilst I've fought for the liberation of my country, then so be it.* He concluded with *Saoirse d'Eirinn*, which evidently means *freedom for Ireland*."

Smitherman dropped the paper onto his desk. "So, today's hearing'll be a formality. The charge'll be read out, guilty plea entered, Smythe may or may not say anything, the judge'll weigh up all the evidence, and then" – he smiled wickedly – "McGreely'll be sentenced and taken to where I hope he spends the rest of his natural life." He was looking pleased. "So, as you're not in court, DS McGraw, you've more time to look into what I was referring to at Saturday's briefing regarding Adrian Bowketts. Where are we with this right now?"

I brought Smitherman up to date with our search for Bowketts and the fact that I had Drake Mahoney in my sights, then went back to work, relieved at not having to go to the Old Bailey.

*

Just after midday: I parked on the Millennium Way and crossed over to the car park by the O2 arena, heading towards North

Greenwich tube station. On the opposite side of the road was a small row of refreshment stalls, and I could see the man I was here to talk to serving two customers.

Tyler Watts was the father of Chapman Watts, or Chappy, as everyone knew him, who, before his disappearance, had worked with his dad at the stall. But Chappy's involvement on the very periphery of Cormac McGreely's bombing campaign, helping the late Gary White to steal the cars used for the bombings, had seen his father being arrested, after explosives had been found in a lock-up garage he rented from Newham council. Tyler had eventually been cleared when Chapman had finally been pressured into making a statement exonerating his father, who'd faced the very real likelihood of a lengthy prison sentence had he not done so. The statement had only been made after I'd leaned on Chappy quite forcibly to do it, though stopping just short of using violence. But his delay in making it meant John McGreely, who'd sublet the lock-up from Chappy Watts without Tyler knowing, had been released from custody, and he'd disappeared by the time we had reached the address he'd given to arrest him.

I approached the stall when the customers moved away. Tyler's brief flirtation with anti-terrorism didn't seem to have harmed his business in any way. I'd also heard through the police grapevine Tyler seemed none the worse for his ordeal.

"Tyler, how you doing?"

"Gawd strewth, it's the Old Bill," he said cheerfully, cockney accent still firmly in place. I noticed, since my last visit a number of weeks back, he'd redecorated his stall. It looked cleaner and more colourful, though his menu hadn't changed too much. "Yeah, I'm fine and dandy." He grinned. "Oh yeah, congrats. My sources tell me you're a married man now, got hitched to some reporter at the *Evening Standard*."

"How'd you know this?" I was surprised.

"Oh, you know me, ear to the ground an' all that. I hear a lot of things from the various other coppers I know who use this place. One of them knew I knew you, and he told me."

He poured me a tea without my asking. I fixed him with a direct stare and, immediately, recognition of why I was here dawned on him.

"So I bet you can guess what I'm going to ask you, then, can't you?" I said, quietly but forcibly. I saw his facial expression change slightly.

He nodded, looking serious. "Yeah, and I don't know where he is either."

"Has he *really* gone abroad?" I asked, sceptical.

"That's what he told me he was gonna do, and that's what I told those other detectives who asked me where Chappy's gone."

"When did he tell you this?"

"Oh, about two, three weeks ago. He left just after."

"He say why he was going, or for how long?"

"Nope," he said firmly. "Just said he needed to clear his head for a while, y'know, get away from everything. The kicking he took really traumatised him, and what with his mate Gary being killed, it all got a bit too much, so him and his girlfriend have taken off."

As he spoke, he looked directly at me, but his eyes told me his focus was elsewhere. I knew Tyler, and a decade of experience being a police officer was whispering that he knew more than he was letting on.

"But is that what *you* think?" I asked.

"Yeah, it is," he replied, maybe a little too quickly. "I don't blame him wanting to get away, forget about it all. His position, I'd scarper as well."

Chappy had taken a severe beating after the Chackartis had discovered he and Gary White had stolen the car of an off-duty police officer and attempted to pawn it off to a Chackarti chop shop. But this had happened a few months ago. Why'd he gone now?

I sipped my tea for a few seconds, looking directly at Tyler.

"Tyler, Chappy's testimony would help put an IRA terrorist away for years, get the bastard taken out of circulation so he can't put any more bombs on London's streets," I said quietly, hoping to appeal to his sense of patriotism. "You remember how *you* felt when the anti-terrorism people picked you up here and took you to Paddington Green? Wasn't a good feeling, was it?"

He didn't respond.

"If I'd not pressured Chappy into making a statement, *you* could have gone down, and for several years. You know this, don't you?"

Still no response.

"Also, a friend of mine, a good police officer, was killed looking for the people who placed the bombs. Stabbed by the same guy who killed Gary White."

I looked directly into Tyler's eyes as I spoke. He knew I was reaching out to him, not only as a detective, but also as a sort-of friend.

"Yeah, I know, and I'm sorry, but I don't know where he's gone. He just said him and her were gonna go off somewhere, and he left."

I didn't believe him but, for the moment, decided not to push him. I sipped some tea.

"So, who's this girlfriend he's gone off with?" I was curious as, last I knew, he'd not been seeing anyone.

"Oh, I dunno." He shook his head. "I've only ever seen her the one time. She came to meet him here 'cause they were going to see something over there." He nodded towards the nearby cavernous O2 arena. "Quite a good-looking number she was, got lovely long 'air and great legs. Spoke really well. Think she's a student. Classy piece, I'd say."

I laughed. "How would Chappy come across a woman like this?"

"Met her through his mate Gary, didn't he?"

"Gary, the one who was stabbed to death?"

"That's 'im, yeah, the one supposed to be renting my lock-up."

Something about what Tyler Watts was saying set bells ringing in my head. My police radar told me there was a connection to be made here, but I couldn't see where. Something about the description of this girl was resonating with me, but I couldn't get a handle on what it was.

"He sent you any postcards, saying *wish you were here?*" I asked, half-jokingly.

"Nah, nothing like that."

This wasn't the reply I'd been expecting. There was something not quite kosher about Tyler Watts' last comments, which convinced me more than ever he knew where his son was. Tyler didn't seem overly concerned at not knowing his son's whereabouts, or even having heard from him, and this didn't smell right. I knew they were close from my time using Tyler as an informant, so I'd have expected him to be a lot more concerned if he hadn't heard from Chappy for all this time. My every instinct as a police officer told me Tyler wasn't exactly lying; he was simply being economical with the truth.

For the moment I didn't push the issue.

"Okay, Tyler, but if he *does* contact you . . ." I drained my tea.

"I'll get him to give you a bell."

*

Taylor and I met up in Islington for what we referred to as a *work date*, and we were having a coffee in a Caffè Nero before our 'date' began. I was in a particularly good mood this evening because, just before I'd left the office, I'd heard the good news. Cormac McGreely had been sentenced to life imprisonment, along with a judicial recommendation he serve no less than thirty-five years. At his age this was virtually a whole life sentence.

This *was* good news because, as well as being a bomber, I knew he'd been responsible for the torturing and killing of two UVF personnel who'd murdered his father several years earlier. The details of what had been done to both men, alongside the pictures of their mutilated bodies, had made for gruesome reading.

He'd also been the main suspect in the kidnapping and kneecapping of a sixteen-year-old girl who'd innocently danced with a plain-clothes, off-duty British soldier in a hotel disco. The girl had been grabbed on her way home from work next day, taken to a remote farmhouse and had her left kneecap blown out. Everyone in the area knew it'd been done by McGreely, and the RUC had pressed the family to name him, but the family had relocated to England, too scared of any IRA reprisals if they testified against McGreely. For this cowardly and despicable act alone, the bastard deserved every minute of his sentence, and I hoped he lived to serve every one of them.

Tonight's work date was because the radical Islamist cleric Gheziel Ayah, a Muslim from Yemen now residing in the UK, recently released from a short prison term for inciting religious and racial hatred against Jews, was to address a public meeting at a hall in Islington about the spiritual role played by Muslims in the world. In previous public meetings he'd openly called for a jihad against the Western world, and demanded Muslims in the UK be tried under the precepts of sharia law.

Several of his more inflammatory comments had incited the

wrath of the media, notably the right-wing tabloid press. He'd celebrated the attack on the Twin Towers in 2001 by stating at Speakers' Corner it was *no more than the Great Satan deserved,* which'd led to a degree of public disorder as several Americans listening on, worried about family back home but unable to fly due to the temporary closure of American airspace, had taken exception to his comments. Police had had to step in before the situation dissolved into violence.

He'd also publicly praised the perpetrators of the 7th July public transport bombings in London in 2005, which had killed over fifty people, declaring the UK was *reaping the bountiful harvest from the seeds it had sown in Afghanistan and Iraq*.

When Private Lee Rigby had been slaughtered in Woolwich in full public view, stabbed and then hacked to death, in May 2013, by Michael Adebowale and Michael Adebolajo, Ayah had loudly praised the actions of *these two glorious warriors* at an open-air public rally, and this had led to clashes between his supporters and counter-demonstrators, though police had been able to contain it before it became a riot. I remembered this one as I'd still been in uniform at the time, but about to take one step closer to God by becoming a DC.

Ayah was a person of interest to the security service and monitored continuously while he went about his daily business. His continued presence in the UK had incensed the majority of the press, which almost unanimously believed his inflammatory presence in the UK was an ongoing threat to national security and, not only should he be deported, he should be declared *persona non grata* and never be allowed into the country again.

So this evening, because of the very real likelihood of demonstrations against him being held outside the hall where the meeting was occurring, there was a sizeable police presence in the vicinity, either visibly outside the hall, marshalling the pro- and anti-Ayah factions and keeping them on opposite sides of the road, or in vans parked discreetly in side streets in case reinforcements were required. A similar meeting several months back had seen police initially overwhelmed by the unexpectedly large numbers of counter-demonstrators, and a young police officer, PC Dan Jones, having his throat slit open, so no chances were being taken this evening.

Taylor was covering tonight's meeting for the *Evening Standard*, but I wasn't here for Gheziel Ayah; I was here because of the certainty Mehmet Tabzouni and Sam Alorami would also be present. After being told I had *the look* by the youths at Selwood's building, I'd obtained false credentials and tonight, if challenged, I was here as a journalist from a left-leaning Dutch political magazine.

Taylor and I sat near the back so I could scan the crowd and also keep an eye on the two pilgrims I was observing. She was focused and in full-on journo mode, scribbling a few notes and initial observations in shorthand before the speakers began, whilst I was looking around at the audience. There was a smattering of all the usual suspects I'd expect to see at such a meeting, as well as a sprinkling of representatives from several fringe left-wing groups and the three mainstream political parties. I was also looking closely because I was wondering which one of the attendees might be MI5's informant.

Taylor nudged me and nodded towards the other side of the hall, where Richard Clements was talking to two other scribes. Further back from him, however, I saw another familiar face, finishing up his conversation with a stranger. The person he'd been talking to went down to the front, and the man I'd spotted was left alone, scanning the audience with an expression of utter loathing and distaste. I wasn't surprised to see him here, knowing his role at his country's embassy in London.

Telling Taylor I'd be back in a minute, I strolled casually through the crowd and came up from behind on the man I'd just seen. He clocked me without even turning his head.

"Evening, detective," the man said calmly.

Joachim Balpak was a London-based operative with Israel's Institute for Intelligence and Special Operations, the Mossad, and he spoke and moved with all the easy confidence of someone who knew he could, and would, kill you in a heartbeat if your actions or intentions were in any way inimical to those of Israel.

I'd first come across him when his name had arisen during my investigation into the death of PC Dan Jones. Balpak had ultimately admitted to the killing of Jones by slitting his throat, and I knew he'd also been directly involved in the deaths of two other persons, but, as he was accredited to the Israeli embassy, ostensibly he was a diplomat and therefore protected by diplomatic immunity, meaning he was beyond the reach of UK domestic law.

I'd been told, as a consequence, an official protest was going to be lodged by the Foreign Office with the Israeli ambassador to the United Kingdom, though whether it ever had been and, if so, what had been the outcome, hadn't permeated down to my pay grade.

"Now, fancy seeing you here." I smiled at him.

"You're not the only people with an interest in the likes of Gheziel Ayah." He turned slightly, so he could look at me while still keeping an eye on the hall. He didn't appear to like what he was seeing. "You know what really amazes me about your country, what *really* takes my breath away? Your government allowing known terrorists to hold public meetings, right here, almost in the heart of London." He shook his head slightly. "Have you English learnt nothing from your history?"

"He's a scumbag, I agree," I said, looking towards Ayah, "but until he breaks the law here, he's at liberty to do as he pleases."

"The law," Balpak said quietly to himself, shaking his head. "Such a wonderful thing."

I was about to mention Ayah had been imprisoned for incitement to racial hatred, but there was nothing to be gained from a jurisprudential discussion with Balpak. "So, what's Israel's interest in Gheziel Ayah?"

"Israel has a permanent interest in the words and activities of people like Gheziel Ayah," he began, "and we monitor them carefully, and we bide our time until the time is right." He grinned as he spoke. I knew what he was implying. "But tonight I'm not here for him; there're others here doing that. I can tell you why *I'm* here this evening. I'm here because *my* interest's in Mehmet Tabzouni, and it's personal." He nodded knowingly.

"Business personal or *personal* personal?"

He paused for a second or two. This answered my question.

"A couple of months ago, when he was in Turkey," – he jutted his chin towards where Mehmet Tabzouni was standing by the stage, talking animatedly to tonight's speaker – "he was the instigator of an attack on a young Israeli national who was visiting Istanbul, a backpacker who'd been travelling around Europe and had stopped off in Turkey to see a friend whilst on his way back home to begin his national service."

He gritted his teeth, as though the next words would be painful.

"The night before he was due to catch his plane to come home, he was set upon by a group of three drunken Turks, who'd been incited by Tabzouni."

He paused for several seconds and took a long, deep breath.

"They dragged him into an alleyway and they beat and kicked him, like he was an animal." He spat the words out. "They sliced and stabbed him several times, laughing as they carried out this cowardly attack. It was a particularly vicious attack. The young Israeli boy died in hospital later the same night from his injuries, died alone and in great pain."

"Sorry to hear this," I said.

"The boy was unarmed and defenceless, simply walking along the road back to his friend's house." He'd raised his voice slightly and his words were infused with venom. He had a look in his eyes which I knew screamed murder. "The young Israeli boy who died that night was my nineteen-year-old nephew, Sol, my older sister's son. An innocent boy who died alone and in agony in a foreign country, with nobody to stand up for him."

He paused.

"When his body was returned to Tel Aviv, such was the nature of his injuries, I wouldn't let my sister see the body of her dead son," he said, quietly. "Her life was already ruined; I didn't want it made worse by the memory of seeing him like that."

He stood silent for a few seconds, then turned to look directly at me. "But *I* looked, *I* saw his battered body, and what I saw broke my heart."

He was silent for several more seconds, focusing his thoughts. His silence had an intensity surrounding it I could almost touch.

"The Psalms tell us *a righteous man will rejoice when he sees revenge*, so, at that very moment, looking at Sol's mutilated dead body, I swore vengeance on the perpetrators." I could sense cold anger in his posture as he looked towards Tabzouni. "I took a personal interest in the progress of this case and, after Sol's burial, I went to Istanbul to investigate this killing, because my good friend Moshe, whom you met in London, is now based in Turkey, and he was able to pull a few strings." He smiled.

I nodded. I knew of Moshe. He'd been with Balpak the first time I'd met him.

"Through Moshe's contacts in the Turkish police I found out Tabzouni had organised the attack; he'd been the ringleader. A police informer had heard him saying something like, *There's some fucking filthy Jew coming; anyone willing to exact revenge against an Israeli?* and he paid these three *bubkes* to attack Sol."

Somehow, I had the feeling I knew what was coming next.

"We got lucky," Balpak said. "One of our informers tipped off the Turkish police and they quickly rounded up the three others who were involved, but they missed Tabzouni; he'd already left for Paris the day after."

"Did Tabzouni himself take part?"

"Not as much as the others, but yes, he did."

"Why this kid? I mean, why'd he do this?"

"Why does *scum* like him do anything?" He spat the words out. "The victim was an Israeli national and he was alone and defenceless. That's all the reason he needed."

He turned away, nodded to himself while looking around.

"But there's been some degree of justice," he said quietly. I could hear a trace of a smile in his voice. "The three other assailants were quickly rounded up, as I said, and two of them are now in a Turkish prison, where they'll stay for some time. But, as we'd done favours for the Turkish police, they allowed *me* to deal with one of the attackers, the one who'd taken the knife to Sol, and laughed as he did so, taunting him and calling him *Hymie* and *Jewboy* with every cut, because I had a personal interest in this hateful crime. They allowed him and me to be in the same room, with no guards anywhere."

He turned back to face me with a disconcertingly wicked look on his face.

"The youth concerned will never walk again without crutches. It could even be he spends the rest of his miserable life in a wheelchair. I made him a cripple."

He smiled. At least I think it was a smile.

"They told me he was one of the most promising young football players of his generation in Turkey. He played for Galatasaray's youth team and, at seventeen, was on the verge of breaking into their first team. He was also being watched by a couple of top Spanish and German clubs, so ..." He paused, almost savouring the moment. "After I'd beaten him almost senseless, I broke both his legs and his ankles in three different places." It looked like he was enjoying reliving this memory. "I used a heavy pointed hammer. I smashed his legs completely, at the knees and the ankles. I took his life from him while leaving him alive to suffer the aftereffects of my actions. Now he will never play football again, which pleases me. He will never even walk properly again, if he even walks at all. I taught him what the price of innocent Israeli blood was."

He paused for several seconds.

"Him?" He jutted his chin towards Tabzouni, who was still talking to Gheziel Ayah by the platform. "I'd like to put a bullet between his eyes, right now, but he'd die much too quickly. So I won't do that just yet, because I want him and his family of jackals to suffer as my nephew suffered. I want his family to weep bitter tears, as my sister wept for her son, as *I* wept for the senseless death of my nephew, a boy I'd held in my arms when he was only one day old. A boy who had his manhood taken from him."

There was an acidic bitterness in his voice I could almost taste.

"Do whatever you want to him." I shrugged. "Just don't do it in this country, huh?"

He turned to look me in the eyes. It wasn't a pleasant look.

"Wherever I get the opportunity." He smiled coldly.

*

The meeting eventually started and ended peaceably, despite some jeers from a small contingent of around fifteen England First supporters outside after the meeting, contained well back behind police lines, as the attendees dispersed.

Gheziel Ayah had spoken in a mix of Arabic and English for nearly an hour. Taylor had taken notes on his speech and the impact it had on the audience, and I'd no doubt his every word was being recorded by the security service and analysed word by word, nuance by nuance. For the most part his speech had been educational and with a historical theme, with no calls for a jihad or praising of suicide bombers, and he'd said nothing inflammatory he could be arrested for.

Outside the hall, several minutes after the meeting ended, Taylor was swapping notes with two other journos who'd been present when I saw Ayah coming out the hall. His bodyguards bundled him into the back of a waiting car, and he was driven away.

Tabzouni and Alorami then came outside. They looked around, and a car waiting just along the road pulled up. They got in quickly. I made a mental note of the registration number, and I attempted to see who was driving, but there was darkened glass all around the vehicle.

As the car pulled away I saw Joachim Balpak looking at it as well. He'd also be logging the registration and the occupants. He nodded at me, turned and walked away. Richard Clements then approached me.

"You converting to Islam?" He grinned.

"I'm with Sally." I nodded at Taylor.

"Oh, okay. You around in the next day or so? I've heard a couple of things you might be interested in hearing."

I told him to call me tomorrow. Taylor and I took a cab home.

ELEVEN

Wednesday

In the office I checked out the registration number of the car Tabzouni had got into. It was listed as being owned by Mehmet Tabzouni, though Tabzouni himself had no driving licence.

The address given for the car's documentation was the same as on his file. It was an address in Southgate, an affluent area in North London, and I wondered how an LSE student could afford to live in such an area.

A check of the property, however, revealed it was owned by a Turkish businessman, Raol Buotrenni, who owned and ran a large property development company in North London. Amongst other ventures, his firm had done some of the work in building the new Tottenham Hotspur stadium recently, as well as the London stadium for the 2012 Olympics. He was listed as being Tabzouni's uncle, sponsoring his nephew's studies in the UK and underwriting the cost of his courses at the LSE. There was nothing listed on the PNC police database system about him, other than that he was a successful businessman.

*

Taylor's interview with the delectable Debbie Frost had been published as a two-page spread in yesterday's *Evening Standard*, under the banner headline *A woman for the future?*, and I'd read it on the bus to work.

It was more or less what I'd expected it to be. Frost had expounded her views on a number of contemporary political issues, and why she believed she had a contribution to make to the nation's political life. She came across as the voice of an erudite young woman and all her answers to Taylor's questions carried the clear assumption she knew she was destined for great things. She'd outlined her views on several of the main social issues of the day, in particular how maintaining law and order and internal security was the first responsibility of any government, and how police should be given greater powers to deal with terrorism. Immigration to the UK should also be greatly curtailed, she said, as currently it was a threat to national security, and any foreign national who supported or espoused views purporting to support terrorism should be deported immediately. Asked where she hoped to be in ten to fifteen years' time, she'd stated her ambition was by then to be a Cabinet minister, hopefully in charge of one of the great departments of state, such as the Home Office. If she achieved this, I mused, it would make her the parliamentary head of the internal security service, MI5.

The article took up most of pages eight and nine and it read well. Taylor had done a good job writing up the interview, and I suspected her boss, Frost's fiancé, would be pleased by how she'd been portrayed in the media. I had to admit, as a man, that the picture used next to the article showed Debbie Frost really was a very attractive woman, though of course she was far below Taylor's class.

But I could see behind the surface image portrayed. I knew just how cunning and venal she really was, and I was only too aware of some of the things she'd had direct involvement in. Her comments about stronger law enforcement and police powers were interesting, as I knew she'd been instrumental in having Louis and Paulie Phipps killed. She'd arranged for Phil Gant, a top-class, ex-US Special Forces hitman, to take out the brothers who'd been blackmailing her, and I'd been standing next to them when it'd happened. I also knew of her late fiancé, Darren Ritchie, helping to launder money on behalf of a terrorist organisation.

It was a safe assumption the Conservative party selection committee in the Norfolk constituency she was due to contest hadn't known anything about these matters when they'd selected their new parliamentary candidate.

*

Richard Clements had said he'd wanted to talk to me. I dialled his number but got his answerphone. I didn't leave a message.

Taylor and her sister Penny were hoping to see a play at the National Theatre, on the South Bank, Friday evening. It hadn't been possible to book tickets online last evening as the National's website had been down, so, as it was only on the other side of the Embankment, I said I'd go across and buy the tickets.

Strolling across Hungerford Bridge, I felt increasingly dejected by how the London skyline, when looking left towards the east of the city, was increasingly becoming a hideous collection of tall and very ugly, misshapen stainless steel and glass structures, like City Hall, the Lloyds building and the appallingly shaped Gherkin edifice. I took no comfort in the fact the ugliest buildings on the London skyline had yet to be built. Walking along the South Bank towards the National Theatre complex I tried imagining, if it were to be built today, just what kind of glass-fronted edifice it might be, and shuddered at the thought.

Inside the National foyer, approaching the box office, I spotted a familiar face in the tea room next to the bookshop. He was sitting at a table, up close to and gazing into the eyes of his female companion who, even at this distance, I could see was staring at him doe-eyed, with a mixture of love and lust. They were laughing about something with what appeared to be an easy familiarity. They were more than just casual friends, this much was obvious, and I knew the woman wasn't his wife.

Engrossed in whatever they were talking about, Richard Clements and his lady friend hadn't seen me coming as I reached the table. The woman next to him looked familiar, but it took me a moment to place her. She worked in the café near the *New Focus* office in Little Turnstile, Holborn, and I knew she was seriously hot for him because she'd made this patently obvious when he and I'd been in there recently. This explained why he kept returning. It now appeared he was responding to her overtly lustful desires towards him.

He suddenly became aware of my presence after a couple of seconds.

"Holy shit," he exclaimed. "Christ, Rob, you made me jump."

The woman with him immediately stood up, looking like someone just caught in bed by her lover's wife. She grabbed her coat and bag, avoiding all eye contact with me, and hurriedly muttered something about having to get back to work but seeing him soon. He stood up, they hugged, and I watched her walk across the concourse, then took the seat she'd vacated. I grinned facetiously at him.

"I don't suppose you were talking about the current precarious geopolitical situation in the Middle East, were you?"

He didn't respond.

"Janet know about her, does she?" I smiled wickedly, nodding at the fast-disappearing figure of his companion, who was now talking on her phone.

Janet was Clements' wife. She was also Commander Smitherman's daughter, and he was a devoted family man and doted on her. If he had even the *smallest* notion his son-in-law, someone he didn't particularly like to start with, was playing an away match, he'd be apoplectic.

"Hang on, no, wait, let me guess: *you're just good friends.*" I was enjoying his discomfort.

Clements sat quietly for a few seconds, biting on his lower lip, staring at me.

"No, of course Janet doesn't know," he said, shaking his head vigorously. He paused for a few seconds, looking worried. "You're not gonna . . .?"

"No, I'm not gonna tell your father-in-law," I assured him, intrigued by the thought of what Smitherman would do. "What you do's your own affair." I laughed at my unintended pun. "Just be aware of what *he'll* do if he *does* find out."

He didn't say anything.

"So, you finally decided to go for it, eh?" I asked.

"Ah-ah, not me. She did." He smiled. "I was in the café a few weeks back and she comes sits at my table. She looks straight at me and says, *Look, I like you a lot, and you keep coming in here, smiling at me and staring at my tits, so what're we gonna do about it, eh?* She left me her mobile number, so I called her later that day, we met up next day after work and went for a drink, then back to her place, one thing led to another . . . you know what I mean?" He looked like a cat who'd just licked up a full bowl of fresh cream. "She lives near here, actually, got a council flat in the block over by Southwark tube station. She's separated from her partner."

He sipped his tea while reading my mind.

"Oh, I'm not leaving Janet, nothing like that. I'm not *that* stupid. I'm married and I wanna stay married, but come on, Rob." His smile suddenly became a lecherous expression, as though we were two men of the world comparing past conquests. "You're offered access to a pair of tits and a body like hers, and you don't even have to work for it; she puts it on a plate for you, I mean, come on, what you gonna do, huh?"

"*Just be careful* is all I'm gonna say."

I went to the counter and bought a tea, then sat back down at the table. He changed the subject abruptly.

"Saw Sally's piece about Debbie Frost in yesterday's *Standard*." He sounded like he was in control again. "She interview her?"

"Last Friday."

He sighed and shook his head. "God, this unprincipled bitch could even become an MP if the political tide in her area turns. Where she's standing in Norfolk's only a marginal seat; wouldn't take too big a swing against the Lib Dems to get her elected."

"So Sally says." I nodded, grinning as I realised my use of alliteration.

"Did you know she's engaged to Sally's political editor, Paul Grayley?"

"Yeah, I did. It was him wanting her interviewed."

"The bitch's landed on her feet there, she has." He shook his head again.

"How so?"

"Oh, he's well connected is our Paul. His father, George, is chairman of Buckinghamshire county council. Tried for years to get a seat over there in the palace of varieties," – he jutted his chin towards the Parliament building across the river – "but could never get the nod to stand anywhere. Runs a successful haulage business and he's loaded. He's also got a relative who's a spook, something to do with the higher echelons of the security service."

"You know who it is?" I was curious.

"No, 'fraid not."

He drained his coffee. It was unusual to see him without a beer, but then it was still before midday.

"But it's actually him I wanted to talk to you about." He lowered his voice as he put his cup on the table and looked directly at me.

"Paul Grayley?"

"Yeah. It's just as well he *is* well connected, because I've found out something about him recently, and I thought you might be interested in knowing about it, given the proximity in which Sally works alongside him."

"Okay." I shrugged and sat back in my chair. "Like what?"

He leaned forward and shuffled his chair closer to mine. He spoke softly. "You're aware Alexander Bressington was taken in for questioning recently, aren't you?"

I was. It'd been me who'd taken him in.

"Yeah," I replied, "I'd heard."

"And I'm guessing you know why as well." He wasn't asking.

I nodded my agreement.

"Well, did you know Paul Grayley's name also came up in the same investigation?" He spoke quietly and looked serious, as though he were revealing a state secret.

"Grayley? How'd *he* get involved in this?"

"Well, it would appear Grayley got himself caught up in the same online scam. Police found he'd logged on to some of the same extreme porno sites Bressington did. But he was doing it because he was attempting to access the *really* hard stuff, you know, the stuff the more extreme paedos like watching which you have to access from the Dark Web, which is what he thought this site was offering. The kind of films where children get used."

"*Children?*" I wasn't liking what I was hearing.

"I mean, he *knew* what the site was really offering, and he was attempting to access the sites offering children and child grooming, some Asian site offering kiddie porn, kids as young as eight being involved, orphans mainly, no parents or relatives, used by grooming gangs for cinematic purposes. But even though he used an alias, like most of them, he'd had to use a credit card to log on to the site." He smiled broadly. "And, you won't believe this, he was dumb enough to use his real card. This alerts Interpol. They became involved and they tip off the police here. Grayley gets taken in but isn't charged. His name doesn't even get placed on the register of sex offenders. You know why? Got a relative in the security service, hasn't he, and strings get pulled *et cetera*. You know how backs get scratched, don't you?" He sounded world-weary.

I grimaced, feeling nauseous. Clements read the look on my face.

"Oh, it's all true." He nodded, sounding certain of his facts. "He's been interviewed by a couple of detectives from the Obscene Publications unit, but his relative got the records buried deep, and no action's been taken so far as I'm aware."

I thought about the situation for a moment.

"He doesn't actually do anything with children himself, the fucking pervert; he's not a practising paedo," Clements said. "He just likes watching films where they're used, if you get my meaning. Gets him off watching kids being submissive."

I sat stunned at what I'd just been told. The thought immediately struck me: did Debbie Frost know what kind of man she'd attached herself to? If, as Clements was saying, his kick was prepubescent kids, what went through his mind when he had sex with Debbie Frost? Whatever I might think of her, there was no doubt she was an attractive, sexy woman. Was she in his life purely for the sake of appearances? Was her body capable of arousing him?

"There's something else as well." Clements nodded, almost portentously. "Two, three years ago, he went on holiday to Thailand and Malaysia, and gets himself arrested in one of these countries, don't remember which one, attempting to smuggle a couple of kiddie porn mags out the country in his bag. He's deported from whichever country back to England, but the whisper was he'd a family friend or relative working at the embassy in whichever country it was, and his uncle, being a spook, had a few words in the right ears to get the matter hushed up. Local stringers for the UK press out there don't get to hear anything about it, and the uncle managed to get his nephew back, on condition he seeks professional help from a therapist. Grayley agrees, and the matter stays quiet." He shrugged.

"The media didn't report it," I said.

"The media never knew," he asserted, shaking his head.

"What about the therapy? Did he do it?"

He grinned ironically. "If he did, doesn't seem to have worked, does it, if he was caught trying to access a kiddie porn site?"

I sat quietly sipping tea, thinking about what I'd heard. He continued.

"The same source told me a few people in the media have heard certain stories about his, eh, misadventures in the Dark Web, but haven't written anything about it." His grin turned malicious. "Be an interesting story if it was ever published. If I could get hold of tangible proof, I'd write it up myself."

There was a lot to take in here. I thought for several seconds.

"So, who told you? Where'd you get all this?" I asked.

His expression changed. "Uh-uh. I don't name sources, Rob, you know that." He shook his head. "As I said, I'm simply telling you this because Sally works with this guy, and I assumed you'd wanna know what kind of fucking freak she's the deputy to."

I thanked him for this information. For the moment, I certainly wasn't going to tell Taylor what I'd heard, but I was at least pleased I knew. I briefly wondered what Debbie Frost's reaction would be were she ever to discover the secret, perverted sexual proclivities of her new fiancé.

"Who knows we're talking this morning?" I asked.

"Nobody." He looked directly at me. "I didn't expect you to be here, did I?"

"Right. Keep it that way. Don't tell *anybody* we've spoken this morning, okay?"

I didn't know what I was going to do with what I'd just heard, whether or not I'd tell Taylor, but I didn't want Clements telling anyone he'd told me what he had. I finished my tea and was about to leave when he stunned me again.

"Did you know Bressington's not gonna be prosecuted either?"

This I *was* surprised at hearing. "How'd you know about this?"

He smiled at me and touched the left side of his nose with his index finger. "Ah, you'd love me to spill the beans, wouldn't you?"

He drained his drink. "The rumour mill in the Lobby says he's gonna be made to take early retirement, spin out some bullshit story about health issues, no longer able to cope with the stresses of the job *et cetera*, then go live anonymously in his Hampshire pile. The word on the street is the security service don't want the aggravation and the embarrassment of a trial, so they're gonna pack him off away soon." He looked serious. "But, for the moment, they're keeping him in place and trawling through his work over the last X number of years, seeing what he's had access to, checking to see if he might have been compromised at some point. You know the deal: someone tells him, *We know your dirty little secret; tell us what we wanna know and it'll stay secret.*"

He stood up and picked up his shoulder bag. "Honestly, Rob, some of the top Lobby correspondents, they know more about what's going on than the fucking Cabinet."

He then looked at me inquiringly. I knew what he was thinking.

"No, I'm not gonna let on about you and whatever her name is."

I bought two tickets for Friday's play and we left the National, going in different directions. I returned to the office.

*

I'd intended to talk to Smitherman about what I'd just heard concerning Bressington, though not who told me, but I immediately picked up that something was amiss when I entered the office. There seemed to be a sense of some kind of panic, from all the movement and people talking in hushed and concerned tones, anxiously looking at computer screens. I saw Smitherman talking to someone I didn't recognise, and both men seemed agitated. As I sat down at my desk Smitherman's visitor walked past looking worried about something, and, when Smitherman saw me across the office, he gestured for me to come over.

I followed Smitherman to his office. He sat down, looking upset, and immediately fixed me with a worried look.

"We've just had a bad break, a very bad break," he said solemnly. "I've just been informed by MI5, Sherif Rizwi was found dead late last night, stabbed several times."

I remembered the news on the radio earlier, discussing yet another stabbing victim in the capital, but I'd not taken too much notice as Taylor and I had been talking while getting ready for work. Was this who the news had been talking about? The name meant nothing to me. "Where was this?"

"Entrance to an alleyway, on a side road by Highbury & Islington tube station."

"Was anything caught on CCTV?"

"Well, yes and no."

"Meaning what, exactly?"

"It means, yes, there's CCTV coverage of the area by the station, but, no, there's no images of Rizwi or any of the attackers. The thing is, around the time of the attack, there's a gap of twenty to twenty-five minutes. Either the system's at fault or, and this is what I think, there's been a hacking into the CCTV relay and someone's cut out any of the images involving Rizwi."

"Anyway, I've no clue who this Rizwi character is, so why's this bad?" I asked.

Smitherman looked very serious. "No, you wouldn't have. I've only just heard it myself. The reason you wouldn't have heard is because he's MI5's man inside Muearada, or, rather, he was." He sighed, shaking his head. "He'd been working undercover on the fringes for a while and had managed to worm his way into a position of trust with the leadership, and it'd been considered a major coup getting someone placed so close to the leadership of this group in the UK. It was Rizwi who told MI5 about Asou el-Taccouli and Adrian Bowkett being seen together, overheard them talking about doing something to bring London to its knees. He'd been inside Muearada for over a year, doing his job and keeping his head down, reporting what he heard or knew to his controller, and he'd provided some good tips about people inside."

"You think Muearada found out about him?" Muearada was a ruthless terrorist organisation. It wouldn't have been good for him if they had.

"This we don't know yet."

"Does MI5 know *why* he was killed or who might've killed him?"

"I've not been told. I know he went to the public meeting last night, the one Gheziel Ayah spoke at, primarily to observe and to report on who he saw there. He was supposed to have reported to his controller after the meeting but didn't arrive at the rendezvous point. Nobody hears from him for a while, then a dog walker reports finding a body in an alleyway by Highbury & Islington tube station, and it was later identified as Keema Bondami, otherwise known to MI5 as Sherif Rizwi. He'd been stabbed three times, all in vital organs. This was clearly the work of someone who's been trained how to use a knife properly."

If Rizwi'd been there last evening, this meant it was quite likely I'd seen him but hadn't realised who he was. I wondered if he'd recognised me.

Smitherman sighed. "So, did you see him at the meeting last evening and, if so, who was he talking to?"

"I've no idea. I don't know what he looks like."

Smitherman immediately produced a picture from a file on his desk and passed it to me. "You see this person last night?"

I looked closely at the picture for six seconds. The face was familiar.

"Yeah, saw him talking to the Mossad agent Joachim Balpak. They spoke, then this guy" – I nodded at the picture – "walked down to the front and took a seat. I went across to speak to Balpak soon after."

"You see him again?"

"Perhaps, but I wasn't aware of who he was, so, if I did, I didn't take any notice of him. Was Rizwi working with Israeli intelligence as part of his undercover role?"

"I can't answer this, DS McGraw," Smitherman stated officially.

I then realised I'd seen Rizwi before yesterday. While I'd been monitoring the movements of Mehmet Tabzouni and Sam Alorami, Rizwi had been one of the people at their table in the LSE library, playing backgammon with them and placing some quite considerable wagers.

"Having eyes and ears inside Muearada has been invaluable," Smitherman stated, "but temporarily we're now deaf and blind and, after what he heard a little while back, this isn't good." He shook his head.

As Smitherman was speaking my mind flashed back to what Joachim Balpak had told me last night, about Mehmet Tabzouni's organising a brutal and, ultimately, fatal attack on his nephew. Was Rizwi's death more of Tabzouni's handiwork? If so, how would he have even known who Rizwi was?

Smitherman was still talking. "The more worrying thing, though, is he's a skilled operative who'd not take unnecessary risks, so how'd they find out about him? How'd they know who he was? He's one of the best undercover operatives the security service has, lots of experience doing this kind of dangerous work, so it's unlikely he did anything to draw attention to himself. He'd be too experienced for something as basic as that."

"Did he give any indication he thought his cover might have been blown?"

"Haven't heard if he did," Smitherman said. "So, this suggests either he was careless and let his guard down, which I personally don't believe, or, more likely, someone tipped off Muearada about him."

I leapt in. "We've gotta start applying pressure, then. We can't assume this was just talk on their part, especially if Adrian Bowketts's also in the country. We have to assume they're planning something and we have to find out what it is. I'm gonna go rouse Drake Mahoney. He's been seen with Bowketts, so I'm gonna chase him down, see what he knows. His comeuppance is long overdue, anyway." I grinned.

Smitherman agreed that my plan made sense. I was going to lean on Mahoney. He was always into something crooked, so I was planning to check out his last known activities and see what I could use against him to coerce him to talk.

But then fate played its way right into my hands.

On my desk was a message asking me to call Kentish Town police station, next to a number and a name I didn't recognise. I returned the call and identified myself, stating I'd been asked to call. I heard muffled voices as the phone was passed to someone else.

"DS McGraw?"

I agreed I was.

"Oh, right, thanks for returning the call. I'm DC Withers, and I'm calling because we're holding someone on suspicion of receiving and handling stolen goods, but" – he paused for a moment – "he gave *your* name when told he could make a call, and he's claiming to be one of your informants." He sounded sceptical. "Now, the man we have in custody is a scruffy, dishevelled little scrote and, frankly, I thought he was full of shit, so I decided to call his bluff and contact you, then I'm gonna go slap him around a bit for wasting all our time."

The description sounded familiar and I realised I knew who was being held. "The person you're holding, is it someone named Andy Harris?"

"Yeah, yes, it is. You actually *know* him?" His voice had risen in surprise.

I adopted a serious tone. "Yeah, and he *is* an informant of sorts for the Branch."

"Bloody hell," Withers gasped, sounding amazed. "Harris's a well-known local tea leaf, stealing and pickpocketing his way round all the local markets. I've pulled him once before when a foreign student claimed he'd stolen her purse, but he hadn't got anything on him, so I had to let the scrote go. You're saying the Branch actually *uses* him?"

"Yeah, we do. We know about some of what he gets up to, but he's also doing something quite important for the Branch at the moment, so I'd consider it a favour to us if you could see your way clear to releasing him from custody. I'd owe you one."

The line was quiet for several seconds.

"Sorry 'bout the delay, just checking it wasn't April first," he laughed. "Okay, if he's doing something for your section, come sign him out and he's all yours."

*

Forty minutes later I was finishing up at the front desk at Kentish Town police station, having signed the requisite *release from custody without charge* forms. Harris was brought up from the cells into the hallway and, when he saw me, his face exploded into a big smile.

"Aw, thanks, Mr Jack." He looked contrite.

As we were about to leave the station, I was suddenly aware of a plain-clothes senior officer walking purposely towards me. He was probably early to mid-sixties, six foot, smartly dressed in a dark suit and white shirt, and he didn't look especially happy. He stopped a few feet away and fixed me with a very quizzical expression, one bordering almost on disbelief.

"Detective Chief Inspector Renwick, CID. You're DS McGraw, Special Branch, aren't you?"

"Yes, sir, I am."

He looked Harris up and down for two seconds, didn't like what he saw, then turned to me.

"Are you really telling me this man here's an *informant*," – he sounded incredulous – "or is this some kind of ruse to get a friend of yours out of trouble? Because if it is . . ."

"No sir, he's one of my informants," I stated formally, "and at the moment he's helping us with an investigation we're pursuing, which, of course, you'll appreciate I'm not at liberty to discuss with you." I didn't say what he was actually doing was sitting in pubs listening out for gossip.

Renwick kept me in his line of sight for a few more seconds, then nodded. "Your superior officer is Commander Jack Smitherman, isn't it?"

"Yes, sir."

His face took on a lighter, almost nostalgic expression. "Commander Smitherman and I go way back, y'know. We were rookie coppers together back in the day, walked the beat in the West End together many, many times. We've each had each other's backs more than once when a few drunks or yobs got mouthy and tried it on with us." He smiled at the memory. "Jack Smitherman's an ex-Marine, and you didn't mess with him or give him any lip if you knew what was good for you."

He paused for a few seconds.

"I just hope you're right about this." He nodded towards Harris, turned and walked away.

*

Harris and I were in a greasy spoon café opposite Camden Market. After bailing him out of custody, I thought the very least he owed me was a large cappuccino.

Once we'd been served, and I'd got over my dismay at the mug of foaming froth I'd been handed, we took our drinks and went towards an empty table against the far wall. Harris, it seemed, knew everyone in the place and nodded at or spoke briefly to several people. It was noticeable a few people avoided my glance, and some stared at me very suspiciously, including the two guys at the table by the window, who immediately got up and left when I looked in their direction. I wondered if those four black guys were right about my having *the look*.

"Funny us meeting like this, Mr Jack, 'cause before I was busted, I was gonna call you last night. I got something to tell you."

"Oh yeah?" I took a small sip of what was supposed to be cappuccino and grimaced.

"Yeah. One of them blokes you asked me to look out for, the one whose wallet I nicked for you in the market?"

He was referring to Drake Mahoney.

"What about him?" I asked.

"I was in the pub the night before last, the one just along the road from here, by Chalk Farm tube station."

I nodded. I knew which one he meant.

"This bloke was in there," he said. "So, I gets me a beer and I go sit in the corner and talk to me mate Charlie, but I'm still keeping an eye on this bloke. Anyway, a little while later, there's a bit of a row and he gets himself into a spot of bovver, like."

"What happened?"

"He 'as an argument with some other geezer at the counter, something about him spilling this geezer's beer. There's a bit of argy bargy, like, there's a bit of pushing and shoving, and then it all starts getting a bit nasty and a few punches get thrown an' all that, but it's all quickly dealt with. Pub bouncers jump straight in and sort it out, tell 'em both to behave themselves or they're out on their ears." He looked nervous for a moment. "Honestly, Mr Jack, you don't wanna upset them bouncers. Real 'ard bastards, they are. I mean, the pub's a Chackarti family place, ain't it, which is why there ain't ever any trouble there." Harris said this almost ominously. "*Nobody* wants to fall out with the Chackartis."

"So, what happened after this?"

"The other geezer leaves in a huff, the bloke I'm watching stays and talks to a few people round the bar."

"You recognise anyone?"

"No, sorry. Anyway, soon afterwards, I see him leave, so I follows him from the other side of the road, like. He goes down the main road, past Camden tube, and turns left. I assume he's going 'ome, so that's what I did. I thought you might wanna know about the fight."

"You got any more details on this *argy bargy*?"

Harris launched into an account of the fight. As I listened, I started to see a way I could take a run at Drake Mahoney.

"Is this any use to you, Mr Jack?"

"Oh, more than you know, Andy." I slid £20 across the table to him, took another small sip from my disgusting cup of froth, spat it back into the cup and left.

*

Mahoney lived in nearby Pratt Street. I parked across the street, next to a *no parking* sign, and rang the doorbell. No answer.

Back in the car, I checked the time and decided to wait a while, see if he returned or came outside. Eighteen minutes later my waiting was rewarded when I saw someone pulling the curtains back slightly to look out of the window.

I walked back to the front door and rang the doorbell again. Five seconds later it was opened by a thickset man I didn't recognise, about my height, with white walls above his ears, short-cropped hair on top and an off-white Adidas T-shirt revealing arms with several tattoos. He had a small scar on his forehead just above his right eye and a dark-coloured crucifix tattooed on the right-hand side of his neck, which looked to be recent. He was probably mid-twenties but looked older.

"Yeah, what you want?" he snarled. His accent was pure Birmingham.

"You Brummies are real classy people." I smiled at him. "Where's Drake?"

"You being funny, pal?" he hissed, squinting and leaning into me in an aggressive manner.

I pushed him away with my right hand, walked into the hallway as he backed up, and produced my ID. "Special Branch. Where's Drake?"

"He ain't here."

"Yeah, right. Get out the way."

I went to walk past him to the door of Mahoney's bedsit, and this character grabbed my right-side jacket collar and attempted to pull me back.

"I said he ain't here," he snapped. "You fucking deaf or something?"

I took a step backwards, moving in sync with the pull, and, as I spun around to my right, I drove my left fist upwards into his solar plexus. I was standing close enough to put real force into the punch. He hadn't been expecting this and let out a loud, painful gasp, wrapped both arms around his chest and dropped down to one knee, gasping and breathing erratically. I pushed him to the floor with the heel of my left foot. He curled up into the foetal position, coughing and spluttering.

"Don't touch me," I snapped at him.

At that moment Mahoney himself came out into the hallway. He looked surprised to see his friend getting up off the floor while holding his chest. He looked even more surprised to see me standing near him.

"What the fuck's going on?" His Irish accent was very pronounced as he looked between us.

"Your friend" – I nodded to the prostrate figure on the floor – "needs to learn to respect boundaries."

There was a palpable silence for a few seconds. I kept Mahoney in my sightline the whole time.

"You want something here?" he finally said.

"Yeah. Get rid of him." I jutted my jaw towards his friend, who was now gingerly getting to his feet. "We need to talk."

Mahoney looked at his friend and jerked his head slightly towards the front door. The man went into the flat and emerged two seconds later with his jacket, and left without saying a word.

Mahoney turned and walked into his flat. I followed and closed the door.

His flat, actually a large bedsit, maybe thirty-five feet square with an adjoining kitchen and bathroom, was as unkempt as when I'd last visited. Clothes strewn everywhere and several not-quite-empty pizza and fast food boxes, beer cans and bottles on every flat surface. The bed hadn't been made and the air in the room smelt smoky and stale. I looked around the room and shook my head. People actually *chose* to live like this?

Before I began, I told Mahoney to take it under advisement that he was being cautioned, which meant anything he said would be noted and could and would be used if and when any charges were preferred against him. I then formally cautioned him, and he nodded when I asked if he'd understood what I'd just said.

"So talk, then." He sounded irritable as he slouched down into an armchair. I moved to stand close by.

"You're in trouble, Drake, you know that?" I smiled at him. "I could arrest you right now for what you've done."

"Huh? How? I've not done anything; how can I be in trouble?"

"Oh, really? Leaving aside the fact you've been identified consorting with several known terrorism suspects, which I'll come back to, you were also seen fighting in a pub the night before last. That's how."

He seemed surprised I knew this. This told me he wasn't about to deny it.

"Yeah, alright, I had a bit of a scrap. So?" He shrugged.

"So, the guy you were fighting," I said slowly, "was rushed into hospital yesterday afternoon. He collapsed at work with a suspected brain haemorrhage, which came about as a result of his being hit by the beer glass you were seen holding on the pub's CCTV. I've also got two witnesses who're prepared to state they saw you using it against this man."

When describing what had occurred, Harris had said, during the struggle, Mahoney had grabbed hold of an empty pint pot and had attempted to strike the other person with it, but had only caught him with a glancing blow before pub security broke it up. But just hearing this had been enough, because it had been at this point I'd formulated the plan for what I was doing now. Harris had also said the man Mahoney had brawled with was from out of town and just looking for a pub to have a beer in, so, as he was someone Mahoney wouldn't be able to trace and check up on, I was attempting to play on Mahoney's gullibility and scare him into talking.

Mahoney was staring at me in disbelief. What I'd said seemed to have had an impact.

"Two morons throwing a couple of drunken punches is something we'd usually ignore, unless there's a real risk to public order, but using an offensive weapon to cause GBH, which is what this is, we don't. So you're gonna be taken in, which answers your question about why I'm here, and it's not gonna look good for you if this other guy dies or suffers a permanent brain injury."

Mahoney sat quietly, alternating between looking at the floor and at me.

"A beer glass isn't an offensive weapon," he challenged me.

"On its own, you're right, it isn't, but it comes under the category of objects which have a lawful usage but which, in the wrong hands, *and*" – I strongly emphasised the word – "used with the intent to inflict serious injury, are classified at law as being offensive."

I paused a few seconds to scare him further.

"And," I said, with a smile, "using an offensive weapon to cause or inflict GBH compounds the offence, you know, makes it much more serious."

He sat back in his chair, breathing deeply and biting on his lower lip. I didn't speak for several seconds, hoping to make him realise, as things stood, he was jammed up.

"What if this bloke doesn't die, though?" he enquired.

"You still used an offensive weapon to cause GBH," I stated firmly, "so you'd still be looking at a serious charge and maybe several years inside if found guilty." I paused for several seconds to let the words register with him. "You've also got a criminal record, if you know what I mean, which won't do you any favours with the judge."

"Fuck," he said quietly to himself, exhaling.

I left him to his thoughts for several seconds. The expression on his face told me he was very worried. I was enjoying his discomfort.

"But there could be a way out of this for you," I said at last, staring directly at him.

"Like what?" He looked hopeful.

"Well, you may well have some information we want to know, and it's the terrorist angle we're mainly interested in." I paused for a few more seconds. "So, as it isn't necessarily you we're after, you answer a few questions and, if the answers you give lead us anywhere helpful, the charges against you might not be quite so severe, you know, no GBH, that kind of thing. Maybe just unlawful wounding, S.18 off the table. That could make a big difference in any sentence."

I looked into his eyes as I spoke. He was dumb, but he wasn't stupid. He'd had enough dealings with police down the years to realise I was offering him a lifeline.

He stared at me for a few seconds, then nodded. "Such as?"

I produced my mobile phone and brought up a picture for him. "Start with him. You know this man?"

I was showing him a picture of Asou el-Taccouli. He stared at it for four seconds.

"No, I don't. Who is he?"

"Now, that's the wrong answer." I paused for a second. "Your credit rating's very low with us, Drake, and you need to start building it up if you're hoping to stay out of prison, 'cause bull-shitting isn't gonna help you. You see," – I smiled at him – "we've got pictures of you talking to this guy in more than one location. He's what we call a *person of interest*, someone we keep our eye on, and you've been captured on film talking with him." I sighed. "So I'm gonna ask you again. You know who this guy is?"

A few seconds' pause. "Okay, I do, yeah."

"What's his name?"

"I don't know his full name. I just know him as Asou."

"Asou." Right answer. "Okay, where do you know him from?"

"I've just seen him around, y'know? He's not a friend or anything, just someone I see about once in a while."

"You know anything about him, what he does, where he goes, this kind of thing?"

"No, nothing. I just know him 'cause I've seen him about, you know what I'm saying?" He was starting to sound nervous. "We're not close or anything, I just see him about, like, y'know?"

"Say it a fifth time and maybe I'll be convinced," I said. "You were seen talking to him outside a mosque one of his friends had been sermonising in. What were you talking about?"

"I don't remember. I was just there and he comes up and starts talking to me about all manner of crap. I wasn't really listening."

"Really?" I was sceptical. "Why were you even there in the first place? What's a good Irish Catholic boy like you doing outside a mosque anyway?" There was sarcasm in my voice.

"I was supposed to be meeting a mate, but he don't show, so I was going home." He didn't sound convincing.

I produced another picture. "What about this guy? You know him?"

I was showing him Adrian Bowketts.

"No, I don't."

"Oh, so if I were to tell you we have you on file pictured in a pub not too far from here talking to *this* guy as well – fairly recently, in fact – you'd deny it," I said airily.

"Me?"

"Yeah, you."

He looked away and didn't respond. It was as clear as day he was lying, and I was sick of being in this pigsty of a room.

"I'm trying to do you a favour here, Drake, but you're not helping me or yourself." I reached into the inside pocket of my leather jacket and produced a set of hand restraints. "Stand up, put your hands behind your back. Drake Mahoney, I'm arresting—"

"No, no, don't, I'll tell you who he is." He sounded panicked. "I know who he is."

"One chance only," I stated firmly. I put the restraints away and showed him Bowketts' picture again. "Right, tell me who this person is."

"I don't know him but, yeah, I saw him in the pub, we got chatting."

"What's his name?"

"He told me his name's Ade, don't know his full name."

"When'd you last see him?"

"Probably about a week or so back. It was only the once."

"Where did you see him?"

"In a pub up around the market, or actually it might have been one in Kentish Town. One of those places."

"You know who he is and what he does?

He didn't answer. He looked around the room, which suggested to me he had an idea about what Ade really was.

"His name's Adrian Bowketts, and police want him because he was involved in Red Heaven's thwarted attempt to cause an explosion around the Albert Hall last year, but he managed to slip away." I stared directly into his eyes. "Shall I tell you what he does, Drake? He puts explosive devices together, very nasty ones as well, with ball bearings and nails, all kinds of good stuff like this inside. If we hadn't stopped them, a lot of people, including women and children, would have died or quite likely have been very badly injured." I paused for a second to let my words sink in. "You don't seem to pick your friends particularly well, do you?"

"He's not my friend, I told you." He sounded irritable. "I just saw him this one time. I don't know him or anything."

"Whatever. What I *really* wanna know is, where's he holed up? We know he's in London somewhere, so where can I find this guy?"

"I don't know," he replied too quickly.

"Do you know any of his associates, who he might be likely to be staying with? He wouldn't be staying at a hotel, so someone's gotta be putting him up, and I wanna know who."

"I don't know that either."

I didn't believe him. He might not know exactly, but I suspected Mahoney would have some kind of idea of where to find Bowketts, or how to get in contact with him. He was sitting looking at the wall and nodding almost imperceptibly. His body language told me he wasn't telling me everything he knew.

I withdrew the hand restraints, told Mahoney to stand up and put his hands behind his back. He complied without a murmur and I cuffed him and drove him to Kentish Town police station, where I told the desk sergeant to hold him on charges relating to section 18, an assault causing GBH, and there'd probably be other charges as well. I'd be back to interview him soon.

*

Late afternoon. After a visit to the office to check up on a few matters, type up my encounter with Drake Mahoney and apprise Smitherman of the situation, I was back sitting opposite Mahoney in an interview room. The interview room here wasn't as depressing as the one at Brick Lane, but it was still spartan and soulless, lit by harsh, too-bright overhead strip lighting, walls painted a miserable shade of gunmetal grey. The metal table and chairs were cold and hard, not to mention bolted to the floor and immovable.

Mahoney was fidgeting in his seat, looking nervous. I had a copy of his file in front of me, which I was perusing. I closed it and looked him in the eyes. I didn't want to spend any more time with him than was necessary, so, before I began, I reminded Mahoney he was still under caution and anything he said from here onward would be included with his earlier comments.

"Okay, Drake, from the top. Your record's not exactly Persil white, is it? Convictions for assault and ABH, as well as several misdemeanours as a youth, shoplifting and causing criminal damage to a parked car by smashing its wing mirror, not to mention stealing another kid's bike and breaking the lock to do so. You've also stood trial for complicity in manslaughter, and, even though you were acquitted, the very fact of being charged, especially in the company of a known IRA man like Diarmuid Carty, won't look too good to a judge."

While I'd been investigating the activities of rogue MI5 operative David Kader last year, Kevin O'Hanlon, someone who'd involuntarily offered information I could use in my search for an Irish bomber believed to be working with Red Heaven, had been killed by Diarmuid Carty, struck hard on the head with a heavy object. Carty had claimed it occurred after a struggle which'd arisen because O'Hanlon had attacked him, though it was my belief Carty had intended to kill O'Hanlon. Carty had been found guilty of manslaughter and sentenced to eight years' imprisonment. Drake Mahoney, despite having been with Carty, claimed not to have been in the room when the assault had occurred, and, as we'd no evidence to put him in the room, he'd had to be acquitted. I believed he'd been an active participant in O'Hanlon's killing, but the evidence against him had been inconclusive.

"So, we attach a charge of conspiracy to any GBH charge, and add on the word *terrorism* to it . . ." I didn't have to finish the sentence. He knew what I was alluding to. "The judge'll get to see all this before he sentences you, and it's pretty certain he'll not be too impressed either." I paused to close the file. "You see, Drake, conspiracy's a catch-all offence. The fact we have you on film talking to someone we know to be involved in terrorism, and not just in this country, means, given we also know you're an IRA sympathiser and from a family of Irish nationalists, we've a good chance of making a conspiracy charge stick."

I gave him a few seconds to digest my words.

"You know what's beautiful about a conspiracy charge?" I looked at him. "We don't even need to prove you were planning anything. We just put you together with others like you. You get the picture?"

His expression said he did.

"Best guess?" I said. "With the charges you could currently be facing, you'll go down for at least five to eight years, though if the victim dies it'll be a murder charge rather than unlawful wounding." I sat back in my seat. "And it's highly unlikely prosecuting counsel will agree to a plea of manslaughter either, not in the current febrile climate, so this'll mean a life sentence, which means you'll do twelve to fifteen, absolute minimum. You've not spent any real time in prison yet, have you?" I fixed him with a direct stare. "Well, you're gonna lose your cherry on this one, unless" – I paused momentarily – "you've got something to tell me."

"But I didn't hit him hard enough to cause a brain haemorrhage," Mahoney protested. "Yeah, alright, I swung at him with the glass, but I only caught him with a glancing blow. I was just trying to scare him, like, get him off me."

"Doesn't matter. As I mentioned earlier, you used a lawful object, but in such a way as to construe it as an offensive weapon." I grinned at him. "And, also, the *thin skull rule* comes into play here."

"Huh? What the hell's that?" He looked bemused.

I held his stare for a moment. "It's the legal principle which says *you take your victim as you find him.* Simply stated, it means some people have thick heads, you can smash a beer bottle hard over their head and they don't feel a thing, but some people have very thin skulls. So, even if you only tap them on the head lightly in the commission of an unlawful act, and they suffer major head injury or trauma, that's just your bad luck." I smiled at him. "And hitting someone with a beer glass is an unlawful act."

He sighed and settled back in his chair, swallowing hard and looking worried. He exhaled. "Can I get a drink of water or something?"

I locked him in the room and went to make two teas. I could have had them made and brought in for us, but I wanted him to have time alone to consider his options. He was jammed up and had few ways to turn.

After eight minutes I returned and put a tea in front of him. He muttered, "Thanks," quietly, picked it up and began drinking.

He sighed. "So, what are my options here?"

He'd used these minutes to do some thinking.

"Options? You don't have any options," I said as I put my cup down, smiling, "but you *do* have choices. You can either stonewall me with more bullshit, in which case you're looking at an S.18 charge, causing GBH, which puts you inside, *or*" – I emphasised the word – "you can tell me everything you know about what I was asking you earlier. You do this and, as I said, we go easy on the charges. GBH might not be included in the charge sheet, and this'll make a major difference to whatever sentence you get. That's if you even get charged."

He looked nervous for a moment. "If I talk, what guarantee have I got that anything I say doesn't make it back to the people I'd be talking about?"

"Look around the room, Drake. I'm the only one here, and *I'm* not gonna tell them."

I didn't tell him the room was wired for CCTV and sound and we were being tape recorded.

"Yeah." He frowned. "That's what the other detective, Glett, once said, but then he was as bent as a thirty pence note."

I'd once seen Glett accepting a package from Mahoney at Portobello Road market, but I'd only Mahoney's word it contained dirty money and I'd refused, then as well as now, to believe he was corrupt until evidence I couldn't ignore was presented to me. I ignored Mahoney's smear. "What's it to be?"

I sat back in my seat and waited for Mahoney. I wondered what his reaction would be were he to know the situation I'd described earlier, his assault victim suffering a brain haemorrhage and being rushed to hospital, was a false one. But it was imperative we get a fix on Adrian Bowketts, so, if jamming up a fringe player like Drake Mahoney was what it would take, I was okay with this situation.

Mahoney sighed.

"I don't know why Ade's in London." He spoke quietly. "I've only met him the one time and it was in the pub I mentioned earlier."

"What we *really* wanna know is, where can we find him? He can't be with anyone we know about, like this Asou character, because they're all under constant surveillance, so it has to be someplace below the radar. You any ideas or names?"

He paused for a moment.

"I don't know how relevant this is, but I've heard mention of someone called Little Des."

The moment he said the name it resonated with me. *Little Des*; I'd heard this name before, and fairly recently, but I couldn't remember when, or even who Little Des was.

"Little Des? You're sure that's the name you heard?"

"Pretty sure, yeah," he replied. "Heard it in the same sentence as Ade's. The impression I got was they might be living together."

After a few more perfunctory questions and answers I'd learnt all I was going to from Mahoney. I called in the duty sergeant and asked him to keep Mahoney in custody until I returned.

DC Withers was still on the premises, so I asked to speak with him. I was escorted to the CID squad office. He was typing at his desk and I sat down in the chair alongside it.

"Does the name Little Des mean anything to you?"

"Little Des? Yeah, I know the short-arsed little runt." He sniffed derisorily. "I've pulled him a couple of times but never been able to make anything stick on him."

"Who or what is he, then?"

"Des? He's a well-known fence around these parts. You steal something valuable and don't know where to unload it, you go see Des. He takes it off your hands and places it, usually with someone working for the Chackartis. I'm guessing you know who they are?"

I indicated I knew them and their rep, having had dealings with their top brass.

"Des is more of a freelance villain but he also works for them, which is why he's not been found headfirst in the Grand Union Canal, bound and gagged. You operate as a fence around here, or you try selling stolen goods or pushing drugs in any large quantity in the pubs round this way, the Chackartis have to give you their blessing, *and* you have to pay them a percentage to operate, or you don't last too long; know what I'm saying? There's no such thing as a wholly independent trader north of King's Cross. Even the local USGs know this and pay the Chackartis."

"USGs?"

"Urban Street Gangs," he said. "Groups of kids based around the estates they live on, like the Queen's Park posse, based on the Queen's Park estate."

"Has he ever had any involvement in terrorism?" I inquired.

"Des? *Fuck*, no." He laughed at the thought. "Little bastard probably can't even spell it. He's just your average common or garden tea leaf; he's not a terrorist. Whatever made you think he might be?"

I omitted several key details, but I explained briefly how his name had arisen in a Branch investigation, and I was simply trying to find out more about this person as he wasn't on our radar. Withers assured me again that Little Des was just a crook and an all-purpose lowlife, and had never been connected with terrorism.

"Where does this character live?" I asked. "I'm gonna go check him out."

"If I remember right, on Islip Street, just across the main road from here. Lives in the place on his own, but God knows how he can afford it."

It then dawned on me where I'd heard the name Little Des before. When I'd been investigating bribery allegations against my ex-boss, Commander Neville Thornwyn, I'd come across a character named Bernie Rayes, known to everyone as Bernie the Buck because of his failed attempt to pass off poorly made counterfeit US dollars. He was an informant of Thornwyn's and was being used as part of a blackmail scheme Thornwyn had been operating at the time. Rayes had also been sought by my late friend Brian Turley, as Rayes apparently owed him money, and so had been hiding out at Little Des' house. He'd been hard to find, as Des hadn't been on our radar.

I remembered where Islip Street was, so, after thanking Withers, I left the station, crossed over the main road and walked along Islip Street to the house where Bernie Rayes had been found hiding. I walked past the house on the opposite side of the road and looked back at it. I remembered following Rayes here from a pub not too far away. What was the pub called again? I knocked on the door twice, but there was no answer.

Back in my car, I phoned Andy Harris and asked which pub it was where he'd once pointed out Little Des. He told me. I remembered it was on Prince of Wales Road, not too far away.

"I'm just on my way there now," Harris said. "Gonna watch sports on their big-screen TV."

"*You*? *You're* gonna watch sports?"

"Oh, I ain't interested in sport, Mr Jack. I'm just gonna collect me winnings." He sounded delighted. "I won a couple hundred on the gee-gees earlier today, and I'm gonna put a few bets on the NBA games they'll probably have on."

"Right, before you pocket your ill-gotten gains, listen carefully, 'cause you gotta do something for me. If Little Des is there, or he comes in while you're there, call me and just say *yeah*. Nothing else, just *yeah*. Got it?"

"Alright, Mr Jack, I'll do that for you."

Twenty-eight minutes later I received a call from Harris.

"Yeah." He rang off.

I waited outside the pub for another forty minutes. I texted Taylor to tell her I'd be late back as I was working in North London. She immediately replied with a kiss and a loveheart emoji. I'd just sent my almost embarrassingly syrupy reply when I saw Des leave the pub, walk along the road, and then turn left onto the main Kentish Town Road. I got out the car and followed him.

His name was well chosen as he wasn't an inch over five foot. He had no reason to suspect someone would be behind him, so he wasn't looking out for a tail, just strolling along without a care in the world. I was certain of his destination, so I alternated between walking in front of and behind him on the opposite side of the road.

At the entrance to Islip Street, he turned right. I dashed across the road, ignoring the irate horn and what sounded like an expletive from an oncoming taxi, and saw Des unlocking a front door and entering the premises.

I contacted Kentish Town police station, asked for DC Withers and told him I'd like somebody to sit on Little Des' house. If anyone came or went, I wanted to be notified.

"How does a scrote like Little Des come to Special Branch's attention anyway?" Withers sounded mystified.

"You'd be surprised." I laughed and rang off.

*

Back at the Yard, I brought up Little Des' file on the PNC. Withers had been adamant Des was just a fence and had no connection to terrorism, but, if this was the case, why had Mahoney heard Adrian Bowketts might possibly be holed up with him?

William Desborough was thirty-six with a string of petty convictions, mainly to do with stolen property, and had served nearly eleven months of a two-year sentence in Maidstone prison five years back. He was known to be a small-time operative on the fringes of the Chackarti family, though he wasn't a target criminal. He wasn't considered sufficiently important to merit keeping an eye on.

But I was intrigued to note there was a red flag attached to his file. This usually meant the person mentioned in the file was either a person of interest to the security service or was related to someone important. How would this apply to Little Des?

I checked his family connections and immediately realised why. My eyes opened wide and I gasped loudly when I read he was the adopted stepson of Sir Alexander Bressington. Elizabeth, Alexander's wife, had borne a son, William, via a fling with a tutor at Cambridge, which hadn't lasted long after she'd come down. She'd met Bressington at the Ministry of Defence when she'd worked in the same office, him being her senior executive officer and, according to the file, already being tipped to achieve great things in the civil service.

Little Des, the stepson of Sir Alexander Bressington. A thought then occurred to me. When I'd gone to take Bressington into custody two weeks back, his wife had initially asked, *Is this about William? Has he actually gone ahead and done it?* What was *that* all about?

TWELVE

Thursday

Mahoney had been released from custody on police bail last evening, initially without charge, though he had been told he was still in the frame for unlawful wounding at the very least, and the investigation was still ongoing. I'd stressed that he'd want to keep a low profile and avoid any contact with the individuals I'd mentioned earlier or serious charges would most definitely follow.

Mid-morning in the office, I took a call from DC Withers. No movement of any kind last evening, but this morning Little Des had just had two visitors, one being an Arab. As the officer watching hadn't recognised either man, he'd photographed them both, together and alone. They'd stayed maybe twenty minutes and then left.

I was also told Des had gone shopping at the nearby Tesco Express while the two men were in his house and had returned home with two sizeable bags of groceries. One of the plain-clothes officers who'd followed him to the shop had enquired about the purchases after he'd left, and had been told Des was a frequent customer, though usually only buying cigarettes, alcohol and scratch cards, and never normally buying as much food as he just had.

"Sounds to me like Des's got company," Withers said.

"Could be," I mused. "I'm on my way."

Before leaving I told Smitherman that Adrian Bowketts might be hiding at Little Des' place. I assured him my suspicion was reasonable, based on my interrogation of Drake Mahoney, and he granted permission to enter the premises, without the owner's consent if necessary, and effect an arrest.

*

Just along the road from Des' house I met up with DC Withers and two others, one plain clothes, one in uniform. One of them showed me the pictures of the two visitors Des had received. I recognised Sam Alorami. The other person was the man I'd seen at Drake Mahoney's flat yesterday.

I explained my belief about a wanted terrorist suspect possibly being on the premises, and the importance the Branch attached to apprehending him. Withers and I were going in through the front door. I told the other two to go around to the back of the house and take up position there. Withers knew Des, so it was agreed he'd do the talking.

After waiting a couple of minutes for the other two to get into position, we approached the front door, with me walking behind. I could feel my heart beating slightly faster as the adrenaline surged through my body. If Bowketts *was* on these premises, it was unlikely he'd yield to police requests to come quietly, so I was psyching myself up for a potentially hostile situation. I also reasoned he'd likely be armed, so I checked my firearm again as we moved.

Withers rang the front door bell. Nine seconds later he rang it again. I was standing slightly behind Withers to his left, clenching and unclenching my left fist, trying to keep my breathing steady and my thoughts focused.

The door opened by slightly over one foot and Little Des stood sideways between the door and the wall. He looked surprised to see us.

"DC Withers, so nice to see you again," he said, calmly but with a slight tinge of sarcasm.

"Morning, Des. Need to talk to you about something. Open the door."

He hesitated for a moment. "Er, it's not actually a good time just now. Got a woman in here, know what I mean?" He winked.

We both knew this was untrue. I could see the tension written across his face. He was attempting to appear calm, but his demeanour suggested he was nervous.

"Now, come on, Des." Withers moved forward and pressed on the door. "Be a good boy. We won't be here long. We just need to ask you a few questions about something."

"No, no, it's not a good time, really." Des had raised his voice slightly. He was attempting to stop Withers opening his door but not succeeding. He was clearly starting to panic.

Withers and I both knew this was a delaying tactic, so he pushed the door fully open. "Don't sod me about, Des, or I'll have you for obstruction. In you go."

Des backed up a few paces, now looking very scared.

I followed Withers into the hallway. There was a room to the left of the front door and the corridor led directly on into the kitchen.

I was looking down the corridor when, suddenly, a shape appeared in the kitchen doorway, only about twenty-five feet away. It was pointing a gun at us.

The person fired the gun three times in quick succession and the noise seemed deafening in such a small enclosed space. The instant I'd seen the person appear and raise his arm I'd shouted *get down* as loudly as I could and I'd dropped to the floor. The shots fired had been hurried and they missed their intended targets, though one bullet hit the wall uncomfortably close to my left calf. Des let out a strangled cry.

The instant the shooting stopped, the gunman disappeared from sight. I waited another second, took a deep breath, got up and ran towards the kitchen while withdrawing my gun.

The back door was open and whoever the shooter was had gone out through there. I ran out into the garden and saw the gate in the back fence was open. I was about to go through it when I heard four more gunshots in quick succession. I threw myself back up against the fence and waited for a few seconds, aware my heart was beating fast, took a deep breath, then ran through, weapon drawn and pointing in the direction of the shots. Whoever'd been firing had vanished.

I could see the two police officers walking towards me, the uniform holding his forearm and the other escorting him. He'd been hit and looked to be in pain.

"I'm alright, it's just a graze. Stings like a bastard, though," the uniform said, trying to smile.

"Whoever it was ran off down there." The other detective nodded in the direction of Kentish Town mainline station. There were several trees and bushes and I couldn't see anyone through them. The shooter could have gone in any direction once through there.

"You see who it was?" I asked.

"No. I saw someone come out from there," – he nodded towards the back of the house – "and when he saw us he started firing, so we ducked down. Didn't get a clear look at him."

I took out my police radio and requested an ambulance and a

forensic team. I also issued an alert for the shooter, and I gave Bowketts' name plus a brief description from what little we'd seen and the direction he'd been heading in, stressing this person was armed and dangerous. The shooter had escaped, but I was sure I knew who it was. For the moment, we'd lost the bastard. But we had Des.

*

Little Des had been taken into custody after being arrested. Withers and I were sitting opposite him in the same room where I'd spoken to Drake Mahoney yesterday.

Des was nervous and fidgeting with his fingers, tapping them on the table. I noticed his fingers were short and heavily nicotine-stained. He was agitated and protesting his innocence to Withers, claiming he'd not done anything wrong and hadn't known the person we were now after was armed.

"I mean, come on, leave it out, DC Withers." He sounded worried. "You know me, you know I ain't ever had nothing to do with guns."

I ignored his ramblings and began by emphasising the seriousness of the situation he was in. Whoever he'd been hiding in his house had fired shots at police, injuring one officer in his arm, and had evaded capture. This also made Des culpable as the man had come out of his house. Des started to look very worried.

"You know what police think about having shots fired at us, Des, don't you?" Withers said, menacingly. Des avoided eye contact with him.

I withdrew my phone and showed him Bowketts' picture. "This your guest, Des?"

He looked at the photo for three seconds. "Yeah, that's him, but I dunno who he is, honestly, I don't. He was just supposed to be staying at my drum for a week or so."

"You ever seen him before he came to stay with you?"

"No."

"So, how come he ended up at your place, Des?" Withers asked. "When did you start running a hotel?"

"He's a friend of a friend, isn't he? A mate asked if this bloke could stay at my drum. Couldn't stay at my mate's place as his missus has just had another kid."

"Why'd he need to stay at your place?"

"I dunno. Didn't ask, did I?"

"Who's this friend of yours? What's his name?" I asked. "I wanna talk to him."

"Just someone I see in the pub once in a while, don't know his name or nothing."

"He's a mate and you don't know his name," I said slowly and disbelievingly. "Obviously a close friend, then."

"Well, you know how these things go, don't you?" He grinned. "You see someone in the pub and you get talking to them, so I suppose he's a sort of mate, yeah."

"One close enough to ask a favour like this, eh? Must be some friend."

He was now looking very nervous. I let him stew for a while.

"You're in well over your head here, Des, you know that?" I looked him in the eye.

He swallowed hard and took a deep breath, but he didn't respond.

"We believe the person staying in your house is in this country to help prepare for, or to perpetrate, some kind of terrorist act," I said, slowly but firmly, "and your allowing him to stay with you constitutes an act preparatory to the commission of such an act. That's S.5, Terrorism Act 2006, Des. You wanna guess how many years you could get for this, especially as a police officer's just been shot by your guest?"

Still no response. Still the nervous look on his face.

"The officer was only grazed, Des, but just think how much more shit you'd be in if he'd been fatally wounded," I said.

"That's a life sentence right there, Des," Withers interjected.

Des was looking very scared. I waited several seconds. I was about to speak when Des looked up at me.

"Look, honestly," he said nervously, "I was asked by a friend of a friend if this bloke could crash at my drum for a few nights. He paid me for it."

"What's the name of your guest?"

"I was never told. They said it'd be in my best interest not to know."

"Who're *they*, Des? Who was it who asked if this guy could stay at your house?"

"Again, I don't know," he said softly, looking worried. "I mean,

I've seen him in the pub now and again, but I don't know him."

I contacted the desk sergeant and asked him to arrange for a suspect to have a look at the rogues' gallery. All pictures of known criminals and others of interest to the police were now kept on computer, rather than kept in bulky files of dog-eared paper.

The desk sergeant brought a laptop in, logged on to the appropriate page and scrolled down. The first pictures appeared.

"Right, scroll down through these," I said. "You recognise him, tell me."

He began. He looked at each picture carefully. I could tell from his eyes and his expression he'd spotted a few of his friends. Twelve slow minutes later he paused and pointed to a face. "This is the bloke who asked."

I recognised the picture. It was Sam Alorami. "You're absolutely certain of this?"

"Yeah." He nodded. The desk sergeant took the laptop away.

"He's one of the men who visited the house earlier, isn't he, Des?" Withers said.

Des nodded.

"What did he want?" Withers asked.

"I don't know, honest. He just told me to go out while he talked to this other bloke, the one you're after, said they'd something important to talk about. I had some shopping to do, so I nipped up the road to Tesco to get some groceries, and, when I came back, the ones who'd been visiting left." He sounded a little less nervous. "Soon after, you blokes turn up. You lot staking out my drum?"

I ignored his question, left the room and contacted Smitherman. I informed him of what we'd learnt from Des, and he put out a message to have Sam Alorami picked up. I returned to the interview room.

"So, Des, what exactly did this joker want you to do?" I demanded.

"He said he knew I had a couple of spare rooms. There's only me lives there, y'see, and I take in lodgers occasionally, helps pay my rent. He asked if I'd mind putting someone up for a week or so, possibly a little longer."

"Did he say why he was asking?"

"No, just said it'd be a big favour to him if I did." His voice was quiet. "And he gave me four hundred, cash, no questions asked."

"The guy in your house? As I said earlier, we believe he's in this country to carry out a bombing or some such atrocity, so we've gotta find him, and quick. You have *any* idea where he might have gone or who he might stay with?"

"How would I? I don't even *know* him, and he hardly ever spoke to me, just stayed in his room the whole time he was in. He went out occasionally, but I don't know where to."

I looked at my watch. "Well, the room he stayed in's being fingerprinted and systematically taken apart as we speak, looking for any clues about him or why he's here in the UK. Then they'll go through the rest of the house as well. Remember what I said about S.5, Des? They find anything which hints at terrorism, it's not gonna look good for you. So, you got *anything* to say which'd help us find this person, now would be the time to say it."

"Do yourself a favour, Des," Withers said.

Des swallowed nervously and shook his head. I concluded the interview.

Des was led away by Withers and taken to the cells to be held on remand, prior to being considered for being charged with offences pertaining to preparatory acts of terrorism.

*

Back in the Branch office, I was told anti-terrorism officers had raided the address where Alorami was known to be staying, but had discovered he'd moved out a few days back, leaving no forwarding address. The room in Des' house had been searched and fingerprinted, as had the rest of the house, but nothing incriminating had been found, though there were several sets of fingerprints taken. The same process had been repeated with Tabzouni's residence, but, again, nothing. To complete the set of bad news, we had nobody on file to match the person who'd visited the house with Alorami.

We'd missed picking up both Bowketts and Alorami. *Fuck it.*

THIRTEEN

Friday

Smitherman spoke to several Branch detectives at an early briefing in his office. An unspecified number of premises across North London had been raided last night and a few individuals taken in for questioning, but nothing of any significance in the search for Alorami and Bowketts had been obtained. We'd had one break in that amongst the fingerprints found at Little Des' house were those of Adrian Bowketts.

"Bowketts wouldn't be back in the country unless it was to do something, so it's imperative we find him, and *quickly*." Smitherman emphasised the word.

After he finished, he asked me to wait behind for a moment. I did, and I knew why he'd asked. I'd heard on the grapevine yesterday the news of my refusal to accept a commendation for bravery had finally filtered down to Smitherman, and the word was he'd been amazed by my decision.

I sat down and he stared at me with a quizzical expression, as if to say, *What the . . .?*

He began by stating how much consideration went into proposing commendations for bravery, and how even being considered said much about the actions of the officer in question.

"So why didn't you want your name to go forward, Rob?" The fact he'd used my Christian name, and spoke in an almost paternal tone, suggested he wasn't asking as a superior officer wanting to know why an order had been disobeyed but, rather, as a colleague curious as to why a course of action he couldn't understand had been taken. "I mean, any awards for acts of conspicuous bravery will look good on your record when promotion's being considered. Did you take this into account?"

"Wasn't the issue." I shook my head. "I refused because Glett's dead and Ferguson escaped, so it wouldn't have felt right, me accepting an award for bravery. If I'd been a bit more alert, maybe Glett wouldn't have been stabbed."

My mind flashed back to the day in question. When I'd arrived at the pub, it'd been Glett who'd asked to make the arrest. I felt a momentary shiver because, had he not done this, it might well have been me being stabbed and dying. I mentioned this to Smitherman.

"You don't know this for certain," Smitherman said, "and I remember you saying there was some bad blood between Glett and this Mick. I read your report, and neither of you knew this character had been armed with a knife."

Glett and I had gone to effect the arrest of someone named Mick, on a charge of stabbing Gary White to death. As Glett had been about to place Mick in hand restraints, Mick had quickly produced a knife and stabbed him in the stomach. Glett had died next day. I'd managed to disarm Mick and get him on the ground. But I'd beaten myself up constantly about whether I could have acted quicker, or should have realised Mick might have a knife.

Later the same day, I'd been in Harry Ferguson's flat and, after a struggle, had just overpowered a wanted IRA suspect when Ferguson had slugged me with the butt of a pistol, knocking me out. He'd escaped, and we still hadn't apprehended him.

"You arrested Glett's killer and he's now inside for life," Smitherman said. "This means something, surely."

"Yeah, perhaps, but accepting an award just didn't feel right, so . . ." I let the sentence hang. There was no need to finish it. Smitherman knew what I was trying to say.

He sat quietly for a few seconds.

"Well, it's your decision, DS McGraw." Smitherman said this in a way which made it clear he didn't approve, but our talk was over, and I returned to work.

*

Late afternoon. I was reading about Cormac McGreely's well deserved life sentence, and wondering when his son John would be joining him in Belmarsh, now that we didn't have Chappy Watts to give testimony. I was mentally cursing Chappy for his disappearing act when a sudden thought flashed through my brain, one I decided was worth checking out.

I recalled my conversation with Tyler Watts two days ago, and his description of Chappy's girlfriend. His description of her had rung a faint bell in my memory.

I logged on to the Branch database and brought up details of my pursuit of the McGreelys. I focused on an arrest I'd made, noting the details of the individuals concerned. A moment later, I was reasonably certain I knew who Chappy's girlfriend might be and, more importantly, where he might be holed up. I made a phone call before leaving.

*

Taylor and her sister Penny were at the National Theatre this evening, so, instead of being home in the flat, at 7.35pm I was sitting in my car, parked in Antill Road, just south of Victoria Park. I was off duty and, as Taylor was out, I'd had no particular plans for this evening, so I was here to check out my hunch.

Tyler Watts' description of Chappy's girlfriend had stirred a memory in me. When I'd gone to arrest Gary White, he'd been staying with his girlfriend in Antill Road, and Tyler's description tallied exactly with White's girlfriend, Helen, who was also a student. White and Chappy had been friends, so, if my hunch was correct, Chappy had made a successful move on Helen, and hadn't even let Gary's side of the bed get cold before he'd moved in.

I suspected, however, part of the reason for Chappy's disappearing act was because he believed he was still on the Chackartis' shitlist, so I needed to ascertain the exact situation in the event of my hunch about Chappy's location being correct.

Thus, before coming here, I'd contacted Ehmat Chackarti. I identified myself and he remembered me from the time I'd gone to his house on a Sunday morning a few months back when pursuing the McGreelys, just after a shooting on the premises had been reported. Later, soon after Glett'd died, Chackarti had claimed it'd actually been Glett shooting at him, though he wasn't certain whether it'd been a warning shot or one with the intent to kill. Either way, I wasn't sure I believed him. I still wanted irrefutable evidence before I believed what had been said about my friend Paul Glett being dirty police.

"Shame about DI Glett, wasn't it?" Chackarti had said when I'd called, though he didn't sound too sorry. He'd then made a couple of barbed comments about how Glett was happy to take the Chackartis' money but didn't always live up to what was expected of him. I'd felt my temper slipping.

"Careful what you say about him to me, pal," I'd said forcefully.

"He wasn't just another copper; he was also my friend. You prepared to give me any evidence or facts to back this up?"

"So, to what do I owe this pleasure?" he'd asked.

Right now, I could see a light was on in flat 5, second floor, 28 Antill Road, which was Helen's. I was chewing over whether to go up and just knock on her door, but decided to wait it out. I was hoping to see who went in or came out, because I couldn't get a warrant. Courts of law don't accept police intuition as proof.

Before coming, though, I'd checked out ownership of number 28. It was one of several properties in this road owned by an American property company, Bertram Moors, which was registered in the Cayman Isles, though flats were being let out by Meadowes, a lettings agency on the Mile End Road which specialised in short-term student lets. I'd checked with the agency and asked about the tenant in flat 5, 28 Antill Road. It had been let to a Ms Helen Mathison, a twenty-one-year-old student studying economic geography and international relations at nearby Queen Mary's, which was also Taylor's alma mater. I'd then run Helen's name through the PNC, but there was nothing on file about either Helen or her family.

At four minutes to ten I was getting very stiff, bored and antsy. There was nothing on the radio, I was out of coffee, and I was wondering why I was wasting my night off this way. I was considering whether I should just go on up and knock or call it a night when a Mini pulled up near to where I was parked, on the opposite side of the road. I saw a man get out and cross the road. In the dark he looked familiar, though I couldn't clearly identify him. He pressed a button and the front door opened four seconds later.

On a whim, I exited my car, noted the registration number and contacted my office, asking for the registered owner of the car.

The answer confirmed my suspicion. The Mini's registered owner was a Mrs Joan Watts, of Bethnal Green, London. Chappy's mother. But it hadn't been her who'd just emerged from the car. There was only one reason why Tyler would be visiting Helen Mathison.

I rang the bell labelled *Mathison* and, amazingly, a buzzer sounded and the door came off the latch. I entered and went up two flights of stairs to flat 5. I'd already checked my weapon for readiness while in the car, so I knocked on the door. Helen opened it three seconds later and, when she saw me holding up my ID, her stunned expression immediately told me she'd recognised me from my previous visit.

I didn't wait to be invited in. I brushed straight past her and into the main room, and there, sitting on the couch across from his father, was one Mr Chapman 'Chappy' Watts.

"Good evening, gentlemen," I said loudly, with a smile.

"*Fucking hell*," Chappy gasped. He couldn't have looked more surprised if I'd been dressed as the Grim Reaper. "How the fuck did . . .?"

"Jesus," Tyler said quietly, more to himself than anyone, slumping back in his seat and shaking his head.

Helen came into the room, apologised to her guests for not stopping me entering, slumped down next to Chappy and folded her arms, almost as a gesture of defiance, while looking at me with some degree of distaste.

There was an embarrassed silence for several seconds. I could see Chappy shaking his head slightly and looking depressed as he stared out the window, and Tyler sighing to himself. I stood in the middle of the room, looking at the assembled personnel.

Helen snorted; she was in a huff. "You can't just break into people's homes like this."

"I didn't. I knocked and you invited me in, remember?" I smiled at her. She turned away.

Tyler looked up at me, more in sorrow than anger. "How'd you know?" he asked softly.

I explained how I'd been looking into whom Chappy knew who might be able to give a lead as to his likely whereabouts, and I was here to check out a hunch. I said I'd seen Tyler arrive, so my hunch had paid off.

As I was speaking, Helen curled up next to Chappy and gave him a look of genuine warmth. It was a look which suggested they'd been together some while. A thought dawned on me.

"Were you two . . .?" I looked between Chappy and her.

He knew what I was trying to ask. "Yeah, Gary never knew about us."

"So, you found Chappy," Tyler said, sounding concerned. "What happens now?"

"Now? Well, I'm gonna call for backup and have him" – I

nodded at Chappy – "taken into custody and charged with obstruction and wasting police time, which you *can* go to prison for, and also you and her" – I jutted my chin at Helen – "for being accessories before and during the fact, and for conspiracy to pervert the course of justice."

This produced a few startled looks. I paused to let my words sink in.

"*Or*, he" – I looked towards Chappy again – "could agree to testify against John McGreely. He's already sworn out a statement, and his testimony could help put this bastard away for a lot of years. He agrees to do this, I *could* develop amnesia about where I found him hiding."

"Oh, no," Chappy immediately responded, shaking his head. "You saw what happened last time I cooperated with police, with *you*." He gave me a dirty look. "I got my fucking head kicked in. I'm not going through that again."

I fixed Chappy with a stare, leaving him in no doubt of what I thought about what he'd said. "You got your head kicked in because you and Gary stole a policeman's car and tried to unload it onto a Chackarti chop shop, which caused all kinds of ructions inside the family. You denying this?"

He was silent for a moment.

"Yeah, well, whatever." He shrugged, petulantly. "I'm still not putting myself at risk. Once Hel's finished at QM and got her degree, we're leaving London." He pulled her closer to him, and she curled up around him and closed her eyes.

There was silence for six seconds.

"You should listen to what he's saying, son," Tyler said quietly, nodding towards me.

"Why? So I can put myself in harm's way again?"

"You've already done that," I said, "but I'm offering you a way out of all this."

"A way out?" He sounded doubtful. "How?"

"Because the Chackartis don't want anything to do with terrorism or bombings. Did you see, a couple of days back, McGreely's father got thirty-five years?"

Tyler and Chappy both nodded.

"We got him because we had help from the top of the Chackarti family. They didn't want their name associated with terrorism, so they provided some help for us to get him, and we did. You'd be doing *them* a favour, Chappy, as well as us. This'll put you in their good books."

I'd distorted the facts somewhat, but there were several grains of truth in what I'd just said. The Chackartis, in the shape of Ali Chackarti, the titular boss of the family, *had* expressed their displeasure at various people inside the family doing favours for the IRA, and weren't keen on the notion of being closely identified with them.

"The last thing the Chackartis want is round-the-clock attention from Special Branch and the security service," I said. "Their businesses would suffer considerably, and this they *don't* want."

"And you know this *how*?" Chappy sneered.

"From the Chackartis themselves," I replied immediately. "Before coming here I spoke to someone I know at the very top of the family, and they're *not* after you." I held Chappy's hostile stare as I spoke. "I've had an assurance from this person they're not coming after you, nor do they have any plans to either."

"And you trust this person?" Tyler asked cautiously.

"Yeah. Yeah, I do." I was adamant. "I mean, I despise the bastard, but his word means something. If *he* says they're not coming after you, you can believe him."

"You can't keep running away, Chappy." Tyler turned to face his son. "You should agree to testify in court, put an end to it, especially after what he's just said about the Chackartis." He nodded towards me. "You get them off your back, you're a big step towards putting your life back together again."

Chappy sighed a few times and looked at Helen. She seemed to be agreeing with Tyler.

And then, a perfect moment in bad timing.

My police radio buzzed, sounding the emergency tone, rather than the usual tone. This was the special tone telling the recipient something *very* serious had just occurred and *everyone* was needed, on or off duty. I could hear Tyler saying, "What the bloody hell's that noise?" as I moved out into the corridor to answer. It was Smitherman.

"There's an emergency situation, DS McGraw, an explosion in Whitehall, somewhere close to the Downing Street gates, a suicide bomber, and there're reports of several fatalities. Drop whatever you're doing and get down there, see what the situation is."

I quickly told the trio I'd be back and, "If I find Chappy's gone again, I'll put a nationwide alert out to have all three of you arrested."

I took the stairs three at a time running back to my car, hit the siren and drove very fast to Whitehall.

*

Southbound traffic was at a standstill, backing up past Cambridge Circus on the Charing Cross Road and all around Trafalgar Square as Whitehall had been cordoned off, with police diverting all traffic either along Duncannon Street, towards the Strand, or along Pall Mall. The situation was not helped by an ambulance at the scene of a traffic accident by Leicester Square tube station.

The siren and a couple of uniforms on the street enabled me to get through and I pulled over into Cockspur Street, by the Admiralty Arch entrance to Pall Mall, parallel with a police van. Two nearby uniforms, one female and a man with an automatic weapon strapped around his neck, saw me and approached, with him shouting aggressively, "Oi, you, move the car, now; you can't park there."

I identified myself as a police officer and showed ID. He nodded his acceptance.

"What's the situation?" I asked.

"I've only been here a few minutes, sir, but, from what I can gather, some Arab walking along by the Cabinet Office's just blown himself up." He sounded angry.

"Any fatalities apart from the bomber?"

"Yeah, the word is there's at least three or four, including one of us." He shook his head. "I've heard he was approaching this bloke to challenge him when he detonated whatever he was carrying. Poor bugger didn't have a chance."

"Okay, thanks." *Fuck, a dead police officer.*

My ID let me pass by the two squad cars perpendicularly parked across the north end of Whitehall, blocking access to the road, and through the wooden barriers indicating a crime scene. This time on a Friday night the area would usually still be buzzing with traffic, diners, theatregoers and tourists, but, instead, there were crowds of people standing silently by the police cordon, many looking dazed and sorrowful, trying to see and make sense of what had occurred about 250 yards away. Police had ordered the evacuation of all nearby pubs, restaurants and other places of entertainment. I could see BBC and Sky TV vans and cameramen setting up, a few journalists taking their positions and talking into microphones under hastily erected arc lights. A couple of reporters saw me going through and shouted questions, but I didn't respond.

I walked along the pavement, past the Clarence. Further ahead, on the west side of the road, I could see a series of flashing red and blue police car and ambulance lights all along Whitehall towards Parliament, giving an almost eerie feel to the situation. There was a fire engine parked by the Cenotaph and several firefighters were standing in the road. Despite the situation, there was a strange, almost unearthly silence in an area that would usually have been bustling with people and traffic.

I walked into the middle of Whitehall diagonally by Horse Guards Avenue. I could see several people wearing white boiler suits and face masks examining the pavement, the walls of the Cabinet Office and the surrounding roadway microscopically, inch by inch, looking for evidence of how much explosive might have been used or, more gruesomely, any human remains for forensic examination and to help identify whoever the remains were once attached to. There were a few medics treating the wounds of people who'd escaped with only superficial injuries.

I felt numb at seeing a number of white sheets in close proximity, laid out over the dead bodies until they could be removed. A quick count suggested about eight or nine. I knew one of the dead bodies was a colleague, a fellow police officer, the others simply innocent passers-by now caught up in a situation they'd known nothing about.

Looking at this sight, I began to experience the out-of-body sensation of emotional and sensory displacement which arises in the aftermath of all such major incidents, where lives had been needlessly lost and reality temporarily suspended, and where the sights, sounds and smells, the full horror of what has just occurred, are beginning to sink in.

I kept moving forward and, in the middle of the road, I was approached by a uniform fingering an automatic weapon and a man in plain clothes. The uniform had the look and demeanour of someone who wanted just one reason to use his weapon.

"Who the *fuck* are you?" I was challenged brusquely by the uniform. "If you're a reporter, you can just turn around and fuck off back up there behind the police line." He nodded towards Trafalgar Square.

I was still holding my ID and I raised it for him to see. "DS McGraw, Special Branch."

He nodded, muttered, "Sorry, sir," and turned away.

The other man walked across. "Apologies for that, detective. He's trying really hard to hold himself together." He nodded towards the bodies covered in sheets. "That's his best mate over there who's just been killed, blown to pieces in front of him."

"'S okay, no problem." I knew what it was like to lose a friend acting in the execution of his duty by violent means. I'd been standing alongside Paul Glett when he'd been stabbed.

"DCI Daisley, S015. You know what's happened here?"

I indicated I'd been sort of briefed, though not in any real detail.

"That one there's one of ours." As we moved forward he pointed to a sheet on the ground about twenty yards away, which was surrounded by people in white overalls and uniforms. "Poor sod never knew what hit him." He shook his head. "This bastard took out at least eight or nine members of the public as well." He looked at the bodies covered with white sheets. "There're several more've got nasty injuries, a couple of which're life-threatening, including the other officer who was moving forward to back up the first officer." He sighed, nodding towards an ambulance.

He then walked onto the pavement. I followed him.

"This is what happened. The officer was walking along here," – he nodded to the main door of the Cabinet Office – "going to intercept someone who'd been picked out by AFR."

AFR was Automatic Facial Recognition, a system designed to identify those persons police had more than a passing interest in if spotted in particular locations where their presence would immediately arouse suspicion.

"The thing is, though, it seems police at the gates" – he nodded towards Downing Street – "didn't get the message about this person being someone of interest until he was about there, just by the door of the Cabinet Office, and there were still lots of people walking around. Police by the gates were finally alerted about this person looking suspicious, so, while the rest were getting all the people walking past and standing around to move back, two officers come out to challenge this person. One officer stopped about twenty feet from him, pointed his weapon at this person, told him to remain where he was, take his hands from his pockets, put them in the air and then get down on his knees, slowly. The man didn't move for a few seconds. The officer moved closer, repeating what he'd said, and the bomber shouted *Allahu akbar* and hit the initiation button of whatever device he was carrying, blowing himself and our man to kingdom come, and badly injuring the other one. The second officer was standing just there." He gestured to an empty space behind a white sheet. "There'd have been a lot more casualties if the officers by the gates hadn't stopped the public from going past the entrance to Downing Street. They were calling for the few who'd walked on as the bomber approached to come back just as the explosion occurred."

"Do we know who this joker was?"

"As of yet, no, we don't. We'll get it off CCTV."

My phone buzzed as he was talking. I excused myself and took the call.

"You're needed here in the office, DS McGraw." It was Smitherman.

"On my way." I dashed back to my car, again, ignoring reporters' questions.

*

There were seven other detectives in the room when Smitherman finally stood up to speak. He was accompanied by a woman I didn't recognise, who I assumed was from MI5.

"Right, first off, for anyone who's come straight here and hasn't heard the news, as well as at least eight members of the public, a police officer's also died in the suicide bombing this evening," he announced in a solemn tone. "His name was Jacob Marshall, aged thirty-one, ex-army, been on the force six years. Got a wife and a year-old son. Another officer's been injured and his injuries are critical; medics think his chances don't look too good."

He nodded to the woman alongside him, and she stepped forward. She was short and quite slim, maybe in her late forties, and was wearing a brown business suit over a pale blouse. She had a severely short-cropped hairstyle and wire-rimmed glasses. She looked like an intelligent woman and reminded me of one of my tutors at King's.

"The bomber's finally been identified from CCTV, though his details are not being released to the media just yet. AFR initially picked him up as he was spotted getting out of a taxi on the south-west corner of Trafalgar Square, by Admiralty Arch, and we're attempting to trace the cab." She paused for a second, looking troubled. "The disturbing thing is, though, there seems to have been a full half-minute gap between AFR picking the bomber out and the message reaching police at the gates. CCTV finally picked him out walking along Whitehall. From the bulky look of his coat, and the fact his hands and arms were hidden inside it, it looked very much like he could well be carrying something underneath, strapped to his chest, which we now know to be a PBIED. Once it'd been realised he was a person of interest to us, *and* closer examination on CCTV told us, from the contours of the coat, the very real likelihood was he *was* carrying something under it, a message was flashed to police at the Downing Street gates to intercept and detain this person, and the message from AFR had also been received, so a vehicle was dispatched to pick him up. Police spread out to apprehend him, but, as PC Marshall approached to intercept and ordered him to stand still, the bomber set off his device. We don't yet know how powerful the blast was, but it's safe to say PC Marshall didn't suffer, and it would have been quick."

We all nodded sombrely. I just hoped she was right.

"He was just a few yards away. From that distance, he wouldn't have stood a chance."

She paused for a moment's reflection, and I took a deep breath and thought about what I'd heard.

Every police officer in this room, and across London, indeed across the whole United Kingdom, would tonight be feeling the impact of the loss of a colleague to cold-blooded murder, and experiencing the outrage felt when a copper, *any* copper, falls in the line of duty. I wouldn't have recognised Police Constable Jacob Marshall if he'd sat on my lap and kissed me, but he was part of the tribe, a member of the family, therefore he was *one of us*, and his loss would be felt across the force. He'd been a soldier and had died while operating as a firearms protection officer standing guard at the gates of Downing Street, and thus would have been aware of, and trained for, the dangers his position entailed. But the awareness of the risks involved in his position still didn't make his horrific, contemptible murder any more acceptable. I silently hoped he had died instantly and hadn't suffered.

"PBIED?" someone asked.

"Oh, sorry, jargon. It means *person-borne improvised explosive device.*"

"A posh way of saying *suicide vest*, then," the interrupter said.

She resumed her talk. "Anyway, the bomber's been identified as Shamir Ali Alorami, also known as Sam, an English-born Muslim, a mature student at the LSE. He's been on our radar as a potential suicide bomber for a while, but, it would appear, someone took their eyes off the ball and he wasn't being watched. As a result of his actions tonight, the UK terror threat level's now being raised from *substantial* to *severe*, until we know whether tonight's was a one-off action or the start of a wider campaign, and there's to be a meeting of COBRA soon, which the Home Secretary will be chairing."

Fucking Alorami, I was thinking to myself. I was hoping against hope he'd stayed alive just long enough to experience some extreme pain levels.

She turned to Smitherman. "There was an attempt made to arrest this Alorami the other night, wasn't there?"

"Yes, but he'd vacated his flat, and no one knew where he'd gone," Smitherman replied.

"The other two we're after are missing as well, sir, Mehmet Tabzouni and Asou el-Taccouli," another detective said. "We've been looking for them."

"And we're going to find them," Smitherman stated, looking angry. "They have to be somewhere because there's no evidence they've left the country, which means *someone* knows where they might be."

He held up a piece of paper.

"I've a list here of several names supplied to us by MI5 whom we're going to be rounding up and bringing into custody, *tonight*," he emphasised, "so come see who you've drawn and go get that person. Don't come back without them, either. Finding these people is now *the* absolute top priority for all of you."

*

Twenty to midnight, and I was in my car. Before setting off I texted Taylor to tell her I'd be very late back, if I even got off duty at all tonight, because of the terror alert and the hunt for the bomber's accomplices. She'd obviously seen the news and was aware of what had happened, because she replied instantly with *Stay safe, McGraw, I LOVE YOU.* I sent her back several emoji blowing kisses, then set off for Islington.

There was frenetic police activity as early morning house raids were now occurring right across North and East London. Police had a list of about twenty persons they wanted to talk to concerning what had occurred recently in Whitehall, all known associates of Mehmet Tabzouni or Sam Alorami and all known to be frequent attendees at the Islington mosque where Tabzouni had conducted the radicalising sessions: messages which Alorami had clearly taken to heart.

I was going to apprehend someone I'd encountered a few months back when I'd been investigating two persons who'd been identified standing outside Conway Hall, Holborn, where a police officer had had his throat slit open and had bled to death. Alimi Akeel had been one of the two bodyguards to the late and extremely unlamented Khaled al-Ebouli. The other one had died in the attack which, a day later, had also killed al-Ebouli, and I was sure I knew who'd fired the shots, but had been unable to prove it.

Outside Akeel's residence in Islington I could see a police car and a detective standing by it. I recognised him. DS Roberts. He saw me get out my car.

"Evening, detective. The shitbird we're after's in there." He nodded towards a darkened house. As he spoke I noticed three uniforms disembarking from a police van parked further along the road. "Let's go wake up Sleeping Beauty, shall we, and not with a fucking kiss either."

He led the way up the few steps to the front door. One of the heavily padded officers had a thumper with him. Roberts rang the doorbell.

"Right, hit it," he ordered.

The uniform hit the door latch hard and the door crashed against the wall.

"Armed police!" someone shouted loudly. It dawned on me the person shouting had been a female officer. The three police officers piled into the corridor, lights on their weapons lighting up the hallway, and I followed them into the house, holding my gun ready. The hall light came on and Akeel could be seen standing at the top of the stairs, looking alarmed.

"What's going on here? My children are sleeping."

As he was speaking, two uniforms ran up the stairs and put Akeel into what appeared to be a very painful armlock. They almost dragged him downstairs to the hallway.

"Remember me?" Roberts smiled. "You're under arrest, pal."

*

Akeel sat facing me and Roberts in the interview room at Kentish Town police station. He was looking disoriented and nervous, breathing heavily and muttering in Arabic to himself.

"Why am I here? What am I supposed to have done?" he asked at least four times, but neither Roberts nor I spoke at first, which made Akeel look more worried.

"You know what's just happened?" Roberts finally snarled. "Some Arab maniac blew himself up in Whitehall a couple of hours ago. He's killed several innocent civilians *and* he killed a police officer, blew the poor bastard to pieces and left his young family stranded. There's also another police officer who's critically injured and undergoing emergency surgery as we speak."

"I'm very sorry, but why come to me about this?" Akeel shrugged and spread his hands out, trying to remain calm. "I had nothing to do with it, and I have nothing to do with any of these people."

"And what people might *they* be, huh?" Roberts demanded.

"People like these, people who kill other people with their homemade bombs."

Roberts appeared not to be happy with this response.

"Can you account for all your movements over, say, the past week?" I asked.

"The past week? I've only been back in London a couple of days."

"Back from where?"

"Beirut. I've been to visit my brother."

"I'll go check it out." Roberts got up, giving Akeel a look which could kill. I took out my iPhone.

"You recognise this man?" I showed Akeel Sam Alorami's picture.

He looked closely, then nodded. "I've seen him in the mosque when I go to pray, but I don't know him."

I explained Alorami was the suicide bomber in Whitehall responsible for several deaths, as well as his own, and that we were after those who had worked alongside and encouraged him in what he had done, because *someone* had to have helped him. But Akeel simply repeated he didn't know the man in the picture.

"What about these two men?" I showed pictures of Mehmet Tabzouni and Asou el-Taccouli.

"The same: I've seen them in the mosque. That's all. I don't know any of them."

During the next ten minutes, Akeel again denied having any contact with any of the three men in the pictures, denied he'd ever sat in on any talk given by someone intent on radicalising young Muslims, and fervently denied being a jihadi and wanting a caliphate in the West, or the establishment of sharia law for Muslims.

"But the man you were bodyguard to, al-Ebouli, *he* was a jihadi, wasn't he? He was all for the establishing of a caliphate in the West, wasn't he?"

Roberts re-entered the room before I got an answer. "Flew out to Beirut, via Paris, two weeks ago. Arrived back at Heathrow early Wednesday morning, direct BA flight from Beirut." He sounded disappointed as he sat down. "His story checks out."

We questioned Akeel further but were unable to pin anything on him. His every movement could be accounted for since arriving back in the country. I believed him. Suicide bombings have to be planned; they don't just happen on a whim. Akeel was led away by another officer to write out a statement outlining his movements since returning from Beirut.

*

Two fifty-five. I was back in the office writing up my account when I heard the depressing news: of the twenty persons police had set out to bring in, only fourteen had been located and brought into custody, with Tabzouni and el-Taccouli amongst those who hadn't been found. Adrian Bowketts hadn't been found either. Police on the ground were continuing the search for these men, but, when I left the office ninety-five minutes later, they'd still not been apprehended.

FOURTEEN

Saturday

I was suddenly aware of being kissed lightly on my left cheek. I slowly came back to life with the aromatic scent of a rather sensuous perfume wafting under my nose.

"Oh my God, it lives! Aaarrgh!" I heard Taylor shriek playfully.

I opened my eyes, blinked a few times, gradually came to and saw a smiling Sally Taylor sitting next to me on the edge of the bed. She was looking radiantly alive and wearing a white shirt and faded black-grey jeans, her straight-from-the-shower mop of strawberry blonde hair flopping down around her shoulders and her glasses. Has any man ever awoken to a more divine sight?

I looked at my watch: nine forty-six. I'd only got to bed at six minutes past five, after a working day lasting nineteen hours.

"Hey, sleepy." She smiled. "I've made you some coffee. I'm off to meet Steve; we're gonna work on our story today. He's made a lot of progress putting it together, some great stuff as well. Tell you all about it tonight."

She kissed me on the cheek again and then left.

*

The suicide bombing and the death of a police officer was the headline story on the front pages of every newspaper. A couple of the broadsheets had somehow managed to obtain pictures from the scene, showing white sheets covering dead bodies, though how they'd managed to get past the police cordon and close enough to obtain these I'd no idea.

Several newspapers carried a picture of PC Jacob Marshall on their front pages, with poignant eulogies about how yet another brave young police officer had died a hero's death protecting his country. Even though he was thirty-one, he looked like someone who'd not long left school, and I felt a lump in my throat when I saw a picture of him and his wife and baby son, taken on a recent holiday: a young couple at a poolside table alongside several others, laughing and looking like they were having fun, and with their whole lives ahead of them. Now, the family had been broken.

At only twenty-seven, his wife Judith was now a police widow, and his son Aaron had lost a father.

The identity of the bomber had not been made known, and the statement issued by the Assistant Commissioner of the Metropolitan Police was a masterpiece of PR spin. It said all the right things in the right order but, ultimately, was just empty rhetoric.

I was supposed to have had a rare Saturday off duty today, but every officer was being mobilised, so I'd gone into the office and spent part of the day reading statements taken from those who'd been brought into custody after last night's atrocity, attempting to make connections between statements made, and logging patterns of movements against the known activities of terrorist suspects. I'd drawn a blank.

I looked at reports from informants concerning the movements and activities of persons of interest but found little of any real substance. A few other persons had also been apprehended and taken into custody earlier today, and a further two houses in East London had been raided and meticulously searched, but nothing useful had come from interrogating these people, and nothing incriminating had been found in either of the houses. The three people police most wanted to question were still at large.

As the terror threat level had been raised to severe, security was tighter and much more overt, and everyone in London today would notice the presence of more armed police in strategic locations. But the reality was that, unless and until the police got a break, we were in the lap of the gods.

The day hadn't been a complete waste, though. Mid-afternoon I drove over to Tyler Watts' tea stall, where he was at work.

"I knew you'd do it," he said, beaming, before I could get a word out.

"Huh? Do what?"

"I knew you'd realise who I was talking about," he said. "When you came here last Wednesday, I gave you a description of that Helen, and I knew you'd soon put it together. That's why I did it. I *wanted* Chappy found, but I didn't wanna give away his location. I mean, I'm his dad, you know what I'm saying? So I thought, if I gave you a coupla clues, you'd figure it out. Don't let on, eh?" He grinned evilly. "Chappy asked, after you left last night, how you'd known where to find him. I told him you were pretty smart for a copper."

"So, is he still gonna do it?"

He knew what I meant. "Yeah, I'll give him a call."

"Then my lips are sealed."

I collected Chappy and Helen from the flat and drove them to Kentish Town police station. I again emphasised he was safe from any reprisals from the Chackartis, which made him feel better.

Chappy told the detective he spoke to that he'd been away and had heard police wanted him to testify against John McGreely, so he'd returned and was prepared to give evidence. I contacted Smitherman, who was delighted to hear about Chappy coming in voluntarily and agreeing to testify, and said he'd contact the requisite authorities so the trial process could be initiated. I said nothing about finding him hiding out.

Chappy then gave a sworn statement agreeing to testify, which meant John McGreely was looking more certain to go join his father in Belmarsh because a trial date could now be set. Although there was no guarantee of a conviction, Chappy's testimony would go some way towards stacking the odds in favour of police. If we could nail McGreely with being involved with the presence of Semtex and other bomb-making resources at Tyler Watts' lock-up, the travelling on a false passport wouldn't necessarily be needed. I'd also have to testify to his arrest at the garage where a range of materials which could be used in the making of bombs had been found, as I'd been the arresting officer, but I was more than happy to do so.

I returned to the Branch office a little happier than when I'd left, though no further arrests and no progress looking into the suicide bomber had been made.

*

I'd only really seen Taylor once this week, Tuesday evening, due to both of us working long hours, so we'd decided, no matter what, tonight was going to be *our night*. Unless someone killed several members of the Government or the royals, tonight was for *us*, and everything we were involved with would just have to wait its turn.

We'd been particularly looking forward to this evening as well. Tonight, we were dining out in Chinatown, in the very same restaurant we'd been to on our first real date, and I'd even managed to book the same table. I had *so* many happy memories of this place. It'd all started in this restaurant. Although we'd been out for a drink the previous evening, it'd been here, sitting in this very spot, where the realisation had struck me of just how much I *really* liked Sally Taylor and wanted to be with her. Those feelings have since grown almost exponentially.

Coming out of the National Theatre and walking along the South Bank yesterday, Taylor said, she'd been aware something sinister had happened because of the number of emergency service vehicles she'd seen crossing Westminster Bridge, which had been blocked off to all other traffic, and the number of sirens she could hear over towards Whitehall. She and her sister had managed to get a taxi at nearby Waterloo station, as she'd heard the entrance to Westminster tube station had been closed, and had been told by their driver, *Some fucking Arab nutter's just blown himself up in Whitehall.*

I gave her a few points about the suicide bombing, though I omitted several key details. I also mentioned a few things about our search for the suspected terrorists earlier in the week, though I didn't mention being shot at two days back. Some things Taylor doesn't need to know.

"So, that's my week. How about you?" I squeezed her hand lightly. "What've you been doing?"

The play, it seemed, was *absolutely fricking brilliant, McGraw*, one of the best they'd seen for quite some while. Given I'd paid £144 for the two tickets, I was pleased to hear this. She told me about a couple of items in the *Standard* she'd been involved with this week, including her account of the public meeting we'd attended on Tuesday last.

"So, how's your other story going?" She'd know which one I meant.

"Oh yeah," she said excitedly, "got some news there."

She'd been mainly researching the state of the law in the early seventies, looking up what legal protection, if any, soldiers had for any deaths occurring in the course of an armed conflict like the one in Northern Ireland, which technically wasn't a declared war. She'd also been looking at comments made by the press and Government politicians around the same time, comparing them with what she'd heard from Pencourt and, in particular, with what some of the soldiers on the programme we'd watched Monday night had said, plus what Jacobs had been discovering. They'd already begun putting a first draft of their story together.

I asked if she'd come across mention of any actions where the SAS had been involved, remembering what George Selwood had told me.

"They weren't officially deployed in Northern Ireland until early in 1976; that's when the first accounts of their involvement were made known. But there're several stories where it's claimed the SAS were involved before then, either providing intelligence or engaged in military action against the IRA, though none have been officially confirmed."

I remembered what Selwood had said concerning the role the SAS had played. Perhaps he'd been telling the truth after all.

"Steve's really been making some progress, though," she said, "checking through the names Pencourt gave us, and he's been to see a few of them."

"Like who?"

"We've whittled the list down somewhat. Of those listed, four of them are now dead, one has a severe case of Alzheimer's and is in a nursing home 'cause he's got no family, and one has the onset of dementia. A few others are either living abroad or else Steve's not been able to trace them yet. But Steve's identified ten who're still with us and he's obtained current addresses for all of them."

She paused to sip her wine.

"There were four soldiers in Two Unit, and Steve's managed to talk to one of the soldiers Pencourt mentioned, guy named Michael Mercer. He was the other uniform with Pencourt when Brendan Morgan was killed."

"He's spoken to him?"

"Yeah." She was excited at this. "Steve called him up, told him what he was looking into, and Mercer came straight out and said he'd be perfectly happy to be interviewed about Two Unit and what they did in Northern Ireland, and he'd no problem with going on the record either. Steve's been to Suffolk to see him."

"Was Pencourt's name mentioned?"

"Only once to confirm something."

"So, what'd he have to say?" I enquired.

"Oh, Steve gave him the whole nine yards about what our

story's looking into, and this guy wasn't fazed at all, admitted everything." She raised her eyebrows as though this was no major surprise. "He agreed Two Unit went hunting for known or suspected IRA personnel and killed them wherever they could be found. He'd *no problems* at all with what they did, was quite matter-of-fact about everything. In fact, he's the guy Pencourt'd met at the regimental reunion who said he'd been pleased to be exacting revenge against the Irish."

"Did he talk about the Morgan case?"

"Steve asked him if he remembered this particular incident, and he did. Steve told him all the available evidence suggested Brendan Morgan had had nothing to do with the IRA. He put it to Mercer the officer in his unit had killed an innocent kid, someone with no involvement in the Troubles. You know what? Mercer sort of shrugged and said, I quote, *Ah well, shit happens, doesn't it?* No remorse at all, evidently. His view? They were taking the war to the IRA, and *this* was the important thing."

I thought for a moment as I sipped some rather splendid Chinese beer. "So, how did Steve even find this Mercer guy? Aren't personnel details like this supposed to be locked away somewhere in army records?"

"Oh, they probably are," she agreed, "but Steve's got some really good sources."

"Yeah, so it seems."

I knew who two of them were. His partner, Trish, worked for Lantanis and I'd little doubt she could access all kinds of classified information from there. I also knew Jacobs' brother was a major in the army, and I suspected he was leaking the occasional titbit to Jacobs, whenever he could do so in such a way as not to violate his oath of loyalty to the Crown or contravene the Official Secrets Act.

"Steve's also contacted two others who served in groups like Two Unit, but they've refused to talk," Taylor said. "One slammed the door in his face, called him a *fucking traitor*. The other was a bit more pleasant about it, agreed there were things went on in Northern Ireland which probably shouldn't have done, but he saw no point raking over all the ashes now the Troubles are over and there's peace once again. Steve asked him if he'd go on the record just saying this, but he wouldn't say anything else. Steve's gonna write it up as a tacit admission of involvement."

We finished our drinks. The instant our glasses hit the table a smiling Chinese waitress magically appeared. "You like more drinks?"

"Be rude to refuse, wouldn't it?" I grinned at Taylor. "Yeah, why not?"

Taylor went off to the ladies'. I watched her walking back to the table, in thrall to just how gorgeous and sexy she was. Our drinks arrived and Taylor continued with her story.

"The thing *really* exciting Steve, though, is" – she paused to sip her wine – "he's discovered the identity and the whereabouts of the doctor who signed off on Brendan Morgan's death certificate, amongst others."

"Yeah?" I briefly wondered what his response to being called out on this would be.

"Yeah. He lives in Mid Kent and Steve's asked me to go down and talk to him in the next few days. As it's only an elderly doctor, he thinks I'd be quite safe doing it without him."

"Mid Kent?" I perked up. "That's my neck of the woods. Whereabouts in Kent?"

She told me. My eyes opened wide.

"That's only just up the road from where I come from," I said, excitedly. "Look, I know the area well and I'm owed some time in lieu. I'll come with you, show you where it is."

"Oh, that'd be great, thanks." She smiled warmly.

"Who's the doc, anyway?"

"Someone called Dr Redfearn; he's a GP now, but still in practice."

My eyes opened wide in sudden surprise. Taylor saw my expression.

"What is it?" She smiled, curious.

"Do you mean Dr Niall Redfearn?"

It was Taylor's turn to look amazed. "You know this person?" Her eyes were open wide.

"Do I know him?" I gasped. "Dr Redfearn's our family's GP."

Taylor stared at me with an astonished look on her face. She then laughed and shook her head. "Oh my God, you know this man."

"Yeah," I agreed, "known him since I was in school when he moved to the area. It was him strapped up my ankle when I damaged it playing football."

"So, what's he like, this doctor?"

"Seems like a nice guy, I suppose. I've only ever seen him in the surgery. I mean, I knew he'd done time in the military, but I knew nothing about this."

She smiled. "And you're gonna come down with me to see him?"

I agreed I most certainly was.

*

We spent a very enjoyable couple of hours in the restaurant, just talking about whatever came to mind. We reminisced about our very first time in this restaurant, and about what it'd felt like when we'd each realised we were falling heavily for the other. Afterwards, we took a slow stroll around the West End, holding hands, occasionally window shopping and simply enjoying being with each other again. The sight and sounds – so many people with smiling faces, out enjoying themselves, going to theatres, restaurants, nightclubs and whatever else amid all the noise, the bustle and excited chatter – were in direct contrast to the eerie silence and the sight of white sheets and flashing lights from emergency vehicles which I'd experienced last night.

We took a taxi home to Battersea and, in the flat, we slumped down on the couch in our favourite position, leaning against the back and wrapped around each other, neither of us talking, just luxuriating in each other's company. Tonight, all I wanted was to hold Taylor close and feel her warmth.

The flat was our haven, our little *sanctum sanctorum,* where the outside world didn't intrude, where we didn't *let* it intrude. In this place, we temporarily forgot everything about our jobs and what was happening in the outside world. In our little sanctum, there were no suicide bombers, no preachers of hate radicalising their disciples with brilliantly distorted logic about what the Koran really meant, no dead police officers, no terrorists intent on taking the lives of non-combatants, and no fanatical adherents to those warped ideologies which seemed to require their followers to provide the constant reinforcement of their beliefs with blood extracted from the bodies of the innocent.

Tonight, the only two people in our little world were Sally and Robert, and, for this sadly all too short a time, the rest of the world with all its incumbent horrors was a light year away.

FIFTEEN

Sunday

I was working at my desk and trying to concentrate, though my mind kept flashing back to last night and how good it'd felt reliving our early days in Chinatown. I finally snapped out of my reverie and began looking up details of the life and times of the McGraw family doctor, Niall Redfearn.

I already knew he was of Irish parentage, though born in Surrey. He'd joined the army and had qualified as an army doctor, serving twenty-one years in places like Northern Ireland and Germany. He'd also been a medic with the task force sent to the South Atlantic in 1982 before returning to Civvy Street in 1991 as a family GP, first in London and, for the last twenty-two years, in Mid Kent. He'd been married forty-six years and had two adult children, one a doctor, the other in the military.

His army record was spotless and he'd left with an honourable discharge. His private life showed nothing untoward; no brushes with the law, not even a parking ticket. He'd an excellent credit rating and no blemishes anywhere. In every respect he was a model citizen.

But it was Steve Jacobs' contention Dr Redfearn had been complicit in the covering up of how several Irish nationals, some of whom were innocent, had died, and had signed off on an untrue cause of death, according to all we knew about the Brendan Morgan incident. I was wondering whether this complicity had been paired with full knowledge.

Pencourt had said Morgan'd been shot three times in the chest and neck, and he'd seen this happen, but, according to Jacobs, Dr Redfearn had signed off on a post-mortem report stating Morgan had died from two gunshot wounds in his back. Had he actually examined the dead body or even *seen* it? Did he know the real cause of death? Had he even wanted to? Had he been in agreement with what bodies such as Two Unit had been doing?

Pencourt had also said one man had died from his injuries after being beaten by soldiers, with the lead officer playing a main role in his death, and Jacobs had obtained a copy of the post-mortem report, where it'd been written up as the deceased being hit by a vehicle and dying from the resulting injuries.

Was it the case that Dr Redfearn had simply signed off on whatever had been put in front of him? If so, in how many more cases like this had he been involved in covering up the real cause of death?

I was trying to imagine the Dr Redfearn I knew, the kindly elderly man with the unruffled exterior and the soothing bedside manner, being involved in any cover-up of the casualties of a shoot-to-kill policy. Had he even *known* such a policy existed and, if so, had he been in full agreement concerning covering up the real cause of death? This was significant because, if the integrity of a post-mortem verdict was cast into doubt, this was potentially grounds for a criminal prosecution, with all the consequences this might involve.

I was still thinking about this when Smitherman asked to see me. He began with some sad news.

"There's been another fatality from Friday night." He shook his head and sighed. "The husband of one of the two women who'd died at the scene died just after midnight from his injuries. They'd only been married five months and were on a belated honeymoon, a week in London. This makes it eleven fatalities now."

Five months. I sighed to myself. Only a little longer than Taylor and I'd been married; no time at all. It was a sombre thought that last evening, around the same time that Taylor and I had been wrapped around each other and enjoying golden time together, an innocent victim had lost his fight to stay alive, and another innocent family had been broken and would now be weeping for its dead.

We were both silent for a while.

I don't know why it came at this moment, but a memory from my last school speech day came to mind. The main speaker had been an old boy, now a C of E priest, who'd told us about the joys of Heaven and of the eternal life waiting for us all in paradise when God eventually called us to his side. He'd said God would call us in a manner of his own choosing. I wondered briefly why he'd chosen such a horrific way to call these eleven people to his side. I must have looked miles away.

"Anyway, it's not all bad news." Smitherman refocused me. "The other police officer on the scene has survived a second round of emergency surgery, pulled through after a seven-hour operation. It's still serious, but he's gonna make it, so that's good. Also, there's two other pieces of good news. We've got CCTV images of the last few minutes of Sherif Rizwi's life."

"Where from? Didn't you say there was a gap in the tape and no images found?"

"Yes, I did," he said, nodding, "but it seems there must have been a backup recording or something, and we've been able to see some of what occurred that evening. First thing, I'd like you to go downstairs, take a look at the CCTV. I'll tell you the other development afterwards."

I went down to the central operations room, a room with a wall laden with CCTV images from right across London, giving the place a slightly surreal feel, and asked for these newfound images to be uploaded. They'd been taken from the cameras directly adjacent to the station and on the road by the roundabout at the top of nearby Upper Street. There were still a number of people about despite the late hour.

From the road camera, I recognised Rizwi walking out the station and turning right towards Highbury Station Road. Three seconds later a man, closely followed by another man, followed him in the same direction. Both men were looking down and had their heads slightly turned to the right, almost like they were trying not to be caught on CCTV. Consequently, even fully zoomed in, it wasn't possible to obtain any clear facial images of the two men from either camera.

There were no cameras in Highbury Station Road, so they were out of sight for nearly six minutes. Both men were then seen running back across the causeway in front of the station, and a car travelling south on Holloway Road screeched to a halt. Both men quickly got in and the car sped off, heading south along Upper Street.

A few minutes after this, I could see a man and a woman coming out of Highbury Station Road and gesticulating at a station employee, who went off-camera for a few moments, then returned to enter the station. Four minutes later, an ambulance and a police car arrived.

I rewound the tape and focused on the car, noting the registration number. As I did, something told me I knew this number from somewhere else.

Back at my desk, I entered the number into the PNC, which a second later flashed back *SEARCH BLOCKED* in bold red capital letters. Curious, I entered the number again, only to receive the same answer. It was then that I realised where I knew the number from.

I brought up my notes from a previous investigation into the murder of a young London police officer, and, after a moment, I knew for certain why the car number was familiar. This was the registration number of the car Joachim Balpak had been in the first time I'd come face-to-face with him. This meant the car the two men had got into was a diplomatic vehicle, supposedly used only for the business of an embassy. Had the Mossad, Israeli intelligence, been complicit in the death of Sherif Rizwi? Why would the Mossad want to kill an undercover MI5 operative?

This wasn't making any sense, but, before I raised this with Smitherman, I decided to check it out with Balpak. I contacted the Israeli embassy but was informed Mr Balpak was away and currently unavailable.

*

The better piece of good news was that the taxi driver who'd driven Sam Alorami to Trafalgar Square, Reggie Cox, had finally come forward. After Alorami had got out the taxi Friday night, the driver had signed off for the evening and had immediately driven up to Norfolk because, next morning, his nine-year-old grandson was due to be operated on for a minor ailment, and he'd wanted his beloved grandad present. Cox had arrived not long after midnight to be there when the kid awoke Saturday morning.

Cox was a widower and lived alone, so there'd been no one at his flat in East Ham to answer police inquiries, and neither his work colleagues nor his neighbours had known where he'd gone. Reporting for work earlier today, he'd been told police were looking to speak to him, so he'd contacted East Ham South police station and had been asked to report there to await an interview with a Special Branch detective. I drove very fast across London to talk to him.

Reggie Cox was about mid-sixties and had the rugged, chiselled facial features, plus the gnarly knuckles, of someone who'd spent his entire working life doing hard manual labour, rather than having been a thirty-five-year taxi driver. My old granny, bless her heart, would have said his face looked *lived in*.

Did he remember his last fare on Friday evening? Yeah, it was some Arab bloke, around nine fifteenish. Where'd he been picked up? Somewhere along the Euston Road, between King's Cross and Euston. Had he been alone when he'd flagged the taxi down? Yeah, but he'd been talking to another man, who'd turned and walked away once the taxi had stopped; Cox hadn't seen the man's face, but hadn't thought anything of it. Had Cox seen where the other man had gone? No, he'd not been looking.

Did the passenger say anything? No, just got in the back seat and said, *Admiralty Arch, please.* He say anything on the ride? No, just sat back and stared out the window. He looked like an Arab but he sounded English. He'd not even spoken when paying the fare, just put a twenty and a ten-pound note in Cox's hand. Had Cox noticed anything strange about the man's behaviour? No, nothing that stood out. What about the fact he had a hood up? What about it? It wasn't unusual in London.

Which route had they taken? The quickest way, back along Euston Road, left into Tottenham Court Road, straight on into Charing Cross Road and round the square to Admiralty Arch. Had the man seemed nervous? No idea, and he hadn't really been looking, to be honest. Had Cox noticed he looked unusually bulky, like he might have been carrying something beneath his coat? No, he hadn't really taken too much notice; he'd just wanted to finish so he could get on up to Norfolk.

"Were you aware, once he got out of your cab, the man walked down Whitehall and, by the door to the Cabinet Office, he detonated the explosive device he'd had strapped to his body and blew himself to pieces, also killing a police officer and several members of the public?"

"No. I'd not known anything about the explosion till I saw the news last night, and they mentioned this person getting out of a taxi, and, when they mentioned a place and time, I thought, *Christ, was that the bloke I dropped off?* So I got in touch with you blokes this morning when I returned home."

His particulars were noted. I thanked him for his help and left the station.

Back in the central operations room, I requested the CCTV footage of the area between Euston and King's Cross, north side of the main Euston Road, for Friday last, circa 9pm. At nine twelve, I saw Alorami coming out of a nearby amusement arcade, talking to another man. I zoomed in on the man and froze the picture. It was a little fuzzy but clear enough for me to recognise him. It was the man I'd put on the floor at Drake Mahoney's flat last Wednesday. They'd both been clocked at Little Des' house last Thursday, and now he and Alorami were having what appeared to be a heated discussion for a couple of minutes, with Alorami gesticulating with both hands. Alorami then walked to the kerb and flagged a taxi, and I saw Reggie Cox's cab pulling up, whereupon Alorami got into the cab and the other man turned and walked back into the arcade. The taxi then did a U-turn in the Euston Road and headed west, carrying Alorami to serve whatever deity or political *-ism* he was about to sacrifice the lives of eleven innocent people in the name of.

I informed Smitherman of what I'd found, and he told me to go bring this man in, plus anyone else on the premises. Five minutes later, I was in my car behind a police van carrying another detective and a number of armed uniforms from the anti-terrorism squad, and we set off for the Euston Road. Very fast.

We screeched to a halt outside a two-storey building. The Merrie Jackpot was on the ground floor, and we discovered it was closed on Sundays. I tried the main door. It was locked and it looked dark inside, aside from a few flashing lights from slot machines. I looked up and noticed the lights were off on the first floor of the building. Was this part of it? I intended to find out.

"Right, you and you," – I nodded at two of the uniforms – "see if there's a back way into this place. If there is, call me and let me know."

"Okay, skip." They set off around the corner into Chalton Street. We waited a minute. Several passers-by gave us very nervous looks. My radio crackled into life.

"Yeah, there is, skip, leads out into Weir's Passage. It's locked, though."

"Okay. We're gonna go in through the front. Anyone comes out, grab 'em."

"Will do."

"Check your weapons," I told the other uniforms. We did.

I rang the bell. No response. Rang it again. No response. I took out my weapon and used the stock to smash the glass by the lock, and was surprised not to hear an alarm as I cleared glass from the door, then gingerly inserted my hand and unlocked it.

"Armed police!" I shouted loudly, which echoed around the empty room as I entered with the other uniforms, guns pointing in front of us. We were surrounded by slot machines, pool tables and various other gambling facilities, such as one-armed bandit machines offering legalised extortion to suckers. The room was sizeable, maybe fifty to sixty yards long and half as wide again, and it felt eerie with most of the machines switched off, lit as it was only by a couple of dull overhead security lights in the middle of the room, contrasting with the flashing lights from several slot machines. We fanned out and looked slowly and carefully around the floor, but nobody was here.

"There're stairs over here, skip," a uniform shouted.

By the refreshments counter, there was an open door with a flight of stairs clearly visible.

"Wait here," I ordered the uniform at the counter. "Anyone other than us comes down . . ."

I went through the door.

"Armed police!" I shouted again at the top of the stairs, which led into a short corridor. There were three doors, two on the left, one on the right. I gestured to the DC to go with me to the one on the right.

I listened by the door. No sound. I held up three fingers. The DC nodded as we stood either side of the door. I turned the handle slowly; it was unlocked. I left the door slightly ajar, we both counted down from three, and then I kicked the door open and entered, gun held in front, followed a split second later by the DC.

We were in an untidy bedroom, the only furniture being an unmade bed with a few soft porn mags next to it, a couple of chairs and an open wardrobe with a few clothes.

We repeated the process with the next room, which was a lounge of sorts, with a settee, a couple of armchairs and a large-screen television. There was a coffee table piled with magazines and newspapers, including the most recent edition of *New Focus*.

Some of the magazines were Arabic publications. From the window, you could see and hear traffic and pedestrians on the Euston Road. The smaller room was a bathroom with toilet. There were no cooking facilities I could see.

I radioed control and requested a forensic team to go through these rooms. I wanted this place fingerprinted to within an inch of its life.

While we waited, the DC and I searched the premises, ensuring we wore plastic gloves so as not to compromise what I was hoping would be a fruitful crime scene. In the lounge there were tins of food in a cupboard, an opened bottle of rancid milk in the small fridge with a smell so sour it made me retch, plus several cans of beer and some items of male clothing in the drawers. There were a few DVDs next to the television. The whole flat had a very empty, very spartan feel.

And I knew why. I knew exactly what this place was. It wasn't a home; it was a dosshouse, a crib, a place someone stayed in temporarily, or was hidden in, before moving to wherever they were going on to next. Was this where Mahoney's friend was staying while in London?

"Wait here for forensics," I told the DC. "I have to visit a suspect."

I was after Drake Mahoney. It'd been his friend I'd seen on the CCTV earlier, and I needed to know who and where he was. I turned right at Eversholt Street, drove north past Mornington Crescent and onto Camden. I parked close by Mahoney's flat and rang the bell. No answer. I rang a few more times; no answer. I put in a call to central operations to have Drake Mahoney taken into custody if he was seen, on suspicion of involvement in terrorism.

*

Back in the office, I checked out the ownership of the amusement arcade. As the flat was clearly being used as a stop-off point, I needed to know who owned and controlled it.

The building was owned by a leisure company, Maynards, which operated several such arcades around the central London area and which in turn was owned by, though an independent subsidiary of, the Ladbrokes group. Their offices were open seven days a week, so I found their London address and phoned their registered office. A woman answered. I identified myself as a Special Branch detective and stated I needed to ask a few questions concerning premises owned by her company. She replied she was the general manager at Maynards and was able to answer any such questions.

"Who's the manager of the Merrie Jackpot, on the Euston Road?"

"Oh, that'd be Florian. In fact, I've just been trying to get hold of him." She sounded agitated. "The front door's just had a window smashed, someone said there've been people going in and out of there and I wanna know how and why it's happened."

"How it happened's easy; police did it." I didn't say it'd been me.

"Huh, why?

"We've reason to believe this Florian's allowing the premises to be used by people we know are complicit in acts of terrorism, so, as the doors were locked and this is an emergency situation, police took the necessary action to gain access."

"What do you mean, *emergency situation*?" She sounded astonished. "How're *we* involved in any emergency situation?"

"You remember the suicide bomb, two nights ago, by Downing Street?"

"Yes."

"About half an hour before the explosion, the bomber was caught on CCTV coming out of the Merrie Jackpot and getting into a taxi outside your premises."

"*What?*" She gasped. "Coming out of *our* premises?"

"Uh-huh," I said. "That's why there're police officers on the premises now, fingerprinting and turning the place over, to see who's been using the flat upstairs as a base, and I'm pretty certain we're gonna find something there. What's this Florian's surname?"

"It's Coyake," – she spelled it out – "though he pronounces it as Coy-yark-ee."

"Is the flat there his permanent address?"

"No, only uses it when he works late or he's opening up early next morning. Flat's mostly empty otherwise."

"What's his actual home address?"

"I dunno."

As she was speaking I noticed Maynards' address was located just off Chancery Lane.

"Well, find it, and quick," I ordered. "I'm on my way to your office."

*

As I drove away I contacted the office and asked for all the relevant details we had on a Florian Coyake, including all known associates, as soon as possible.

In Chancery Lane I pulled up by the corner of Breams Buildings and saw the ground floor offices for Maynards. I went in without ringing the bell. There was a woman sitting at a desk by the reception counter. She was dressed casually, bright sweater and jeans, and with her dark hair tied back in a bun. I guessed she was in her early thirties.

"Are you the . . .?" she began.

"Yeah." I showed ID. "You got Florian's home address?"

"Actually, erm, no, we don't seem to have one for him." She looked embarrassed. "I've just been looking at his personnel file, and I remember now. When we interviewed him for the job, he said he was between flats and currently had no official residence, so he was dossing on a friend's couch till he found somewhere."

"Did he say which friend?"

"I don't really remember, sorry."

I didn't like what I was hearing. "But you still employed him."

"Yes, we did. He was the best candidate we interviewed, the only one who didn't have a police record, so we, or, rather, I offered him temporary usage of the flat till he found somewhere."

"Very noble. How long's he worked for you?"

She thought for a moment. "About a year and a half now, I think."

"A pretty long temporary," I suggested.

"Maybe so, but you know what?" Her eyes opened wide. "He's as honest as the day's long. Books always in order, and there're no large or sudden unexplained cash shortages. He's not skimming off funds for his own purposes, so, as the previous two managers had both been dismissed for getting caught with their fingers in the till, the issue of his tenancy kind of hasn't come up again." She shrugged. "You know what I'm saying?"

I didn't but hadn't the time to ask her to explain. "What's his contact number?"

"It's the one for the Euston arcade."

"No, I want his mobile number."

She stared at the screen. "We don't appear to have one for him."

I was now agitated.

"Not every day's a long day. Think about that one," I said as I turned to leave.

*

There'd been a message left on my phone to contact the office.

"Florian Coyake, twenty-eight, parents are Spanish but he's English. Family lives in the Cotswolds somewhere. University dropout. He was a sciences student at Westminster but didn't finish the course. He's clean, no arrests and no record of any run-ins with police, *but* he's a known associate of several people we've got on file."

"Okay, gimme some names."

She listed four names, and none were familiar.

"There's also a Gary White, and a Chapman Watts, known to all and sundry as Chappy, both known to be active on the fringes of the Chackartis."

I knew White was now dead but Watts was very much alive. "Thanks for this."

I drove to the O2 car park and saw the Watts' tea stall was closed. This was unusual; it always opened weekends, as the car park was always in use. I contacted police and asked for Chapman Watts to be picked up at his family's house and, if not there, at his girlfriend's flat, and taken into custody. I gave both addresses.

Soon afterwards I received a message. Chapman Watts wasn't at his parents' house, so police had been to the flat in Antill Road. There was nobody at the flat, and police had been told by a woman in the next flat the girl who lived at number 5 had left late Saturday evening with her boyfriend, both seen carrying bags.

I drove almost recklessly fast to Tyler Watts' house in Bethnal Green in an agitated state. He answered the door. I stated I needed to speak to Chappy but I'd been told he'd moved out, along with Helen, and it was imperative that I find him. As I was speaking, it was noticeable that Tyler was avoiding eye contact with me.

"So, where the fuck's he gone this time, Tyler?" I was trying to remain calm. "This rather contradicts what he said yesterday."

He stared at me somewhat glumly.

"On my life, detective," he said solemnly, "I didn't know he'd left till earlier today when I went round there. His mum's been crying all morning, and no, I don't know where he's gone either. That's the God's honest truth, as true as I'm standing here. I'm sorry."

You little bastard, Chappy, I swore loudly to myself.

"If he turns up, I'll bring him in myself." Tyler sounded contrite.

I was about to leave when I had a sudden thought.

"Has Chappy ever mentioned, or do you know of, someone called Florian Coyake?"

"Florian? Yeah, I know who he is; we call him Florence." He grinned. "He's a mate of Gary's, or he used to be. They were friends at university. Both of them dropped out together, stupid pair of buggers."

"You know where he lives?"

"Last I heard, he was staying in a gaff over some amusements place on the Euston Road."

"I've been there; he's not there now. Any other places he might be?"

Tyler looked impassive for a moment. "He used to stay at my lock-up one time."

"The lock-up?"

"Yeah, he did. I didn't know it at the time. He had nowhere to stay, so, as I was subletting to Gary, he told Florence he could stay there if he wanted till he found a gaff. He kept his car there and he slept in that."

I remembered, when I'd arrested John McGreely the first time, a few months back, it'd been at Tyler's lock-up, and there'd been a Peugeot inside nobody had known the ownership of. There'd also been bomb-making resources, including Semtex, plus a couple of firearms. Had Coyake had anything to do with these?

"You still have the same lock-up?" I asked.

"Yeah."

I knew where it was. "Thanks."

*

I turned off Bethnal Green Road and pulled in quietly, parking thirty yards away from the lock-up. I checked my firearm and approached silently on foot. I listened carefully at the door and heard what sounded like a radio and somebody moving around inside.

I banged on the door. The radio stopped.

"Yeah?" a nervous voice said.

"It's Chappy," I said, subtly disguising my voice.

The small door inside the bigger garage door began to open. As it did, I swivelled to my right and kicked hard against it with the heel of my trainer. The door swung open and hit the person opening it. A second later, weapon withdrawn, I moved quickly inside and pointed it at the inhabitant, who was looking angrily at me while rubbing his right shoulder.

I was facing an unshaven, bleary-eyed man in his late twenties, dressed in black jeans and a dirty grey hoodie. The lock-up stank of oil and petrol fumes. He'd been out for breakfast as I could smell fresh coffee, and I saw Burger King wrappers on the floor.

"Hands behind your head, lock your fingers together," I ordered. He saw the gun and complied immediately.

I looked at the man for six seconds. I then identified myself. "You're Florian Coyake, right?"

He nodded.

"Turn around, face the wall. Very slowly, put your hands behind your back."

He did. I kept my gun trained on the base of his neck while putting restraints on his wrists and reciting his rights to him.

"You're under arrest, pal."

*

Brick Lane police station. I was in the same depressing interview room I'd used on several other occasions. Somehow, this being a Sunday afternoon, it felt even more depressing. Coyake was sitting opposite, looking around at nothing and sighing.

"Okay, Florian, let's make this quick and painless, shall we?" I began. "You know why I've arrested you, and why you're in here, don't you?"

He shook his head. "No, not really," he said quietly.

"I'll spell it out for you, then." I sat forward.

I explained that Friday's suicide bomber had been caught on CCTV leaving the premises Coyake was the manager of. "So, this is your current situation. *You're* the manager, therefore *you're* equally culpable because premises under *your* control were used for purposes relating to the commission of a terrorist act, one which has so far taken eleven innocent lives. Now, this joker couldn't have carried the device across London; that'd be too dangerous, and too conspicuous. So this means it has to have been strapped on him in the flat above the arcade. As I've said, you're the manager, so, unless you can convince me you weren't involved, this'll mean several years in Belmarsh, Florian, because either you aided and abetted or, even worse, you turned a blind eye because you were indifferent to what was about to happen. So, which one is it?"

He looked down at the table and sighed. Then he shook his head.

"Did you know who the bomber was?" I asked.

He didn't answer.

"Did you know he had a suicide vest strapped to his body, and what this person was planning to do when he left your premises? Who else was on the premises with him? Were *you* there at the time?"

He didn't reply. I waited ten seconds.

"The bomber was also seen talking to someone on the pavement, who then went back onto the premises after the bomber got into a taxi. Who's *this* person? How long did he remain on the premises for afterwards?" I knew who it'd been, but I wanted Coyake to tell me.

No reply. Silence for another eight seconds.

"Look, Florian," I said, "if you don't wanna spend the next twenty years in prison, you need to get yourself in front of this."

I waited a few more moments.

"A police officer was murdered two nights ago, Florian, *murdered*," I said, with emphasis, "and this crossed a line nobody crosses, because it means we don't cut *anyone* any slack until we get the bastard who did it. There're no favours done, no deals cut, no *nothing* till we find the killer. But, in this case, we know who did it, so who we really want now are the people who primed him. Someone had to have strapped what was quite likely a very complicated device on him. He *had* to have had an accomplice – no way could he have fitted this device on himself without risking self-immolation – so we want this bastard as well." I waited for a moment. "Was this what the other person there was doing? Was he an accomplice?"

No response. I looked directly into his eyes.

"Anything you can tell us which'll help grab these pilgrims will count in your favour, you know what I'm saying? *Any* names you can give us will go some way to getting time off your likely sentence. Judges take things like this into account."

Silence for the next fifteen seconds. I called the duty sergeant and told him to take Coyake into custody and hold him incommunicado overnight until I returned.

"Hey, what about my rights?" he began to protest. "I've got the—"

"What about your fucking rights?" I replied, indifferently. "We're talking terrorism, pal, which means you don't have any rights where dead police are involved."

The duty sergeant led him away. I called Smitherman to bring him up to speed. There'd been no sightings of Drake Mahoney, nor of Mehmet Tabzouni or Asou el-Taccouli. Adrian Bowketts hadn't been picked up either.

SIXTEEN

Monday

Before returning to Brick Lane, I went to the Yard and learnt the rooms above the amusements arcade had been fingerprinted. Several different sets of prints had been found, and not all of them were in our database. But, of those that were, I recognised the names Drake Mahoney and Chappy Watts. Coyake had been fingerprinted yesterday and his prints had been found.

The second floor was simply a series of empty rooms, but the more interesting discovery had come when anti-terrorist police had ripped the first-floor flat apart, and had found a small storage space which'd been carved out of the ceiling above the bathroom, with the access to it cleverly disguised. They'd had to break a lock to search it. As well as a couple of handguns and a very specialised high-powered rifle, a Russian-made Kalashnikov AK-47, police had recovered a few bags of fertiliser, several small bottles of nitroglycerine, a bag of ball bearings and sundry other materials which could be used in the making of improvised explosive devices. They had also found several short lengths of steel tubing, making them believe someone was planning to construct a pipe bomb.

What gave police even greater cause for concern, though, was that, apart from the AK-47, everything which'd been found was a lawful product which could easily have been bought over the counter. Anyone with even a half-decent knowledge of chemistry could have used these ingredients to devastating effect.

According to one of the bomb squad officers who'd been in the flat, there'd been more than enough resources found to construct several more suicide vests with at least the same explosive intensity of the bomb in Whitehall three nights back, and the immediate sense had been one of relief because, had this find not occurred, who knew what carnage might have followed? This was a significant discovery, and anti-terrorist police were certain they'd broken up something before it had had a chance to get properly underway. So now finding the missing suspects was our top priority.

*

Back at Brick Lane. Coyake was sitting opposite me looking bleary-eyed, as though he'd not slept much the previous evening.

I spelled out exactly what had been found just above the bathroom, going into considerable detail as to the nature of the materials found, their likely usage had someone with the required nous been able to utilise them, and the potentially fatal consequences had police not intercepted them before they could be used. I left him in absolutely no doubt, based on what police had found yesterday, of the gravity of the situation he was now facing. Just for good measure I threw in the AK-47.

"So, in view of what I've just said, and also to refresh your memory, Florian, this is how your situation looks," I said. "You're the manager of premises where firearms and equipment which can be used to make bombs have been found, *and* which a suicide bomber was seen leaving last Friday, going off to where he later killed himself *and* eleven other people, *all of them innocent*, with one of the people killed being a police officer."

I spoke slowly but emphasised every point, especially the last one, looking directly at him. I paused a moment.

"Now, I don't give a *fuck* about people like Sam Alorami," I stated forcefully. "I don't care if they wanna die in a thousand fucking pieces and go to Valhalla to meet however many virgins they think are waiting for them, but I care very much about innocent people being killed by fanatics like him, *especially* when a young police officer gets taken out as well."

He was beginning to look worried.

"Incidentally," I said, "did you know it's only an urban legend about virgins awaiting the suicide bomber wherever they end up? There's nothing mentioned in the Koran about it. I wonder if Alorami was aware of this?" I grinned.

I waited several seconds. Coyake said nothing. Time to focus him.

"Someone's going down for this, Florian, someone pays, so, as we've got you, you wanna try guessing who it's gonna be?"

He was looking more nervous and breathing deeply. What I'd said had registered with him.

"So, unless you've got something to tell me which is gonna help us find the other people involved," I said, looking directly into his eyes, "*you're* gonna take the full rap. You're gonna be charged under the 2006 Terrorism Act. This means a life sentence, pal, and you'll do thirty minimum. Judges come down hard on police killers; that's a fact. You may not have killed him yourself, Florian, but you're just as culpable as the one who did."

Silence for a few seconds.

"Depending on the charges we decide to bring, you may even draw a whole life sentence. This means the whole of the rest of your life behind bars, Florian, with *no* likelihood of parole, so . . ." I paused. "What's it to be?"

I waited almost a full minute. The silence was almost tangible. He didn't answer, just looked at the wall behind me.

I stood up. I was about to speak when he sat forward.

"It wasn't supposed to be like this," he said quietly, as though he were talking to himself. "I didn't know it was all gonna come down to this."

I sat down again. "What didn't you know?"

He sat quietly for a few seconds, composing himself, then sighed.

"Okay." He exhaled. "A guy I know came to the flat over the arcade one time, and—"

"Hold on, who was this? Which guy?" I interrupted him.

He paused for several seconds. "Drake Mahoney."

"How'd you know Mahoney?"

"Just seen him around, y'know? I see him in a pub once in a while and we talk."

I didn't believe him, but for the moment I told him to continue.

"He said he's got this friend just come down to London, looking for a place to stay for a while, and asked if he could doss down in the flat till he got things sorted out. The story was the guy's ex-wife was after him with a court order for something or other, something about being behind on payments for his kid."

"When was this?"

"Couple months back. Drake said this person couldn't stay at his place; said he was on a police watchlist because he'd been turned over after the couple of IRA car bombs about the same time. So I said it'd be okay. I mean, I usually stay at my girlfriend's place in Brixton anyway, so the flat's empty most of the time."

"Who was his friend?"

"Danny someone, didn't get his surname and I didn't ask."

"English?"

"Yeah, a guy from the Midlands, got a real heavy Brummie accent."

I produced several enlarged pictures I'd brought with me and laid them across the table. I pointed to one of them. "Him?" It was the man from Mahoney's flat.

He looked closely, then nodded. "Yeah."

I left the pictures on the table.

"Anyway," he continued, "a few weeks ago, on a Wednesday, I came back to the flat 'cause my girlfriend wasn't all that well, so I thought I'd stay away till she was better. So, I go upstairs, and I see this Danny guy" – he nodded at the same picture – "and two other people. He has a rifle and he's showing them how to strip it down and reassemble it. There were also a few handguns on the table."

"Who were the other people there? Any of these pilgrims?" I directed his attention to the pictures spread across the table.

He scanned the pictures for several seconds.

"He was one of them." He pointed to a picture.

This was interesting. He'd pointed to a picture of Sherif Rizwi, the MI5 undercover operative.

"Who was the other person there?" I asked.

"Don't know. I'd seen him before but didn't know his name."

"Did you talk to anyone about these illegal firearms?"

He paused for a moment, then sighed. "Well, I mentioned it to Drake. Told him this Danny character seemed to know all about weapons. He said Danny had learnt about them from his time in the army."

"So, what happened after you told him about this?"

"Drake told me it'd be advisable to stay away as much as possible, 'cause Danny was gonna be using the flat to do something."

"He say what this was?" I asked.

"No, he didn't, and I didn't ask. I didn't wanna know." He looked around for a few seconds, still agitated and nervous. "So that's what I did." He shrugged. "I just stayed downstairs when the arcade was open and, when I closed up, I went down to Brixton."

"And I'm guessing this Danny was given a key for the back entrance, so he could come and go without being seen."

"Yeah. I didn't always know when or even if he was there."

"Did you ever see this guy there?" I pointed to Sam Alorami's picture.

"Couple times. I'd see him walk through the arcade to go upstairs, but I didn't speak to him."

"And you also saw him." I pointed out Sherif Rizwi's picture.

"Yeah."

"What about these two?" I pointed out pictures of Mehmet Tabzouni and Asou el-Taccouli.

"I don't think so, no." He slowly shook his head.

"So you're saying you didn't have *any* idea what Mahoney and this Danny were using the flat for?"

He shook his head again. "No."

"Weren't you even curious?" His response had amazed me. "Someone using *your* flat to give instructions on how to use firearms, and you take *no* interest?"

"'S right," he agreed. "I didn't wanna know what they were doing."

The flat was a bomb factory of sorts; this much was clear. This was why they'd wanted Coyake to stay away. I wondered whether he was just a useful dupe, allowing premises under his control to be used, and seemingly indifferent to what the flat was being used for. This seemed dubious and wasn't going to count in his favour.

In any case, I could now tie Mahoney to the flat through his fingerprints and Coyake's admission it'd been him asking if Danny could use the flat. I had the bastard. This, at least, was good news. But I was wondering what Rizwi had been doing there.

I left Coyake locked in the room and contacted the MOD, asking to speak to someone about army personnel. After being routed to the section dealing with the army, and being passed on to two different people, I was finally connected to someone who could help. I identified myself and mentioned I was looking for details about someone who'd recently come out of the army, maybe a couple of months back, Christian name Daniel, no surname, from Birmingham. Thirty seconds later came the reply.

"Daniel Hunter, twenty-six, and he hasn't left the army; he's gone AWOL. He got into a scrap with a lance corporal and fractured his skull. He was confined to barracks but left his base in

Aldershot without permission eight weeks ago and hasn't been seen since. But we'll get him, sooner or later. They always slip up, and he'll go to the glasshouse for two years, then be dishonourably discharged." He sounded confident.

"Anything else I should know about him?"

"He's a qualified marksman, a specialist. Can shoot the ears off a queen bee from 500 yards firing into a high wind. Knows his way around firearms."

I said Hunter had been seen in London very recently, and I gave a couple of names and addresses. He thanked me and rang off.

Back in the interrogation room, I told Coyake he was going to be remanded in custody while our investigations were ongoing. He meekly acquiesced, seemingly resigned to his fate.

"Am I gonna go down for this?" he asked.

I shrugged. "No idea."

*

Smitherman asked to see me. As I sat, I noticed there was an air of despondency hanging over him; something was clearly bothering him. I asked if he was feeling alright.

"I saw my daughter Janet yesterday, and she's rather worried."

"Oh yeah? Nothing too serious, I hope."

I had the strangest feeling I knew what was coming next.

"She isn't sure," he began cautiously, "but she thinks her husband, that bloody Clements, might be seeing someone else."

"Really?" I did a good job affecting surprise. "How does she know?"

"She says he's seemed a little different somehow these past few weeks, nothing she can put her finger on, but she said he's now more distant, a bit distracted by something. He's spending more time out the flat in the evening, and not always telling her where's he's been either. I mean, I accept sometimes he's out late because he's working, reporting on meetings, interviewing people; that kind of thing's part of his job. But what really made her think, what *really* upset her was, a few days ago, doing some laundry, she smelt a woman's perfume on his shirt: quite a garish one as well. She asked him about it and he said it's probably from a woman in his office he'd hugged when she announced she was pregnant, but it's still got her worried."

"Oh dear," I replied neutrally.

Smitherman looked menacingly angry. "If I find out it's true, and he *is* having an affair . . ."

He didn't complete the sentence. He didn't need to. The look on his face and his tone of voice left me in no doubt Clements would be in for a hard time. I recalled what the DCI at Kentish Town had said about being on the beat with Smitherman back in the day. Even being half Smitherman's age, I'd not fancy Clements' chances one to one against his father-in-law.

I was now facing some kind of moral dilemma: do I tell Clements his father-in-law, a man capable of beating him to a pulp and not even breaking a sweat doing so, now suspects he's up to something which is upsetting his daughter, and he'd better stop seeing whatever her name is, *or* do I simply say it's not my problem and leave him to reap what he's sowing?

I was idly wondering, if Clements got a fat lip or worse from his father-in-law, whether I'd have any responsibility for this, when Smitherman spoke again.

"Anyway, why I wanted to see you. You contacted the Israeli embassy yesterday, and I'm wondering why."

I told Smitherman about the CCTV images showing two unidentified men following Sherif Rizwi into Highbury Park Road and, six minutes later, getting into a car I'd traced back to the Israeli embassy, shortly before Rizwi had been found dead. I also mentioned I'd seen Joachim Balpak earlier the same evening, at the meeting where Gheziel Ayah had been speaking, and he'd been talking to Rizwi. "So I wanted to know what he knew about this, and, in particular, why he was talking to Rizwi. Also, why were these two jokers getting into a car with Israeli diplomatic plates around the time someone on our side was killed, when the circumstantial evidence points to their direct involvement?"

Smitherman didn't initially reply. He sat quietly for several seconds. "I see." He was silent for a moment longer. "I'll have to talk to Stimpson about this, so, for the moment, don't take any further action. Leave it with me."

I pointed out to Smitherman that Sherif Rizwi had also been identified by Florian Coyake as being in the flat when Danny Hunter had been giving a lesson in how to assemble and disassemble a rifle. "Was this anything to do with Rizwi's undercover role inside Muearada? Also, was he looking into something specific and, if so, how would this lead to him being on the Mossad's radar?" I was curious.

"Again, I don't know. I'll mention this to Stimpson as well."

*

The rest of the day involved talking to a couple of informants concerning a separate investigation, writing up a statement and rereading case notes.

Almost three days on, and no sign of the three people we were pursuing. Our hopes had been raised when we'd heard West Midlands police had raided an address in Leicester, acting on a tip-off about three unknown and suspicious persons seen going in and out the back of a bakery inside the last twenty-four hours, but they'd turned out to be illegal immigrants from the Sudan who, having been left there by their couriers, were waiting to be moved on to their final destination. None spoke passable English, so none could explain anything to police.

SEVENTEEN

Tuesday

Just as 2.30pm hit, Taylor turned off the M20 onto the slip road at junction 4, the A28 exit, went across the bridge and headed southbound in the direction of Tunbridge Wells. We were both off duty, so I was accompanying her on her visit to Dr Niall Redfearn, as I knew him and was certain he'd be more willing to talk if I were present. I'd learnt from the surgery receptionist he'd be seeing patients today until three, and afterwards was going to go straight home, so, at ten to three, we parked across from his house and settled in to wait.

I knew this exclusive estate. I remembered these four- and five-bedroomed detached houses, somewhere around forty in number, being built about twenty years back, on land which had at one time been orchards and a paddock. We used to ride our bikes around here when it was mainly grassy because it was too lumpy and stony to play football. The farmer had retired, however, and had sold the land to a local developer, who'd obtained a *change of usage* order, from rural to urban, in order to build houses.

I'd pointed out where I and others had played when we'd been kids, and where we'd done a lot of our early scrumping, with a few stories about other escapades we'd got up to, and I was just debating whether to tell Taylor I'd had my first real kiss from my first real girlfriend here, standing by the big tree on the other side of the field, when Dr Redfearn pulled up into his driveway.

I watched him get out the car and walk towards his house. He was walking somewhat gingerly, as though he were struggling with arthritis. We waited a few minutes after he'd gone inside, then approached. He answered the door on the second ring.

I identified myself and, after a moment, he remembered me, and we shook hands. I introduced him to Taylor and asked if we could talk to him for a moment. He immediately agreed and invited us both in.

We went into his warm and very cosy lounge, which had a good view of the remaining fields from the back window. The room was carpeted, well lit and tastefully furnished with what appeared to be well-preserved antique furniture. Several large, tranquil pastoral scenes of the nearby Kent countryside adorned the walls. I recognised the Hop Farm, just outside Tunbridge Wells, in one of the paintings. He saw me looking at them.

"All of them painted by local artists, and this," he said proudly, pointing to the picture next to the Hop Farm, "this one was done by my granddaughter."

He then invited us to sit, and we sat on the settee opposite him. I'd not seen Dr Redfearn for several years, and I couldn't help noticing he was looking much older and a little frailer than I remembered. This began to make me feel mildly apprehensive about confronting him, but we'd driven all this way to see him, and Taylor had a valid reason to be here, so, after politely refusing his offer of tea or coffee, and a minute of small talk about jobs and our respective families, we got down to business.

"Well, it's nice to see you again, Robert. So, to what do I owe this pleasure?"

"Actually, it's Sally. She'd like to ask you a couple of questions, if you don't mind."

"No, I don't mind. You mean medical questions?"

"No," Taylor began, "about your time in the army." She nodded towards the plastic folder on her lap.

"The army? I left the forces over thirty years ago." His expression changed and he sounded guarded. "Why's my army service a matter of interest now?"

Taylor explained in a little detail the nature of the story she was researching for her newspaper, how it'd come about, though without naming any names, and how the name Dr Niall Redfearn had arisen in their research, and so she'd like to ask him a few questions pertaining to this.

"Shoot to kill?" He sounded incredulous. "This is the British army we're talking about here. The UK army have never been assassins, whatever you might think."

"We're not suggesting they were; we're just looking for information."

An uncomfortable silence for a few seconds. He then sighed.

"What, specifically, did you want to talk about?" He didn't appear too happy.

"You served in Northern Ireland, didn't you?" she began.

"I did, yes. I completed two tours of duty."

She paused a moment to look at her notes. "Dr Redfearn, the reason I'm asking is because we've obtained copies of death certificates which you've signed off on, citing a particular cause of death."

"Okay," he replied, slowly and hesitantly.

"But we've uncovered a few incidents where it's claimed the *real* cause of death has been covered up, and a different reason given for how the victim died."

"Such as what?" He seemed mystified.

Taylor reached into her shoulder bag and produced another plastic wallet containing photocopies of post-mortem reports and death certificates. She pulled one out and handed it to the doctor. "Is this your signature?" she asked.

He looked closely over the top of his glasses. "Yes, it looks like mine." He handed it back.

"Did you sign this certificate on the date given?"

"Of course I would have done; that's standard procedure." He sounded as though he was attempting to keep mild annoyance from his voice. "Everything's dated and signed at the same time."

"On this certificate, you've signed off on the cause of death being from gunshot wounds to the back. The official story is he was spotted attempting to shoot at soldiers, but they opened fire first, and shot him as he attempted to escape."

Dr Redfearn didn't respond for several seconds.

Taylor continued. "But we've heard from soldiers on the ground this particular person was actually shot twice in his chest and once in the throat, and from quite close up as well. Yet, according to this report, the cause of death was from gunshot wounds taken in the back. And you signed off on it."

Again, no response from Dr Redfearn. He appeared to be thinking.

"This isn't the only one either. We've a few other reports of post-mortems where the cause of death given and signed off on is at variance with what's claimed to be the *real* cause of death, and it's *your* signature on all the ones we have."

He breathed out and sighed, but didn't respond. Taylor waited a moment.

"There's another instance where someone died as a result of injuries from being seriously assaulted, yet the signed death certificate" – she held up a photocopy – "maintains death was as a result of being hit by a fast-moving vehicle. But, as you'd know, any person hit by a vehicle moving at thirty miles an hour or more would have more extensive injuries across the body than just facial bruising. The victim here actually had his jawbone driven up into his brain by a kick to the face. This isn't mentioned on the death certificate."

There was a hushed silence for several seconds.

"Can you account for either of these discrepancies, Dr Redfearn?" she asked.

"Now, just hold on a moment." He raised his voice slightly. "Are you saying I deliberately covered up something here?"

"No. That isn't what we're saying, Dr Redfearn. But I'd like to ask you, did you actually conduct *every* post-mortem you signed off on?"

"Off course I did," he snapped. He was evidently beginning to dislike where this was going. "If it's got my signature on it, I'd've conducted the post-mortem. It would've been my responsibility to do so, and I'd have done it to the best of my ability with all the facts at my disposal, plus the evidence from looking at the body of the deceased."

Taylor put the certificate back into the wallet. I knew she was thinking about her next question. I'd never seen her in full-on journo mode before. I was impressed.

"You see, doctor," she said, "what we're wondering is this. Was it ever the case that a report outlining a cause of death was written out for you by someone else, an officer perhaps, and you were simply asked to put your name to it without conducting your own examination to ensure that what'd been written down was the *actual* cause of death?"

I'd been observing what'd been happening, and I noticed a subtle change in Dr Redfearn's eyes when Taylor asked this question. His eyes opened slightly wider and, for a second, there was a look of genuine surprise. It was fleeting, but I noticed it.

"There's no suggestion you've deliberately misled anyone, Dr Redfearn, and we're not naming names or looking to pin any blame on you," Taylor tried to reassure him. "I'm simply asking if you were satisfied with the cause of death on *every* post-mortem report and death certificate your name appears on."

He sat back in his chair and looked deep in thought for several seconds.

"Or let me put it like this," she went on. "Was it ever the case you were asked to look the other way, Dr Redfearn, while someone wrote out a report for you, or could it have been that someone wrote it out, forged your signature and you didn't even see the report?"

No response given.

Taylor looked directly at Dr Redfearn. "Dr Redfearn, were you aware of allegations of a shoot-to-kill policy being conducted by various small army units in Northern Ireland in the early seventies? The reason I'm asking is because all the people in these reports" – she held her plastic wallet up for Redfearn to see – "are claimed to be victims of this policy, and quite a few of them were innocent, like the shooting victim I told you about just now."

Taylor had brought along four death certificates and post-mortem reports for victims where there was genuine doubt about any IRA involvement on their part. They'd either been in the wrong place at the wrong time or, in the case of Brendan Morgan, specifically targeted by members of Two Unit.

"Are *you* investigating this as well?" He turned to look enquiringly at me. "Is this a police matter?"

"Me? No, I came with Sally because I know this area, and I know you. I'm not here in any official capacity."

Silence.

"Presumably you're aware of the seriousness of posting misleading information on post-mortem reports?" Taylor asked. "As a medic you're responsible for—"

"Don't tell me what my responsibilities are," he suddenly exclaimed, looking angry. "Do you know how many years I've been a medical man?"

Nobody spoke for five seconds.

"So, would you say you're completely satisfied with the cause of death in *every* report your signature appears on, and everything mentioned is true and correct, Dr Redfearn?" Taylor calmly asked, holding her plastic wallet.

After another brief silence, Redfearn spoke. "I'm bound by the

Official Secrets Act not to mention army regulations, and my oath as a doctor means I really can't talk about individual cases. I'm sorry, but I can't answer any more of your questions." He sounded apologetic.

"So, not answering my last question: does this mean you're *not* satisfied with the actual cause of death in all these cases?" Taylor asked.

"Don't put words into my mouth, young lady." He was now sounding agitated. "I'm simply saying I'm prohibited by law and duty from answering your questions."

He stood up abruptly, suggesting this interview was over. We did the same.

"This isn't an attempt at character assassination, Dr Redfearn," Taylor said. "We're not out to discredit you as a doctor, and you'll not be named in the story we're putting together."

He didn't respond.

"Dr Redfearn, you should be aware there's very *real* substantial doubt about the causes of death given in every one of these." She held up the plastic wallet with the documents she'd brought. "We have a witness who's sworn this is the case, plus another person who's testified he was part of the unit doing the killings, including the first case I mentioned. Even the man in the unit says that victim was innocent."

I thought of George Selwood, who had claimed to know of the existence of this policy, plus the involvement of the SAS.

"So, coming back to my earlier question, doctor, were you under *any* pressure to change the reported cause of death, or to bring it more into line with how the army wanted the report to read?"

"I think we're done here, don't you?" He walked out of the room. We followed. "As I said, I'm legally prohibited from answering these questions."

He was sounding very displeased. Taylor's questions had probably brought back memories he'd not thought about for some considerable time.

"Well, thank you for your time, Dr Redfearn," Taylor said in the hallway as he opened the door. He looked at her as though she were invisible. We stepped outside.

"Goodbye, Dr Redfearn," I said. "I hope we didn't . . ."

I went to shake hands, but he stepped back inside the house, looked at me with what appeared to be a sense of disappointment and slammed the door shut.

We got in the car and set off. I could see Dr Redfearn in the front room window watching us pull away. I was wondering if he'd report our visit to someone.

"Well, that went swimmingly," Taylor laughed as she turned off the A28 onto the M20 and joined the early evening rush hour traffic heading west towards London.

EIGHTEEN

Wednesday

"So, it's been decided by the powers that be, those on the top floor who're closer to God than us mere mortals," – Smitherman's eyes flicked upwards – "no charges are to be brought against him. He's to be given a decent interval to do so, but he's been told he's got to announce his impending retirement sometime in the next couple of months."

I was in Smitherman's office. He'd called me in, amongst other things, to inform me no charges were to be laid against Sir Alexander Bressington. Apparently MI5 had spent the past couple of weeks trawling through every highly sensitive issue Bressington'd had access to in the past decade, attempting to ascertain whether anything critical had been leaked, because the scam site he'd logged on to had been operated by members of the FSB, the successor body to the KGB. Bressington had managed to convince the security service he wasn't being blackmailed, and there appeared to be no evidence any of this material had been seen by persons outside the charmed circle of those authorised to see it.

As there was no evidence of undue influence being employed by the FSB in the daily work of Bressington, and nothing to suggest he'd been compromised, the conclusion had been that Sir Alexander was just a sad, immoral individual with a fetish for watching porn involving children, making him wholly unsuited for the high office he held. He'd been told that if he resigned quietly, citing ill health, his knighthood could be kept, his pension would not be at risk, and his reputation would not be publicly sullied as details of the real reason for his early retirement would be known amongst only a very few. If Clements was to be believed, though, knowledge of this was commonplace in media circles. How long before someone leaked the sordid details and made them public knowledge?

More importantly for MI5, however, they knew any trial in open court would have raised media questions about the efficacy of positive vetting undergone by those destined for high office in the civil service, and whether an old boys' network had simply covered up the truth. The media would also want to talk to and about Bressington, so MI5 were determined no such questioning was to be encouraged. Thus a security blackout had been imposed and a very high-flying, distinguished career was going to come to a publicly dignified, though privately ignoble, termination.

I didn't let on to Smitherman I'd already been made aware of this, as Clements had told me something similar a week ago. I also wondered whether Smitherman knew about Paul Grayley being caught in the same scam as Bressington. Grayley was just the political editor of the *London Evening Standard*, and he didn't have the ear of senior Cabinet members and the Prime Minister, or access to highly sensitive documents. But what he *did* have was a relative in a high place who, Clements had said, had managed to hush up some of the more disagreeable aspects of his nephew's sexual proclivities, so he could be allowed to remain in place as there was no likelihood of his being a potential blackmail case.

"There've long been whispers about some kind of organised paedophile ring within the highest echelons, involving top politicians and senior civil servants," – Smitherman seemed aghast at the thought – "though, despite all the rumours and innuendo, there's no direct evidence of any such body. Maybe Bressington'll be the first one to be caught."

He sat quietly for a moment.

"Anyway," he said, his mood changing, "there's something I'd like you to check out, as it may have a connection to your recent investigations. You know someone named William Desborough, I believe?"

I was about to say I didn't when it dawned on me this was Little Des' birth name. I agreed I knew who he was, and said it'd been at his house that Adrian Bowketts had been hiding out and had fired shots at police on two occasions, injuring a uniform.

"He was attacked in his home last night, sometime mid-evening, assaulted rather nastily it seems, and he was treated at University College Hospital but, as his injuries weren't life-threatening, he was discharged and allowed to go home. Police spoke to him at the hospital and he wouldn't give any details, but he was clearly shaken up. So it might be something wholly unconnected, but, given who he's had in his house recently, and the fact he's on police bail until they decide if he's going to be charged with anything, I think *you* should go talk to him, see what you can find out."

*

He opened the door the second time I knocked. His face was heavily marked, with some painful-looking bruises around his swollen bottom lip and under the eyes, one of which was very vivid, and his left arm was in a sling from suffering a dislocated shoulder. He recognised me immediately, sighed, turned and walked back into his kitchen, his jerky movements suggesting he was in some degree of physical discomfort. I followed him. It was from this kitchen doorway that Bowketts had fired shots at me and DC Withers, and there were still bullets marks on the wall by the front door.

He sat down and I stood by the table, looking around. The kitchen was a mess. There was a pile of dirty crockery on the draining board, some plates still with uneaten food on, and a full basket of unwashed laundry by the back door.

"Your cleaning lady not back from her holiday yet?" I asked, facetiously.

I looked at Des. He looked like he'd been told he'd less than a week to live.

"You look like you've been in a car crash, Des." I nodded at his face.

Little Des snorted and shook his head.

"So, who did this to you?" I got serious. "Bowketts? Someone connected with him?"

My hypothesis was his injuries were, in some way, connected with the company he'd been keeping, and on the way here I'd speculated on whether Bowketts or others had blamed him for police uncovering where Bowketts had been hiding. He had other worries apart from his association with suspected terrorists, though. Operating as he did on the edges of the Chackarti family, buying and selling all manner of contraband, he was forever at risk of crossing the line and doing something the family disapproved of, such as fencing the right stolen goods to the wrong buyer, and punishment beatings for those stepping out of line were not unusual in this area of London.

He didn't answer, just sat and stirred his drink with his right hand.

"Come on, Des, talk to me. Who did this to you?"

He looked at me with a strangely sad expression, rather like a dog who couldn't understand what he'd done to deserve being beaten by his owner. I waited for about fifteen seconds.

"Don't forget, Des, you're on police bail because of what happened here last week," I said sternly, "so, if you don't want those charges brought forward, you should do yourself a favour and get in front of whatever this is. You cooperate with us, things could be a lot easier for you."

He sat still, sighing to himself and looking dejected. I was getting irritated with his silence by the time he started to talk.

"My stepfather had this done to me," he said calmly, nodding towards his sling. He paused for a few seconds, then looked up at me. "You know who my stepfather is?"

I did, but I wasn't going to let on I knew. I was interested in what Little Des might have to say about him.

I shook my head. "No, I don't. Should I?"

"Oh, yes. He's an important man, is my *beloved stepdad*," he sneered ironically.

"Okay. Who is he, what's his name?" I asked.

"Alexander Bressington. Oh, I'm so sorry, *Sir* Alexander Bressington," he said, sarcastically. "Knighted by Her Majesty, no less, a real VIP. He's some kind of mandarin, a top civil servant, respectable pillar of the community and all that. To see him and hear him speak, you'd think when he farted it gave off lavender," he sniffed, "but he's a bloody perverted freak, and he knows *I* know what he is." He said this with an undisguised rancour which bordered on hatred.

I waited a moment. "What do you mean?"

"What do I mean? He's a bloody kiddie fiddler, is what he is, and he knows I know it."

"How do you know this?"

He laughed for a few seconds, grimacing as he moved his shoulder too quickly. "How? It's me who gets him those filthy bloody books he reads, and all them DVDs, or at least it was up till recently; that's how I know. I was able to get them imported through some front company in Soho, and I used to collect them from the newsagent's they were delivered to and take them round to his place when he lived in Chelsea."

I was about to say *he still does*, but I caught myself just in time. "I don't suppose he willingly admitted this to you, so how did you discover his, ah, exotic tastes in literature?"

"I first found out five or so years ago, back when *mummy dearest*," he scoffed, "was still speaking to me. I went to his flat one evening. I still had a key at this time, so I let myself in. He'd not heard me entering. I went into his front lounge and I caught him watching a kiddie porn flick."

"Like what?" I was sure I wouldn't like the answer.

"Mainly girls under ten getting undressed, then getting into the bath and then washing themselves all over, or washing each other, the sick bastard. He had quite a few such films and a few magazines as well. He knew he'd been sussed out." He stopped talking and breathed out. "He panicked, and at one point I thought he was gonna cry, but I told him to calm down, I wasn't gonna tell anyone, because" – his face suddenly lit up – "immediately I knew a business opportunity had just fallen into my lap."

"A what?"

"A chance to make a bit of dosh." He laughed, though his wincing suggested the bruising around his mouth made it hurt to smile. "I knew people who knew people who could access this kind of stuff from Scandinavia and the Far East."

"Through the Chackartis," I said.

He shrugged but didn't confirm. "Anyway, we talk and eventually we come to an arrangement. I'll keep schtum and get him more of what he likes to read and watch, and, in return for keeping my trap shut, he'll *see I'm all right*, and he does." He raised his eyebrows. "He pays the rent for this house. Check his bank statements. Every month there's a payment for the rental here. I mean, I couldn't afford to live here on my own."

There was silence for several seconds, as though the effort of talking was draining him of his strength.

"So, effectively, you're blackmailing him."

"Am I?" He laughed suddenly, wincing again and rubbing his mouth lightly. "Nah, he's just buying my silence, isn't he? How's this blackmail?"

At this point I began weighing up Bressington and Little Des against each other morally, trying to ascertain which of the two I was more repulsed by. I looked at Des with some degree of disgust. "So, how does this cosy little arrangement lead to him having this done to you?" I nodded at his face.

"Oh, he didn't do it himself. Not got the bottle, has he? Three weeks ago, I got an irate phone call from my dear mother. Apparently, *Daddy*" – he sneered at the word – "had had a visit from police the night before, concerning what I was just talking about, and they'd taken him off somewhere, and she thinks I had something to do with it. I hadn't."

"Does she know *why* police took him in?" I asked, not saying it'd been me who'd done it.

"Oh yeah, 'course she does," he said knowingly, "and she knows he pays the rent here. She's known about his sick and twisted fantasies all along, but, as he keeps it to when he's alone and he doesn't actually go near young girls himself, she goes along with it. With his money and connections, he can give her a *good life*, the kind of life she believes she deserves, mixing in upper-class society. That's what matters to her."

He laughed ironically again. "You remember the advert where some woman says a bloke'll do anything for her, *because I'm worth it*? That's my mother. She thinks she's worth it, so she goes along with him and turns her head and ignores what he does."

He paused for a moment and sighed. "Anyway, I get home last night and this big geezer was in here, sitting in this very chair, waiting for me. Another one comes out from behind the door and grabs me in a painful armlock. The one sitting here says I'm to be a good boy and listen very carefully. He then says I'm to say nothing about Sir Alexander or anyone else in the family to anyone, *ever*, if I don't wanna get hurt. I say, *What about Sir Alexander? He's my stepdad,* and this geezer says he knows, this's why they've been told to *be gentle* with me. He then smacks me a few times, and the bastard holding me does this." He nodded to the sling. "Dislocated my fucking shoulder. The other one says, say nothing to anyone about Sir Alexander or anyone else in the family or there'll be more of this, and next time they won't be so gentle. Then they leave."

"You recognise them, seen them before?"

"No, didn't know who they were." He shook his head.

"Describe these two, what they look like."

"About your height, I suppose, both wearing suits. The one who spoke to me sounded quite posh. He had a bit of a scar round here." He ran his finger just below his right eye.

"And you think your stepfather sent them along to do this."

"Who else? No one who knows me knows who my stepdad is, so it ain't likely to be one of those, is it? Gotta be 'im, innit? Especially after what my mother had said, and what these two guys said."

I left, but only after advising him to remember he was still on police bail and to say nothing about his claims to anyone until I'd had a chance to make a few inquiries.

And then, a break. A message had been left on my desk telling me Chapman Watts and Helen Mathison had been stopped at Dover yesterday evening, as they'd been attempting to board the last cross-channel ferry of the day. He'd shown his passport and, as the message had been put out on the wire to arrest him if seen, he and Helen had been taken into custody by Kent police and held overnight. They'd been returned to London this morning. Helen had been released on police bail, and I went down to the holding cells to talk to Chappy.

He was looking very forlorn when he was led into the interview room, as though the realisation his absconding had landed him in serious trouble had finally caught up with him. He sat back in his seat and sighed loudly. I looked at him. He was blinking rapidly, like someone adjusting his vision in a dark room. That he was frightened wasn't in doubt. I wondered if I could tap into this.

"Pretty stupid move, eh, Chappy?" I said slowly. "I mean, fancy using your own passport. Didn't I tell you, you run off again and we'll be looking for you?"

He didn't respond. I waited a moment.

"So, why'd you run, eh? You told me on Saturday you'd be willing to cooperate with police, testify against McGreely, then you disappear. Why'd you do it?"

Silence again.

"Anyway, for the moment, it doesn't matter, because you're here for reasons other than this, though that's serious enough," I looked him directly in the eye as I spoke. "You're here because a suicide bomber killed eleven people in Whitehall last Friday night, which is why I had to leave Helen's flat as quickly as I did. This bastard was seen leaving premises on the Euston Road, and when we raided the place Sunday, guess what, Chappy?" I smiled at him. "We found *your* fingerprints amongst several others, including a couple whom we know to be terrorist sympathisers."

He was looking down at the table. No response.

"And, just to make things even worse, they also found explosives, detonators and the resources needed to make all kinds of explosive devices on the premises, as well as an AK-47. The place was a terrorist's weapons storage dump."

He bit his lower lip and shook his head slightly.

"Now, I'm hoping you're not stupid, Chappy," I said quietly, "because you've gotta realise this spells trouble for you, *real* trouble. The *only* way out of this for you is to cooperate, tell me exactly why we found *your* fingerprints in a flat known to be a base for a suicide bomber."

I paused a moment. "It's like this, Chappy. You answer some questions honestly, and it'll make a big difference to whatever charges you face, which could mean a *lot* less jail time. Maybe even none at all, depending."

I waited fourteen seconds.

"It's your choice, Chappy." I looked at my watch. "And you don't have too much longer to decide, either."

Eleven seconds later, Chappy looked up at me. He sighed. "What do you wanna know?"

I began by asking how he came to be in the flat in the first place. It'd been through his friend, the late Gary White. White and Florian Coyake had become quite close friends at Westminster University, and they'd both dropped out at the same time. He'd gone to the flat for the first time over a year back, when Florian had got the manager's job at the arcade. Had he gone there many times? Not too many, no. Had White known Coyake was allowing the flat to be used as a base for stashing explosives and bomb-making equipment? Chappy didn't know. Did Chappy know White was at one time on the fringes of Red Heaven? No, he didn't. I was doubtful but didn't push it.

Chappy also said there were certain times when he didn't go to the flat with White because there'd be *all these fucking Arabs* on the premises and he didn't like them.

I produced a few photographs. Did he recognise anyone here? He recognised Sam Alorami and Mehmet Tabzouni. How? He'd seen them in the flat on a couple of occasions. What did they talk about? He didn't know, said they mainly talked in Arabic amongst each other.

"How well do you know Florian Coyake?"

"Not that well. I mean, I knew who he was, but that's about it. I only went to the flat 'cause Gary was his friend."

"You knew him well enough to let him stay in your dad's lock-up, though, didn't you?"

"Just doing it as a favour to Gary." He shrugged.

"When I arrested McGreely at the lock-up, were they his cases of explosives we found or were they anything to do with Coyake?"

"I don't honestly know whose they were. I'd never seen them before."

The bags had been fingerprinted but no prints had been found. McGreely had predictably denied any knowledge of them. Were they to do with Muearada?

"What about Sam Alorami?" I asked. "How well did you know him?"

"I didn't. I mean, I knew who he was, but I wasn't friends with him."

"You ever talk to him?"

"Don't think so."

There was something about the way Chappy's eyes were moving which made me think he wasn't being entirely honest with me.

"But did you know *what* he was?" I asked. "Did you know he was an active adherent to the philosophy of Muearada, a proscribed terrorist body, and had been radicalised into becoming a militant jihadi? Last Friday he took his own life and the lives of eleven innocent people. *Eleven innocent people, Chappy*, one of them a police officer. Think about that one."

"I didn't know this about him." He shook his head.

"What about Coyake? How close was he to Alorami?"

He waited a moment before he answered. "If I tell you a few things, will doing this get me time off my sentence?"

"I've no idea. A judge decides what you get, so that's beyond police control. What *is* in our control, though, is it could mean less serious *charges* being brought. As I said earlier, Chappy, cooperation counts."

He sighed. "Who gets to know anything I tell you in here?" He sounded concerned.

"I do." I grinned. "I'm sitting right opposite you."

"No, I mean, will you tell anyone else?"

"Only my boss, but that's 'cause he has to be told; he has to know everything."

Chappy agreed to this. He then told me in some detail about how Alorami'd made the suicide vest himself, but the chemicals used to make an explosion of sufficient magnitude had been mixed by Coyake. Coyake knew how because he'd been a chemistry student at university and had done lots of research on the topic, and he'd always claimed he knew how to make a devastatingly effective explosive pack, one capable of causing maximum devastation over a short distance. Could Alorami have done this without Coyake's help? No, he would have needed Coyake.

"So Coyake was directly involved in helping Alorami with the suicide vest," I said.

"Yeah, Gary and him. They both knew about chemicals and making bomb packs." He paused for a moment. "That's how Helen and me got together. She liked Gary and all that, but she didn't like some of the things he talked about," – he looked directly at me – "or some of his friends, especially Coyake, who she thought was a creep. So, anyway, she was feeling down one night 'cause they'd had a big row, so her and I went out for a drink, and we just hooked up from there. She was gonna split from him, but he died before she could tell him."

I didn't care about him and Helen. I held Chappy firmly in my line of sight. "Are you willing to make a sworn statement to this effect, as well as testify in court against Coyake?"

He nodded. "Yes, I'll do it. My dad's right. I can't keep running."

I was pleased to hear this. Testimony from Chappy would help put Coyake away, as well as John McGreely.

"It was all getting too heavy," he said, almost mournfully. "'S why I went into hiding. I'd been told by police I was expected to give evidence against John McGreely, but when I had an idea what these people were thinking about, I just had to get out. If the Chackartis knew I was talking to police and giving evidence in court, they'd quite likely think I was spilling what I knew about them, so I decided to lie low, put the story about I'd gone abroad."

"That's not the case now, I told you this, so why'd you leave Saturday evening?" Based on what he'd just told me, I was certain I knew why, but I wanted to hear him say it.

"The identity of the suicide bomber had just been given on the news. I thought, *Oh, fuck, how long before they connect me with the flat?* I told Helen and she agreed we should get away for a while. We stayed with a friend of hers for a few days, then tried to go away yesterday. My dad had come through with some money for me."

"Did he know where you were after you left?"

"Not till yesterday, no, he didn't."

"What about Danny Hunter? What's his role in all this?"

"Is that the Brummie?"

I nodded.

"Yeah, I came across him. He's on the run from the army, isn't he? Bloke's a freaking headcase, always talking about killing people. Him and Sam were very friendly."

"What's his role in all this?"

"Far as I know, he's the weapons man, claims he can get guns and stuff if wanted."

I thought about where we were so far. If Chappy was to be believed, Florian Coyake wasn't the innocent bystander he'd claimed to be earlier. He'd been an active participant in what'd happened. Also, I could now connect Drake Mahoney to the flat via his fingerprints, which would give him some explaining to do. I also knew Danny Hunter was involved as it'd been him talking to Sam Alorami outside the flat before setting off to blow himself and others away, and Hunter knew Mahoney. All this wasn't in doubt.

But what I didn't know was why Sherif Rizwi had been present.

As I was thinking my iPhone sounded. It was Andy Harris.

"Mr Jack, the bloke you told me to look out for?" He sounded excited. "The one whose wallet I nicked in the market?"

I knew who he meant. "What about him?"

"Just saw him, didn't I, in the pub he had the fight in."

"Where is he now? Is he still there?"

"Nah, left to go home. I followed him to a house in Pratt Street. Saw him go in and so I called you."

"Thanks, Andy. Don't hang about in case he spots you. I'll catch you later."

I summoned the desk sergeant and had Chappy taken back to the cells to await my return. I then contacted Kentish Town police station and asked for DS Withers. I explained I'd like a couple of uniforms to meet me in Camden. He agreed to it.

Twelve minutes later, after a fast siren-aided drive to Camden Town, I parked around the corner from Pratt Street. I could see two uniforms further along the road, and they came across when they saw me. One couldn't have been older than twenty, but the other had the kind of eyes suggesting he'd seen quite a bit of life's dark side. I explained briefly that the guy I was here for had a connection to a flat where a suspect, his friend, plus explosives and other resources had been uncovered, and it was the same flat the suicide bomber had left from last Friday, so this guy had some explaining to do. They nodded their agreement.

"Nobody's left since we've been here, skip." The older one nodded to Mahoney's building.

"Okay."

We approached the house carefully. There was a short path from the street leading to the front door, and two full-to-overflowing wheelie bins against the wall. Mahoney lived on the ground floor and I could see the bay window curtains of his flat were closed.

We crept quietly up to the front door. I pressed the top buzzer. A voice answered.

"I've a pizza delivery for flat two but their bell's not working," I said. "They're not answering."

The buzzer sounded and the latch came off the front door. We entered the hallway quietly and snuck up to the door of Mahoney's ground-floor flat. I delicately grabbed the door handle and turned it slightly. It was unlocked.

I nodded to the two uniforms and then at the door. They knew what I had in mind. They stood either side of the door, tensed and ready. I withdrew my shoulder weapon, checked it, nodded a count down from three and then kicked the door open.

"*Police!*" I shouted loudly.

Mahoney was standing by the sink in the corner, looking startled, and immediately dropped whatever he'd been holding. It broke. He saw me pointing a weapon at him. But there was something different about the way he was looking at me I couldn't immediately put my finger on.

"Hands where I can see them," I ordered in a loud voice.

He raised his hands to shoulder height and stared at me.

"Hello, Drake," I said sarcastically. "You're coming with us; you've got some questions to answer." I nodded to the younger uniform. "Cuff him."

The uniform produced a set of hand restraints. As he took hold of Mahoney's left arm, Mahoney turned quickly and punched him full in the face, and he went down. The other uniform lunged at Mahoney. Mahoney broke his grip and headbutted him. The officer staggered backwards with blood pouring from his nose. In the same flowing movement Mahoney produced a small can of Mace and gave a short squirt to both men in the eyes. They began yelling and rubbing their eyes against the stinging sensation the spray produces when it hits the naked eye. I'd been unable to take a shot as the second uniform had been obstructing my view and I had no clear target.

Mahoney turned to face me, apparently spoiling for a fight. It was then I realised what it was that had made him look slightly different. From the glazed look of his eyes he was under the influence of some kind of stimulant. Drugs? Alcohol? Whatever it was, he was staring at me very aggressively. I had the feeling he wasn't going to come quietly.

"Gonna shoot me, are ya?" He grinned, his Irish accent now very accentuated. "Come on, then, shoot me." He spread his arms wide and thrust his chest forwards. "Come on, here's your target."

I kept my weapon aimed at the centre of his chest. "Drop the spray, Mahoney."

He laughed and shook his head. "Y'know what I think? I think you've not got the stones to use that thing," he sneered, "so I'm just gonna walk right on outta here, and you're not gonna stop me."

He began inching his way around the room, still pointing the spray at me. I took three short steps backwards into the doorway, keeping my weapon targeted at Mahoney. He moved closer until there were only five or six paces between us.

"Only way out of here's through me," I said calmly, and lowered my weapon while maintaining eye contact. "Remember what happened to you last time you came at me?"

A few months back, I'd turned up here to question Mahoney, and he'd come at me as I'd gone to put hand restraints on him. I'd dropped him with a hard chop to the throat, which'd hurt considerably, and he'd struggled to talk or swallow for a few hours afterwards.

He was staring at me with ill-disguised loathing. If looks could kill I'd be dead. I held his stare, mentally psyching myself up to be ready for whatever he was going to do. Whatever substance he was under the influence of had stimulated his aggression levels. But, whatever he'd taken, there was no way I was letting him escape. I'd wanted him too long to allow that.

The stand-off lasted thirteen seconds. I could see one of the uniforms getting up from the floor and rubbing his eyes when Mahoney let out a loud yell and ran at me, squirting the spray wildly. I ducked, shuffled to my left and, as he drew level, I jabbed out my elbow, which connected with the side of his arm. He dropped the spray and I turned and kicked it across the room, out of his reach. I could smell and almost taste the sour odour, but I could still see; none had caught my eyes.

I holstered my weapon. I wasn't prepared to shoot him at such close range; besides, I wanted him alive.

I could see in his eyes what he was planning to do. I began flexing my fingers and shrugging my shoulders.

"This is still the only way out," – I nodded to the door – "and you gotta get past me."

This was his cue. He charged at me, wrapping his arms around my chest, and drove me back into the door jamb. He'd been quicker off the mark than I'd expected and the slam against the door jamb jarred my back. I shrugged him off and we spilled out into the hallway.

He threw a punch which I turned away from and it hit the top of my left arm. He lunged at me again and, this time, I wasn't so quick to move. His punch caught me full on the left cheek. I felt it. My head shuddered under the impact and my eyes watered. If I'd not been fully aware there was no chance this situation would end any way other than very violently, I was now.

I moved further back into the wide hallway and he circled around me, his eyes almost feral. My cheekbone was throbbing and I was rapidly blinking, but, for the moment, I ignored the aching. I saw the younger of the uniforms came out the room, rubbing his eyes. I shouted for him to stay by the front door and, if Mahoney got past me, take him down using whatever means available. I saw him withdrawing his night stick.

Mahoney lunged at me again. I stepped aside and jabbed him hard on the side of his right knee with my right heel. I heard him yelp; it had hurt. He turned and made a grab for my jacket and, as he pulled me towards him, attempted to headbutt me. I quickly turned my face away and his forehead caught my right ear, and it stung. For a moment the ringing in my ear made me feel like I had tinnitus. I broke his grip with a downwards chopping motion using both arms, and then, in the same flowing movement, hit him hard with a left jab, which knocked him back against the wall. He shook his head, wiped a trickle of blood from his lip, pushed himself off the wall and came at me again.

But I was now fully in the zone because his punch had brought me sharply into focus. I was ready for him. I'd been trained by experts to think rationally in situations like this, and I knew how to stay focused and how to use force effectively, not wildly or randomly: only in any situation where an advantage was there to be gained.

I stepped aside as he lunged, and he stumbled past me. He came at me again swinging wildly and, again, I sidestepped him. He leapt at me full-on and, this time, I stood my ground and drove my right fist into his stomach. He felt it, doubled over and gasped loudly. I saw an opportunity and took it. I punched him hard on the side of his head and he dropped down onto one knee. He shook his head for two seconds, then scrambled hurriedly to his feet and came at me again.

Only, this time, he wasn't quite as quick. He was weary, his guard was down and his eyes were unfocused. I saw my chance.

I feinted with my right and he recoiled slightly. In that same second I tilted my body angle slightly to my right and threw a quick left jab onto his nose, which drew blood, and, a split second later, followed it with an almighty right cross to his chin, putting as much power and strength into it as I had left. I connected perfectly and a shuddering pain shot up my arm to my shoulder.

He went back two steps, hit the wall, dropped to the floor and rolled over onto his back, groaning audibly and trying to get up.

I looked down at him. I was breathing heavily, sweating slightly, and my right knuckles were bruised and aching. I was still psyched and the temptation to kick him in his exposed groin was considerable, but I resisted. He was finished.

"Good one, skip." The young uniform smiled approvingly as he put his night stick away, rolled Mahoney onto his front and put hand restraints on him. He dragged Mahoney to his feet and threw him against the wall, head first. He then spun him around.

At this point the older uniform who'd been headbutted suddenly appeared from nowhere and punched Mahoney in the stomach. Mahoney gasped in pain, dropped to his knees and doubled over. The uniform went to hit him again.

"*That's enough*," I ordered. "Get him in the car."

They dragged Mahoney outside. I followed. Once Mahoney was in the back of their car, I looked at both of them.

"You ever pull a stunt like that again," – I paused – "at least make sure I'm out the way so I can truthfully say I'd didn't see what happened."

"You got it, skip," the older uniform said with a grin.

*

Mahoney's face had been cleaned up, though he was bruised in a few places. The effects of the stimulant he'd been under the influence of a couple of hours ago appeared to be wearing off. I'd been told all the symptoms suggested he'd been using skunk, a very high-grade potent marijuana which, in some users, stimulated violent aggression.

He sat staring at me as though he didn't recognise who I was, or even where he was. My heart rate had returned to normal, though my left cheek was sore and bruised and my knuckles were still aching. The pain had lessened after a couple of minutes with my hand in ice water, and I could at least hold a pen properly. I reminded him he was still under caution.

"Well, assaulting a police officer, as well as using Mace against police: these'll be added to what I told you last week, Drake. Throw in conspiracy as well and you're looking at the tail end of quite a long stretch."

He didn't reply. He sat back in the chair and folded his arms.

"And, to make your late afternoon even more enjoyable for you, Drake, we raided a flat on the Euston Road a few days back, found all kinds of goodies: bomb-making resources and firearms, and" – I smiled at him and sat forward – "we found *your* fingerprints as well."

He looked up at me.

"Yeah, we did, honestly," I said. "Not on any of the weapons or bomb-making stuff, sadly for us, but they were all over the coffee table and on a couple of the beer glasses. We probably wouldn't even *need* a conspiracy charge with all this evidence. The fact of your fingerprints being found there ties you in with the suicide bomber." I paused. "Unless, that is, you've got a better story to tell me."

He looked nonplussed.

"So, what *is* your connection to this flat?" I asked.

He didn't answer.

"Florian Coyake says you took Danny Hunter there and asked if he could stay a while as he needed somewhere anonymous to doss down. I mean, I suppose he would, given he's an absconder from the army."

Mahoney looked up, surprised.

"You didn't know this?" I put on an amazed look. "He's done a bunk from the army: injured a lance corporal in a fight and he's done a runner."

"Told me he was out the army, he'd done his time."

"Well, he's obviously as full of shit as you are, Drake." I paused again. "He went AWOL and military police are looking for him. So, we add giving refuge to a fugitive from justice to the list of charges you're facing, and you're up to your thick Irish neck in it."

Mahoney looked bewildered. He snorted to himself and then sighed. I called for the duty sergeant.

Mahoney stood up. "What am I being charged with?"

"I don't know yet." I grinned at him. "I'm spoilt for choice."

He was led away to be detained in custody overnight.

*

Six twenty-nine pm. I had Chappy Watts brought back to the interview room, and I told him I was going to give him the benefit of the doubt and release him on police bail, provided he guaranteed he'd stay in London, preferably somewhere I could find him at short notice when I needed him. He agreed he'd stay at the flat with Helen.

"I have to come looking for you again, Chappy, I'm gonna rip your fucking ears off."

The look on his face told me he'd got the message.

*

An hour later. Taylor was working on her story with Jacobs and wasn't due back till around nine, so I decided, before going off duty, to look up details of Lady Elizabeth Bressington. I'd been intrigued and not a little disturbed by Little Des' withering statement that his mother had known but been relaxed about Alexander Bressington's, to put it mildly, esoteric sexual peccadilloes, and that she stayed with him because his money and position gave her the life and social status she thought she deserved. I'd been somewhat distracted earlier today, so, as tomorrow I'd planned to talk to Alexander Bressington about the assault on Little Des, I decided I needed to know more about his wife.

Elizabeth Bressington, aged fifty-eight, had been born Elizabeth Clarissa Elspeth Desborough and hailed from a well-to-do family in an affluent part of Oxfordshire. She'd attended a private school in Buckinghamshire as a day pupil and, at eighteen, had gone up to Lady Margaret Hall, Oxford, to read PPE.

The year she'd graduated she'd given birth to her only child, William Anthony, but she'd broken off the relationship with William's father, her politics professor, when she'd moved to London to take the entrance exam to join the civil service. She'd passed and, after joining the service, had initially been based inside the Ministry of Defence. There, a short while later, she'd met Alexander Bressington, who at the time was a senior executive officer and already being tipped to become a high achiever inside the service. They'd married, and Alexander had formally adopted William and raised him as his own child.

I looked up her family antecedents. Her father, now deceased, had worked for a major American oil company at senior management level, and her elderly mother had at one time been a trainee nurse before becoming a stay-at-home mother. There was nothing about the family that stood out; all I found were the usual activities associated with the upper-middle-class Oxfordshire county set: riding to hounds with a local hunt, memberships of tennis clubs and bridge clubs, gymkhanas, Crufts, being active in the National Trust and so on. She had one sibling, a sister named Rebecca, but what I read next about her made me sit bolt upright and gasp in utter surprise.

Rebecca Mildred Desborough had married an Oxfordshire businessman named George Arthur Frost. George was the brother of Andrew Frost, and Andrew, a businessman who ran a haulage company, had a daughter, Deborah Anne Frost.

Alexander and Elizabeth Desborough were Debbie Frost's uncle and auntie.

Debbie Frost was cousins by marriage with Little Des.

Immediately I wondered whether Debbie knew anything about her uncle Alexander's fetish for very underage girls. Which then led me to speculate further on whether she'd any idea about her new fiancé's sexual proclivities.

I suddenly realised the driver who'd said he'd had to smuggle Adrian Bowketts into the country was driving for the haulage company owned by Debbie's father.

Another thought then dawned on me. Earlier today, Little Des had said the two men who'd assaulted him the night before had told him to say nothing about Sir Alexander *and anyone else in the family*. Did this mean Sir Alexander knew about his niece's fiancé's perverse sexual tendencies as well, and was attempting to protect his niece from any unfavourable exposure, given she was now a prospective parliamentary candidate?

I was almost beginning to feel sorry for Debbie Frost. If any of this ever became public knowledge, and her new constituency association got to hear about it, her aspiration for a political career would be dead in the water before it even left the harbour.

*

At twenty-five to nine I parked my car, locked it and began to walk towards the rear entrance of our building.

"Detective McGraw."

I heard my name being called out. I turned and saw a man exiting a car and walking purposefully towards me. Even in the semi-darkness I knew it was Joachim Balpak. I noticed his car had the same CD registration plates as the vehicle the two men suspected of killing Sherif Rizwi had got into by Highbury & Islington tube station.

He stopped alongside me. I looked around.

"I'm alone," he said.

"You here officially or unofficially?" I was curious.

"I'm just here," he replied. "You tried to contact me three days ago. What did you want?"

I told him about seeing Sherif Rizwi on CCTV leaving a tube station and being followed by two men who, a few moments later, had got into a car with CD plates. "The one behind you." I nodded to his car. Soon after this Rizwi had been found dead, stabbed. I wanted Balpak to explain this sequence of events to me because, *prima facie*, the evidence would appear to suggest Rizwi had been murdered by the Mossad, thus my call to him. I also told him about the initial gap in the CCTV records, and how, soon after Rizwi's death, the footage had suddenly reappeared.

He absorbed what I'd said for a few seconds.

"Your man was an undercover MI5 operative. How would I know this?" he said, matter-of-factly. "We too have people inside Muearada as well as MI5. This is how I know."

He stopped talking for a moment. I was about to speak, but he continued.

"I'm not going to give you any details, but what I *can* tell you is your man Rizwi died because his actions had interfered with an Israeli operation we were in the process of conducting against Muearada, and it cost one of our agents his life."

I was surprised. "What, here in London?"

"Doesn't matter where; it happened, and this is all you get to know. His actions interfered with Israel's legitimate interests, so we had him eliminated." He shrugged as though what he'd just described was simply a routine procedure. "There're lots of stabbings in London about now, so he was stabbed in such circumstances to make the media believe this was just another unfortunate fatality following a street fight."

This was in fact the line media reports of the death of Sherif Rizwi had taken.

"Of course," Balpak said, "your superior officers know the reasons why this occurred. They may or may not tell you, but they know what I know."

I thought about the evening I'd last seen Balpak. "I saw you talking to Rizwi in the hall last week. What were you talking about?"

Balpak shrugged and didn't reply.

"Did you *know* this was going to happen when you and I were talking in the hall a few hours before he was stabbed?"

"I don't discuss Mossad operations with non-Mossad personnel," he stated formally. "What I do or don't know doesn't concern you."

"Rizwi was in the hall." I nodded knowingly. "Were you there following him?"

Balpak remained silent.

I thought about something else for a moment. "Rizwi had also been identified as being in a flat where a man was demonstrating to him and others how to disassemble a rifle and put it back together again. Did this have—"

"Don't ask; I won't answer any of your questions," he said firmly. "I'm just here to tell you the matter of why Rizwi was killed is known in higher circles, so you'd be wasting your time if you investigated it any further." He paused for a moment. "Also, the two men you saw on the CCTV are no longer in this country, so you have no suspects either," he added, looking pleased.

I was thinking of a response when he spoke again.

"This is also why the images on the CCTV have been restored. As the people in your security service now know why he was killed, there was no necessity any longer to keep the gap in the tape."

There was silence for a few seconds.

"And now you people are looking for Tabzouni and his cohorts, aren't you? We know about the dragnet last Friday evening and your people not finding them. We're looking for them as well, and *we* don't ask as nicely as you English do." Was that a smile?

I knew what he meant. If the Mossad is on your tail, your chances of longevity are usually not too promising.

"I ought to tell you," he said, ominously, "Tabzouni had better pray to whatever deity he worships you people find him first. If *I* find him, and the opportunity presents itself, you know what I'm going to do to him, don't you, and it won't be quick *or* clean."

He turned, walked back to his car and drove away.

*

"You're not gonna believe who Steve's managed to get in touch with," Taylor said, very excitedly. We were in the kitchen. I was making coffee while she stood next to me. "He's managed to track down an ex-SAS officer, someone who's served in Northern Ireland, and been to talk to him."

I turned to look at her in surprise. "Ex-SAS?"

"Yeah, and he had some very interesting things to say about his time there."

I finished making the coffee and poured two cups. As I passed her a coffee she was looking at my left cheek.

"Where'd you get the bruising?" she asked.

"Oh, would you believe some idiot tripped up balancing his coffee and a file and headbutted a wall while trying not to drop either?" I replied casually.

She laughed. "You're still handsome, though, McGraw," she said softly, lightly kissing my cheek.

We took our coffees into the lounge and took our usual seats.

"So, how'd he come across this SAS guy? How'd he find out about him?" I was very curious. "Ex-members of the special forces don't exactly advertise to journos."

"I've no idea." She smiled. "He won't let on, won't even tell me the guy's name, says I don't need to know. But, whatever, he agreed to talk on the record, had no reservations about doing it, so we're gonna feature his role quite prominently."

"He say *why*?" Ex-SAS men don't usually agree to talk to the media either, especially on a matter as sensitive as the one Taylor and Jacobs were looking into.

"I wondered about that as well. But Steve said this guy believes he'd been shafted by the military top brass, so he's prepared to talk."

"Shafted in what way?"

"He said he'd been hauled up over a botched operation, and it'd been recommended by his commanding officer he be RTUd as a punishment, because of his rank, and he's still deeply resentful about their decision to demote him, even after all this time. In actual fact, he'd felt so resentful, rather than be RTUd, he resigned his commission, left the forces altogether."

"RTUd?" I'd forgotten what this meant.

"*Returned to unit*," she said. "Means you're being kicked out of the SAS and sent back to whatever regiment you came from."

"So, what'd he done? Why'd they kick this guy out? I would

imagine you've gotta fall down pretty badly to be kicked out the SAS."

She sipped her coffee while settling back in the chair. "He was caught up in the aftermath of what happened in Dunloy."

"What was this?" I asked.

She explained.

Sometime in July 1978, John Boyle, a sixteen-year-old Catholic, had inadvertently discovered what turned out to be an IRA arms cache, hidden in a churchyard in Dunloy, Co. Antrim, and he informed the RUC. They in turn alerted the SAS, who were sent in. The SAS mounted a round-the-clock operation to watch the cache, and to apprehend whoever came back to collect the arms. But, for reasons unknown, the teenager came back to look at the cache.

She stopped talking to look at me. In that moment I knew what was coming next.

"These two SAS guys didn't know who he was, they think he's IRA and they shoot him dead. But the thing is, he *wasn't* IRA, he was just an innocent kid, and there was a riot in Belfast later that evening when the news was made known. The two soldiers tried to claim the kid had raised one of the rifles in the arms cache and pointed it at them, which was why they shot him, but according to the RUC he was shot in the back. And a forensic examination revealed none of the kid's fingerprints were on any of the rifles."

I thought about this for a moment. "So what happened to the two soldiers?"

"Because the kid was only sixteen, and it was known he was shot from behind, they were both eventually put on trial for manslaughter, but they were both acquitted."

We took a drink from our coffees.

"But the point about this incident is, the guy Steve spoke to?" Taylor went on. "He was the SAS captain in charge of the surveillance operation, their commanding officer. He was charged with some kind of dereliction of duty – I don't remember the exact wording of the actual charge Steve mentioned – and was court-martialled and found guilty of falling well below the standards expected of an SAS officer in the field on active duty, which had led to a non-combatant dying. He was ordered to be RTUd with immediate effect, but he refused to accept this. He resigned his commission and left the army instead."

We sat quietly for several seconds.

"This ex-SAS bloke believes he was treated very unfairly, says he'd given the two soldiers very clear instructions about what to do if anyone came to the churchyard and looked like they were after the arms cache hidden there, but a court acquits them despite their not following orders, and *he* gets ordered to be reduced in the ranks. So he says he was punished for what these two soldiers did and he's nursed a grudge against the army ever since, which is why he agreed to talk to Steve about his experiences."

As she was speaking, I remembered Christine Simmons telling me Taylor should be careful about spending too much time associating with Jacobs. Had she known something about this when she'd told me? "So, what else did he have to say?"

"Oh, don't worry, he was careful about what he told Steve," she said, "and he said there were things he'd never talk about or give details of. But he agreed there definitely *was* a shoot-to-kill policy, *and* it'd been decided upon at the highest levels of Government."

"Highest levels?" This surprised me and I sat forward. I'd heard this recently, but hearing it said by someone who'd been on the front line with the SAS gave it an added piquancy. It appeared George Selwood had been telling me the truth. "How high are we talking?"

"According to this guy, the matter was raised in a special Cabinet committee, whose recommendations were then discussed by the full Cabinet. I'm about to check the National Archives for details about this, because this was just after those three Scottish soldiers had been ambushed and killed, sometime in the summer of 1971."

She then told me about this case. Three young Scottish soldiers from the 1st Battalion, Royal Highland Fusiliers, off duty, in civilian clothing and on a night out, had been lured into a honeytrap by two young women whom they'd met in a city centre pub. They had been driven to the outskirts of Belfast and then assassinated by the IRA, with their bodies being found in a ditch later the same evening after it'd been assumed by the army they'd gone AWOL.

"This was really controversial at the time, McGraw," she said.

"Two of the soldiers were brothers, and one was only seventeen, so, according to this SAS guy, the Cabinet discussed the case and decided it was time to get rough with the IRA, hit back hard. Peacekeeping didn't seem to be working, so the decision was the IRA was going to be hit where it lived. Shoot-to-kill came out of this discussion."

"Was this guy part of it?"

"Yeah, said he was with the first squad of SAS men to be sent to Ireland in the summer of 1971, which is five years before it's officially recorded the SAS were being deployed in Northern Ireland. He said he was part of the intelligence team, 14 Intelligence Company, who found out those reputed to be IRA members and where they lived, and, instead of passing them on to army intelligence and the RUC for information purposes, he'd give the details to a body like Two Unit. They'd follow up on it and take out those who'd been named."

I remembered, recently, when I'd been talking to the odious George Selwood, he'd said the SAS had been involved in the implementation of shoot-to-kill by passing on intelligence to the soldiers on the ground. I was beginning to realise my initial doubts that such a policy had ever existed were now rapidly dissolving. Taylor was on to something here.

"We've told Hugh about this," Taylor said, "and he was initially worried about our including any references to actions carried out by the SAS. Steve said it confirmed the existence of the policy, though, because the SAS operate directly under political orders, and they'd only have been in Ireland, doing what they did, if the Government had ordered them to be there."

She went out to the kitchen to pour two more drinks. When she came back, she passed me a coffee and sat down on the couch next to me. "So Steve convinced him we should keep the SAS reference, especially after this kid was shot in the back despite the soldiers' claim to the contrary. This is what Pencourt was saying right at the beginning, wasn't it, so Hugh's gonna go with it." She sounded very excited about this. "Steve's got one or two more people to speak to in the next day or so, and these will be the last ones. Then, with what I've found during my research, and with what I'm hoping to find when I look through the National Archives tomorrow, we can start formatting the story and putting it together."

We drank our coffee.

"We're almost there, McGraw." She sounded very pleased. "Steve's got the testimony of several people, ex-soldiers and others with stories which contradict the verdicts on the death certificates, plus what I've found through what I've been looking into."

She leaned into me and turned around to face me. "This could well be a *big* impact story, McGraw, at least as big as the piece we put together about Blatchford, maybe even bigger, and it's starting to read really good so far, so *you* ..." She curled up next to me, smiled sexily and touched my nose lightly. "You mustn't say *anything* about this to *anyone*," she said softly.

I put my arm around her, pulled her closer and kissed her. "My silence can be bought, y'know," I said quietly, grinning at her.

"Oh yeah?" She put her coffee down and returned my kiss with a *much* better, and longer, one of her own. "How much?"

I started nibbling her ear and her neck.

"Oh, as much as that, eh?" She laughed. "You drive a hard bargain, McGraw."

NINETEEN

Thursday

Florian Coyake was led into the interview room. I was already there waiting for him. He sat down, and the uniform left the room. Coyake stared at me with a combination of indifference and bewilderment.

I had Coyake's file in front of me. The decision had already been taken to bring charges against him, and it was now just a question of what his full culpability was. This would be another step towards ascertaining it.

"Science student, eh, Florian?"

"Used to be." He shrugged. "What's this got to do with anything?"

"I've just come off the phone with one of your ex-tutors at Westminster. You remember Dr Carol Reed, your chemistry tutor?"

"Yeah, what about her?"

"She says, despite the official record giving your desire to leave, the unofficial word is you were asked to leave Westminster University before you were kicked out. Something about you ignoring repeated official warnings and using university facilities to try to make an explosive device, endangering staff and students and, on one occasion, causing one of the science blocks to be evacuated during exam preparations. Any of this sounding familiar?"

He didn't reply. I continued.

"And I've also just looked at the report from a Major Allsopp, the bomb squad officer who examined those pieces of Sam Alorami still left in Whitehall." I paused, ensuring I had Coyake's attention. "Simply stated? His report says the PBIED used by Alorami, from the nature of the injuries suffered and damage to nearby property, had to have been quite a sophisticated model and, as such, would have had to be strapped onto his body by someone with a knowledge of chemistry. His opinion? There's *no way* any suicide bomber could have strapped this device onto himself, because the extreme volatility of the chemicals used was such that he'd have run the risk of blowing himself up in the flat." I paused again. "So our hypothesis is he *had* to have had assistance, an accomplice, someone with a good working knowledge of chemistry, to help make the device and *then* strap it onto his body in such a way that he could travel in a vehicle without the risk of premature detonation."

I remembered, recently, when I'd been looking into a car bombing in London, a second explosion had occurred on the road behind the Festival Hall on the South Bank, caused by a faulty design which had detonated the bomb prematurely as the vehicle had crossed over a speed bump, blowing the driver to pieces. I remembered seeing the pictures of the grisly remains of the driver and wanting to vomit.

Neither of us spoke for a few seconds.

"So, you see where I'm going with this?" I asked, raising my eyebrows. "Alorami had to have help, so our reasoning is, with you having a chemistry background, *and* being the manager of the premises he came out of..."

He didn't respond.

"You need me to draw you a picture?" I looked directly at him. "We're saying the accomplice was *you*, pal, so, unless you can convince me otherwise right now, you're gonna be charged with this under S.6, Terrorism Act 2006, to wit: *having a direct involvement in the planning of and preparing to commit a terrorist act.* That's an automatic life sentence right there, Florian, quite possibly a whole life sentence, because eleven people died very nasty deaths, including a young police officer," I snarled.

I paused to let my words sink in. Then I opened the file and laid four pictures on the table in front of him. They were all extremely gruesome, showing the victims of the explosion last Friday night. All the pictures showed burned, blood-splattered and mutilated bodies, a couple with limbs missing and someone with half their face gone: people who, seconds previously, had been flesh-and-blood sentient entities enjoying a Friday night out and, in the case of PC Jacob Marshall, carrying out an extremely important duty.

They were all tragic, but the saddest case had been the civil servant who'd only been caught up in the explosion because, police had been told, leaving the Treasury building earlier, he'd realised he'd forgotten something and went back to retrieve it. But for this, he'd have been well past the scene of the explosion when it'd occurred.

Looking at these for the first time, a couple of them had almost made me retch, and I'd seen similar pictures previously.

"This is some of Alorami's handiwork, Florian," I explained. "Look at these. This is what the bastard did after leaving *your* arcade last Friday."

His eyes looked down at the pictures but didn't appear to register any emotion.

"Look at this one," I ordered, pointing to a picture of what was left of a man lying against the wall of the Cabinet Office, his face a bloodied mess, his clothes torn and shredded and hideous burns all over his body. "*Look at the picture.*"

He did.

"This guy was on his honeymoon, he was only twenty-six, had everything to live for. This one here" – I pointed to the mutilated remains of a young woman – "was his wife; she was only twenty-five. Can you explain to me what they did to Alorami and others like him to deserve this, and why *you* helped him do it?" I challenged him.

Coyake didn't speak. He sighed to himself. I nodded.

"I hope you haven't made plans for the next couple of decades, pal, because you won't be keeping them," I stated while collecting up the pictures.

He sat back in his chair and crossed his arms. I looked at him. From his look of seeming indifference, I might just as well have been telling him what I'd had for breakfast.

"So," I said, "you have *anything* to say before the duty sergeant takes you off to be charged with the offences I mentioned just now? This is your final chance to do something to help us catch the other pilgrims Alorami associated with, and also to do yourself some good, maybe even earn yourself a little mitigation."

He didn't reply, simply sat looking smugly at me. His indifference to these pictures had left me wanting to wipe the smugness off his face, but I knew the room was covered by CCTV, so I suppressed my desire for violence. He was led away and taken into custody, pending charges and an appearance at Westminster Magistrates' Court tomorrow.

*

My intention at this time had been to visit Sir Alexander Bressington to talk about the assault on his stepson, but Smitherman had vetoed this plan.

"The security service wants him completely isolated for the moment. Remember what I told you yesterday morning?"

I did.

"Well, until all this is through, they want him left alone, so, for the moment, don't talk to him. You'll be told when he can be approached."

I spent the rest of the afternoon typing up my report on Florian Coyake and my reasons for recommending he be charged under the appropriate legislation, the 2006 Terrorism Act. I became mildly frustrated with the situation as I was typing because his evasive manner made me think he knew more than he was letting on, but, whatever, we had him in custody and, as we had more than sufficient *prima facie* evidence against him, he was to be charged with the assistance I was convinced he'd given Sam Alorami last Friday. I finished typing, uploaded my report, sent it on to Smitherman and went off duty late afternoon.

Thinking I'd leave my car in the Yard's underground car park, I decided I'd walk to Victoria and take a bus from there. I walked along Victoria Embankment and, at Portcullis House, turned right into Bridge Street. Walking past the crowds entering and exiting the nearby Westminster tube station, I paused to pick up an *Evening Standard* and look at the headlines. As I did, a man leaving the tube station collided with me on my right side, and the bag he was carrying struck my right knee. Whatever was in his bag was solid and I felt a temporary jolt. Being jostled and bumped into wasn't exactly unusual at this time, five thirty-five, as there were always crowds of tourists and office workers moving in and out of the tube station.

I turned to apologise in case it'd been me in the wrong, and I immediately noticed he was of Middle Eastern appearance, a little shorter than me and probably around twenty, with a full beard, a shock of thick, black curly hair and some kind of large Arabic red-and-white chequered scarf around his neck, which covered both shoulders of his army camouflage jacket. Our eyes connected only for a split second but, instantly, something inside me clicked into life. There was something about his deep-set eyes and, even in this microsecond, I could see he was looking nervous. He muttered something under his breath I didn't catch and walked away towards Parliament Square. As he did so, I noticed he was wearing dark army canvas trousers, tucked into a pair of military boots.

But I was more interested in his bag. It was an ordinary supermarket bag for life, though, rather than holding the handles, he'd folded the top over and was holding the bag close to his body, in such a way that it wasn't possible to see inside.

A few paces away, he turned to look back at me and our eyes met fleetingly. There was something about those eyes I didn't like. I wondered if I knew him from somewhere but drew a blank.

He hurriedly turned away and walked on towards Whitehall. There was something about this person's mannerisms making me suspicious. I couldn't explain it, but I knew everything about this person was somehow wrong. There was a vibe I couldn't shake.

I took out my police radio, stepped inside the tube station concourse and sent a message to the police command post in Whitehall, outlining my suspicion about this person, along with a description. I advised officers in Whitehall to be alert for his presence, to keep an eye out for him and, if considered necessary, pull him over and frisk him.

When he was ten yards away, I decided to follow him to see where he was going. I was still thinking about his eyes, which were what had set me on edge, and I couldn't help thinking there was a kind of nervous tension about him.

At the corner of Whitehall and Parliament Square he stopped for a moment and looked into his bag. I paused and moved back out of his line of sight as he glanced around for a moment. He kept walking. I followed, ensuring I could see him as he passed through the crowds heading south along Whitehall towards the square. He walked past the Red Lion, political Westminster's main watering hole, and then he stopped a hundred yards further along, placing his bag on the ground by the iron railings, just past the Cenotaph, and stood motionless, staring across the road at the gates to Downing Street.

I stayed as close to the wall as possible as I inched my way towards this man. I moved into the forecourt of Richmond House and crept forward until I was only about fifteen yards from him.

He stood motionless for several seconds, then picked up the bag again. I could see he was now fingering the top of his bag nervously. He put it back down against the railings. I could also see his lips moving and his head nodding slightly.

Across the road, I could see two police officers getting out of one of the police emergency response vehicles parked alongside the Cenotaph and preparing to cross the road in the direction of this person. At the same moment people on the west side of Whitehall were being moved back as the gates of Downing Street swung open, traffic in both directions was halted and then a police motorcyclist and two black Daimlers drove out and began to turn right, heading down Whitehall towards Parliament. As the gates were opening, the man quickly reached down and put his hands inside the bag.

In this split second, it hit me: what it was about him that had unnerved me.

This bastard's on a suicide mission.

I immediately started running towards him just as he was pulling out an automatic rifle from his bag, yelling loudly to the crowd of people around me to *get down*. Several people recoiled as they noticed the weapon and many people began to panic and scream and run. I collided with a forty-something man, who dropped his briefcase, stumbled backwards and slipped over. The two police officers immediately raised their rifles when they saw the man's gun and heard my yelling, plus the panic beginning to ensue on the pavement.

The gunman fired several shots at the two cars, hitting both of them with the spray of bullets, but none penetrated the armour-plated doors and reinforced windows. The cars swerved slightly but kept moving forward.

One second after he began firing, I rugby-tackled him, hitting him full on his left hip with my left shoulder and wrapping my arms around his upper thighs, knocking him to the floor. The rifle fell from his hands as he went down. In one flowing movement, I scrambled up and across him, grabbed his left wrist and sharply bent it backwards, and he yelled out in pain. I flipped him over onto his front, dropped my right knee into the small of his back, grabbed his other wrist and, as I was doing so, shouted to the oncoming uniforms not to shoot: 'I'm a police officer!'

I pulled out a pair of hand restraints, and I was cuffing him as I became aware of two police officers now standing alongside me, pointing their guns twelve inches from this person's head, and loudly shouting instructions to him not to move.

I stood up and hauled the gunman roughly to his feet. The tension and nerves I'd seen in his face just a few seconds earlier had receded. He'd carried out his mission, or at least had attempted to, and he was now looking almost serene. He was talking to himself in whatever language or dialect he spoke.

The two police officers were soon joined by two others, who'd come across to assist us. One of them I recognised as the uniform who'd challenged me last Friday night when I'd been walking towards the scene of the suicide bombing by the Cabinet Office.

"Should've let me shoot the bastard," I heard him say to no one in particular.

"Did I hear you say you're a police officer?" one of the first uniforms asked.

"Yeah," I exhaled, pulling out my ID. "Special Branch." I turned to face the gunman. "You're under arrest. You speak English?"

He looked at me blankly. I looked at the officers holding him and nodded towards the van.

The gunman was bundled into the back of the police van, which had moved across the main road, and driven away. I leant back against the railings, put my weapon away and took a few deep breaths as my adrenaline rush began to subside. Police officers were ordering pedestrians and others to *keep on moving, it's all over, folks, come on.* Traffic, though, which had been halted, was now being temporarily diverted out of the area.

As I took a deep breath, the enormity of what I'd just done was now beginning to sink in. I'd acted instinctively when I'd seen the rifle, and everything had then happened so quickly, so I was still trying to piece together the exact sequence of events in my mind. Had I not been fortuitous enough to collide with him by the tube station, whatever he'd been intending might well have succeeded, though he'd undoubtedly have been shot dead. Maybe this had been what he'd wanted.

But the thought occurred to me ... had I not been as near to him as I was, might he have had time to turn and shoot at me as I'd snuck up on him?

He'd only fired the one burst of bullets, and the two vehicles, containing whoever it was, had continued on to their destination. Apart from several small dents in the sides of the cars, there was little damage and, more importantly, no one had been injured or died, though I suspected several pedestrians had been shaken up by the sound of gunfire.

I crossed to the other side of the road, where a senior officer with pips on his shoulder was asking the uniforms a few questions. One of the uniforms nodded towards me.

"I'm DCI Elson, SO15," the senior officer said. "Your actions just now were commendable, not to mention very brave. This constable says you're a police officer. Who are you?"

"DS McGraw, Special Branch." I showed ID. "I was in the area."

"Had you been tailing this man? Is this why you were nearby when he started shooting?"

I explained briefly how this situation had come about and how, but for the fact he'd bumped into me and I'd noticed his eyes, I'd be waiting for the bus home about now and wouldn't have known anything about what had happened.

"Well, one up for the good guys, eh?" He smiled and patted me on the shoulder. "About bloody time we had some luck here. Anyway," – he looked around and gestured to a car – "get in, quick, there're media people over there in Downing Street who've heard all the noise and are heading this way. Come on, we'll get you away from here before they see you."

"Thanks."

I was driven back to the Yard, where I spent the next hour and a half having a detailed Q&A session with an MI5 officer who was about to go and interview the shooter. After being told someone else would probably want to talk to me tomorrow, I was allowed to leave.

*

Taylor and I were watching the BBC news at ten. She'd not long been back home as she and Jacobs'd been interviewing someone about the story they were putting together, and she'd decided to take a shower, so we'd not yet talked about our respective days.

The lead story was, predictably, *another terrorist outrage in Whitehall*, this time a lone gunman's failed attempt to kill the passengers in the Daimlers, who I now learnt were the Israeli ambassador and two other senior Israeli diplomats. The reporter quoted security sources saying the worrying question was how this gunman had known about the ambassador's visit, which had not been publicised, and in particular how he'd known, almost to the minute, the exact time the ambassador was going to be leaving No. 10 and been in position ready to fire. The name of the would-be assassin wasn't given.

There'd also been considerable media speculation, though, about the identity of whoever it'd been who'd tackled the gunman. A few-second CCTV clip, from a camera on the wall of the Foreign Office, had shown the gunman being rugby tackled, but the tackler's head had been blurred out. Police had revealed no details about this person beyond stating that it was lucky he'd been so close by, and that his intervention at the time had undoubtedly prevented any loss of life.

A BBC journalist who'd been in Downing Street had been able to interview a few pedestrians who'd been on the pavement close by. I recognised the pedestrian I'd knocked to the ground. He was telling the reporter about the man who'd tackled the shooter shouting out he was a police officer, and showing what looked like some form of ID to the uniforms, though he'd not caught the name. I was just hoping nobody had been quick enough of mind to record my actions on their phones.

DCI Elson had refused to answer any questions relating to the tackler's identity, leaving the reporter to speculate on whether the officer concerned had been security service, and whether the gunman had been apprehended so quickly because he'd had an MI5 tail.

"Oh, wow, that's right by where the suicide bomber killed all those people last week. Lucky this guy was near enough, eh, McGraw?" Taylor said. "You know anything about this?"

I didn't answer for a few seconds. However, Taylor knew me far too well by now; something about my expression must have triggered her journo instincts, because she fixed me with the look which I knew meant *come on, McGraw, what is it?*

"Eh, yeah, I might do, actually." I grinned. There was a look on my face she recognised.

Taylor's face took on an expression of pure surprise, mouth and eyes wide open.

"Oh my God, McGraw," she exclaimed excitedly, nodding at the television. "Was that *you* brought this guy down?" She moved across and sat down next to me.

"Yeah, yeah, it was." I then stressed she was *absolutely* to keep this to herself. She agreed she would.

"So what happened?"

Being circumspect, omitting several key details, and with one white lie, I gave her a potted account of what had occurred, stating it was possible I might be able to expand on this later on. We both knew our jobs came with limitations on what we could tell each other.

"There'll be a follow-up story tomorrow about this, for sure," Taylor said. "If I'm involved in writing it up, I'll call and pick your brains."

I said I'd like that very much.

TWENTY

Friday

I was in Smitherman's office. He began by telling me the gunman had been interrogated by MI5 overnight, and had been identified as Rahid Sulluman, aged twenty-one, a Lebanese national and the half-brother of Asou el-Taccouli. He'd also been on an MI5 *person of interest* watchlist, though he hadn't been picked up by AFR yesterday and nobody had been watching him either, which had caused issues inside the security service. Late last evening, the chief of MI5 had been summoned to Downing Street and asked why nobody had been watching this person, and evidently he'd annoyed the PM by replying that, with somewhere around 20,000 persons of interest on their files, potential terrorists one and all, they'd no chance of keeping them all under close scrutiny without extra manpower and resources.

This morning Sulluman was due to appear before Westminster Magistrates' Court to face charges relating to the commission of an act of terrorism, and also one of attempted murder, and would then be remanded in Belmarsh before being tried.

Sulluman was in the UK on a one-year student visa, and was described as being a student at Queen Mary's, which offended me greatly as this was also Taylor's alma mater. It dawned on me I'd heard about someone else being a QM student recently, and I was trying to think of who it might be as Smitherman was talking. More significantly, though, Sulluman was also known to be an attendee at the Islington mosque where Mehmet Tabzouni held his radicalising sessions with impressionable wannabe martyrs.

Sulluman's English was extremely limited, and he hadn't always been able to understand the questions asked, so his interrogation had taken place with the assistance of an interpreter from the London School of Oriental and African Studies. But, if his command of the local language was as poor as was said, how the hell had he managed to obtain a place at a leading London university?

The rifle he'd been firing had also been a cause for concern for the security service. He'd been firing an AK-47, one of the assault rifles favoured by specialist military units in Russia, which was an expensive model and not exactly available over the counter in your local gun shop. Where would he have got this from? One of these had also been found in Coyake's flat last Sunday.

After bringing me up to speed regarding Sulluman, he sat back in his chair.

"Congratulations on yesterday, DS McGraw." He almost smiled.

He'd been apprised of the whole story, so he knew everything that had occurred, including my initial suspicions about Sulluman. He'd also read the statement I'd given the MI5 officer yesterday evening, and he agreed the likelihood of my having to give a further statement was minimal, as what I'd said last night had been exhaustively detailed.

"You'll probably get another commendation for this. You going to *accept* this one?" he inquired, looking at me over the top of his glasses.

"I dunno. I was just doing my job." I shrugged.

"Well, if you're nominated again, do so." He made it sound like an order. "Nobody died this time, so you've nothing to reproach yourself about."

I said I'd consider it if it ever happened. He then got back to business.

"Police turned over Sulluman's place last night; tore it apart, they did. He'd a small bedsit in Islington, but there was little of any note on the premises, apart from a few radical tracts which'd been downloaded from the internet. Most of these were in his native tongue, and he'd admitted he knew nothing about computers, so someone had to have helped him with the downloading. Nobody in the building seemed to know anything about him; he was a loner, just kept himself to himself. Also, several other addresses were raided, addresses of people this man's been known to associate with, and some of them are still being questioned now. Most of them are students, though, and just know him from QM, so not much progress has been made."

"You think he was acting on his own?"

"MI5 doesn't think so. Someone has to have told him what time to be where he was, and also get him the Kalashnikov, so we need to find who these people are."

*

Back at my desk I logged on and looked at the transcript of the interrogation of Rahid Sulluman. I noted he was a student of economic geography and international relations. This instantly set bells ringing. Someone else studied this subject. Who was it?

I brought up my case notes to date. That's when it hit me. Chappy Watts' girlfriend Helen Mathison was a student of the same subject at QM as the would-be assassin. Chappy'd been to Coyake's flat, and Coyake had been arrested in the Watts family lock-up.

I pulled up outside the Antill Road flat after a fast siren-aided dash through London. I'd contacted DS Roberts and he was waiting when I arrived. I quickly brought him up to speed as to why we were here. We rang the bell and entered when the latch clicked.

Helen was wearing a Kurt Cobain T-shirt and jeans with several strategic rips, and her long hair was in a ponytail. She registered surprise when she saw two detectives showing ID. "Chappy's at work; he isn't here."

"It's *you* we're here to talk to, not him," I said as we walked past her without waiting to be asked in.

"*Me?*" She appeared startled and followed us into the lounge.

"Yeah. Do you know someone named Rahid Sulluman?" I asked.

"Rahid? Yeah, he's on my course, we're in the same seminar set. Why are you asking?" She looked nervously between Roberts and me.

"How well do you know him?"

"We do the same course and I suppose we're sort of friends, that's how. I help him out occasionally. Why are you asking me these questions?" She sounded nervous.

"Help him with what?" Roberts asked, ignoring her question.

"With his studies. His English isn't very good, so I help him with the language sometimes when he doesn't know the meaning of a word or how to phrase something. He's also not very computer savvy, so I occasionally help him out with using his laptop when he's stuck."

"He's at a top London university. Didn't it strike you as odd he couldn't even speak the bloody language?" Roberts asked forcefully.

I changed tack. "Have you ever helped him download materials from the internet?"

"Only once."

I looked at her and nodded, as if to say *go on.*

"In the university library a couple of weeks back. He said he wanted to download some school materials but didn't know how, so I showed him how to get on to the internet, how to bring up whatever website he wanted and what to press to begin downloading."

"You know what site it was?"

"No. He just said it was to do with the course. He then went off and printed off what he wanted, and he thanked me when he'd finished."

From the worried look in her eyes, I believed her.

"When did you last see him?" I asked quietly, trying to keep Helen calm.

"Hmm, probably a week or so ago, I think. He's not been into college the last few days. He missed Wednesday's seminar."

"Has he ever been here, to this place?"

"A couple of times, yeah. He stayed here for a night, couple of weeks back when he had to leave his flat and had nowhere to go. I said he could crash on the couch. Chappy was okay with it."

"You know where he lives now?"

"Said he'd got a place in Islington, I think, but I don't know the address."

I looked around the room and a thought hit me. "Has he ever asked you to hold on to something, or to store something for him?"

"Like what?" She sounded suspicious.

"I don't know. Something like a bag or a package, perhaps?"

She thought for a moment.

"Yeah, he did," she said. "Said his new place was too small for all his stuff, so could he leave a bag here with some of his things till he got a place with more storage space."

"We need to see this bag," Roberts quickly said. "Where is it?"

"Why? It's private property." Helen sounded indignant.

"You see the news last night?" I asked.

She nodded.

"Your friend Rahid tried to kill the Israeli ambassador in

Whitehall. Someone hadn't intercepted him, he'd have been shot dead where he stood." I didn't say it'd been me.

"Oh my God, *that was Rahid*?" She was open-mouthed.

"Yeah, it was. Where's this bag?"

She looked bemused, muttering something to herself and shaking her head as she led us into the small bedroom. She nodded to the wardrobe. There was a large military-style holdall on top.

I grabbed a chair, put on a pair of plastic gloves, reached up and gently felt around the bag. I gingerly prodded it around the sides, and the contents mainly felt soft, like clothing, with what felt like a few hardback books as well.

I carefully brought the bag down and slowly placed it on the bed. I was almost certain it wasn't booby-trapped, but I wasn't taking any unnecessary risks.

The bag was locked, but I used a kitchen knife to break the lock and carefully unzipped it. Inside, the bag was packed with clothing, plus a few academic textbooks with four- or five-syllable titles I suspected Sulluman probably didn't understand and couldn't even pronounce.

And, tightly wrapped in thick cellophane, inside a taped-up carrier bag, inside a tightly rolled pair of jeans, were two Sig Sauer P226s and an H&K G36 rifle, plus a number of ammunition clips.

"Quite the study aids. They issue these during freshers' week, do they?" Roberts scowled acidly. "Your friend's a terrorist, sweetheart, and you're helping him out, storing his stuff for him."

"Oh my God, I, I didn't know they were in there." Her voice was strained and the open-mouthed expression on her face flickered between amazement and fright. "He just said it was all clothing and books."

"Get your coat, Helen; you need to come with us."

*

Back at the Yard, Helen was led away by a young female officer. I could see Helen was trying hard not to cry, so I'd assured her she wasn't in any trouble yet, but we needed to talk to her about the bag in her possession. The bag was taken away to be fingerprinted.

Florian Coyake was brought up from the holding cells to the interview room, where I was now waiting for him. He was agitated and clearly going stir crazy being held in custody. I couldn't care a shred less what he felt.

For whatever reason, he'd not yet been charged, as I'd been told was to happen yesterday, and so was demanding access to a solicitor and to be released on bail. I explained carefully to him there was no automatic entitlement to a lawyer where terrorism was at issue. The 2006 Terrorism Act, amongst other things, had suspended the writ of *habeas corpus*, and he could be held incommunicado for anywhere up to twenty-eight days without being charged, given that police had reasonable cause to believe he was involved in terrorism. This shut him up.

I then told him I was going to give him one chance to do himself a favour and, if he was smart, he'd take advantage of it. I placed a picture on the table in front of him. "You recognise this person?"

It was a picture of Rahid Sulluman, taken in custody. Coyake looked carefully at it for several seconds.

"Yeah." He nodded slowly.

"Well?"

"I think his name's Rashid, or something like that."

"Close enough. Where d'you know him from?"

"He's been to the flat a few times."

"What was he doing at the flat?"

He sat quietly for several seconds. "If I talk, how does this change my situation?"

"It doesn't, though of course police having a word in the right ear sometimes helps." I was trying to sound reassuring. "But there're no promises or guarantees where terrorism's concerned."

I didn't bother explaining to him that the phrase *a word in the right ear* didn't necessarily mean anything said would be for his benefit. It could even mean police would bend the right ear and request more serious charges being brought if it was believed the suspect deserved this, based on any information produced from his interrogation. I was hoping this would be the case with Coyake, as I was convinced he hadn't just turned a blind eye to the events of last Friday; he'd helped Alorami by strapping the PBIED to his body, and a police officer had died a violent death, as had ten ordinary civilians. I had absolutely no intention of doing him any favours.

"Okay." He nodded. "You remember me saying about this Brummie showing a couple of people how to disassemble a rifle? I pointed out one of them in a picture."

I agreed he had.

"Well, this guy" – he nodded at the picture of Sulluman – "was the other person there."

I instantly thought about what Joachim Balpak had said concerning Sherif Rizwi's interference with whatever operation the Mossad were pursuing. Was this in any way connected to it? "He come back after this?"

"Might have done, I don't know." He shrugged. "Why's Rashid's name coming up now?"

"Why? He attempted to kill the Israeli ambassador in Whitehall yesterday, that's why. Were you aware of anything like this being talked about or planned?"

Coyake's eyes opened wide in amazement. He shrugged, but he made no comment.

"You ever hear either of these two pilgrims, or any of the others, talking about any specific actions they had in mind? Something like this, for instance?"

"No, I was never a party to any talks they had."

"You just helped with the PBIED, is that it?"

He didn't respond. He was taken back down to the holding cells.

*

Back at my desk I was surprised to receive a call from Joachim Balpak. I was immediately curious as to how he'd know my contact details, but knew better than to ask.

"Thank you for what you did in Whitehall yesterday," he said.

"How'd you know it was me?"

"Do I *really* have to answer that?" He sounded amused.

He was very well informed.

"Did you know who the target was?" he went on.

"Not until I heard the news last night, no, I didn't. I just saw the two Daimlers with blacked-out windows, and then this pilgrim pulling out a Kalashnikov."

"Well, apart from a few bullet marks, nobody was injured and there's no collateral damage. Our ambassador got back to the embassy safely, which is gratifying."

"How would this gunman have known about your ambassador's visit to Downing Street, and when they'd be on the move?"

"This is what *we* want to know, which is why we're keeping a close eye on what happens next," he remarked, "as it's possible the British will not cooperate with Israel on this matter after the death of Rizwi."

There was nothing I could say in response to this.

"There's clearly a leak somewhere, either in your or our security," he stated forcefully, "and I find it hard to believe it's at our end. Our agent who died did so because of a leak from your man Rizwi, which is why we did what we had to."

I wasn't able to respond to this comment either.

"Well," he said after a six-second pause, "I just wanted to extend Israel's thanks for what you did yesterday. Just think: as I recall saying to you, if you people locked up these Arab terrorists and didn't let them walk around as free as uncaged birds, situations like this would not happen as frequently as they seem to. Didn't you lose a police officer a week ago, murdered just across the street from where yesterday's assassination attempt occurred?"

"It's called the rule of law, pal, y'know? You're free to do whatever until you break the law. This mean anything to you?"

"The rule of law, such a wonderful thing in the wrong hands." He sounded like he was being dismissive. "We'll talk again soon." He rang off.

While Balpak had been talking I had noticed a text message coming through on my mobile. It was from Taylor, stating she'd just found a message on her desk fro`m Ms Debbie Frost, asking her for my contact details.

Debbie Frost needed to talk to me? I was intensely curious; why she would want to do this? I texted Taylor back and said it'd be fine to pass my details along. She replied with *I told you, McGraw, she fancies you,* alongside an emoji with a laughing face. I replied with an emoji emitting a sour-faced groan.

Four minutes later my mobile sounded. It was indeed Debbie Frost.

"Oh, ah, hello, DS McGraw." I wasn't sure whether she sounded worried or embarrassed. "Would it be okay if we talked? I think I need your help."

She wanted *my* help? "Okay, in what way?"

"I'd sooner we talked face to face. Could we meet somewhere?"
"When?"
"When are you available?"

*

Ten minutes later I was in Starbucks at the Parliament Square end of Victoria Street, close by Conservative party main offices. I was seated by the window when she arrived. She was wearing a dark, professional business suit and a white blouse opened at the collar, and carrying a slimline attaché case. There was no denying she was a really attractive woman, though obviously, standing next to Taylor, she was a non-starter. She nodded at me, bought herself a black coffee and joined me at my table.

"Thanks for doing this," she began. "I expected you to slam the phone down on me when I called."

"I was gonna do that, I would've told Sally not to give you my contact details. Anyway," – I shrugged – "life just ain't long enough for any unpleasantness, is it?" I sipped my coffee. "Besides, your fiancé's Sally's boss."

"Yes, he is." She sipped her drink. "It was nice talking to Sally the other week, and getting to know her. I can see why Paul thinks she'll go places."

I nodded. "Thanks."

"Actually," – she paused for a moment – "it's him I want to talk to you about."

"Paul? What's he done?"

"Well, it's not all about him." She seemed nervous.

"So what is it?" I asked.

"It's like this." She leapt straight in. "I'm being blackmailed."

"By whom?"

"Someone in my family, actually, my cousin."

I knew who this cousin was, but I wasn't going to let on I did. Not yet, anyway.

She said nothing for eight seconds. Her facial expression and her sighing said she was finding this situation very uncomfortable.

I was going to have to prompt her. "And he or she is . . . ?"

"A very nasty little creep named William Desborough."

"Okay, who's he? And how and why's he blackmailing you?"

She then explained the situation to me.

Little Des had somehow unearthed the details of the abortion

Debbie Frost had undergone when her relationship with Tory MP Christian Perkins had ended a couple of years ago. I knew she'd aborted the foetus when Perkins had decided he wasn't going to leave his wife and set up home with Frost after all. Frost had attempted to resurrect the relationship by stealing documents pertaining to Perkins' involvement in a security service sting operation in the mid-1970s which, ironically, George Selwood had also been part of, and threatening to make them public unless he reconsidered his decision, though ultimately nothing came from her actions, and they'd since repaired their fractured friendship, as I'd once found to my cost.

Des had been aware of Frost's comments in her recent interview in the *Evening Standard*, concerning how the law on abortion should be tightened up, and had contacted his cousin, informing her he knew all about her abortion from her relationship with a much older man, a married MP. He had labelled her a hypocrite and threatened to go to the media with the story unless she paid him a substantial sum for his silence. He had said he'd get back to her with a figure soon.

"How would he have even got hold of those details?" I asked.

"I don't know, which is somewhat worrying." She sighed. "But what's even more worrying is, if news of this ever gets into print . . ."

She didn't complete her sentence, but then there was no need to. I knew, as did she, if this story was ever published, it would undermine her chances of winning the Norfolk seat she was contesting at the next election.

I decided to ask her anyway. "How harmful would publication be?"

"*Very*," she replied instantly, "especially after my comments in the interview with Sally last week." She paused for a moment, looking serious. "You're a man; you probably won't understand this like another woman would, like Sally would, but I felt tremendous, horrible, really horrible guilt after the abortion." She sighed heavily. "It really knocked me sideways. I was repulsed by what'd happened and I knew I'd done the wrong thing for the wrong reason, and I experienced some profound depression before I snapped out of it. So I've done a lot of thinking about this, and I've changed my view on abortion as a consequence." She paused again. "I don't wanna ban it, nothing like that, but you can just imagine what my political opponents might make of this."

"Have you told Paul about the blackmail threat?"

"Yeah, I have." She nodded. She was silent for a few seconds. "He knows all about the abortion, and also about my affair with Perkins."

We were quiet for a moment.

"But, now that he knows, Paul's threatening to go see Desborough and beat the crap out of him. I've told him it wouldn't help 'cause it'll give my cousin another reason to contact the press, but he says he's gonna do it, and that'll get him into trouble."

Just when her world seemed to be on an even keel again after the loss of her previous fiancé, Darren Ritchie ... finally selected to contest a seat, with a favourable press profile and a new love in her life ... along comes Little Des, one of her extended family, to pour sour milk all over her.

"Tell him it's *not* a good idea. Tell him there're other ways of dealing with your cousin." I had an idea in mind.

"So, I'm in a jam." She sighed. "What would you suggest I do?"

I mentioned, as to the blackmail threat, there wasn't much she could do just yet, because, as things stood, it was just her word against his. What she *should* do, though, was attempt to get some tangible proof. So, if or when William Desborough got back to her, she should record their conversation. Try to make him say as much as possible about why he was doing this, get him to incriminate himself, make him spell out *exactly* what he wanted. It'd be particularly important to ensure he talked about money, and mentioned a specific amount, when he wanted it by, and what he'd do if she didn't pay. This'd ensure there were no doubts about his intentions. *Then* she could go to the police, and they would take action, as blackmail was regarded as a particularly heinous offence.

She listened intently to what I was saying. "Hmm, yeah, that makes sense. Thanks." She nodded and smiled broadly. "I'll do that."

I drained my cappuccino. "So, *why's* he blackmailing you?"

"He wants money, why else?" She came straight back at me. "He thinks I'm loaded because I live in Chelsea, and won't miss a few thousand. I'm not, but, even if I was, the thought of paying *anything* to a repugnant little slug like him . . . *yeeuch*." She screwed up her face as though she'd just sat on a wet toilet seat.

She went quiet for a few seconds, staring at me with a quizzical expression.

"Did you *really* not tell Sally anything about me before she interviewed me?" She seemed amazed by this. "Or was she just being polite?"

"No, I really didn't; why would I?" I shrugged. "All I told Sally was about your car being stolen and all that. She doesn't know anything about anything else."

She was wondering whether to believe me or not.

"Well, thanks for the advice, detective." She went to stand up.

It then occurred to me to inquire *why* she'd asked if I'd told Sally anything about her before their interview, but for the moment I decided not to. Debbie Frost and I said our goodbyes and we went off in different directions.

*

Drake Mahoney was sitting opposite me in the interview room. His face still had a small bruise from our encounter on Wednesday, as did I, and he was looking his usual surly self as he tapped his fingers on the table.

"Any chance of getting a smoke?"

"Every chance out there," – I jutted my chin at the wall – "but not inside this building."

I placed a couple of pictures on the table.

"What can you tell me about him?" I pointed to Rahid Sulluman's picture and explained what he'd attempted to do in Whitehall yesterday. I didn't tell him about the role I'd played in preventing it.

He looked blankly at the picture for several moments.

"Anything you can tell us will count in your favour. Don't forget, there's still your scrape in the pub using a beer glass to be considered. You answer a couple of questions, and I might just be able to make any potential charges there go away."

"Yeah?"

"Yeah." I nodded.

He spilled his guts out. Sulluman had apparently been determined to die a martyr's death, either through a suicide bombing or by taking out a hated enemy with him, ideally a Zionist. One time in the flat, Mahoney had heard him proclaiming why he wanted a caliphate in the UK and how the Koran said the blood of the infidel must be sacrificed in his own kingdom to smooth the passage of the pilgrim into heaven.

"I didn't even know what a bloody caliphate was," Mahoney said, with a laugh. "He couldn't speak English very well; one of the other Arabs there had to translate for him. I know he also wanted to learn about firearms, and Danny showed him how to use rifles and handguns, how to reload, how to hide them on your person, things like that."

"Did you have *any* idea what he or others like him were planning?"

"No, nothing specific." He shook his head. "They were always talking about some big plan they had, but I never knew what it was. Didn't want to, either."

"Was your friend Danny in on this plan?"

"He showed them how to use firearms, but, other than that, I don't think so."

"So where's this Danny now? Where would he be likely to be hiding?"

"I dunno. Said it'd be better if I didn't know where he'd be staying."

"Who would he be likely to be staying with? Who else does he know in London?"

"I don't know."

"Danny giving instructions about how to use firearms suggests he's more than just a bit part in some plan to do something. You have *any* idea what he's involved with?"

"No." He shook his head.

*

Helen Mathison was led into the interview room, and the young female officer sat in the corner while I spoke to her. Mathison was red-eyed; she looked small and very frightened and I suspected she'd been crying, wondering how she'd gone from completing an overdue essay to ending up in a police cell.

It was a perfunctory session. No, she'd no idea what had been in the bag Rahid Sulluman had asked her to hold on to. She'd agreed to help him because he looked lonely and didn't know many people. He'd told her the bag contained only clothing and books and he'd take it back soon. No, Rahid had never talked politics with her, she'd never heard him talk about anything terrorism-related and their only real conversations had been about the subject they were both studying at Queen Mary's, and occasionally about his family back home, particularly his girlfriend in Lebanon, whom he said he hoped to marry when he returned home. She said she knew he went to a mosque in Islington to pray, but she knew none of his friends, and she recognised none of the names I mentioned to her. She'd never been to the flat on the Euston Road, though she knew who Florian Coyake was and didn't like him, and she didn't know Drake Mahoney. I believed her. One look at her eyes told me she was telling the truth.

I told her the only prints found on the bag had been Sulluman's and Chappy's. Helen said Chappy had placed the bag on top of the wardrobe for her but hadn't opened it and he didn't know what was inside it either.

After a quick confirmatory call to Smitherman I told Helen she was going to be released on police bail, which was a formality, and, as things stood, it might well be that she wouldn't be charged with anything, but she was to remain at the flat until any final decision was made. She readily agreed to this proviso.

*

Six forty. I was meeting Taylor from work. She'd said she'd be in Covent Garden this afternoon talking to someone about another story she was involved in on the paper, so I was going to meet her in the Sherlock Holmes, a pub a couple of hundred yards from Trafalgar Square.

I'd left the office and started walking eastwards along the Embankment, and I was just turning left by Embankment Gardens when I saw two men approaching me from the direction of Northumberland Avenue. Both were about my height and formally attired in jackets and trousers, shirts and ties. They stopped about three feet in front. One of them I didn't know, but the other looked familiar, and, after a moment, I realised who he was.

"Good evening, DS McGraw," he began.

I nodded. "Ian Gosling, isn't it?"

"Yes, that's correct. How you doing?"

Ian Gosling was the husband of Christine Simmonds, my

friend in MI5. Gosling was also an MI5 operative and, in fact, it'd been him who'd broken the news to me about my friend Michael Mendoccini's association with Red Heaven.

"You have a moment to talk?" the other one asked. He looked a little older than Gosling, probably late thirties, and he sounded very well spoken.

I was curious. I knew immediately their being here at this time was not a coincidence. Why did they want to talk to me, and why here?

I then noticed the man who'd just spoken had a small scar around his eye. Little Des had said a well-spoken man with a scar had assaulted him, and he hadn't been alone. Had it been these two and, if so, why?

"Yeah." I looked at my watch. I had a few minutes before meeting Taylor and the pub was only a couple of minutes away.

We wandered a few yards into the gardens and stopped by the first bench.

"So, is this an official unofficial conversation?" I asked. "I mean, is this gonna be logged?"

"It's like this," the unknown man started, but I immediately cut him off.

"First off, I know he's MI5," – I nodded at Gosling – "so who're you?"

"Name's Deacon, also MI5. We work in the same section." He looked at Gosling and flipped open an ID wallet, which he held up for me to see. I saw the name *Dominic Deacon*.

"Okay."

"We're talking off the record for the moment, detective," Deacon said. "Are you okay with this?"

I nodded my agreement.

"It's like this. Your wife is currently helping to put together an article in conjunction with someone who holds political views most definitely inimical to the better interests of this country."

"Who would this be?"

"His name's Stephen Jacobs. Do you know him?"

"I know who he is, but I don't know him."

"Well, he's an anarchist," Deacon said. "Not a bomb-throwing Peter-Kropotkin-style anarchist; one of the more modern type. Someone who believes in upsetting the established order of things, and doing it from the inside. The article he and your wife are proposing to publish will certainly do this, and it will also cause a considerable amount of embarrassment and anguish to certain well-placed individuals, several of whom are no longer in any position to refute any accusations which might be about to be levelled against them."

"Are they proposing to level accusations against anyone, then?" I asked.

Deacon continued without answering. "What particularly surprises us is the editor of the *London Evening Standard* was a Cabinet minister not a year ago, until he stepped away from frontline politics to take his current assignment, and yet he's sanctioned and commissioned this article. You would think, with his connections to Government, he'd be aware of the danger involved in publishing such a mischievous piece of work."

"Mischievous?" I queried.

"I don't believe this word is too strong, DS McGraw, considering the implications which'll arise if this story reaches the public domain," he stated, sententiously. "Are you aware of the subject matter of this article?"

"Why don't you tell me?"

Deacon then went into a lengthy diatribe about how this article was going to claim British soldiers had been directly engaged in unlawful acts of shooting and killing known IRA personnel. The article was also going to claim this policy had been officially sanctioned, despite public assurances to the contrary, by the then-Government, who'd given the green light to the army to act beyond their remit of being in Northern Ireland purely as a peace-keeping force. And, to rub more salt in the wound, it would claim innocent civilians had been killed as a result of this policy, and an official blind eye had been turned to this. All this I knew, but I didn't let on.

Deacon was still talking. "Mr Jacobs has been talking to several ex-soldiers about this, including, I'm led to believe, an ex-SAS officer, who would of course be prohibited from making *any* public comments concerning his activities whilst a member of this regiment, not least because he's covered by the Official Secrets Act."

I was aware of some of what Taylor and Jacobs had been

researching, but I wasn't quite sure of why Deacon was telling me this, so I made no response. We were silent for a number of seconds.

"This article will make the UK army out to be nothing more than an undisciplined rabble, killing indiscriminately irrespective of the consequences, and there'll be huge reputational damage to the international standing of our armed forces, not to mention the Government of the day, because most certainly there'll be questions asked down there." He nodded towards the Houses of Parliament.

I remained silent for a few seconds longer. Deacon was looking flustered, but Gosling was standing alongside him, hands in his jacket pockets, looking calm and relaxed.

"Are you saying what they're proposing to publish isn't true?" I asked.

"Whether or not it's true is beside the point, DS McGraw," Deacon came back with. "It's the impact the story'll have which concerns us."

I paused for a moment. "Look, this is all very interesting, but why are you telling *me* about it? I've nothing to do with what's being written."

"Oh, really?" Deacon smiled in a supercilious manner. "Is this why you went with your wife to see Dr Niall Redfearn earlier this week: because you're not involved?"

Redfearn had obviously made his displeasure known to somebody in a high place.

"I *know* Dr Redfearn," I replied calmly. "He's my family's GP; he lives in my hometown."

"Whatever the case, detective," he said, "I can tell you he was less than happy at being ambushed in his own home with accusations of malpractice in his duties as a doctor during his time in uniform, especially when he's still getting over the recent death of his wife." I hadn't known about this. "He believes his reputation and professional integrity are about to be smeared across the media."

"I didn't know about his wife, but I was there, and I can guarantee *no* such accusations were made," I stated slowly and firmly. "He was simply asked about certain procedural points relating to what was written on a couple of death certificates. He wasn't accused of anything. Sally simply asked him to clarify a few points concerning actual causes of death."

Deacon and Gosling looked at each other for a moment.

"Be that as it may," Deacon said, "we're talking to you here, off the record, because I'm hoping to impress upon you the seriousness of the damage this article will do when it's published." His voice was quiet but threatening. "And so, to this end, I'd like you to impress upon your fucking wife she really should desist from what she's doing."

"My *fucking what*, pal?" I instantly took a step forward, leant my forehead a millimetre away from his and pushed, rather than butted, him with it, furious at his tone. He recoiled and looked angrily at me. I tensed up. I was ready to go with him.

"Come on, chaps, there's no need for any of this." Gosling stood between us and pushed us apart. "We're all on the same side here."

An uneasy silence for three seconds.

"My apologies, detective," Deacon said softly. "That was out of order."

I nodded, accepting his apology. My anger receded.

"What I meant was this." He looked at me. "Your wife's record so far is unblemished, you understand? She's a vestal virgin so far as my department's concerned, and her loyalty can be counted upon, so it'd be a pity should this record be tarnished by being associated with an enterprise such as this."

"Is this some kind of threat?" I stared at Deacon.

"I believe Christine spoke to you over three weeks ago," Ian Gosling joined in, "concerning your wife working with Stephen Jacobs, and how she'd be doing herself a favour if she didn't get too close to him."

"Yeah, she did," I agreed, "but Sally makes her own decisions about what stories she works on, and her paper's happy with what they're doing."

"If her editor knew what *we* knew, he'd not be quite so sanguine about letting a story like this be run in his paper," Deacon suggested.

"Let's get something straight here," I said. "You're saying you want Sally to pull out of this story because she's helping Jacobs?"

"That would be a part of it, yes." Deacon nodded.

"So what would be the other part?" I asked.

Neither of the two men replied. I waited a moment.

"Or are you saying she shouldn't be doing this because what they're claiming is actually true and you don't want it published? Is *that* why you're talking to me?"

Nobody spoke for six seconds.

"We may talk again, DS McGraw," Deacon said. "In the meantime, consider this just a friendly chat, and also be aware this conversation *never* took place. Both my colleague and I are on record as being somewhere else at this very moment, and this'll be corroborated if necessary, so I'd be grateful if you kept this between ourselves for the moment." He raised his eyebrows as if asking a question.

"Yeah, I'll do that." I nodded.

They began to walk away, then stopped.

"Oh, and well done on yesterday." Deacon smiled. "First-class piece of police work. A fine tackle as well; we could use you at the Harlequins."

Deacon and Gosling then turned and walked away along the Embankment. They were hailing a taxi as I continued on my way to the pub.

Taylor hadn't arrived yet, so I bought her a large glass of wine and a pint for myself. I took a table and spent a few minutes thinking about my exchange with the two MI5 operatives. It was a nailed-on certainty this meeting hadn't been a chance encounter. They'd known where I was going to be at this time, and had waited for me as I was on my way to meet Taylor. There was only one way they'd have known this.

Was my or Taylor's phone being tapped?

She arrived eleven minutes late. It didn't matter; I'd wait much longer for her if I had to. I watched her walk across the bar and look around to see where I was sitting. I felt an intensely warm glow just looking at her. She saw me and came over.

I'd been debating whether to tell her of my recent close encounter with the two MI5 officers, and the advice they'd wanted me to give her, but for the moment I said nothing.

She said she'd not got back to me today because the only follow-up on yesterday's incident in Whitehall was just about Sulluman appearing briefly at Westminster Magistrates' Court and then being remanded in custody at Belmarsh pending trial.

"So, what did Debbie Frost want?" She smiled as she sipped her wine.

I trust Taylor implicitly, so I told her someone Frost knew was attempting to blackmail her, though I didn't say who, and she'd wanted to know what her best course of action was, so I'd given her a few pointers. As I was talking the thought hit me that Little Des was also blackmailing Alexander Bressington with what he knew about his stepfather's deviant sexual tendencies.

"And she was okay with your advice?"

"So far as I know. I await developments."

She took a sip of her wine, looking pleased. I soon found out why.

Her research into the shoot-to-kill story had led her back to the National Archives in Kew, where she'd been examining Cabinet minutes from meetings held in the summer of 1971, where issues relating to the worsening situation in Northern Ireland had been discussed. Some of the papers had been redacted, and others were still unavailable for public perusal, as they'd been exempted from the thirty-year rule, but she'd been going through everything that was available to her.

She'd done this because, when she'd begun looking into the story, and had taken a first look at Government documents, she'd come across a name she'd been interested in, given the position he'd held in 1971. She'd looked up his details and had asked to talk to him. He'd been away on holiday but had finally returned her call. He was living just outside London and had agreed to her request for an interview. Last evening she and Jacobs had been to talk to this person at his home in Petts Wood, North Kent, and what he'd told them had been astounding.

"So, which person was this?"

"Name's William Cardley."

"And who's he in the universal scheme of things?" I sipped some beer.

"Who's he?" She smiled as she moved closer to where I was sitting and lowered her voice. "He was an MP in the early seventies, and also one of the junior ministers in the Home Office involved in the special Cabinet committee GEN 47, which, among other things, discussed sending the SAS covertly into Northern Ireland. Their recommendations were put to the full Cabinet, which discussed everything the committee put forward."

"He was on the committee?"

"Sort of. He took the minutes of the meeting which went on to the Cabinet, *and*," – she beamed – "as a result of this Cabinet meeting, it would appear a tacit acceptance about shoot-to-kill was agreed upon."

"Officially agreed?"

"Oh, no, nothing like that. Just the notion, if the army were to use methods other than those laid down by law and the official army rules of engagement to defeat the IRA, this would not be unacceptable. It was more nods and winks and an implied *you know what I mean* stance, rather than any officially stated policy."

I sipped more beer and took in what Taylor was saying.

Taylor went on. "The legal problem the Government had was the country had never officially declared war on the IRA, even though they had on the Brits, and that complicated the matter as it wouldn't be covered by the Geneva Convention and the laws relating to the conduct of soldiers in wartime."

I thought about this for several seconds. "But he was okay with talking to you and Jacobs?"

"No problem at all. Steve threw a few points at him about the story we're putting together, and he agreed the matter was discussed in the committee and recommendations were put to the full Cabinet." She paused for a moment. "Actually, he was one of the sources for the BBC's programme on shoot-to-kill, the one we watched last week. A lot of what they aired came from what Cardley told them."

We sat quietly for a moment.

"So," Taylor said, "the Cabinet must have approved what was said, because this SAS guy told Steve they were sent into Northern Ireland in the summer of 1971, which was when the policy was instigated. The timeline seems to fit. Officially the SAS didn't get sent to Northern Ireland until 1976, but this seems to suggest otherwise."

She took another sip of her wine.

"It's all beginning to fall into place, McGraw. I think we've almost done it." She smiled. "We've proven what Pencourt said happened was probably correct, certainly on the balance of probabilities. It may well not have been an official policy, but there's little doubt there was something like this in existence. Everything we've been finding out points to it."

I'd heard from people like George Selwood the policy had been in existence as well.

"Great." I smiled at her. As I spoke, I was thinking about my recent encounter with Deacon and Gosling. "So, when's the *Standard* planning on publishing this?"

"Steve's got one more person to talk to, either today or tomorrow. He's not saying who it is just yet, but he says, if what he's hoping for comes off, he'll have hit the jackpot." Her voice rose slightly; she was excited about this. "Then we start putting it all together, and the plan is to have it published in the magazine inside a few weeks, once the editor and the legal people have cleared it."

We both drained our drinks and then got up to leave.

"Let's go get something to eat, then we can go back home and engage in some pillow talk."

"Pillow talk?" She smiled knowingly at me. "This usually comes after sex, doesn't it?"

I raised my eyebrows and smiled.

TWENTY-ONE

Saturday

"Drake Mahoney's going to be released on police bail," Smitherman informed me.

"Huh?" I was dismayed.

"All the evidence against him is speculative at best, isn't it?" he said. "True, we've found his fingerprints in the flat Coyake used, but they're not on any of the explosives or the weapons, are they? We can't definitively prove he was involved, so he's going to be released until we know more. We've got all the conjecture and speculation we can use, but we don't have enough on him to justify continued remanding him in custody. We can't really nail him with anything concrete, can we?""

I was reluctantly forced to agree this was quite probably true. There was plenty of circumstantial evidence against Mahoney, and several coincidences, but nothing definitive which would help ensure a conviction. Most of what we possessed, any half-decent defence lawyer would rip to pieces.

I reluctantly had Mahoney brought up to the interview room and gave him a brief synopsis of the situation. I informed him he was being released, but stressed this *didn't* mean he was off the hook, and I was still going to be investigating him and his known associates. Thus he was being released on police bail, but he ought to be aware a decision was pending concerning his potential culpability for any criminal acts, so, if he was smart, he'd keep a low profile and not associate with any of the people on our watchlist. He knew who I meant.

He was led away to sign the appropriate release from custody forms and allowed to leave. I'd little doubt he'd be back.

Despite an intensive police search across London, with several places being raided more than once, there'd been no sign of Tabzouni and el-Taccouli, or Adrian Bowketts. A watch had been kept on the Islington mosque they were known to attend, but they'd not been attending this past week either. Danny Hunter was still unaccounted for as well, which was also worrying.

My mobile sounded. It was Debbie Frost.

"My pathetic cousin phoned me again last night," she began, "and he came straight out with what he wants."

"Which was what?"

"He said he wants £10,000 immediately or he's going to the media and selling his story."

"Did you do as I suggested?" I ventured.

"I did indeed." She sounded excited. "He called my landline, so I recorded his comments on my mobile and got everything he said."

"Did it come out clear?"

"As a bell." She sounded happy. "Can you come to my office?"

Matthew Parker Street was only a ten-minute walk away, so I strolled along to Conservative party HQ and was shown upstairs to her office. There were no official meetings, so today was dress-down Saturday. Frost was wearing dark, expensive-looking blue jeans and a tight-fitting white T-shirt, which emphasised the swell of her body. Again, I wondered briefly whether Paul Grayley was turned on by Debbie Frost's body, given what I knew of his sexual inclinations.

"Listen to this," she began excitedly as I sat down by her desk. She placed her mobile phone next to me and pressed play.

It was definitely Little Des' voice, no question. He stated he wanted money, £10,000, and if she didn't pay within two days he was going to contact one of the tabloid newspapers and try to sell his story. He said he was sure they'd be interested in the story of a woman, a potential MP, stating the laws relating to abortion should be tightened up, when she herself had aborted a foetus arising from an affair with one of her senior Tory party colleagues, a married man and also an MP. She'd asked why was he doing this, and he'd replied *because you're a fucking hypocrite who deserves to be fleeced.*

What Little Des had said clearly fell within the purview of the 1968 Theft Act. I suggested she take it to the police station nearest to her home and report this. Or, alternatively, she could call his bluff, say and do nothing and let him take the next step. Then, if he went to the media, this would suggest a clear intent to act upon the blackmail threat, which would compound the offence. She agreed to wait until he contacted her again.

*

I was walking slowly back to the Yard and, as I crossed over Whitehall and began walking along Bridge Street, I thought I spotted a familiar face standing in the crowds at the entrance to Westminster tube station. He was with another man I didn't recognise, who was carrying a large canvas holdall and talking on his mobile.

The first man was idly looking around and, as I got nearer, I realised who it was. It was Andy Harris. What would he be doing here on a Saturday? This was usually one of his more lucrative days for thieving around Camden Market as the numbers of foreign student visitors increased. Also, Harris rarely travelled anywhere south of the Euston Road, believing it to be another country.

But something about the man he was with resonated with me. He was about my height and with a large build, though it didn't look like fat. It looked as though his talk on the phone wasn't going too well, as he appeared to be frustrated about something.

He didn't look like someone Harris would usually associate with either. I'd met several of Harris' friends and associates, and they were mostly like him, feckless and gormless, whereas this guy looked like a pub brawler.

I couldn't put my finger on it, but something about this unknown guy was gnawing at my police sensitivities. He and Harris together just didn't look right, so I withdrew my phone and surreptitiously snapped the pair of them several times, whilst pretending to be looking in a different direction.

The unknown man put his phone away just as I'd finished snapping them, looked at Harris and jerked his head towards the tube station. He picked up the holdall and they both disappeared inside.

I'd known Harris for almost six years. I'd just joined CID and started working in Neville Thornwyn's team as a wet-behind-the-ears DC when I'd first encountered him, and in all this time I'd never known him to associate with people like the one I'd just seen him with. Who *was* this guy?

Back at my desk I logged on to the PNC and typed Harris' name. I knew he had a criminal record for shoplifting and various other offences relating to theft. His picture was a few years out of date and didn't do him any justice; he was far more dishevelled than this.

I typed in *known associates* and several names appeared. A few I recognised or knew about, so I clicked on the two I didn't.

Bingo. The first picture looked like the man I'd just seen with Harris. I checked it against the picture on my phone. It was indeed the same guy.

His name was Joe Simpson, aged thirty-eight. He was known to be on the muscle end inside the Chackarti family, working as a debt collector and bouncer at various locations around London, under the auspices of George Duncan, a man I'd once had some dealings with. Simpson'd had one spell inside for aggravated assault and he was suspected of being implicated in several others, though charges hadn't been proffered. His profile described him as *someone to avoid in a one-to-one situation*. What would Harris be doing with *this* guy?

I clicked on to details of Simpson's immediate family and gasped, open-eyed in amazement, when I saw his family connections.

He was the younger brother of Stanley Simpson, a notorious thug who'd been head of security at Las Vargas, a pub-cum-club in Wood Green, which was also a well-known hangout for the Chackarti family. Stanley was now serving eighteen years in Parkhurst on the Isle of Wight. I'd had a small part in his arrest and he absolutely deserved every moment he was inside.

I was then even more amazed to see Joe Simpson's sister was named Stella, and her picture was of the woman I've seen in Harris' flat. She too had a police record, but mainly for offences relating to the receiving and disposing of stolen property.

Dear God ... Andy Harris was shacked up with the younger sister of one of London's most notorious thugs, Stanley Simpson, and I'd just clocked him with Stanley's equally thuggish brother.

*

It was just after six and I was about to sign out. But, despite having had a busy afternoon, I'd also been thinking about why Harris had been with Joe Simpson. Even allowing for Simpson being the brother of his lady friend, why would Harris be out with him? Harris usually spent his weekends working, particularly this time of year, which meant stealing wallets, purses, mobiles and tablets from all the foreign students around Camden Market.

I phoned the landline in Harris' flat from the office, and Stella answered. Even if she dialled 1471 afterwards, my number would be withheld, so I was safe. I disguised my voice to sound like someone Harris would be likely to associate with at the nearby pubs where he drank and placed his bets. I asked where Andy was and why he wasn't down here in the pub, as we'd got a few bets on the rugby and today's racing from Chepstow, and we were going to watch them on the pub's TV.

"Oh, he's gone down south with Joe to see one of Joe's friends. Not sure when he'll be back; sometime tonight, I imagine." Her voice was pure North London.

"I've just rang his mobile and he ain't answering, so I thought I'd see if he was still at 'ome, like."

"No, he's left his phone here as the battery's dead. Sorry 'bout that."

"Oh, that's alright. Who's Andy gone to see, anyway?" I asked. "Didn't know he had any friends on the south coast."

"Nah, not the south coast, South London," Stella said, laughing, "and it's not Andy's friend; it's Joe's. Someone he knows is staying down Brixton way and they've gone to take something down to him."

"He's not gone pinching, 'as he? He don't know the markets round there like he does up this way."

"No, I don't think so." Stella sounded amused. "Andy's just gone with Joe 'cause his mate Beau needs something, and he's unable to come back up this way to get it."

My police instinct instantly kicked in. There was something about this comment I was finding it hard to get hold of. I was certain there was more here, but I couldn't ascertain what it was.

"Oh, okay. Tell Andy I'll see him in the pub sometime."

I rang off before she could ask who was calling.

I went back online to bring up Joe Simpson's file and check out any known associates going by the name Beau, surname and Christian names. I checked Beau, Beaumont, Baudelaire, Bauden and Beauregard, plus others, but no matches. I entered *Beau* into the PNC to check if anyone associated with the Chackartis had this name but drew a blank. I'd get in touch with Harris directly tomorrow. Something sounded off here.

*

Back in the flat. Taylor had arrived home a few minutes before me and was in the kitchen, pouring herself a glass of wine, when I came in. She took a bottle of beer from the fridge and passed it to me. She was beaming.

After a warm hug and kiss, we retired to the lounge and slouched down onto the couch. I was about to ask her what she was smiling about when she told me something which, I was to discover later, would have profound ramifications for her story.

"You remember what I said about Steve last night, about someone he still has to talk to?"

I nodded. "Yeah."

"He met up with him today. Well, actually," – she grinned – "confronted him, more like. Steve found out where he retired to, down in Devon somewhere, and went to see him because he particularly wanted to talk to this guy. When he told me earlier today who it was and, in particular, what this person ended up as, I was staggered. I couldn't believe it."

"Okay, who is it?" I was intrigued.

"You remember me saying Pencourt was never told the name of the officer, the one who shot and killed Brendan Morgan?"

I nodded.

"Well, Steve's managed to uncover the identity of this officer, and that's who he's been to see today."

"How'd he do this?"

"Don't know; just says he has sources he can ply for information." She sipped her wine. "Anyway, Steve travelled to Devon and went to his house. The man was in and Steve said who he was and said he'd like to talk to him. The guy asked about what, and Steve replied with *how about your time in command of something called Two Unit? You were in charge of this unit, weren't you?*"

"How'd this guy respond?"

"Not at all pleased." Taylor shook her head, smiling. "Then Steve told him he knew all about Two Unit and what it was set up for. Asked if he had any comment to make for the story."

"What'd this guy say?"

"Initially the guy stonewalled him, didn't say anything. Steve asked him if he'd like to go on the record about Morgan's death, but the guy said he'd no idea what he was talking about. Then Steve told him he had proof he was in command of Two Unit, and he knew Morgan had been executed rather than just shot dead. He told this guy he'd heard it'd been *him* who'd fired the shots killing this innocent kid, and he had sworn statements from people who'd be prepared to back this up."

We both sat quietly for a few moments.

"Steve also told him about the one they'd pulled off the street and taken to a deserted barn somewhere, the one who died from the beating he got. Again, this guy doesn't respond, just stares at Steve."

She sipped her drink. I took a drink from my bottle.

"But Steve says his reaction suggested he'd touched a nerve, he could see it in his eyes, and the guy *didn't deny it either*, just started stammering. Then, somewhat amazingly, he said something about how *this was all so very long ago* and told Steve to go away as he's not talking to him. Steve said this is all gonna come out in our article, and we're gonna name you, but the guy just slammed the door on him."

We sat quietly for a few more moments. I could imagine his discomfort at being confronted on his own doorstep by someone telling him they knew he was a murderer and they were planning to publish it.

"You said something about where this person ended up," I said. "Where was this?"

"That's the thing. Not long afterwards, this guy leaves the army and joins the police."

She paused but, from her expression, I could sense there was more to come. When it came I couldn't conceal my utter amazement.

"And he eventually ended up becoming the head of Special Branch."

"*Whaaat?*" I sat up so quickly I almost spilled both our drinks.

Taylor recoiled at the speed of my reaction.

"*Special Branch?* When was this?" My voice registered utter astonishment, almost shock.

She waited a moment before continuing. "He retired ten, eleven years ago. Your boss is Smitherman, right?"

"Yeah," I nervously agreed.

"And who was before him?"

I thought for a moment. "Commander Norman Allerton. Smitherman took over from him when he retired."

"Well, this guy was the one before Allerton."

I didn't know who this was. "So, what's this person's name?"

"His name's Paul Deacon, though he's now *Sir* Paul Deacon as he received a knighthood the year he retired. Services to law enforcement."

Deacon? The MI5 officer who'd spoken to me last night had said *his* name was Deacon. Was he a family member, a son, grandson or nephew? I now knew for certain Dominic Deacon meeting up with me last evening was no coincidence.

Jesus. The ex-head of Special Branch was going to be accused of first-degree homicide in this article. This would light a fuse under the security service; there was no doubt of that. What would be their response when this went viral, as it certainly would?

I took a few deep breaths. Taylor saw the amazed look on my face.

"Oh, don't worry, we'll probably not give names in what we write," she assured me. "We'll just mention events and so on. It'll be up to the lawyers whether names will be mentioned anywhere, though the fact Deacon achieved a position of some prominence in law and order circles will be."

I was reeling from what I'd just heard. This was sensational stuff. I took a few deep breaths and sat back on the couch. Did Smitherman know anything about this? "You do realise, don't you, as head of Special Branch, you're considered to be only a few rungs down the ladder from God himself?"

Taylor smiled at this comment, but it wasn't quite as flippant as she assumed it to be. Head of Special Branch was a highly respected and exalted position in the security structure of the UK, with the decisions this person had to take occasionally having wide-reaching implications for public safety and order generally. A failure to consider all available evidence, or getting a decision wrong, could lead to many innocent people dying, or the security of the country being put in jeopardy. It was a highly pressurised position, and anyone holding this office was expected to be above and beyond reproach, yet Jacobs had discovered something in

Paul Deacon's past which should have militated against him ever being in a police uniform, never mind an exalted position of authority.

But Taylor was relaxed and pleased with the results of her and Jacobs' efforts these past few weeks. "We're on the home strait now, McGraw." She was beaming. "We've now traced, or rather Steve has, two of the soldiers in Two Unit, one of whom agreed with what Pencourt said about how Morgan died, and when Steve got back in touch and gave him the name Deacon, he agreed it was him in charge of the unit. And now we've got the officer in charge of the unit, plus we have the evidence the death certificates have probably been doctored." She sounded excited.

We paused for a moment.

"I'm meeting Steve tomorrow and we're gonna start outlining the story, then putting it all together." She was in full-on journo mode. "We're also gonna be talking to the editor next week sometime about everything we've found."

"You guys have done good." I gave her a hug and she leaned into me. We sat like this for a long several seconds. Usually this would be the warmest of feelings, having the woman of my dreams curled up next to me like this, but inside I was shaken up.

For the first time since she'd spoken to Pencourt, I was now very apprehensive for Taylor because of the impact I knew this story was almost certain to have.

*

One oh-nine. Taylor was lying next to me, and I was listening to her breathing softly because I was finding sleep hard to achieve. My mind was spinning with the revelation the ex-head of Special Branch, if Jacobs' sources were accurate, was directly implicated in the cold-blooded murder, execution, of two innocent people. This was without all the other killings Pencourt had spoken about involving Two Unit, which Deacon had been in command of. If even half of this ever became public knowledge, what would be the public reaction, as well as the implications?

I gently extricated myself from Taylor, got up and went into our little office. I switched on my laptop, logged on to the Branch site and then entered the name *Sir Paul Deacon*. As I'd expected, there was a lengthy file on him. I didn't doubt this wasn't the full picture, but it was more than sufficient for my purposes.

He'd left the army in the mid-seventies and had joined the police here in London. But, in the early eighties, as a detective sergeant, he'd been recruited by MI5 and had risen through the ranks, eventually becoming a senior intelligence analyst. He'd remained there until he'd been offered the chance to become head of Special Branch, which he'd accepted, and had held the post until his retirement.

I read some of the comments about him and a brief synopsis of some of the cases he'd been involved in. He'd still been head of Special Branch when the 7/7 bombings occurred in 2005 and he'd been praised for how he'd handled the investigation into, and the aftermath of, the situation. He'd retired with a stellar reputation inside security and he'd been highly regarded by everyone he'd served with, and even the Queen evidently agreed as he'd been awarded a knighthood for his services to law enforcement throughout a long and distinguished career. He was also listed as being a current advisor to the Home Secretary when matters of security came up to be considered.

I checked his family details and discovered he had one son, Dominic, also in MI5, and the picture displayed was of the same person who'd spoken to me yesterday concerning the story and what it was likely to mean. I briefly wondered whether Dominic knew about his father's past and whether, if he did, this was why he'd come on so strongly towards me, as he didn't want his father's reputation besmirched.

But what came as a *real* shock to me, looking at the elder Deacon's family tree, was the discovery he was related to Paul Grayley. Deacon's sister, Edwina, had married George Grayley, and they'd had a son, Paul, who was a journalist and currently held the position of political editor on the *London Evening Standard*.

I took a deep breath. I remembered Clements telling me Paul Grayley had avoided arrest and prosecution after being caught trying to access indecent images of children because he'd a relative in the security service who'd managed to pull strings, hush the matter up and keep him off the sex offenders' register.

This relative I now knew to be Sir Paul Deacon.

TWENTY-TWO

Sunday

Mid-morning. I'd been thinking about my conversation with Stella concerning where Harris had been going when I'd seen him by the tube station. Joe Simpson was with the Chackartis, but Harris' only connection with them was storing contraband in his flat. Why would he be going to Brixton with this Simpson? I wanted to know, so I phoned Andy Harris' mobile, curious about what answers he'd give to my questions. He answered.

"Andy, who was the guy you were with yesterday?" I began.

"Where'd you see me, then?"

I told him where I'd spotted him early yesterday afternoon.

"Oh yeah." He sounded amused. "We'd got the wrong bus at King's Cross, so we got off in Whitehall and got the tube to Victoria, then another tube from there."

"So, who was the guy?" I repeated.

"Oh, 'im, 'e's Stella's brother, Joe," he replied. "He's a bouncer at the pub where that bloke, the one I told you about, got into that scrap. Joe and another bouncer broke it up, told them both to behave themselves or they'll get a slapping from them. You don't wanna mess with Joe, Mr Jack."

"Where were you going when I saw you yesterday?"

"Brixton."

"Brixton? What's down there?"

"Joe had to deliver something to someone he knows who's staying in the area."

"You know where it was?"

"Some place on the Loughborough estate, but I don't know the area so I don't know the address, sorry."

"What were you delivering?"

"Dunno, he didn't say. Whatever it was was in the bag he had."

"Who's his friend down that way?"

"Think he said his name was Beau, or something like that."

"You see this guy? What'd he look like?"

"No, I didn't see him. But that's the funny thing, see. We get off the tube, like, and we go to this estate. Bloody hell, it's really rough down that way, Mr Jack. Anyway, he tells me to go wait in the café on the main road, and he goes off to see this . . . whoever it was."

"So you didn't see who Joe was delivering the bag to."

"No."

"You know anything about this person?"

"No." He paused for a moment. "Only that Joe says it would be in my best interest not to know his mate or where he's staying."

This didn't sound right. "He say why?"

"Nah, didn't say, just told me to go to the café and wait."

Why would Joe take Harris with him, then tell him to wait in a café?

"Joe was a bit narked about having to go down to Brixton; that's why he had the hump. He said it was easier getting stuff to him when he was staying in North London."

"North London?" I was curious.

"That's what he said. Apparently his friend was staying with Little Des at his place for a while, but he's had to move down to Brixton."

Little Des?

A thought flashed into my brain. The name Beau had been mentioned. Little Des had recently had a house guest named Bowketts. Could this Beau character actually be Adrian Bowketts?

I then remembered someone else had mentioned Brixton recently. Who was it?

"Right, Andy, you're gonna keep this conversation all to yourself. Do *not*," I stressed, "I repeat, do *not* tell this Joe or Stella you've spoken to me. You got that? *Very* important you keep this to yourself."

"Yeah, okay. What's all this about, Mr Jack?" Harris sounded puzzled. "Why you asking me all these questions?"

"You don't need to know, Andy, but what you *do* need to know is, if the situation's what I think it is, you could be in some very serious trouble if you get too close."

"Oh, bloody 'ell, Mr Jack." He sounded worried.

"So stay quiet. In fact, try and stay clear of your girlfriend's brother for the next couple of days, until I know the exact extent of the situation. We clear?"

"Righto, Mr Jack, I'll keep schtum."

*

Brixton. Who'd mentioned Brixton? Someone had recently mentioned Brixton, and I was trying to remember who and what the context was.

I brought up the case notes and flicked through them. *Eureka.* There it was. Florian Coyake had said he wasn't always in the flat above the amusement arcade as he sometimes stayed with his girlfriend in Brixton.

I thought about the people involved. Bowketts knew Tabzouni, el-Taccouli and Alorami. Alorami had been the suicide bomber who'd killed eleven people in Whitehall nine days ago, and he'd been assisted, I was convinced, by Coyake, who claimed not to have been in the flat on certain occasions as he'd stayed in Brixton. This was stretching coincidence, but we had no other leads to go on. I put my theory to Smitherman, who agreed there could be something there and to look into it.

Coyake was brought up from the cells again. He was still antsy at being held in custody without having been charged. He sat with his arms crossed, looking very annoyed. I still couldn't care less about how he felt.

I leapt right in. "Your girlfriend lives in Brixton, is this right?"

"Yeah, she does." He looked curious. "What's she got to do with anything?"

"Is it on or near the Loughborough estate?"

"Why?" He sat back in the chair.

"Because we've received information making us think she may have company staying at her place and, as we think it could be someone we particularly want to talk to, we need to check this out. What's your girlfriend's name?"

He sat silent for several seconds. It was noticeable he was avoiding looking at me.

"Okay, here's the deal, pal." I sat forward. "Either you give me her name and address in the next five seconds, or I'll have you charged with obstructing a murder inquiry, plus with conspiracy to conceal somebody wanted in connection with a terrorist offence. This'll guarantee a few more years to your sentence." I paused for a moment. "You forgotten *why* you're in custody, Florian? I can make things *so* much worse for you."

He sighed and bit his lip, looking at me like I was something he wanted to tread on and squash.

"Her name's Grace Vassos," he said reluctantly.

"And her address?"

He told me the address. I asked him to describe the area around her building and how to access her flat to minimise the chance of being seen. He told me. I then asked if she had any family or close friends in the area.

"Her sister lives nearby. Why?"

"What's the name?"

"Denise." He told me her address. "It's quite near Grace's place."

"Name like Vassos, they Greek?"

"Cypriot."

"You've done yourself a favour here, Florian."

He didn't look convinced.

*

Coyake was returned to custody and I ran the Vassos sisters through the PNC. No black marks against either name, though I noted Denise, the younger sister, was also a student at Queen Mary's. Another coincidence. Did she also know Rahid Sulluman?

I contacted Brixton police station, spoke to a DS I knew and asked him if a uniform could meet me on the Loughborough estate. He agreed to this. Fifteen minutes later I parked around the corner from my destination and saw a uniform walking towards me. I identified myself, explained the purpose of my visit to the area and what I'd like him to do.

Denise Vassos lived in a first-floor flat in a terraced row of houses. As it was a Sunday she was home and answered on the first knock. I identified myself and asked if I could come in and talk to her about her sister along the road.

"Grace? She's in here with me. Why'd you need to know about her?"

She stepped aside and I entered. We went into the lounge, where Grace Vassos was sitting on the couch. She stood up as I entered.

The sisters looked alike; both looked like they came from the Mediterranean, and both about five-four with lots of dark hair and big brown eyes. They were wearing T-shirts and blue jeans, torn fashionably in all the right places but revealing nothing.

Grace eyed me suspiciously as I approached her. I showed ID.

"You know Florian Coyake, don't you?" I began.

"Yes, he's my boyfriend, been together over a year. Though I'm starting to get worried as I've not seen or heard from him for the past week or so, and I can't raise him on his phone either, so I don't know where he is, if you're here about him." She sounded defensive.

"Oh, I know exactly where he is."

Her eyes opened wide, expectantly.

"He's been arrested and being held in custody, pending charges relating to the aiding of a terrorist incident a week ago."

She shook her head and sighed resignedly, as though what I'd just told her had come as no real surprise at all.

"But, if you wanna help him, you can answer a few questions," I told her.

"Like what?"

"Like have you ever been to his flat over the arcade on Euston Road?"

"Twice, I think," she nervously replied. Hers were probably among the prints we hadn't been able to identify.

I produced my police phone and loaded up pictures. "You ever see any of these persons on the premises?"

I showed her pictures of Sam Alorami, Drake Mahoney and Danny Hunter.

"Yes, those two." She'd pointed to Alorami and Hunter.

"You know why they were there?"

"No." She shook her head.

"Did Florian ever talk about either of them?"

"Not to me, no," she replied quietly.

"Is there anybody staying in your flat at the moment, apart from yourself?"

She looked nervously at her sister, mouthing something I couldn't understand to her. Denise nodded in reply.

"Yes, been there over a week now, which is why I'm here. I was told to stay out the way."

"By who?"

"By someone Florian knows. I was told this person needed to lie low for a few days, so I was to move into here and give him some space."

"And Florian was okay with this?"

"Yeah, said it'd be a big help to him if I let this person use my flat."

"Help in what way?"

"He didn't really say, just said it'd be a big help to him."

I produced my police phone again. "Is this who's in your flat?"

She looked closely. "Yeah, it's him."

I'd shown her a picture of Adrian Bowketts.

"Anyone else there with him? Two Arabs, for instance?" I asked hopefully, thinking of Tabzouni and el-Taccouli.

"Not that I know of." She shook her head.

"Is he still there now?"

"I've not been told if he isn't."

I remembered something else. "Denise, you're a student at QM, right?"

"Yes." She was nervous.

"Do you know a Rahid Sulluman?"

"Rahid? Yeah, he's on my course. He's in my seminar set."

"Helen Mathison's in the same set, isn't she?"

"Helen? Yes, she is. Why?"

"You friends with Rahid?"

"Sort of," she said guardedly. "We talk occasionally."

"Has he ever asked you to hold on to something for him, a bag or a rucksack, something like this?"

She thought for a moment. "Yes, a rucksack. Said he had nowhere to store it, so he asked if he could leave it with me here until he gets a place to store the stuff in it."

"Where's this bag now?"

"It's in my flat," Grace leapt in. "The guy in there asked me to bring it over to him."

Sulluman was clearly spreading his resources around London. This would make it so much easier to prepare something sinister.

"Right, Grace, gimme the layout of your flat, inside and outside ..."

She did. For the next ten minutes she described her flat in some detail: entrance, the layout of the four rooms, what was in them and, what particularly intrigued me, being a ground-floor flat, the back exit.

After a couple more questions, I swore the sisters to secrecy and told them not to go to Grace's flat today, or to contact it, but to remain where they were in case we needed to speak to them again. They agreed they would do this.

Outside, I told the uniform to patrol the area around the flat.

In Brixton police station I told the desk sergeant I wanted Grace Vassos' flat kept under discreet observation, around the clock. Anyone came out, I wanted to know who they were and I wanted them followed. Anyone went in, same procedure; I wanted to know who they were and where they went. I wanted to know about anyone who even looked at the flat as they walked past.

Smitherman was pleased by the news I gave him, and also by the fact I'd got the flat under observation. He'd liaise with Counter Terrorism Command, SO15, to devise a plan to go in and grab Bowketts. I was pleased to hear I was to be involved in it.

TWENTY-THREE

Monday

I'd texted Taylor mid-evening yesterday, explaining I'd be stopping for the night in a section house just off the Embankment as, very early in the morning, I'd be involved in a counter-terrorism action, and I had to be close by for briefings *et cetera*. She texted back with *I'll look forward to seeing the news tomorrow. Be careful, McGraw, I LOVE YOU.* I replied with something about how gorgeous and sexy she was, after which she sent a smiling emoji. I then began mentally psyching myself up for what would soon be happening.

Four forty-five am. It was still dark. I'd been awake since 4.05 am and, after a team briefing by an SO15 operative, we set off.

London was quiet this time of the morning, and I could feel the adrenaline pumping as we drove towards Brixton. We turned off the main Brixton Road into the Loughborough estate and, as we approached our destination, the engine was switched off and the van glided quietly to a halt. The driver and the five other men inside very quietly exited the van and stood on the corner.

All six of us were dressed appropriately. Four SO15 operatives were head-to-toe body protected, and carrying assault rifles. The officer in charge and I were wearing Kevlar body protectors, stab vests. The area was dark and deathly quiet and I could hear no sound or movement, other than some distant traffic. The officer in charge had ordered police cars to be parked either end of the road to prevent access to the area by other vehicles.

We quietly moved along by the side wall, approaching the door to Grace Vassos' building, and stopped by the front gate. There was a path about twenty yards long leading to the entrance. Once inside, Grace's flat would be first on the left.

One of the officers quietly crept up to the front of the building, did something to the lock and delicately opened the main door. The officer in charge and three others entered the premises, while I and another SO15 operative took up our position behind the building, just inside the back gate. We readied ourselves and I signalled we were in place over the radio.

On a prearranged signal, the officer with the thumper smashed the lock to Grace's flat and all four men entered, shouting *Armed police!* loud enough for me to hear outside. I could see the lights on their weapons in the dark room. Three seconds later the back door opened and I could see a shape running fast down the garden. As he closed on the gate I stepped out from behind a wheelie bin and pushed it into his path. He wasn't expecting this and he collided with the bin. His forward momentum carried him over the top of the bin, and he landed awkwardly on his left shoulder; I heard him yell out.

I immediately leapt over the bin and, as he scrambled to get to his feet, in one flowing movement I pushed him back on the ground, dropped to one knee, spun him over onto his front, planted my knee firmly in the base of his spine, my left hand pinning his head to the ground and my right hand holding a gun to the side of his head. The other uniform stood in front, pointing an assault rifle very close to his head. My gun was also pointed at him.

"You're under arrest, pal, lie still, don't fucking move," I hissed forcefully. I looked up at the other uniform. "Cuff him."

He did. I pulled the person we'd caught roughly to his feet and turned him around. It was Adrian Bowketts, the same person who'd shot at me in Little Des' house. At the same moment the other officers came running outside. Everything from the flat door being forced open to Bowketts' arrest had taken precisely fourteen seconds.

"This Bowketts?" the officer in charge asked me.

"Yeah, this is him."

"Take him in." He nodded to one of his operatives. "Good work, men. We've wanted this one for a while."

Bowketts was led away. I could see a number of lights in the building had now come on, with people wondering about the commotion, plus some shouted comments and torrents of abuse from people unhappy with the police presence. The lead officer looked at me again, shaking his head.

"Fucking people, why do we even bother, eh?" he said quietly, looking disgusted. "Anyway, how'd you know Bowketts was here?"

"A stroke of good luck."

It was, as well. Had Debbie Frost not asked to see me, I'd not have spotted Harris by the tube station, and I'd not have received the break we'd just had.

*

Late morning; I'd showered, had a debriefing session and a couple hours' rest and was now back on duty.

"Well done on the arrest, DS McGraw." Smitherman looked as though he was in celebratory mode. The entire office was buzzing and everyone seemed pleased at the arrest of someone on our wanted list for some time. His expression then changed to one of sheer disbelief. "The flat was searched after Bowketts was led away. You know what was found?"

I shook my head. I didn't.

"A couple of packs of ricin."

My eyes opened in amazed horror. *What?*

"Yes." He nodded. "This bastard was in the process of sprinkling some in padded envelopes. He'd all the gear to do this safely, and was going to post them to those he intended to kill, who we found on the list he'd written out."

"Such as who?"

"People like the Prime Minister, Home Secretary, governor of the Bank of England, prominent MPs, important people like this."

I remembered Smitherman telling our meeting, a few weeks back, about Sherif Rizwi overhearing someone say something about bringing London to its knees. Could *this* have been what they'd had in mind? Had Alorami's suicide attempt been just a sideshow, a diversionary tactic? "How would he have even got hold of ricin?"

"Don't know. This is one of the things MI5'll want to know. They've got him secreted away somewhere and are interrogating him" – he looked at his watch – "about now. But they found a holdall and the evidence suggests it was delivered to him in this."

This was why Grace Vassos had been ordered to stay away from her flat, so Bowketts could work in seclusion and undisturbed. I'd seen Joe Simpson with a holdall Saturday afternoon. He'd been the one delivering it to Bowketts. But had he *known* he was ferrying a deadly poison across London?

"I think I know who by," I volunteered. I explained my thinking to Smitherman.

*

Joe Simpson lived in North London, in a flat just off Wood Green High Street. DS Roberts was waiting outside and I brought him up to speed.

"I know this bastard," Roberts said. "He's Stan Simpson's younger brother and just as big a scumbag."

I agreed he probably was as I knocked. The man answering said, as I showed ID, Joe wasn't in and was probably at Las Vargas having a drink.

Las Vargas was surprisingly full of late lunchtime drinkers, mostly male and watching a sports programme on TV, and I spotted Simpson talking to another man. We approached and he looked up. He made us as police immediately. Maybe I do have *the look*. I showed ID.

"Joe Simpson, get up, you're under arrest," I ordered him.

"What for? I ain't done nothing," he protested.

"Get up, Simpson," Roberts said forcefully, moving past me and towards him.

Simpson sighed and slowly stood up. I took out hand restraints and placed them around his wrists. We led him out the pub, aware of the fact most of the noise had subsided and we were being watched by everybody present. I looked at the counter and saw where my friend and colleague DI Paul Glett had been stabbed. We took Simpson to the car and I drove him back to the Yard.

*

In the interview room I sat opposite Simpson. He was looking like he couldn't understand why he'd been arrested. All the way back he'd asked *What've I done?* ad nauseam, but neither Roberts nor I had answered, and he'd eventually sat silently, sulking.

I had his file. I'd looked at it yesterday and it didn't make any better reading today. I put it down and looked directly at him. "Right, Joe, you wanna know why you're here, don't you?"

"Yeah, I bloody do," he snapped.

"Okay, I'll tell you. Saturday afternoon, we think you delivered a bag, a large holdall, to a flat in Brixton." I told him the address.

He looked surprised.

"You were seen entering the building, Joe. We've had the flat under observation for some while, and you were eyeballed going in carrying a bag, but when you left, not too long after, you didn't have the bag. You denying this?"

He didn't reply.

"And you weren't wearing gloves, so my bet is we'll find your fingerprints when the lab boys finish their examination of it."

He sat silently, nodding to himself, for eight seconds.

"Okay, I delivered a bag; what about it?" he eventually said.

"You know what was *in* the bag?"

He was registering the expressions on my and Roberts' faces, and he was now looking very nervous. I waited six seconds for an answer.

"Well, do you?"

"No."

"It was ricin, Joe. You know what this is?"

"No." He shook his head. "I mean, I've heard of it, but I don't know what it is."

"It's a highly potent toxin, Joe," I stated, "and it's hard to get hold of anything much more lethal than this. Even being exposed to a tiny piece, probably a fraction the size of a grain of salt, can be fatal. You're opening mail and any of it gets onto your skin, and then you touch your mouth or eat something with your hands, you're dead."

His eyes opened wide in amazement.

"And this is what you delivered to Brixton." I paused for a moment to let my words sink in. "You delivered enough ricin to kill several hundred people."

He looked stunned.

"The flat was raided early this morning, and we've arrested the person who was packaging it up into envelopes, the person you gave the bag to. The people he was sending it to wouldn't have opened the envelope. Important people don't open their own mail, Joe, so it'd likely be some poor sod, probably a junior clerk working for minimum wage in the mail room, who'd've done this, and probably died as a result. And," I stressed, "we're gonna find your fingerprints on the handle of the bag."

I sat back and watched him squirm.

"I didn't know what was in the bag," he said, sounding nervous, "and I didn't ask either. I was just asked to deliver it to the address I took it to. That's straight up, on my life."

"Who'd you give it to?"

"The man in the flat. I just knocked on the door, he was expecting me. I went inside, he took the bag and I left. That's all I was asked to do."

"You know who you gave it to?"

Simpson shook his head. "No, never seen him before."

"Really?" I was doubtful.

"Yeah, really."

Harris and Stella both knew the bag had been for a *Beau*, so I knew Joe Simpson did as well, but for the moment I didn't press the issue.

"Well, he's a terrorist, Joe," I said calmly. "He's usually a bomber, but it seems he's going upmarket and looking for a classier, more imaginative way to kill more people."

He didn't respond.

"So," I said, "what we really wanna know is *who* asked you to deliver the bag."

He sat quietly. I waited nine seconds.

"Okay, I'll ask you one more time. Who asked you to deliver the bag?"

Again, no answer. He was now looking very frightened and breathing erratically.

"I admire your loyalty, Joe." I stood up. "I really do, but not answering means you're gonna have to take one for the team on this. The ricin was in a bag, which *you* delivered. Now, if you were to tell us who asked you . . ."

"If I tell you, I'm a dead man," he stammered. "You don't know these people."

"If you don't . . ." I shrugged. He knew exactly what I was implying by this.

He said nothing.

"I can only think you believe his name's worth fifteen years of your life."

I got the desk sergeant to have Joe Simpson remanded in custody.

*

The lead item on the evening news was the arrest of Adrian Bowketts and the discovery of a significant quantity of ricin on the premises, apparently intended to be sent to several people in important positions in Government. It was described as a very successful joint action by anti-terrorist police and Special Branch detectives.

I was watching the news with Taylor, who was curled up next to me on the couch. She knew I'd been involved, though I'd only told her a few things about it.

"How many people could he have killed with the amount found?" she asked.

"I don't know the exact amount he had, this'll probably not be revealed, but even if it'd been only a very small amount, it'd definitely run into several dozen, possibly hundreds."

"Defies belief, doesn't it?" she remarked sadly. It did.

TWENTY-FOUR

Tuesday

In the office, first thing, I'd heard MI5 had learnt there'd been no signs Tabzouni or el-Taccouli had ever been in the Brixton residence. The area had been canvassed and the flat had been microscopically searched, but no evidence of either man ever having been there could be ascertained.

Thinking about what Taylor had said last night had given me an idea. Joe Simpson was known to be connected to the Chackarti family, albeit on the muscle end, and he'd been caught out being involved in terrorism, which was something I knew several persons at the top of the family were wholly opposed to the family having any involvement with.

But it was clear *someone* had to have asked Simpson to deliver the ricin to Brixton, and it could only have been a person with considerable influence near the top of the family. Simpson, at his level, wouldn't usually come across people who'd have access to quantities of ricin. So, if I had a clue as to who this person might be, maybe this was a way I could bring some pressure to bear on Simpson.

Which was why, at 9.49am, I was standing at the front door of Ali Chackarti's very desirable detached property in Fortis Green, close by to where his brothers lived. He was the nominal head of the family and, even though the family business was jointly run by the four brothers, plus their retired father and assorted cousins, all male, Ali was the alpha male of the family, the *primus inter pares*, the first amongst equals.

I'd been here before, so he recognised me. He stood aside and admitted me into his study. He knew this wasn't a social call and Special Branch would only be here if it was serious. He'd be more concerned to know why his network of police informers hadn't warned him of an impending police visit.

He asked what was so important I had to come visiting. I explained to him in graphic detail the purpose of my visit. He sat quietly, listening and nodding to himself, and, by the time I'd finished explaining, he looked very concerned.

"So it's like this, Ali. You people start ferrying dangerous toxins like ricin around, and you're in *big* fucking trouble, and all the police and whoever else you people have tucked away in your pockets won't be able to save you. You have *any* idea how many people could have died if they'd been exposed to the amount of ricin we intercepted?"

He looked up at me. He very likely despised me completely, but he knew I was being honest with him. In a strange way he probably thought I was looking out for him. I wasn't. I couldn't care less for him. I just didn't want ricin falling into the wrong hands.

He looked thoughtful for nearly half a minute. He knew what I was saying was the truth. It looked as though he was grinding his teeth whilst he considered what I'd said.

"I'm asking you to believe this is nothing to do with our family," he said slowly, looking directly into my eyes. "I give you my word, detective; in fact, I swear on my mother's heart" – he stood up and placed his hand across his heart – "this was *nothing* we'd agreed to be involved in. I would *never* allow my family to be used in this way for something so despicable."

In a perverse kind of way, I believed him. True, he was a scumbag, and it was one of my wet dreams to see him and his three brothers behind bars, with the keys dropped down the nearest drain, but I also knew his word meant something. I knew he would never say something like this unless he meant every word.

"The person we have in custody was probably told to do what he did," I said, "and it's very likely he didn't know what was in the bag he was carrying, but *someone* near to the top of your family did, and we wanna know who this someone is."

He nodded slowly and looked upwards, thinking about something.

"Let me make a few inquiries," he said, walking to the door. The interview was over. I left.

TWENTY-FIVE

Wednesday

Things had moved on in the past couple of days. Florian Coyake had been charged with a range of offences under the 2006 Terrorism Act and, even if it couldn't be definitively proven he'd helped Sam Alorami with his PBIED, the fact of CCTV images showing Sam Alorami leaving the amusement arcade where Coyake was manager, and Alorami's prints having been found in Coyake's flat, meant a guilty verdict was assured. He'd appeared before Westminster magistrates yesterday and had been remanded in custody pending Crown Court trial.

Adrian Bowketts was still being interrogated in an MI5 safe house somewhere, but no details had permeated down as to what had been learnt, or, if they had, I'd not been told.

Joe Simpson, despite his continued denials of knowing what the holdall contained, was facing potential liability under the Poisons Act 1972 for the unlawful possession and transportation of dangerous substances. Surprisingly, magistrates had accepted the application for bail, despite prosecuting counsel's claims he was a flight risk, due to his concern for his elderly and infirm mother. He was ordered to surrender his passport. I'd mentioned my conversation with Ali Chackarti to Smitherman and he'd suggested, depending on what we heard, if anything, he might face slightly less serious charges.

But, despite a lot of circumstantial evidence and too many coincidences for comfort, the decision had been taken not to charge Drake Mahoney. The only thing we had was his fingerprints in Coyake's flat, but there were none on any of the weapons or explosives found, and a charge of conspiracy was considered to be unlikely to succeed. Reluctantly, we'd had to let Mahoney off the hook, though I'd no doubt our paths would cross again.

The better news for me was that Chappy Watts and Helen Mathison were not going to be charged. I'd little doubt Helen'd been duped by Sulluman into holding a bag with weapons for him and, apart from her dubious taste in boyfriends, she was clean, so she was being given the benefit of the doubt. Chappy could have faced liability for absconding and wasting police time, but I'd not told Smitherman I'd found him hiding out at his girlfriend's flat, and his agreement to testify against John McGreely had earned him a little credit. I'd been to visit him at his father's tea stall by the O2 in Greenwich and relayed the good news.

"I've gone out on a limb to get you a break, Chappy, so you do anything else stupid ..." My voice trailed off, but my expression left him in no doubt about what I meant.

Tyler Watts looked very relieved. "Whoa, thank fuck for that," he exclaimed. "I've been worried sick; so's his mum."

TWENTY-SIX

Thursday

Late last evening, a message had come through. Two dead bodies had been found in a car which'd been parked by the Alexandra Pavilion, inside the grounds of Alexandra Palace. The park keeper had gone to tell the occupants the park was now closing and they'd have to leave, but he'd been shaken by what he'd found, which'd led him to call for police.

Both men had been badly beaten and shot. Each of them had several cigarette burns, broken bones and extensive bruising all over, and both had been shot in the back of the head. This had been more than just an execution. This had also been a punishment beating, an example made to others.

The two men were identified as being George Duncan, aged forty-two, a top player in the Chackarti family, and Daniel Hunter, aged twenty-six, known to have absconded from the army two months previously. They'd been found in Duncan's car, which had been fingerprinted, but only Duncan's prints had been found. There'd been no witnesses, no CCTV, and no one had seen the car being parked.

Duncan was known to be the driver and personal bodyguard to Ali Chackarti. Police had attempted to contact Ali at his home last evening, to be told Mr Chackarti had had to leave the country unexpectedly on Tuesday afternoon, for family reasons, and wasn't expected back from Turkey until after the weekend. A quick check with immigration revealed a Mr Ali Chackarti had flown from Gatwick airport to Istanbul, Tuesday afternoon last.

I knew this story was a crock. I'd spoken to Ali Chackarti Tuesday morning about someone known to be associated with the Chackartis carrying ricin around London. He'd said he'd make some inquiries, and it now seemed he had done it and hadn't liked what he'd discovered.

I speculated about the likely sequence of events: Ali had had a few discreet inquiries made, he'd realised what had happened and who'd authorised it, and then he'd issued the necessary orders to whoever it was, who'd passed it down the chain of command. Duncan and Hunter had been ordered to be eliminated and, from the nature and severity of their injuries, this had been carried out with extreme prejudice.

When I'd been looking for Cormac McGreely, it'd been Duncan who'd been the family connection to Harry Ferguson, so I could only assume Ali Chackarti now believed Duncan had become a liability, and someone who, despite his position, he could no longer trust. Duncan, as Ali's bodyguard and confidant, would know far too much about family business to be allowed simply to walk away, no matter what promises he made, so Ali'd had him removed. Also, because of the seriousness of the issue, an example had been made of him.

As for Danny Hunter, we could only assume he'd been the one responsible for procuring the ricin, and had used the promise of easy money to rope in Duncan, who in turn had used Joe Simpson to deliver the ricin, though we'd now never know for certain.

*

Joe Simpson was brought back up to the interview room. I leapt straight in and told him I knew it'd been George Duncan who'd asked him to take the bag down to Brixton. I'd been guessing, based on the identities of the bodies found earlier, but his jolting backwards in the seat and the look of surprise on his face told me I'd hit the jackpot.

"I'm right, aren't I?"

He took a few deep breaths and sighed, biting his lower lip.

"Yeah, it was," he said after settling down. "He asked to see me at the club last Friday evening, told me he had a job needed doing. He said he had this friend who needed to get something taken down to Brixton, but this friend couldn't go down himself as he was keeping a low profile."

"He say what this something was?"

"No, just said it's a bag and there's something whoever it was in Brixton needs inside it, so I was to be very careful with it. All I had to do was collect it next morning and take it to an address in Brixton, just give it to the bloke in the flat and come away. That's it, simple." He shrugged.

"Did you see the friend he mentioned?"

"Once, when I picked the bag up Saturday. He was with George when I went to Las Vargas, though I only saw him for about a minute or so."

I produced my phone and showed him a picture. "Is this him?"

He looked closely. "Yeah, it's him."

It was Danny Hunter. Was this why he couldn't be found: he'd been squirrelled away from sight by George Duncan?

"How'd you know it was George?" He looked very curious.

"Him and this one" – I nodded at the picture again – "were both found dead late last night."

His eyes opened wide in surprise. I continued.

"Both of them had some very extensive injuries and both were also shot in the neck from close range. For now we've drawn a blank on where they got the ricin from, though investigations are ongoing."

We were both quiet for a moment. Simpson was digesting the news of George Duncan's death, alongside that of Hunter.

"You have any ideas who might have done this to them?" I asked. "Both of them were tough guys, so you'd need a few people to take them down, especially someone like Duncan."

"No." He shrugged. "Could have been any number of people done it. Something like this would usually be done by people outside the family; there're always people they can count on for jobs like this."

I briefly wondered how many it had taken to subdue Duncan, who'd be a formidable opponent in any fight, then quickly moved on. "You were also seen with someone else in Loughborough Road; who was this?"

"Oh, him. That was Andy; he lives with my sister. He's nothing to do with the Chackartis, so I took him along for insurance."

"Insurance? Against what?"

"Against me not coming out the flat," he quickly replied. "There was something about this bloke's eyes" – he nodded at Hunter's picture – "I didn't like the look of. I've done stuff for George before, and I trust him, but I didn't know or trust this other bloke, there was something not right about him, so I bring Andy with me. When we get there, I tell Andy to go have a coffee and call my mobile if I'm not back in twenty minutes and, if I don't answer, get the police."

I thought about everything I'd heard in the last few minutes.

"Does Ali know George's dead?" Simpson asked.

I shrugged. "I've no idea; he's in Turkey."

"He'll be livid when he finds out George's been murdered."

I didn't respond to this.

"So where does this leave me?" he asked. "I didn't know it was ricin in the bag."

"That's for my boss to decide."

*

I was surprised to receive a text message from Taylor. *Hi hun, call me at work.* I did.

"You're not gonna believe this," she began. She sounded excited. "I arrive at the office this morning and I'm told by the news desk they've received a message from someone claiming to have *something sensational* for the paper."

"Yeah, what about?" I was wondering why she was telling me this. News of interest to the *Evening Standard* isn't usually my forte.

"Whoever he is claims to have evidence about a top civil servant, someone in a *very* senior and important position who's even been knighted by the Queen, being an active paedophile."

Immediately I thought of Alexander Bressington. I was wondering if the message had been from Little Des when Taylor continued.

"But the really *amazing* piece is he also claims to have information about someone who's just been selected to contest a parliamentary seat having had an abortion last year, and the putative father was a senior MP in her party, someone almost twice her age she was having an affair with." She paused for a moment. "This guy gave a name and they haven't told me who it is yet, but I'm wondering if he means Debbie Frost." She sounded like she couldn't believe this. "I mean, she's just been selected to fight a parliamentary seat, and you said last Friday she'd told you she was being blackmailed by someone. Could this message be from the same person?"

The conjunction of these two pieces of information left me in no doubt this message to the paper was from Little Des. He'd already threatened to blackmail her, and now it seemed he was proposing to act on his threat and take down his whole family.

"Do you think it might be Debbie?" She sounded amazed.

"I don't know." I did, but I wasn't telling Taylor for the moment.

"He sounded very convincing, McGraw, says he can prove it as well."

"Has this person suggested what this evidence is?"

"No, not yet. He wants to talk to someone about the information he has."

"So is your paper acting on it?"

"It's with the editor at present; he's talking to Paul Grayley about whether this person's a crank or whether this might be something in the public interest."

Frost had told me Grayley knew about her affair with Perkins, so, when he heard what was been offered to the paper, he'd put two and two together and realise it was his fiancée being spoken of. I doubted he'd want knowledge of this blasted across the newspapers, and certainly not if leaked by a family member.

"Debbie gave me a name last Friday, so I'm gonna go check this out," I said. "I'll get back to you and we can compare names."

"Okay, hun."

*

I made a phone call and then drove to Little Des' house in Kentish Town. On the way I wondered how he'd be able to offer proof against Alexander Bressington without directly incriminating himself, if what he'd told me was true.

Little Des answered the door after I'd knocked twice. I could see he recognised me, and he looked irritated as I walked straight past him, practically knocking him aside, without waiting to be asked in.

"Oi, you can't just barge in here like this," he said loudly as he closed the door and followed me into the kitchen. I turned to face him. He was looking indignant. I ignored his feelings and nodded to a chair.

"Sit down there and *shut the fuck up,*" I ordered him.

He recoiled but complied, looking like a seven-year-old who'd just been wrongly admonished. "What's all this about?"

I looked at him for a moment. He was a pathetic individual. It was almost surreal to realise he had a familial connection to a knight of the realm, and was a part of Debbie Frost's family tree.

He started to squirm slightly in his seat, looking uncomfortable. I leapt in.

“So, you’ve decided to go public with your blackmail threats, then.” I wasn’t asking him.

“What blackmail threats? I’ve not made any.” He didn’t sound convincing.

“Ah, don’t give me this crap. You’ve been in touch with the *Evening Standard*, haven’t you, offering dirt on a member of your family.”

His eyes opened wide in surprise. This told me everything.

“First off, I should tell you they’re not going to run either of your stories, and no other paper will either.”

He sat back, shook his head and sighed. “How d’you know this?” he asked sullenly. “Did they tell you?”

“No paper *ever* takes a story like this without checking the facts. The first thing they do is verify what’s been said, so the *Standard* contacted the intended victim, a Ms Debbie Frost, and asked for her comments about what you’d implied. She then played them her tape of your conversation last Saturday.” I smiled at him. “She’d recorded the conversation to protect herself. It’s clear to the paper you’re attempting to blackmail her, and she denies the story you’re claiming anyway, so they’re not going to run it, irrespective of whether it is or isn’t true.”

He looked down at the floor with another loud sigh.

“The paper’s probably gonna come after you because you’ve attempted to scam them with a story based on blackmail, and they don’t like being duped either.”

I’d no idea if this was true or not, but it produced a worried look on Des’ face.

“At this moment,” I continued, “Debbie Frost’s with police giving a statement about your attempt to blackmail her, and playing them her recording of what you were demanding last weekend. She wants them to press charges.”

He was open-eyed in disbelief. I gave him a few seconds to regroup his thoughts.

“Also, your claims against your stepfather are covered by a DSMA notice, which means the paper couldn’t publish any details even if they wanted to.”

I didn’t say the notice was a voluntary arrangement, but it had the desired effect. He sat quietly, looking very morose. His dreams of extra money and scoring one against his family were now in tatters.

"Why'd you do this, anyway?" I asked quietly. "You surely didn't think she'd just pay up and hope you went away, did you?"

His expression instantly changed to one of pure detestation.

"Lying bitch has got money, hasn't she," he snarled, "so why shouldn't she pay? She's a fucking hypocrite. She's *had* an abortion after getting knocked up by a married man more than twice her age, yet she tells the paper the law on it should be tightened. Fucking slut."

"Who told you this, anyway?"

"Actually, it was my dear stepfather first told me, and I just took it from there. I logged it" – he touched the side of his head – "as I thought I could use the info at some point, and her being selected as a parliamentary candidate gave me the chance."

"Cute," I said. "Another opportunity to extort money from your family, just like you do with your stepfather."

"Why not? They've treated me like shit for long enough. Anyway," – he shrugged – "my dear stepfather and I have a business arrangement. It's not blackmail."

I left him to stew in his rancour for a few moments.

"Plus I know about her new fiancé." He had an evil grin on his face. "I went to the *Standard* because, if they didn't publish my story about my stepfather, I was gonna go to another paper and say the *Standard* knew about it but wouldn't publish because they've also got a bloody nonce working for them."

"Well, I'm afraid you're out of luck on this one as well. So, add on to this the fact we know you allowed a known terrorist to stay here ..." I paused for a moment. "Bowketts is now in custody; he's going down for a long time, and he knows it. So, if I ask him to name you as his accomplice in letting him stay here and I say it could reduce his sentence, you think he won't take it?"

Des looked at me open-mouthed. "You wouldn't ... would you?"

I'd scared him.

"Look at it like this," I said. "You drop the blackmail, say *nothing* about your family to anyone, and I don't talk to Bowketts."

He sighed, then nodded his agreement.

I then told him to stand up as he was under arrest, and I informed him of his rights. He was taken to Kentish Town police station and I told DS Withers why I'd brought him here. I said I'd be back to question Des soon.

"Oh, don't worry, take all the time you want." Withers smiled like he was on a promise. "We've a cell I've wanted to see this scrote in for a long time."

Des was led away.

I drove away wondering why I was protecting Debbie Frost.

*

I contacted Debbie Frost and told her about her cousin's message to the *Evening Standard*.

"Yes, I know, Paul's been in touch with me about it. What's gonna happen to the slimy little weasel anyway?"

I then told her of Des' arrest on charges of blackmail and other offences, and that police would probably be in touch with her about her recording.

The relief in her voice was palpable. "Oh, that's great, thanks for this," she gushed. "You and Sally *must* come round to our place sometime soon and have dinner with us."

I felt my stomach churning at the thought. I'd sooner chew rusty barbed wire.

"You never know," I said.

I then contacted Taylor and told her the story she'd mentioned earlier was now dead. The person who'd left the message had been arrested and was going to be charged with blackmail.

"Yeah, I heard. Paul said we're not taking it up. He told the editor he'd a personal interest in the case."

We were quiet for a couple of seconds.

"They've still not told me the name of the woman, but, if Paul says he'd a personal interest in this, then it *had* to be Debbie Frost this guy was referring to, didn't it?" Taylor asked, sounding concerned.

"Yeah, it was," I agreed.

"Oh, poor Debbie."

I wasn't sure I agreed, but I remained silent.

TWENTY-SEVEN

Friday

Sitting at my desk. I'd just returned from Kentish Town police station, where I'd been to interview Little Des. Well, it was more like me telling him he was a detestable little maggot. I'd informed him that I'd initially been ready to give him the benefit of the doubt concerning Bowketts lodging at his house, given what DS Withers had told me about Des being mainly a local tea leaf, but his blackmail efforts had left me completely unsympathetic, plus he was going to be charged with allowing his premises to be used for the purpose of aiding and abetting a known terrorist. He hadn't looked too happy about this.

"You can't do that," he'd exclaimed.

"Oh, really? See you in court." I'd left him to his dejection.

After five days, Bowketts' interrogation had produced little of any real value. He'd refused to say who obtained the ricin for him, though the list of names police had found left them in no doubt of what he'd intended to do with it. He'd refused to confirm he knew either Danny Hunter or Sam Alorami, even though CCTV images showed them talking together. He'd said he'd never heard of the Chackarti family. Nobody'd believed him, and so he'd now been charged with sufficient offences under the Terrorism Act 2006 to keep him in prison until his grandchildren drew their pensions, and was being held in Belmarsh pending trial.

*

Smitherman asked me to come to his office. He had a very serious expression on his face.

"Sir Alexander Bressington's dead."

I was jolted back in surprise.

"An accident?" I asked.

"If you can call an apparent suicide an accident, then yes."

He recited the facts as were known. Lady Elizabeth Bressington had gone to an operatic recital last night at St John's concert hall, Smith Square, and her presence there with two other persons had been confirmed. Upon returning home by taxi at about 11pm, she'd found her husband slumped in an armchair, with a line of blood down the left side of his face. There'd been a small pistol lying on the floor by the chair, which was thought to be a Ruger LC9. She'd said in a statement she'd not known he even owned a gun.

She'd called the security service number all persons deemed to be of sufficient importance in the political hierarchy were given to use in emergency situations, to ensure certain sensitive issues did not enter the public record, as every call to 999 was routinely recorded in case of litigation. An ambulance, several men and a woman had arrived soon after. The body had quietly been taken away and the woman, an MI5 officer, had stayed with Lady Bressington to get a statement.

Only Sir Alexander's prints had been found on the gun. Circumstantially, everything pointed to Sir Alexander taking his own life.

"Do we know why? Did he leave a note of any kind?"

"I've not heard about a note, but we've learnt from his wife he'd been contacted by his stepson ..." His voice tailed off. I knew who he meant. "Apparently she said the stepson, Des, had been in touch with a couple of newspapers and was going to blow the whistle on his whole family. Evidently he couldn't be talked out of it, said Sir Alexander was going to pay for the beating he'd taken. Lady Bressington and her husband said they knew nothing about him getting any beating, but Des said they were lying."

He stopped talking for a moment.

"So, sometime last night, while Sir Alexander's wife was out ..." He shrugged, as if to say, *You know what happened next.* "The press's had a DSMA notice slapped on it for the moment and, as his early retirement was going to be for health reasons, they'll mention this. I'm not sure what they'll list as the cause of death," he said formally, "but it won't be a gunshot wound to the head."

*

Six forty-five pm; I was meeting up with Paul Grayley after I'd phoned and told him I'd like to speak to him. He'd been curious as to why, but he had agreed to this. I'd told him he wasn't to tell Taylor we were meeting.

This wasn't a social meeting. Frankly, I despised him and I was meeting him because of my belief he deserved to be in prison, but

I'd no tangible evidence I could use, so my intent was to put the frighteners on him.

We met up at South Kensington tube station as it was equidistant from both our homes. The station was crowded, so we moved outside and stood by a shop doorway.

"So, why'd you need to speak to me face-to-face? We could have done this on the phone."

"No, we couldn't."

I began by stating I knew he'd been the instigator of the vicious assault Little Des had received in his home a week ago. I'd done some thinking about this after both Sir Alexander and Lady Elizabeth had said they'd nothing to do with it. I believed the attack had been carried out by Dominic Deacon and Ian Gosling, as they matched the description Des had given, and Deacon was Grayley's cousin.

Grayley looked alarmed when I spoke, but after a few seconds he smiled, became calm and didn't deny a word I said.

"Yup, I had the little shit roughed up." He looked smug. "The bastard was planning to jeopardise Debbie's chances of becoming an MP, and I wasn't gonna let that happen, no chance." He shook his head firmly, looking serious.

"So you had a word with your cousin Dominic, and he—"

"Yeah." He cut me off. "He went round to, ah, explain the situation to Des, but he clearly hasn't got the message. I was gonna have the message reinforced, but he's now been arrested, so I can't get to him."

"I know; it was me who arrested him."

Grayley's expression was hard to read for a moment.

A thought then struck me. Little Des had said he'd found out about Debbie Frost's abortion from his uncle, Sir Alexander.

"You know anything about why Sir Alexander Bressington killed himself?" I asked.

It only lasted a second, maybe not even that long, but the look in his eyes told me he was involved in Bressington's death. Either he'd arranged it, maybe using his cousin Dominic Deacon, or he had pressured Bressington into doing it himself. Either way, I couldn't prove it, but I knew Grayley had been involved.

"Anyway, he got what he deserved, didn't he? They both did," he said, dismissively.

He looked smug. It was my cue to wipe the smugness from his face.

"Sad though it is to say, pal," I said, staring at him, "not everybody gets what they deserve."

"What does *that* mean?" He looked curiously uncomfortable.

I moved closer till my face was twelve inches from his.

"Just remember one thing," I said, quietly and firmly. "I know all about you and how your uncle Paul kept you off the sex offenders' register after your, ah, regrettable incident in Thailand, plus your being caught recently in an internet porn scam which featured children, along with Des' stepfather."

The shocked and horrified look on his face told me he wasn't about to refute this. He stood silent for several seconds, considering what he'd heard.

"You know what happens to nonces like you in prison, don't you?" I asked. "You'd have to spend your whole life looking over your shoulder in case someone's behind you. You think Uncle Paul could protect you from this?" My cynicism was showing.

He didn't respond to this.

"Must give you a real sense of satisfaction and a belief in your own infallibility knowing you've a connected uncle who can pull strings, eh?"

He looked at me with a knowing smile. "Ah, *now* I know why you're here. You're planning on blackmailing me, aren't you?"

"No, I'm not." I waited a moment. "Well, actually, yes, I am, but it's like this. If anything happens to Des while he's in the prison system, anything at all . . ."

My voice trailed off. I didn't have to say anything. He knew what I meant.

He sighed and shook his head. I wasn't sure if he was about to cry, from the expression in his eyes. There was an uneasy silence. I was about to leave when he spoke again.

"I'm doing my best, you know? I have these feelings inside me, I hate them and I want to be rid of them, but it isn't easy. Getting rid of any addiction isn't easy," he said plaintively.

This was probably true, but I wasn't here to debate with him.

"Does Sally . . .?" he said softly.

"No, she doesn't know about you, and she won't either, so long as you stick to what I just said. We clear on this?"

He nodded his agreement. "Yeah."

"More importantly, does *Debbie* know about you?"

He sounded very worried. "No, and she mustn't either."

"Same as before, then: she won't if . . ." I looked him in the eye.

He nodded his agreement, then took a couple of deep breaths. "Actually, Debbie and me, I don't know how much longer we're gonna last. She's really hot for this other guy; talks about him all the time, she does, about what a great guy he is and how he's been helping her out."

I didn't say anything. He waited a moment, then he absolutely floored me with his next comment.

"You wanna know who this other guy is?" he said quietly. "It's you."

"*Me?*" I blurted out. I thought Taylor'd been joking when she'd told me she thought Frost might be interested.

"Yeah, you. I mean, c'mon, detective, why'd you think she phoned *you* when Des first tried blackmailing her, rather than me?"

I shook my head and tried not to laugh at the implausibility of the situation.

He looked at me and almost smiled, said he wouldn't let on to Sally his fiancée was after her man, then turned and walked away. I watched him disappear into a nearby taxi.

Debbie Frost fancied me. Dear God. I decided I would never tell Taylor this.

TWENTY-EIGHT

Saturday

Taylor and I had a table booked for eight at our favourite Italian restaurant and, as I was running slightly late, I was hurriedly parking my car behind our building at seven oh-nine. As I got out the car, salivating at the thought of an intimate evening in my favourite restaurant with my all-time favourite woman, I saw a familiar face approaching me.

"Good evening, detective."

It was Joachim Balpak. He was looking very pleased.

"I won't take up too much of your time," he said. "I have some news for you."

"Oh yeah? Like what?"

"You'll probably be told this in more detail tomorrow, but you can call off your search for Mehmet Tabzouni and Asou el-Taccouli."

"Why? We haven't found them yet."

"No, *you* people haven't." He sounded disapproving. "But *we* have, or, rather, *I* did."

"*You* found them both?"

"Only one of them. El-Taccouli has left the country, believed to be in Syria, but Tabzouni has been found."

"Where'd you find him?" I was curious. "We've been looking for him for several days."

He sort of smiled and nodded at me. "When *we* want someone, detective, we don't let the rule of law get in our way. I believe I mentioned to you before how we Israelis don't ask questions as nicely as you British." He paused. "There're no Marquess of Queensbury rules with us, detective, no notions of *fair play, old chap* and *oh, that's not cricket, old boy*," he said, spoofing a highbrow English accent. "If *we* want information from someone, information vital to Israel's continuing security as a nation state, then we use whatever means we can to extract it."

I looked at him for a few seconds.

"Yes, this includes torture, if this is what you're thinking, detective. I asked a few people about where to find Tabzouni, and, ah . . ." He paused. "Eventually I got the answers I wanted and I found where he was hiding."

"And I don't suppose they just gave up the information you wanted freely either."

He knew what I meant.

"Oh, not willingly." He laughed, or was it an ironic chuckle? "Let's just say one or two people had to be, ah, persuaded to my point of view, but in the end they all told me what I wanted to hear, and eventually I found Tabzouni."

"Where'd you find him?"

Balpak shook his head.

"So where is he now?" I asked. "Is he in Israeli custody?"

"Commander Smitherman will complete the picture for you tomorrow. Good night, detective. Enjoy your evening."

He turned, walked back to his car and drove away.

TWENTY-NINE

Sunday

Tabzouni was in a critical condition in Charing Cross hospital and had undergone extensive surgery for his injuries, several of which were life-threatening. He'd been found unconscious in Finsbury Park early Saturday morning by a dog walker who'd called the emergency services.

"He's not regained consciousness yet," Smitherman said. "Whoever did this really did a number on him. This wasn't just a beating; this was sadistic torture. Someone went to great lengths to ensure he didn't die. The supposition is he's been tortured by someone well trained in torture techniques, someone who knew enough to cause pain without killing the victim."

I knew who this someone was as well. I was deciding whether to tell Smitherman when he continued.

"We've also received information about el-Taccouli. MI6's belief is he's in Syria, and they're trying to work out how he left the country."

He was quiet for a moment.

"Well," he said, "at least we stopped a ricin attack, and whatever it was that was supposed to bring London to its knees, and we've got people in custody who're gonna go down for this. Small victories, DS McGraw, that's what our working life consists of, but they're better than no victories at all. I'll take all the small victories we can get, especially if they get the likes of Bowketts off the streets."

He took a sip from his coffee cup, and then he beamed broadly. "Oh, and I've had some news as well, though I'm not sure if it's good or bad."

"Yeah? What's this?"

"We had a family barbecue at my son's place yesterday. Clements was there and, when I saw him get up and go into the kitchen, I followed him in and closed the door, cornered him, just the two of us. I knew Janet had already confronted him, told him she'd suspected he was being unfaithful to her, and he'd denied it, so I went up to him and asked him straight out if he was seeing someone else. He said he wasn't. I looked him in the eye and said, *You wouldn't be lying to me, would you?* and he repeated he's not seeing anyone, promised me he wasn't. So Janet's accepted his word, they've resolved whatever the problem was and she's happy again, which is good news. You ever have a daughter, DS McGraw, you'll soon learn her happiness is everything to you, and if anyone's hurting her you want to kill them."

But the smile then left his face as quickly as it'd appeared. "But in a way I was almost hoping the little shit'd say yes, as I'd have been tempted to smack him one." He looked disappointed, like a source of pleasure had been denied him.

Lying to Smitherman while he looks you straight in the eyes. It was a skill I'd yet to acquire. I'd have to ask Clements how he'd managed to carry it off.

THIRTY

Friday

The news of Bressington's untimely death had finally been released on Tuesday evening and had made the press next day. The *Times* had reported the story of a senior civil servant, someone tipped to be the next secretary to the Cabinet, having died from a heart attack. He'd been due to announce his retirement on grounds of deteriorating health very soon, but nature had interceded and hastened his departure. His eulogies had been impressive and there'd been several fulsome tributes from ministers, both past and present, and top civil servants about Bressington's invaluable contribution to the machinery of Government down the years and how sorely he'd be missed by everyone. I wondered who, amongst the higher echelons, knew the real truth about Sir Alexander.

I'd received a call yesterday morning from Clements, asking if I fancied a coffee in the National Theatre café, rather than the one near his office in Holborn. I did.

I bought a coffee and sat at his table. I knew there'd be a work reason for asking me for a coffee, and he immediately asked if the stories of Bressington's heart attack had been true or a convenient establishment cover-up. I assured him the heart attack had been a fact, pointing out even people like Bressington were not immune to ill health. For the moment he seemed satisfied with my answer.

"So, you lied to your father-in-law, eh? How'd you keep a straight face doing it?" I asked, with an ironic smile. "You know what he'll do when he finds out you've bullshitted him, don't you?"

"I didn't lie to him," he protested.

I looked him in the eye. "Oh, really? So the woman I saw leaving here the other week, the one with the great tits, didn't really exist, eh?"

"It's true. I stopped seeing her the start of the week before last." He grinned wickedly. "So, when Jack asked if I was seeing anyone, I could truthfully say, hand on my heart, I wasn't. But it's just as well he didn't think to ask me *had* I been seeing someone, 'cause I'd have been in dead shtuck then, wouldn't I?" He laughed.

We were quiet for a moment while we sipped our drinks.

"So what happened with you two, then?" I was more curious than interested.

"Aw, she was quite boring, actually. The sex was great, but you couldn't talk to her about anything; she doesn't take any interest in current affairs or anything like that, never reads newspapers or watches the news. She's actually as thick as cow shit, if I'm being honest."

He sipped some more coffee. "Also, and you probably won't believe this," – he looked almost remorseful – "I had an attack of the mega-guilts, I really did." He paused for a moment. "Weekend before last, I looked at Janet, and I'm probably not explaining this too well, but I saw what I'd always loved about her, right from when we'd first met. Some kind of strange feeling swept over me. I looked at Janet and I thought to myself, *Why the fuck are you doing this, eh? Janet's a lovely person; do you really prefer this pneumatic blonde to her?* and the answer was no, I didn't. I finally came to my senses. I mean, this chick *has* got great tits and she's really hot, but there's gotta be more to it than just that, surely." He paused again. "So I spent the weekend with Janet, took her out to dinner. Really spoilt her, I did. Told her I'd been working too hard and neglecting her, and I apologised for that. And then when I met Cheryl on Monday – that's her name, by the way – I was gonna tell her it's over."

He broke out into very amused, ironic laughter. "But Cheryl beat me to it." He shook his head as he laughed. "She said she'd seen her ex-partner again over the weekend and they'd had a long talk and decided they're gonna try again, so she told me it's over between us. I agreed it made sense as she clearly still has feelings for this guy, and they'd been together several years before they'd split up. She asked if I was okay, and I said yeah, I'm cool with it. I didn't tell her she'd saved me telling her the same thing."

He then leant forward and looked businesslike. "She said the initial reason for the split had been because he'd been arrested. He's a bit of a hard case, apparently, and police had pulled him in for being involved in a serious assault. You know the Chackartis, don't you?"

I agreed I did.

"Oh, of course you would, you're ex-CID." He grinned. "Apparently, this guy's something in the Chackartis."

This I was very interested in. "So who's the guy?"

"Name's Joe Simpson."

My face betrayed my surprise.

"You know who he is?" Clements looked surprised.

"I know the name, yeah." I described him. I didn't say I'd arrested him a few days back, or that he was on bail for ferrying ricin across London.

"My God, small world, eh?" He laughed.

*

Taylor and I had both been fully occupied with work since before last weekend. We'd been so busy we'd spent hardly any time together this week, just the occasional coffee at breakfast before one of us had to dash off. I'd been involved in an investigation at work which had kept me out late a few nights, and meanwhile she'd been working long hours with Jacobs, engaged in last-minute interviews to confirm what they'd been told with a couple of sources for their story, and then finally formatting and writing up their account of the shoot-to-kill strategy, based on what they'd learnt.

I'd seen Taylor for about ten minutes at breakfast today and she'd initially been excited, saying the story was now mostly completed. This morning they were going to finish *tarting it up*, reread it to make sure it all made sense and contained no grievous errors, then they were forwarding it to Hugh Blackbourne, the editor, for his opinion.

"I'll tell you how it all pans out this evening." She'd sighed softly. "If we're both here at the same time, that is, 'cause it's not happened much lately, has it?"

She'd then leaned into me and given me a long, extra-warm hug, and exhaled. From the expression on her face, if I hadn't known her better, I'd have said she was feeling guilty about something.

"You okay?" I lightly touched her cheek.

She put her hand on top of mine and looked directly into my eyes. "You realise we've hardly seen each other this past couple of weeks? We've both been much too busy at our jobs, so this weekend we've *got* to make some time for us," she whispered knowingly. "You know what I'm saying? *We're* the important thing here, McGraw, *us*, not our jobs. I really don't want us becoming one of those couples who're so busy all the time they lose sight of each other and end up drifting apart. Promise me we won't let this happen, McGraw."

I agreed: we were the important thing and it was time to refocus our priorities. "You got it, let's take a step backwards. Sod our jobs; how about a date tonight, babycakes?" I gave her my poor impersonation of Bogart, holding her close.

She beamed and lightly bit the tip of my nose. "You're on," she said softly.

Tonight had been sheer delight. We'd eaten in a Thai restaurant near Sloane Square and had had a lovely meal. She told me about the article, which they'd now virtually completed. Her editor had looked over it and declared himself happy with how it read so far, and it had now been passed on to the managing editor, who was going to read it over the weekend. Taylor was pleased with how it'd turned out and was looking forward its being published in a couple of weeks.

As she was talking about it, I was remembering Christine Simmons' comments, more than five weeks ago, about Taylor getting too closely involved in working with Stephen Jacobs, plus her husband telling me last week I should talk to Taylor about stopping the article. But I'd heard nothing since, so I wasn't too concerned.

After a little window shopping, with Taylor drooling over a pair of jeans costing more than we'd spend on a weekend away, we'd taken a taxi back to the flat. I was now feeling blissful, lying in bed with the naked body of the woman of my dreams, the woman I fantasise over, wrapped around me. How many men ever get to make love with their fantasy woman?

THIRTY-ONE

Friday, seven days later

Taylor had mentioned two days ago her managing editor had finally read the completed article, twice, all twelve and a half thousand words of it. He'd liked what had been written and had approved it for publication. He'd particularly enjoyed the implied tension between polemic and factual comment and had commented to the writers they'd got the balance between the two just about right. He'd said it'd been an absorbing read and, assuming the lawyers raised no objections to anything written, publication had been set for Thursday week.

This week, Adrian Bowketts had appeared before Westminster Magistrates' Court and, after a short and perfunctory hearing, where he'd said nothing other than confirming his name, had been remanded in custody. As the arresting officer I'd been present in court but hadn't had to take the witness stand. The evidence was factual and the defence wasn't disputing anything, so it'd been a formality. The trial date had been set for later in the year.

Mehmet Tabzouni had died on Tuesday afternoon, however, without ever regaining consciousness. The nature of his injuries had been such that doctors, despite emergency surgery, had been unable to save his life when he'd haemorrhaged internally after a seizure and begun to flatline. His death had made national news, with the cause of death being given as injuries suffered in a car crash. Few, if any, in the media mourned his departure. Gheziel Ayah had immediately disputed the reason given and had blamed rogue elements in the Mossad for the death, claiming they'd been following Tabzouni all the while he was in London. The British police were also blamed for not providing protection for Tabzouni in the face of what was referred to as *Zionist aggression*.

The injuries Smitherman had described had been horrific and, while I'd lose not one second's sleep over Tabzouni's demise, what Balpak had done to him had been brutal. A bullet between the eyes would have been far more humane and produced the same outcome.

Joachim Balpak had contacted me Tuesday evening at home.

"The world is a better place tonight, detective." He sounded exultant. "Have you seen the news?"

I knew what he was referring to. I agreed I'd seen it.

"The death of one more sworn enemy of Israel is always a cause for rejoicing. Tonight, we will drink kosher Scotch to his departure." He sounded like he'd already started.

"Pretty barbaric, what you did to him, wasn't it?"

He didn't reply. He didn't need to. We both knew the truth. And, even in the unlikely event of my obtaining incontrovertible evidence it'd been Balpak who'd tortured and killed Tabzouni, he was protected by diplomatic immunity as he was an accredited diplomat.

"All that matters, detective," he solemnly intoned, "is my nephew Sol can finally rest in peace. His death has been avenged. *Shalom*." He hung up.

*

Early evening; I was just coming to the end of my shift, completing a report about an investigation I'd been involved in earlier in the week, which had concluded successfully with an arrest. I'd just finished uploading it when Smitherman approached and sat by my desk.

"I'd like you to be at this address at nine o'clock tonight," he said casually, handing me a piece of paper. I looked at the address written on it. It was close by: Lord North Street, Westminster.

"Why's that?" I was curious.

"Let me put it like this, DS McGraw: it would be in your best interest to be at this address later this evening."

The expression on Smitherman's face made me realise I wasn't being asked if I'd like to be there. I sighed. "Whose place is this, anyway? Am I supposed to be meeting someone?"

"All will be revealed when you get there." He got up and went to his office.

Taylor was seeing a play with her sister and a friend, so I texted her saying I was going to be working late this evening. I hung around the office until after eight, then strolled around to the Red Lion, Whitehall, and sank a quick beer while wondering just whose residence it was I was being asked to visit in Lord North Street. Shortly before leaving, I'd looked for the registered owner of the property online, only to discover I needed the appropriate security clearance to access such details.

Lord North Street was very short, about one hundred yards, and came off Great Peter Street into Smith Square, right in the very heart of political Westminster. I found the number I was looking for and rang the doorbell. It was opened instantly by a very intense, unsmiling man who gestured me in. He was about my height and build, around thirty, and was wearing a very casual jacket and trousers. Was this *his* house? I discounted this thought the moment I noticed the gun in the shoulder holster under his jacket.

He closed the door. "Your phones, your weapon and your wrist-watch, please, detective," he said curtly. He wasn't asking.

I gave him my watch, my police radio, my mobile and my firearm. After being thoroughly searched and expertly patted down, I then followed him along a short corridor and up a flight of stairs, whereupon we turned back on ourselves, went along another short corridor and entered a room which overlooked the street. There were two men already there, standing by the window and talking quietly. Had they been watching me arrive?

I looked around. The room was perhaps twenty feet square and lit by a warm glow from the two table lamps in opposite corners. It had a thick, dark carpet and several paintings of naval battles on the walls. There were two armchairs by the windows and a mahogany table in the middle of the room, with two chairs alongside. I could smell coffee.

The men stopped talking ten seconds later when they noticed I was in the room.

"Good evening, detective; thank you so much for coming," the older of the two said in a pleasant tone, as though I were a welcome house guest at a dinner party. I nodded but didn't reply as it seemed churlish to point out I wasn't here by choice. He was distinguished-looking, probably mid-sixties, and wearing a formal business suit with what looked like a regimental tie. He had very silver hair and was wearing wire-rimmed glasses. The other man was less formally dressed, jacket and trousers, probably mid to late forties, and didn't say a word.

"Please, have a seat." The older man smiled and gestured to a chair by the table. I did. Each of the two men took a small armchair by the window and we sat about nine feet from each other. The man who'd led me to the room poured coffee from the pot on the table into three delicate, chintzy bone china cups with matching patterned saucers and handed us one each. He then left the room without speaking and closed the door.

We sat silently for five seconds. I was wondering if this was an audition or an interview.

"Do you know who I am, detective?" the older man finally began.

I shook my head. "No, I don't."

"And this gentleman?" He gestured to his left.

"Same."

"And this is how it's going to remain," he said formally. "I'm telling you this because it's important you understand what's happening here never took place. I am somewhere else at this very moment, as is my colleague here, and this will be a matter of record. Do you follow?"

I did. He was telling me they were both important people, each of them was *someone*, and this meeting was absolutely unofficial, off the books and covered by the Official Secrets Act. This explained the surrender of my phones and my gun and the patting down when I'd entered the premises, to ensure I wasn't wired and couldn't record anything said.

"Am I in some kind of trouble; is that why I'm here?" I asked hesitantly.

"Oh, good Lord, no." The older man smiled benignly, shaking his head. "Nothing of the kind. And even if you were, that would be something for Commander Smitherman to deal with. No, this is simply an informal chat. I just wanted you to appreciate the ground rules before we begin."

"Okay." I nodded, somewhat relieved.

"So, as to why you're here, my purpose here this evening is to put you in the picture regarding something which, had it proceeded as planned, might have caused some considerable degree of embarrassment to past and present members of Her Majesty's Government, and also to tell you why we won't be allowing it to go ahead."

He spoke slowly, as though considering every word before he said it. But how did what he was about to say affect *me* in any way?

He'd read my mind. "What I'm about to tell you involves your wife, Mrs McGraw."

I grinned involuntarily.

"Oh, I'm sorry, have I said something funny?" he asked.

"No, my apologies." I stopped grinning. "It's just I've never heard Sally referred to as Mrs McGraw before. She hasn't taken my surname; she still goes by Taylor. So, when I heard *Mrs McGraw*, I thought of my mother and wondered what she'd done."

"Fair enough." He almost smiled. "For our purposes, I shall thus refer to her as Miss Taylor."

I nodded.

"Miss Taylor," he went on, "is one of the authors of a forthcoming article about an aspect of British military policy in Northern Ireland in the early seventies, along with her collaborator, Stephen Jacobs, is she not?"

I agreed she was. *Then* it hit me why I was here. These guys were senior MI5 operatives, and I suspected they were displeased with what Taylor and Jacobs had been doing. Was *this* what Christine Simmons had meant about Taylor getting too closely involved with Jacobs?

"The article is currently with the *Evening Standard*'s managing editor and chairman, and, as I understand it, the paper is making plans for this article to be published in its magazine in the very near future. Am I right about this, detective?"

"I don't know." I shrugged. "I don't work for the *Standard*."

"Well, it's our information this is what they're considering."

It's our information. This clearly suggested the security service had sources at the top of the *Evening Standard*, who had informed MI5 of what the paper was planning on publishing. This would explain the approach made two weeks ago by the pair of MI5 jokers who'd advised me to tell Sally to stop what she was engaged in.

He paused to sip some coffee. I did the same. It was really good coffee. The other man didn't touch his. I noticed he was staring directly at me the whole time, eyes unblinking, observing my responses and my body language, so as to gauge what I was thinking.

"Have you read the whole article?" the older man asked.

"I haven't read *any* of it."

"But, presumably, you are aware of its subject matter and its direction, even if you don't know all the specifics."

"More or less, yeah."

"We've seen the article." He nodded. "It's very long – around twelve thousand words, I believe I'm right in saying – and it's a very thoughtful, very considered piece of work. It's well researched, cogently argued and well reasoned, and, given what we know about the political sympathies of Mr Jacobs, it offers a surprisingly balanced look at the issue in question. There's very little of the left-wing polemicising we usually read from him. Maybe Miss Taylor's had a moderating influence on him." He smiled. "But I have to tell you, detective, the article as it currently reads will *never* see the light of day in this country. Simply stated, it's *not* going to be published."

He paused to sip more coffee. I made no response.

"Well, actually, let me put this another way. It will be published, but *only* after it's been heavily redacted and several of its more pertinent points have been removed."

He was looking directly at me as he spoke. Again, I didn't respond.

"This is because the article contains several facts and details concerning events we would rather did not become public knowledge, for reasons I will now come on to explain."

I was attempting to look calm, but I was experiencing a mixed set of emotions. I wasn't completely surprised to hear it wasn't going to be published as submitted, given what Taylor had told me it contained, but I was curious as to why they were telling me this.

"But first, detective, let me give you some context." He put his cup down on the table, sat back and folded his arms. "The basic premise of the article is correct. Two Unit *did* exist and, yes, its function *was* what the article alleges it was. And this came about because, I'm sorry to say, the British rather mishandled the situation in Northern Ireland, right from the start. When the situation in the province became really serious in the late sixties, and British soldiers were finally sent there in 1969, the powers-that-were at the time saw this, more or less, as just another little colonial difficulty. They responded as though they were up against the Mau Mau in Kenya or a tribal uprising in Malaysia, and they attempted to resolve the situation through the use of a disproportionate and unreasonable level of force. But what had *not* been considered by our people, or perhaps had been underestimated, was the sheer depth and strength of the support the two warring communities were receiving from their people on the ground." He paused for a moment. "They'd seldom come across this before, but it didn't affect their thinking. And the failure to consider this, and the failure to win the hearts and minds of the nationalist community, in keeping the situation containable, is ultimately what led to the pursuit of a shoot-to-kill policy. It was believed this would have a demoralising effect on the IRA, but quite frankly, if anything, it did the opposite."

He stopped talking for a moment and looked around the room. "But we continued, even though we could see after a while there would have to be a political solution as, quite clearly, we weren't going to succeed militarily. I'm afraid this inability to find any satisfactory political solution contributed to extending the Troubles for much longer than should have been the case." He nodded. "This is the starting point for Miss Taylor and Mr Jacobs' article. Their contention is this strategy was one that would only ever be attempted by a government still clinging to notions of empire, wholly devoid of any viable strategy for handling the situation by any method other than force."

I wanted confirmation of what I'd just been told. "So, shoot-to-kill *was* a reality, then."

"Yes, detective, it was; it most certainly was." He paused. "Which is part of the reason why the full article must not, and never will, be published in this country. Her Majesty's Government will never, *ever* admit to it either, for reasons which I'm sure you'll understand. Which is why certain sets of Cabinet minutes from the time are exempt from the thirty-year rule, and will be kept secret for much longer."

I could imagine a few reasons. I remembered Taylor mentioning certain sets of minutes she'd been unable to access at the National Archives.

He said nothing for several seconds. "Can you imagine the response of those dissident supporters of the IRA whose belief is the Good Friday agreement was a sell-out when they read the British government was actively seeking them out and killing them, bypassing the courts and the rule of law? Can you imagine the galvanising effect this would have on the IRA? We'd very likely be looking at more civil unrest and possibly British soldiers back on the streets of Belfast again, and this we cannot allow to happen. The last twenty years, there's been peace in the province, and we cannot and will not allow this to be taken away."

I thought about this for a few seconds.

"Do you have any questions, detective?" he asked.

"Just one for the moment. You used the word *facts* when you were talking about the problems with the article. Does this mean everything in the article is actually true?"

He didn't answer for several seconds. "For the most part, yes, though there're one or two inaccuracies, and I will not say what these are. But, for our purposes, yes, there're several very pertinent points made in what has been written."

He finished his coffee, then continued. "There're also other reasons why this article will not be being published as written. Firstly, the writers are claiming they've interviewed an ex-SAS soldier. They've not named him, but we know who he is. He's confirmed the fact of a shoot-to-kill strategy, and he says he was there in 1971 helping put the strategy into place with others from a division in the same regiment." He nodded slowly. "Now, as you'll doubtless know, this claim contradicts the official position of the UK government of the time, because it's a matter of public record the SAS did not get sent to Ireland until 1976. To admit otherwise would be to admit the Government lied about its Northern Ireland strategy at the time, and raise all manner of questions." He stopped for a moment. "Also, to admit to this would be to hand a major propaganda victory to the IRA, who've claimed for years the SAS were in the province, carrying out covert undercover operations against them, and they must never be allowed *any* such victory. Do you follow?"

I nodded. "Yeah."

"Similarly, for any doctor to falsify medical records is a very serious offence, and it would appear, from what's been suggested," – he looked directly at me – "the two writers have obtained documentary evidence to prove this, haven't they?"

"Why ask me? I'm not writing the story."

"But you went to visit Dr Redfearn with Miss Taylor, did you not?"

"I went with her because I'm from the area, and I know Dr Redfearn; he's our family's GP. So I made the introductions, but I took no part in any of the questioning."

"Well, in any case, we cannot allow it to be said in public that doctors working for the British army were party to any such situation." He paused momentarily. "Just think what the implications of this would be. Every death certificate for an IRA person would now be subject to doubt, and this'd be another propaganda victory for them. And, also, any claims someone had been tortured in Castlereagh or Long Kesh by the RUC or the army would now be given more validity. Put another way, these claims would be taken more seriously if it had been said in the media death certificates had been falsified, particularly if those certificates were published, albeit with names removed. This situation we can't allow. If the integrity of death certificates were to be called into doubt . . ."

He didn't finish the sentence, but the implications of what he was saying were clear.

"You see the point I'm trying to make, detective? They cannot be allowed to claim such a propaganda victory here either."

I did. "Yeah." I nodded. "*Were* they falsified?"

He was silent for a moment, then continued. "But, perhaps most serious of all, detective, you know who Sir Paul Deacon is, don't you?"

"Yeah, he's the ex-head of Special Branch."

"He was indeed, and, in a long and very distinguished career, he served this country well behind the scenes. However, this article is going to claim not only that he was in command of a small unit killing suspected IRA personnel, with or without firm evidence of any terrorist activity, but also that he personally killed two people in cold blood rather than in combat, and it describes the abduction and shooting of one of these persons in graphic detail. Sir Paul isn't named, of course, but his rank and the battalion he served in are, plus the dates when he was in the province, which means any half-competent investigative journalist would be able to establish his identity from the details of what's been written."

He paused again. "There's also the claim he was party to a suspect dying after being seriously assaulted by members of the

Parachute Regiment. *Tortured*, I believe, is the word the writers use."

I sat quietly for a moment, thinking about what I'd heard. "As I mentioned, I don't know the whole story, but are these allegations true? *Did* he kill these two people in cold blood?"

I already knew the answer, but I was wondering what they'd say about it.

The man nodded slowly for several seconds. "What may have happened was indeed regrettable, detective."

"May have happened? Innocent people being murdered? I'd suggest it's more than regrettable," I stated calmly.

"I agree." He smiled pleasantly. "And, as you may be aware, the strategy of shoot-to-kill was abandoned primarily as a result of this incident. Deacon left the army soon after this; his chances of further promotion were now scuppered."

"Didn't prevent him achieving high office in the security service, though, did it? Was there no background check carried out before he joined MI5?"

Again, silence for a few seconds.

"I explained some of the context of the situation earlier, detective," he said, patiently, "and the mistakes which were made. But the situation with Sir Paul is now in the past, and nothing can be gained by bringing him or the service into disrepute."

I was thinking of my reply when he continued.

"Besides which, there's another reason why Sir Paul's identity must never be made known in this context, which is . . ." He paused and fixed me directly with a stern look. "Sir Paul's mother, Elspeth, was the second cousin and lady-in-waiting of Her Royal Highness, Elizabeth, later Queen Mother, while she was the consort to King George VI. Under *no* circumstances is it *ever* going to be allowed to have the royal family mentioned, even in passing, in the context of Northern Ireland." He stressed these words very strongly.

I was absorbing all I'd heard, as there was a lot to consider. Taylor and Jacobs had really rattled a few cages with their story.

He shook his head. "You can also just imagine the kinds of questions which'd be asked in the House if this story is published as it currently reads. The current Government would be forced to defend a policy it had no part in, and whatever answers given would probably never be enough. The whole history of the situation would be rewritten. There'd probably also be calls from some of the more excitable elements in the press for Sir Paul to be prosecuted, or at least to have his knighthood removed, were his identity to be established, which'd then raise other issues."

He sat forward in his chair. "There are other potential dangers in publication as well, detective, but I'm unable to share the reasoning with you, which I'm sure you'll understand." He nodded again. "So I hope I've made it clear why, despite all the scholarly work put into the article, and its attempts to be objective, we simply cannot allow it into the public arena without considerable redacting. The paper already knows this, and the writers will soon be informed."

Silence for a few more seconds.

"Anything you wish to add, detective?"

"No." I shook my head. "Thanks for the heads-up."

"You're probably wondering why we're telling you this."

I nodded. I was.

"It's because Northern Ireland is now a peaceful nation and economically prosperous. If this article helps to reawaken the IRA, this peace will be threatened, and it'll be people like yourself who'll be on the front line looking for Irish bombers and their sympathisers, which I believe was a situation you found yourself in very recently, was it not?"

This was a reference to Cormac McGreely. I agreed it had been.

"So," he said, "this little chat is simply to assure you there're very valid security reasons why your wife's story is being curtailed, and that you'd be affected by its implications, therefore we thought you should have some idea why we cannot allow it to be published as it stands."

I nodded. There was nothing to say to this.

"Well, thank you for coming this evening, detective."

Both men stood up, I did the same.

"Oh, and, in case you were wondering, there'll be no black marks attached to your wife's file as a result of this piece of work," the older man said with a smile. "We have no reason at all to doubt her loyalty to her country or her motives in being a party to writing this article. She was simply offered the chance to be involved in a major journalistic enterprise. Also, she's from good family. Her father plays golf with Commander Smitherman, and I'm led to believe he's also something in the City?"

"Yeah, he works for a bank, something to do with investment portfolio management."

"Not my line of country, I'm afraid." He shook his head. "You are, of course, bound by the Official Secrets Act, detective, and every word which has just been uttered in this room is covered by the terms of the act." He smiled at me. "*Any* attempt by yourself to disseminate the details of what was said here this evening will be treated very seriously indeed."

I nodded my understanding.

"So, when you hear the article is not to be published as is, you will act very surprised and not let on you've already been made privy to this information. Are we clear?"

I agreed we were. He smiled and thanked me again for my presence.

"This way, please," a voice behind me said. I turned. It was the same man as earlier. I'd not heard him re-enter the room. I followed him downstairs. He handed back everything he'd taken from me, opened the door and bade me farewell. I left the house.

THIRTY-TWO

Sunday

Taylor had said nothing about the article yesterday, so I was assuming she'd not yet heard from her editor about what was to happen to it. I'd done a lot of thinking about the meeting Friday evening and what I'd been told, and had wondered how the censoring of the article would be sold to the two writers.

Smitherman strolled along and sat down by my desk. "No problems Friday?"

"None I've been told about."

"You're clear about why you were there?"

I indicated I was.

"Any problems with what they told you?

I shook my head. "None. Whose place was it, anyway? I tried looking up details of ownership, but it came back I needed security clearance to access it."

"Yes, I know you tried." He almost smiled. "The search was traced back to you, but you'd have been derelict in your duty had you not done so. Off the record, DS McGraw, strictly between us, it's an MI5 safe house. They've a few in the area; that's one of them."

"And the two guys who were there?" I raised my eyebrows optimistically.

He almost smiled again, got up and left without answering.

THIRTY-THREE

Wednesday

Taylor had arrived home looking very relaxed; remarkably so, considering what she'd been told earlier in the afternoon by her editor. She was sanguine and had clearly got in touch with her inner zen.

Today, she'd been called into the editor's office, asked to sit down and then told the article she and Jacobs had spent the past seven or so weeks researching and writing was not going to be published as it currently read. I didn't let on I'd been made aware of this five days back.

What was going to be published instead would be a largely sanitised account of the situation, mostly repeating what *Panorama* had claimed a few years previously, and with the excision of all references to the SAS, medics giving inaccurate death certificates, Cabinet committee discussions about shoot-to-kill, comrades of Barry Pencourt unapologetically claiming they killed as part of a shoot-to-kill policy, and Sir Paul Deacon.

The editor's reasoning? The *Standard*'s lawyers stating the naming of names would lead to the possibility of litigation against the Government, after agents of the state, ex-soldiers, had claimed they'd deliberately killed in what was designated as a peacekeeping role, and where no official war had been declared. Relatives of Brendan Morgan would have been able to sue the UK government for restitution after the admission he'd been murdered. This would mean, if litigated, the Government would have to go to court and defend its agents, the soldiers, or make financial restitution without admitting liability. Britain would also be seen as intentionally violating its obligations under international law, as the UK was a signatory to the Universal Declaration of Human Rights, as well as the European Convention on Human Rights. Seeing violations of such rights admitted in print would put the Government in an embarrassing situation.

"So you're okay with this?"

She smiled as she sipped her coffee. "I can't honestly say I'm surprised. Even as we were compiling the piece, I think I assumed we'd be lucky to get this past the lawyers, and it seems we didn't. But it's been a great experience, looking at how to put major articles together, and I've learnt a lot from it."

She sipped more coffee, leant back against me and looked at me. "There was sadder news than this today, though." She nodded glumly. "Barry Pencourt died last weekend, so he never got his public confession. I can only hope he'd made his peace before he died."

THIRTY-FOUR

Friday week

Jacobs and Taylor's article had been published in the *Evening Standard*'s magazine yesterday. The sanitised edition read well, though it was several thousand words shorter than the original piece. Even when the more sensational aspects had been excised, it'd raised more than enough questions to be a worthwhile read.

Jacobs, I'd learnt from Taylor last evening, had been very distressed the full piece hadn't been published, even though his commission was to be paid in full by the paper. He was now attempting to have the full article placed abroad, and was seeking discussions with left-wing magazines in the Netherlands, Germany and Italy about this possibility. He'd been convinced that someone in the Government was *leaning on the paper, Sally.* If unable to get it published abroad, he was contemplating attempting a book on the subject.

Nine oh-five. Walking along the Embankment to work, I saw a familiar figure approaching from the opposite direction as I reached the Yard. She was carrying a briefcase and wearing a very smart dark grey business jacket and knee-length skirt with a crisp cream-coloured blouse opened at the neck. She was even wearing heeled shoes. I was dismayed to see her once-flowing hair was now much shorter. She was smiling broadly.

"What are you doing my side of the Thames?" I asked as I gave her a hug.

"Off to a meeting up there." Christine Simmons nodded up at the top of the New Scotland Yard building. "But I got here early because I was hoping I'd run into you first. My meeting doesn't start till nine thirty; you got time for a drink?"

I had. We went to the basement café and I bought two cups of what turned out to be very weak tea. We took a table and sat down.

"Brawling in public, DS McGraw?" she began light-heartedly. "I don't know . . ." She shook her head. I knew what she was referring to.

"*No* man gets to insult Sally and just walk away," I stated.

"Oh, God, *men*." She sighed, sipped her tea, then flashed me an ironic smile. "Didn't I tell you about Sally getting too close to Jacobs?"

"Is this what you . . .?"

She held up her hand and cut me off. "Ah-ah, I'm not going to answer questions, Rob, but what I *can* tell you is we knew Jacobs was about to embark on this story when I spoke to you last, and, as we knew he had good sources in Government departments, we'd anticipated him finding out much of what he did. We were hoping to uncover a couple of the people who've been leaking information to him, and we did. A woman's been sacked from her senior post in the MOD as a result of leaking classified information, and a senior official's been demoted, and both are likely to be prosecuted. Apparently, the woman and Jacobs were lovers at university and they've remained quite good friends, and she was happy to do favours for him." She shrugged. "So a couple of Jacobs' sources have been closed off to him. But we'd *not* anticipated his uncovering of Sir Paul." She paused for a moment. "Can you imagine the furore if this had made it into the press: *ex-Special Branch head complicit in murder whilst in uniform*?"

"Is this why you wanted Jacobs to continue, so MI5 could uncover his sources?"

"Jacobs was put on to this by his brother Neil. Barry Pencourt had been raising an unholy stink about this for some time, so Neil Jacobs agreed, when we asked him, to steer his brother in the direction of Pencourt. We knew Steve Jacobs wouldn't be able to resist this kind of story. In following it up he led us to uncovering two people we'd suspected of leaking classified information for some while, and not just names and addresses either. Where'd you think Jacobs got the SAS soldier's name from?"

I immediately realised the irony of the situation.

"So, all this time, Jacobs was inadvertently working for you?" I laughed. "You think he'd be amused if someone told him?"

She also laughed, but then fixed me with a serious look. "Suffice to say, you're *not* going to whisper *any* of this in Sally's ear next time there's pillow talk, are you?" She was emphatic.

"How about when we're having dinner?" I grinned.

"I warned you about Sally getting too close to Jacobs because we weren't exactly sure how far he'd go with this, and also because

I like her and I didn't want to see her file classification changed to someone we have to keep an eye on."

Journalists on all major papers across the UK covering political, economic and intelligence issues have files kept on them, with detailed lists of their articles and their political leanings. Most are in ordinary buff files, which means they're not under suspicion, but being in a red file means your loyalty is suspect and a watch kept on what you write, especially if it appears to be derived from sources leaking classified information.

"Did they *seriously* think they were going to get the full article published?" She looked and sounded amazed.

"I've no idea. They kept on going, so I can only assume they did."

She shook her head firmly. "Was *never* going to happen. We were following it from a safe distance as it was being put together, which is how we knew about the SAS soldier and Jacobs' uncovering of Sir Paul's identity."

The MI5 operative in Lord North Street had alluded to the service having sources at the *Evening Standard*. This confirmed what he'd said. I wondered if their source was the editor. He was an ex-Cabinet minister. Had he been in on it? This would explain his commissioning the piece.

"The real truth is known," she said, "and most, but not all, of what they wrote was correct."

"So which parts did they get wrong?" I wondered.

She shook her head again and continued. "But it'll *never* be admitted in public, not while memories of IRA atrocities are still fresh in many people's minds. The public image of the British soldier is still a positive one, thus the success of campaigns like Help for Heroes, and nobody wants this image tarnished. In future, who knows what'll happen, but at the moment, no."

There was nothing to say to this.

"So," Simmons said, "she planning any more articles with Jacobs?"

"None I know of." I grimaced as I sipped some very weak tea. I had a thought. "Can I ask you something? No, it's not about this."

She nodded.

"Did you people *really* not know about Alexander Bressington?" I asked. "I mean, how did he keep this a secret for so long?"

She'd know what I was referring to.

She grinned. "Now, you know I can't answer this question, but what I can say is, ah, the situation's a little more complex than you might think."

"In what way?"

She smiled and shook her head.

"Also, did he *really* commit suicide?" I was thinking of my belief Paul Grayley was involved in some way.

She didn't respond. I waited seven seconds.

"Can I ask two other things?"

She smiled. "Yeah, of course, but there's no guarantee I'll answer them."

"A couple of weeks back I was asked to go to a house in Lord North Street . . ."

"Yeah, I know." She smiled, flashing her blue eyes at me.

"Who *were* those two guys?"

She shook her head.

"And, last point, *was* Sally's or my phone tapped? I mean, how else would Ian Gosling and Dominic Deacon have known to intercept me the other week and ask me to tell Sally to stop what she was doing? I don't believe their presence there was sheer coincidence."

She drained her tea, pulled a face and stood up. She didn't answer the question. She wasn't going to either. This confirmed what I'd suspected.

She picked up her bag, came around the table and gave me a quick hug. "Right, one mustn't keep the Assistant Commissioner waiting, must one? Good talking to you, Rob, you take care. Regards to Sally."

She walked away towards the lift. I couldn't face drinking any more tea, so I followed her.

www.ingramcontent.com/pod-product-compliance
Lightning Source LLC
LaVergne TN
LVHW091020080826
845145LV00002B/306